Praise for
JOHN D. MACDONALD

Fawcett Books
by John D. MacDonald

THE BRASS CUPCAKE
MURDER FOR THE BRIDE
JUDGE ME NOT
WINE FOR THE DREAMERS
BALLROOM OF THE SKIES
THE DAMNED
DEAD LOW TIDE
THE NEON JUNGLE
CANCEL ALL OUR VOWS
ALL THESE CONDEMNED
AREA OF SUSPICION
CONTRARY PLEASURE
A BULLET FOR CINDERELLA
CRY HARD, CRY FAST
YOU LIVE ONCE
APRIL EVIL
BORDER TOWN GIRL
MURDER IN THE WIND
DEATH TRAP
THE PRICE OF MURDER
THE EMPTY TRAP
A MAN OF AFFAIRS
THE DECEIVERS
CLEMMIE
THE EXECUTIONERS
SOFT TOUCH
DEADLY WELCOME
PLEASE WRITE FOR DETAILS
THE CROSSROADS
THE BEACH GIRLS
SLAM THE BIG DOOR
THE END OF THE NIGHT
THE ONLY GIRL IN THE GAME
WHERE IS JANICE GENTRY?
ONE MONDAY WE KILLED
 THEM ALL
A KEY TO THE SUITE
A FLASH OF GREEN
THE GIRL, THE GOLD WATCH
 & EVERYTHING
ON THE RUN
THE DROWNER

THE HOUSE GUESTS
END OF THE TIGER & OTHER
 STORIES
THE LAST ONE LEFT
S*E*V*E*N
CONDOMINIUM
OTHER TIMES, OTHER
 WORLDS
NOTHING CAN GO WRONG
THE GOOD OLD STUFF
ONE MORE SUNDAY
MORE GOOD OLD STUFF
BARRIER ISLAND
A FRIENDSHIP: The Letters of
 Dan Rowan and John D.
 MacDonald, 1967–1974

TRAVIS McGEE SERIES
THE DEEP-BLUE GOOD-BY
NIGHTMARE IN PINK
A PURPLE PLACE FOR DYING
THE QUICK RED FOX
A DEADLY SHADE OF GOLD
BRIGHT ORANGE FOR THE
 SHROUD
DARKER THAN AMBER
ONE FEARFUL YELLOW EYE
PALE GRAY FOR GUILT
THE GIRL IN THE PLAIN
 BROWN WRAPPER
DRESS HER IN INDIGO
THE LONG LAVENDER LOOK
A TAN AND SANDY SILENCE
THE SCARLET RUSE
THE TURQUOISE LAMENT
THE DREADFUL LEMON SKY
THE EMPTY COPPER SEA
THE GREEN RIPPER
FREE FALL IN CRIMSON
CINNAMON SKIN
THE LONELY SILVER RAIN

THE OFFICIAL TRAVIS McGEE
QUIZBOOK

JOHN D.
MacDONALD

A
FLASH
OF
GREEN

FAWCETT GOLD MEDAL • NEW YORK

A Fawcett Gold Medal Book
Published by Ballantine Books
Copyright © 1962 by John D. MacDonald Publishing, Inc.

ISBN 0-449-12692-7

Manufactured in the United States of America

First Fawcett Gold Medal Edition: November 1963
First Ballantine Books Edition: December 1983
Twenty-eighth Printing: July 1991

For Sam Prentiss
   Jim Neville
   Tom Dickinson
   And all others opposed to the uglification of
   America

Two old men are fishing from the end of a public pier as the round sun moves toward the gunmetal horizon of the Gulf of Mexico.

The one from Indiana says, "What I want to know, do you ever get to see that flash of green?"

The one from Michigan spits toward a floating tern. "The only flash of green down here to make a wish on is the flash of money you miss out on. I bought one lot for six hundred, held it for five years and sold it for three thousand. I could have bought ten. Make you sick to your stomach."

"But people say they've seen it, the minute the sun disappears."

"Now, it stands to reason, mister, any damn fool stares into the sun long enough, he'll end up seeing exactly what some other damn fool tells him he's going to see."

"Well, I'd like to see it. Just once."

1

WHEN SHE HEARD the rattle of the old tin wheelbarrow, Kat Hubble knew it was after four. On Tuesdays, after he had finished up at the Lessers', and on Fridays, when he was through at the Cable home, Barnett Mayberry would do one extra hour of yard work at her house before getting into his stuttering old car and driving back home to Pigeon Town, the Negro community on the far side of Palm City.

Before Van had been killed, Barnett had come one full day a week, and though now it added up to only one quarter of the time, he seemed to keep the place looking as neat as ever, though of course she had begun no new landscape projects in this past year, and she did more of the work herself.

The arrangement with Barnett had just seemed to happen. Beginning the week after the funeral, he had stopped by to take care of things which obviously needed attention, such as clipping the side hedge of Australian pine, and she had given him a dollar for each after-work hour. In some mysterious way it had become a routine. It so exactly fitted her diminished purse and her needs that she could not help suspecting it was not entirely satisfactory to Barnett, that he had entrapped himself through some murky idea of loyalty and pride in past projects. Yet when she had at last taxed him with it, he had looked rigidly beyond her and shuffled his feet and said, "I got a place for them dollahs, Miz Hubble. It working out good for me."

She had always felt slightly indignant that Van should be able to get along so effortlessly with Barnett and the other Negroes who had worked for them from time to time. But, as he had reminded her, there was quite an environmental gap between a girlhood in Plattsburg, New York, and a boyhood in Orlando, Florida.

She would hear Van out in the yard, laughing with Barnett, and once when he came in she said, "Hee-hee-hee. Yuk, yuk, yuk. I'll bet he doesn't laugh that way when he's with his own people."

Van had stared at her in honest surprise. "Of *course* he doesn't, cutie. And he doesn't talk the same way either. He uncle-toms me a little, but without losing his dignity,

7

and I pull the mahster a little on him, but not too much. It's a protocol thing, Kat, and it makes us both feel at ease because we both know so very damn well the limits of the relationship in which we have to operate. He's just as respected a citizen in his neighborhood as I am in mine. If I try to push him beyond the limits he sets, he'll just get slower and stupider until I leave him alone. And if he tries to take advantage of me, he expects to get chewed."

"But when I go out to tell him what I'd like him to do, he stares into space and acts terrified."

"He probably is. He knows you don't know the rules. He knows you're a Wellesley liberal. You might ask him what he thinks of Faubus. And the next time you listen to us have an attack of the jollies, dear heart, you might note that I probably laugh differently and speak differently than when I'm with *my* own people. He's probably as wary with Burt Lesser as he is with you, and as comfortable with Martin Cable as he is with me."

Since Van's death, Barnett had given her the curious impression he had been trying to put her at ease. He would make some empty remark and then laugh. Five years ago she had bought a little rubber tree in a pot for twenty-five cents. Now it was nearly twenty feet tall and continually covered with the upright bloody spears of new leaf growth. "Heeel!" Barnett would say. "Little ol' two-bits tree." That was their signal for the vague social laughter. But once it had brought too clear a memory of Vance, and one laugh had become a sob and she had fled into the house.

When she heard the sound of the wheelbarrow, she left the letter she was writing her sister and went out into the side yard. The lower Gulf Coast, from Tampa to the Keys, was enfolded in an airless July heat which was so merciless it had little flavor of tropic languor. Instead, it seemed to have a humming intensity, an expectancy, as though any moment the Gulf and the bays would be brought to the boiling point and all the roofs would break into flame. Each afternoon the thunderheads made their lazy, ominous, atomic symbols out over the Gulf. Sometimes there would be a riffle of rain-wet air turning the leaves, but all the storms moved ashore across other counties.

Barnett had trundled the wheelbarrow over to the pile of cuttings under the punk trees. She saw that he was wearing one of Van's discarded shirts, a pale-blue Orlon knit that she had always liked on Van until the sun of Saturday golf had faded it unevenly and he had given it to Barnett. She tested the familiarity of that shirt upon herself, like touching and retouching something which might be a little too hot to hold and then finding, with a certain pride, that you can hold it after all.

Barnett Mayberry was of an unusual muddy saffron hue, and his features seemed more Asiatic than Negroid. When Van had been annoyed with him, he would call him, never to his face, "That damned Manchurian."

"Fixin' to tote thisheer bresh over to burn, Miz Hubble."

"That's fine, Barnett. I wanted to ask you about this thing that's growing up into the live oak."

He followed her across the yard. "I seen him," Barnett said. "This here a strangle vine."

"It's growing awfully fast. Should it come out?"

"Fixin' to take him out. I'll cut him off low now, and next week he lets go enough up there, I pull him down easy. Take a long long time to kill that tree, we let it go. By the time it die, all you can see is the strangle vine aholt all over it."

A car turned into her drive and stopped. It was an old blue Plymouth station wagon. She felt a quick pleasure as she recognized it as Jimmy Wing's car and saw him clambering languidly out from behind the wheel, grinning at her, lifting her arm in a lazy greeting. He came across the yard toward them, loose-jointed, a sandy man in his middle thirties, a man with a long narrow head, a thrusting, fleshy nose, a face more deeply lined than his years warranted. His hair, brows, lashes and his light-blue eyes were not as dark as the slightly yellowed tan of his face. He had a crooked mouth and an ugly crooked grin—both sweet and wry in an attractive simultaneity. He wore a white short-sleeved sport shirt and light-gray slacks. He had the unconscious knack of giving the most ordinary clothes a look of elegance. She had decided it was partly because of the lazy grace of the way he moved, partly because of his spare bony frame, partly because he was so consistently immaculate.

Whenever he recalled how she had disliked him before Van had been killed, she was astonished at how blind she had been. Jimmy had been the only one of Van's close friends she had actively disliked.

"If it's any help to you, it's worse in town, Kat. How you, Barnett?"

Barnett's grin was broad, his voice emphatic. "Fine, Mist' Wing. Just fine."

"You get those pictures?"

"I sure thank you, Mist' Wing."

"She get in up there to Tuskegee?"

"They said for her to come."

"That's one fine girl, Barnett."

"What's this all about?" Kat asked.

She found herself walking toward the house with Jimmy and knew he had effortlessly avoided explaining in front of Barnett. And she knew she had once again violated some obscure clause of the protocol.

"His daughter was valedictorian at their high school last month. Sandra Nan. Not much for looks, but hellish bright and energetic. Barlow got a good picture of her, so I had the darkroom make up three glossies and send them to the family."

"Darn it! I should have known that."

"He's got one good boy, and one boy headed for trouble, so he's batting high in the league."

"Jimmy, do you know everything about everybody in Palm County?"

"Now, if I did, honey, everybody would be paying me not to work on the paper."

They went through the screened portion of the cage at the rear of the house. He slid a glass door open and they walked into the roofed portion of the patio.

"Well, now!" he said, looking at her quizzically. "You've sissied out, Kat."

"And every time I turn the noisy thing on I remember how Van hated air conditioning, and I feel immoral and guilty. You know my tenants stayed to the middle of June, and you know it got hot early this year. So they wanted one and we dickered around, and we finally decided I'd pay a hundred dollars against it, and if they take the house again next year, I'll cut the lease another hundred. It's a three-ton thing, and it's sticking in the wall between the living room and the bedroom wing. What can I fix you to drink?"

"Can of beer is fine, if you've got it."

"Coming up." She went to the kitchen and brought the two opened cans back to the glass-top patio table, sat across from him.

"Will the whosises want the house next season?"

"The Brandts. They say so. They'll let me know for sure by the first of November. Let me make my full confession on the air conditioner, Jimmy. I wasn't going to use it. I was just going to let it sit there. But you know how cold they keep the darn bank all day. When I'd get out, I'd just wilt. I held out until last week, wearing my prickly heat rash like a badge of honor or something. Then I woke up in the middle of the night and my hair was sopping wet and it was too hot to go back to sleep. So like a thief I snuck around and closed the windows and plugged the beast in, and slept so hard I nearly didn't hear the alarm."

"Now you're hooked."

"I've fallen so low I even like the noise it makes."

Jimmy stood up and walked toward the living room to stand and look the length of it. "Looks just the same," he said.

"It is, and it isn't. Jean Brandt had different ideas. I suppose any woman would, really. She moved things around, and she stored things away. I've been getting things back the way they were, but they won't be exactly the way they were. It looks a little different, and it feels different. Do you know? It was our house, but now I feel a little bit as if I were renting it too—from the Brandts. It isn't as important to me as it was, which is very probably a good thing. I'm glad you talked me out of putting it on the market."

He came back to the table. "You would have taken a whipping, Kat."

"I just didn't think I could endure living here."

"We can always stand a little more than we think we can. One thing on my mind, Kat, I've got to drive up to Sarasota next Sunday. Borklund wants me to do a feature on their public beach program. I've got about everything I need, but there's one fellow I want to talk to. And he won't take up much time. So how about you and the kids coming along?"

She studied him, wondering if it was coincidence, then saw his casualness was a little too elaborate. "Thank you, dear Jimmy. I know it's going to be a rough day for me. I've been dreading it for weeks. But I'll manage."

He shrugged. "But if coming along with me would make it any easier . . ."

"It would. Indeed it would, and I'm grateful. But, you see, the neighbors have been conspiring to keep me distracted, and I've given so many polite refusals I wouldn't feel right saying yes to you. Van died on July ninth. Once I'm past this one, it will be over a year. I can manage it. The kids and I are going on a beach picnic by ourselves. I'll have a lot of July ninths to get over. This will only be the second worst. Jimmy, it's nice to have you stop by. I like seeing you in the bank too, but that's when I have to keep being the happy hostess. Ready for another beer?"

"I'll ride with this, thanks." He frowned at his big, bony, freckled fist for a few moments, then looked at her with an odd expression. "I thought you'd come along on Sunday, and it would have given me a chance to talk to you about something."

"You act as if it's something unpleasant."

"It is, and I better give it to you now. It's off the record, honey. You're still active in the S.O.B.'s, aren't you?"

"Recording secretary, but there hasn't been anything to record. Save Our Bays, Inc., has sort of been resting on its laurels."

"It might be a very timely idea for you to resign."

"What is that supposed to mean?"

"That project of filling in Grassy Bay is going to be opened up again soon."

"You can't mean it, Jimmy! You can't be serious. Two years ago we licked it. I never worked so darned hard in my life. And Van too. All those phone calls and petitions and ringing doorbells and going to public meetings and taking all that abuse. We whipped them. We mobilized all the conservation groups and we got a bulkhead line established in Palm County, and nobody can fill beyond that line. Nobody can touch Grassy Bay. We *saved* it! You must be joking."

His smile was bitter. "It's going to astound a lot of other people too. Let's say you saved it for two years. It's a different deal this time. They've been setting it up quietly for almost a year. Last time, it was an outfit coming in from outside."

"Sea 'n Sun Development. From Lauderdale."

"This time it's local."

"Local men?"

"Don't look so incredulous. And the fill project is a little bigger. Eight hundred acres. They have an option on a good big piece of upland to give them access to the bay. The financing has been arranged for. When the county commissioners set that wonderful bulkhead line, they reserved the right to change it."

"But they have to have a public hearing."

"I know. The new syndicate will petition for a change in the bulkhead line along the bay shore of Sandy Key, to swing the line out to enclose eight hundred acres of so-called unsightly mud flats, and request county permission to buy the bay bottom from the State Internal Improvement Fund. The commissioners will set a date for a public hearing, at which time prominent local businessmen will go to the microphone, one after the other, and say what a great boon this will be to the community, a shot in the arm for the construction business and the retail stores. Captive experts will get up and say the fill will have no effect on fish breeding grounds or bird life, and will not change the tide pattern so as to cause beach erosion. It will be nicely

timed, because a lot of the militant bird watchers and do-
gooders will be north for the summer, and they won't give
the ones who are left here much time to organize the opposition. The commissioners will change the bulkhead line and
approve the syndicate application to purchase. The trustees
of the IIF will sell the bay bottom at an estimated three
hundred and fifty dollars an acre, and then the drag lines
and dredges will move in. It's going to be a steamroller
operation, Kat, and it's going to run right over anybody who
stands in the way."

"We can't let it happen."

"We can't stop it this time. Kat, there's a fortune sitting
out there in that bay. I figure total development cost at a
max of three million against a total minimum gross sales
of lots of six and a half million. Where else along this
coast is there water that shallow so close to an urban area?"

"But we must stop them, Jimmy!" She stared at him.
"Why do you think I'd resign now?"

He stood up. "Need another beer. Stay where you are."

She heard the refrigerator door slam. Barnett rapped at
the patio door. She got his money from her purse and took
it to him. He told her he'd cut the vine off close to the
ground, and when he came next Tuesday he'd trim the big
pepper hedge.

She walked, frowning, back to the table where Jimmy
Wing sat. "You should resign because it'll be easier now
than later. The new deal is called the Palmland Development Company. Your neighbor, Burton Lesser, is heading
it up."

"Burt! But he was against . . ."

"Against somebody else doing it. Leroy Shannard is in
on it, handling the legal end. He handled Van's estate,
I know. And the uplands they took the option on is part
of the Jerome Cable estate, and your neighbor and em-
ployer, Martin Cable, is the executor of that estate. A good
piece of the financing has been worked out through the
Cable Bank and Trust Company. And this time the newspaper isn't going to be so scrupulously neutral."

"Ben Killian should have been on our side last time,"
she said indignantly.

"He won't be this time. This is home industry, kid. It's
going to be patriotic to be for it, and like some unspeakable
act to oppose it."

She leaned back in her chair and stared at him in dismay. "But all those men *know* better, Jimmy."

"And they know how much cash is sitting out there on
those flats."

"Grassy Bay is one of the most unique and beautiful . . ."

"You don't have to sell me, honey."

"You helped us last time."

"Not this time."

"Are you scared to, Jimmy?"

"I'm scared of a lot of things. This might as well be one of them. Katherine, you'd better take stock. There's one hell of a difference between being Mrs. Vance Hubble, wife of an architect, and Mrs. Vance Hubble, the young widow who works at the bank."

"I should keep my head down?"

"That's my message. These are men you know, but they aren't going to fool around. It could get dirty, honey."

She stood up and walked away from the table, turned and looked back toward him with a puzzled expression. "So I should give up on something Van believed in? Just like that?"

"I know he took a certain risk in taking the stand he did. He lost some contracts. But he got some new ones to make up for it. So you could call it a calculated risk. I can tell you this, Kat. If he could see the way this one is set up, he wouldn't mess into it."

"That's a filthy thing to say!"

"Why so? My God, the world is a practical place and Van was a pretty practical guy."

"But he fought for what he believed."

"Most men do, up to a point. But when they stand to lose too much, and gain too little, they think up reasons to stay out of it."

"Van wasn't like that."

"It's a point we can't argue. I just don't want you to get into any kind of . . . of a memorial campaign. The bay is gone."

She moved slowly back toward the table. "When Van first brought me down here, I hated it. I missed the hills and the snow and the familiar seasons. One morning very early—it must have been nine years ago, because I was pregnant with Roy—we went to Hoyt's Marina and went out in the boat. It was that old skiff we used to have, and he'd just bought it, used, and fixed it up a little. There was a heavy mist. The tide was going out of Grassy Bay, flowing out through Turk's Pass. It was warm and still. He stopped the old engine and we drifted across the flats. It was a private little world, with the mist all around us. It was a time when if you wanted to say anything, you felt like whispering. I heard the sea grass brushing the bottom of the boat. Sometimes we'd catch and turn slowly

and come free, or Van would push us off with the pole.
I heard fish slap the water, and once we heard the snuffling
of porpoise over in the channel next to the mainland shore.
It grew brighter in the mist. I looked over the side and
watched the sand, the mud, the grass, and a million minnows.
Van told me to look up. Directly overhead the morning
mist was so thin I could see the blue of the sky through it,
and just then a flight of white pelicans went over, much
lower than you usually see them. I saw them through the
mist, and I heard a hushed creaking of their wings. It
was a magic time, Jimmy, and that was the moment when
I began to love this place. The rest of the mist burned
away, and we were out in the middle of the wide blue
bay. Van started the engine and we went chug-chug down
to Turk's Island and spent the day."

"But it didn't add a dollar to the economy. Kat, I've
told you what's going on because I don't want you to be
hurt. I gave my word I wouldn't tell anyone, and I've
broken it."

"I appreciate it, Jimmy. And I know what you're trying
to tell me."

"But?"

"I just couldn't let all the work Van did go to waste.
You can understand that."

He grinned. "I knew what the reaction had to be. But
I had to make the attempt. At least you have some idea
what you're up against. I'll be standing by, Kat. Use me for
a rest camp, a first-aid station." He stopped smiling. "But
I'd rather you keep this to yourself."

"I can't even do that."

"But, honey, if the leak is traced back to me, they'll put
lumps on my head."

She thought for a few moments. "I was at my desk in
the bank and I heard two men talking about Grassy Bay."

"That isn't likely. They've been very careful. I know Sally
Ann Lesser is in on it, because Burt couldn't have come
up with some of the basic money otherwise. So can't you
pry it out of her?"

"Now that I know what I'm after, I can. Otherwise, I
can't tell when she's lying."

He looked at his watch and stood up. "Thanks for the
beer."

"And thank you for the advance information, Jimmy. I
think I really need a project right about now."

They walked through the house to the front door. He
shook his head and said, "Believe me, honey, nobody needs
what you're thinking of taking on. It could break your heart."

"Again? Maybe I'm sort of invulnerable."

"They'll try to find out. You take care, hear?" He stood there for a rare moment of awkwardness, then walked on out to his car. He backed out and waved to her as he drove off down the narrow asphalt of Pine Road, toward the exit gate of Sandy Key Estates.

Katherine walked through the living room. She stopped at a west window. Beyond the pepper hedge the last smoke of the dying brush fire rose in a hazy column, bending slightly toward her as an imperceptible breeze off the Gulf shifted it.

Too many things were moving through her mind simultaneously, immobilizing her so that she could not begin any one of them. But the considerations of strategy had to give way to the homely obligations. She went to the phone to call Claire Sinnat and tell her to shoo the kids home from the Sinnat pool, then decided to walk up the road and collect them. She fixed her lipstick, ran a hasty brush through her cropped red hair, and went outside.

At first she thought it as stunningly hot as before, but in a little while she realized the sting had gone from the sun's heat as it moved closer to the Gulf horizon. But the big black salt-marsh mosquitoes were out early. They whined in her hair and tickled her long legs and needled the backs of her shoulders and the small of her back between her green halter and the waistband of her white shorts.

By the time she reached the Pavilion she was being driven out of her mind by them. Gus Malta, the official caretaker, was hobbling around the Pavilion on his bad leg, fogging the ground, the shrubbery and the low branches of the trees with the rackety gasoline fogger he carried slung over his meaty shoulder. He stopped the motor and called to her in the sudden silence.

"You come over here," he ordered. "You'll get bit to death walking around like that tonight."

She hesitated and went over toward him. She did not like the man. He adopted a pseudo-fatherly air toward all the younger matrons of Sandy Key Estates, and toward the daughters of the older ones, but his manner seemed to mask sly insinuations. He did yard work for some of the residents, maintained the shell roads, the community tennis court and the Pavilion. For his community efforts, he was paid out of the treasury of the Sandy Key Estates Association, replenished by the quarterly assessment levied against each resident, based on the size of his lot.

"Now you stand right there and I'll put a cloud of this

upwind from you, and it will drift onto you. You hold your breath and turn around slow while it's going by."

"But I don't want to get that stuff in my hair."

"Won't hurt your hair," he said and yanked the starter cord, and belched a cloud of bug fog toward the beach. As it enveloped her she held her breath and turned slowly, dutifully, vastly annoyed at herself. *Now if he tells you to go roll in the sand, you'll do that too, you darn ninny.*

It drifted past her and she stopped turning and began breathing. "That's better," Gus said. "Now they won't mess with you, and raise all them red lumps." He grinned at her, exposing the ruin of his teeth. "You coming to the party?"

"I didn't know there was one."

"Now, when you see me fogging this place, you know somebody wants it for a party, Mrs. Hubble."

He always seemed to know exactly how impertinent he dared be, and he altered it to fit the temperament of each target. She knew that if she acted angry, he would pretend to be hurt and bewildered.

The Pavilion was the only community structure. It was open on three sides, forty by twenty, with a slab floor, steel uprights, and a thatched roof. There was a bamboo bar against the single wall. On the beach side was a big barbecue pit, and there were picnic tables under the Australian pines and under the coconut palms. The Pavilion was in the center of the two hundred feet of Gulf beach open to all the landlocked residents of the Estates.

"Who is giving the party, Gus?" she asked evenly.

"It's the Deegans and Mrs. McCall giving it, for about forty people, the way I heard it."

"Thanks for the spray job," she said and walked away from him, heading north on Gulf Lane toward the Sinnat house. The fogging machine did not start up. She resisted the impulse to look back, and knew she would see him standing there, watching her walk away. If she turned, he would grin placidly at her. It was a part of the mythology of the Estates that if a woman appeared in a swim suit in the farthest corner of the area, within ten seconds Gus Malta would find some work to be done within ten feet of her. Eloise Cable swore that she had turned quickly one evening and seen his face just outside the screen of her open bathroom window. It was generally agreed that if he wanted to gamble his job by risking the Peeping Tom act, Eloise Cable was the logical candidate. In spite of his manner, and all the work he left half done, it was agreed that he was very good with the kids.

As she pushed open the Sinnat's garden gate, she heard the concerted yapping of a dozen assorted children, and the sloshing and slapping of the water in their big pool.

2

JAMES WARREN WING drove north along Mangrove Road, the main road which bisected Sandy Key. He wondered vaguely how many times, how many hundred times he had driven this same stretch of road, and how many hundred times he would drive it again.

Once again she had afflicted him with what he had begun to call, with a sense of irony and guilt, Kat-fever. It was a restlessness, a dissatisfaction with all the familiar comforting routines.

He wanted to return to his normal blandness of spirit, maintain an uninvolved equanimity, suppressing the little bulgings of guilt and barbs of conscience. He knew it would be so much easier for him if he could be less scrupulous with himself, less intent on definitions and emotional accuracy. Were a man able to use his own fictions and realities interchangeably, he could be much more at home in a muddied world. Introspection, he had decided, is being bred out of the race because it is not survival-oriented.

So much fuss, he thought, about wanting a woman who does not even know she is wanted. Van, good buddy, rest easy. I've just helped her in a few small ways, and that's all there's going to be.

But he could hear Van's familiar response to that familiar protestation: But you keep seeing one hell of a lot of her, pal.

Because I like her. Is there a law?

Is she so much? Just a spare, high-pockets redhead, boy, skimpy upstairs and flat across the behinder, with angular hips and knobbly shoulders, and eyes which aren't either blue or gray, and monkey wrinkles across her forehead. She moves well and her skin is fine, but she's a slapdash, helter-skelter woman, too smart, too ready to argue. She carried your kids, and loved you truly, boy, and there's nothing there for ol' Jimmy.

But it was becoming ever more difficult for him to think of her as the same woman who had been married to Van Hubble, the same tense, skeptical Yankee bride Van had brought down with so much pride ten years ago. They had never liked each other.

This was a new friendship, one year old. A new friend

—as if Van's wife had died with him. I keep arranging to
see her because I like her.

But there was a hyena cackle in the back of his mind, a
sound of knowing derision. "You mean you'd like to maneu-
ver her into the sack, Wing, on any basis at all, even as a return for past favors, you sick son of a bitch, and you keep
sucking around waiting for a break, because you're too gut-
less to clue her, too afraid she'll say no in a very final way."

So is it so criminal to want a woman? She came into his
mind so vividly it seemed to blur his view of the bright highway, and he quickly sought escape from the impact of his
lust by forcing his mind up into shallow, fatuous levels and
keeping it bobbing there, like a child's balloon on random
currents, turning his head rapidly from side to side and wearing a small strained smile as he inventoried the minutiae of
reality—Ohio plates, a bird feeder, girl on a bike, gull on the
wing, pink house, fat man, For Rent sign.

When the seizure of his need was ended, he dared think
of her again, resenting her because she had made so many
of his assumptions about himself untenable. She had rup-
tured the structure of contentment and let the restlessness in.
She had made him wish for some kind of great change in his
days when he knew that no change could benefit him.

Thus far he knew he had been objective enough to avoid
the most obvious trap: the wishful belief that the very intensity of his awareness of her had somehow generated a
reciprocal tension, and that he need only make the first
hesitant move and she would fall sighing into his arms. It
was a constant temptation to read too much into meaningless things, like the idiots who find codes and prophecies in
Shakespeare. He knew well Kat's relentless honesty, and knew
she could not dissemble, knew she would immediately disclose any feeling she might have for him.

A year ago he would have been hilariously incredulous
had anyone tried to tell him he would become physically
infatuated with Katherine Hubble. It had come about so very
gradually.

In the beginning he had helped her with all the routines,
legalisms and barbarisms of sudden death. She had been
stunned, heartsick and lost—her eyes dull, her hair lifeless,
her skin drab, her movements slow, her voice hesitant and
indistinct. Before she had the heart for any future plans, he
had gone to Leroy Shannard to talk about Van's estate, and
learned that Van's few good years had come too late, the tax
had taken too much of it, and she would have to find work.
He had seen her often, out of a sense of duty to Van, helping her in small ways to find her way back to reality. For a

time he thought she might never recover, but then her pride and spirit began to show itself again.

It all began in such a mild, unanticipated way. It seemed pleasant to be with her, a small triumph to make her smile, a great victory when he made her laugh aloud. He took a possessive interest in her recovery, and when he thought she was ready he scouted the town and found the job for her at the bank, and made her take it before she thought she was able, and saw it work out as he had hoped.

It was during this time of reconstruction that he began to find pleasure in looking at her, at the shape of her hands, the line of her throat, the way she moved and turned, the bold configuration of her mouth. He had never found her as attractive while Van was alive. Perhaps then he had been more aware of flaws than of virtues, because that was the time when they had not liked each other particularly.

The pleasure of looking at her changed, little by little, into an oddly humid speculation. Over the years he had noted small clues to the probability that she and Van had a devotedly lusty marriage, and he wondered just what she had been like with him.

At first his conjecturing was a small game to play, but the game suddenly turned into compulsion and was out of control. He began to imagine her as the insatiable witch of all legend, and felt a revulsion toward himself that his imagination should have led him into such a pattern. It offended his own sense of personal dignity to have become a victim of such a fever. He told himself it was like a recurrence of adolescence. No woman could be so uniquely desirable. It was a delusion which would be vanquished were he ever to have her. He diagnosed it as a disease of immaturity, the imagination festering, and prescribed for himself dosages of some convenient and amiable women he knew who sought amusement as opposed to involvement, yet rose from these encounters with an undiminished thirst.

As his compulsion had become more established, he bemused himself with an ethical equation, analyzing every act to test its plausibility, to make certain he did nothing which could not be explained on some other basis than infatuation. Until this day all his relations with Kat had passed this test, but now he was at a new place in the relationship. He could not bend the requirements of plausibility far enough to permit him to have told Kat about the Grassy Bay plan. Elmo Bliss had told him to mention it to no one. But he had run with it to Kat, almost immediately, like the pebble placed at the feet of the she-penguin.

Now that it was done, he could see clearly his own attempts

at self-deceit. He had told himself it was his duty to warn her, but he had known all the time she would accept the challenge as an emotional obligation. What he had done was make yet another claim upon her gratitude, and had, at the same time, established a basis for their future proximity. He had, in effect, offered to be her spy in the enemy camp.

He prided himself on having been able to avoid thus far that most despicable rationalization of all, that of terming it love, thus giving a noble reason for the most furtive acts.

Love, he knew, was the ever-handy refuge of the scoundrel. And it did heavy duty as the lyrical justification for a million illicit scrabblings each night, on beaches, on back seats, under bushes and on the useful high-density foam rubber of forty thousand motels. Love was that jungly place reeking of Gloria, of death, of madness, with no escape except to the desert beyond the jungle, where, in relative peace, you could allow the bitter sun to bake your skull and toast your heart to an enduring little muffin. Not love, please.

The other rationalization to be avoided most carefully was that philosophical devaluation which asks who will give a damn a hundred years from now. That is the good old kosmic view of kopulation. Tomorrow, baby, they drop the bomb, so live tonight. It is an empty wind sighing through an empty place, and it works equally well for rape, theft and murder.

When he denied his motive the benefit of any ornamentation, it came down to a stark and almost Biblical lust. I want the woman. I want her in spite of all my sickly little requirements of maintaining my good opinion of myself. Unhampered by this tottering ethical structure, I could run faster and score sooner.

He could not think of desire as being a part of any plan, any enduring program. He could not see beyond the first time of taking her. It was a primitive need and a primitive act, and should it ever happen, he did not know what the world would be like until he was beyond her and could see what it was like on that far side.

For a long time he had comforted himself by telling himself that no matter how increasingly strong the compulsion might become, he was safely beyond those puppy years when he might have let it disrupt those other aspects of his life, those reassuring routines and relationships, which he had erected around himself like one of those insect towers of sand and spit which, in time, turn into protective stone.

Yet he had blithely told her of the Grassy Bay project. And that was like kicking the stone to see how solid it had become.

He drove by the small area of commercial development on Sandy Key adjacent to the causeway, and when he was beyond it he looked south along the blue reach of Grassy Bay. The bay was narrowest near the causeway, widening out toward the south. As he crossed the causeway he saw a small white cruiser setting out from Hoyt's Marina, with a stocky brown woman on the bow, coiling a line. Further down the bay he saw a pattern of flashing white on the water and saw the birds circling and diving in agitation. Maybe mackerel, he thought, in from the Gulf. More likely a school of jacks chopping the bait fish. Two outboards were converging on the roiled area.

When he came off the causeway he was stopped by the traffic light at the intersection of Mangrove Road and Bay Highway. After the May and June hiatus, the summer tourist season was gathering a rather shabby momentum. In the winter months the biggest contingent came from the central states, and there were so many of them that at last, to the residents of Palm County, they seemed to become but one elderly couple, endlessly repeated, driving a bulbous blue car with Ohio plates (at wandering unpredictable speeds), the man in Bermudas, the woman with a big straw purse, questing through all the towns of the shallow-water coast, bemused, slightly indignant, frequently bored, like people charged with some mission who had lost their sealed orders before they had a chance to open them.

As was so solemnly and frequently stated by all public officials and all Chamber of Commerce executives, the winter flow of this endlessly duplicated couple was the backbone of the economy, and it often seemed that the supply was inexhaustible, yet Jimmy Wing had noted among the businessmen of Palm City an anxious and almost superstitious attitude toward the continuity of the flow. They heartened themselves with every evidence of repeat business, no matter how questionable the source of the statistics. They fretted about the accessibility of the Caribbean islands. But at the heart of their unrest was the never-spoken conviction that there was really nothing to keep them coming down. It was a fine place to live, and a poor place to visit. They could not quite see how any sane reasonable person would willingly permit himself to be "processed" through that long junk strip of Tamiami, exchanging his vacation money for overpriced lodgings, indifferent food, admission to fish tanks, snake farms and shell factories.

So secretly disturbed were these businessmen about the proliferating shoddiness of the coast that they were constantly taking random and somewhat contradictory action. The more

the beach eroded away, or disappeared into private ownership, the more bravely the huge highway signs proclaimed
the availability of miles of white-sand beaches. As the shallow-water fishing decreased geometrically under the attrition
of dredging, filling, sewage and too many outboard motors,
they paid to have the superb fishing advertised, and backed
contests which would further decimate the dwindling fish
population. As the quiet and primitive mystery of the broad
tidal bays disappeared, as the mangroves and the rookeries
and the oak hammocks were uprooted with such industrious-
ness the morning sound of construction equipment became
more familiar than the sound of the mockingbird, the businessmen substituted the delights of pageants, parades and
beauty contests. (See the Grandmaw America Contest, with
evening gown, talent and bathing suit eliminations.)

So quietly uneasy were the business interests that the few
tourist attractions of any dignity or legitimacy whatsoever
were pointed to with more pride than they merited. (Weeki
Wachee, Bok Tower, Ringling Museums—and "The Last Sup-
per" duplicated in genuine ceramic tile.)

One motel operator on Cable Key had expressed the hidden fear to Jimmy Wing one quiet September afternoon.
"Some season we'll get all ready for them. We'll fix up all
the signs and raise the rates and hire all the waitresses and
piano players and pick the trash off the beaches and clean
the swimming pools and stock up on all the picture postcards
and sun glasses and straw slippers and cement pelicans like
we always have, and we'll set back and wait, and they won't
show up. Not a single damn one." He had peered at Jimmy
in the air-conditioned gloom of the bar, and laughed with a
quiet hysteria. "No one at all."

And this hidden fear, Jimmy realized, was one of the reasons—perhaps the most pertinent reason—for the Grassy Bay
project. Once you had consistently eliminated most of the
environmental features which had initially attracted a large
tourist trade, the unalterable climate still made it a good
place to live. New permanent residents would bolster the
economy. And so, up and down the coast, the locals leaned
over backward to make everything as easy and profitable as
possible for the speculative land developers. Arvida went into
Sarasota. General Development went into Port Charlotte. And
a hundred other operators converged on the "sun coast,"
platting the swamps and sloughs, clearing the palmetto scrub
lands, laying out and constructing the suburban slums of
the future.

In the Palm City area it had not worked the way the downtown businessmen had hoped it would. Buck Flake had de-

veloped Palm Highlands, and Earl Ganson had set up Lakeview Village, and Pete Bender had made a good thing out of
Lemon Ridge Estates, but just as fast as the population
density in the newly developed areas warranted it, the big
new shopping centers went in.

Grassy Bay would be an entirely different kind of proposition. It was a lot closer to downtown than the scrub-land
housing. The waterfront lots would be more expensive, the
houses bigger, the future residents a little fatter in the purse
than the retireds who bought their budget tract houses back
in the piny flats where the cattle had once grazed.

Ahead of Jimmy Wing as he waited for the light was a
typical summer tourist vehicle, an old green Hudson from
Tennessee, the fenders rusting, the back seat full of kids, a
luggage rack on top piled high and covered with a frayed
tarp. A car in the traffic headed out onto Sandy Key honked
and somebody called his name, but he did not turn quickly
enough to see who it was. Two cars later he recognized
Eloise Cable alone in her white Karmann Ghia with the top
down. The yellow scarf tied around her black hair made
her face and shoulders look exceptionally brown. She grasped
the wheel high and held her chin high, looking arrogant, impatient and behind schedule.

When the light changed he turned left on Bay Boulevard
and drove on into the middle of the city, turned left on
Center Street and drove out over City Bridge onto Cable Key.
He drove a mile and a half south, past all the motels and
the beach shops, the bars and the concession stands, and
turned right into the long narrow sand driveway that led to
his rented cottage on the bay side of Cable Key.

It was an old frame cottage of cypress and hard pine, with
one bedroom, a small screened porch facing the bay. The
neighbors on either side were close, but he had let the brush
grow up so thickly along the property line he could not see
them.

The interior of the cottage was orderly, in a cheerless, barren way. Except for a shelf of books and a rack of records, it
looked as if it had been put in order to be inspected by a
prospective tenant, in a semifurnished category. When the
infrequent guest would comment on how it looked as if no
one lived there, Jimmy Wing would be mildly surprised, but
he would look around and see the justice of the accusation.
When he had sold the house in town and moved out to the
cottage on Cable Key two years ago, the habits he had
established had been, perhaps, a reaction to the dirt, clutter
and endless confusion and turmoil of those last few years of

Gloria. But once he had satisfied his need for a severe order around him, the pattern had been fixed, and he had no particular reason to change it.

Breakfast was the only meal he ate at home. He was usually out of the house by ten in the morning. The four house-keeping cottages were owned by Joe Parmitter, who also owned the Princess Motel over on the Gulf side, across Ocean Road from the cottages. One of the motel maids, Loella, had a spare key to Jimmy's cottage, and every morning after finishing up the motel rooms, she would come over and clean the cottage and make the bed.

Jimmy Wing had been for several years a reporter on the Palm City *Record-Journal*, the morning newspaper Ben Killian had inherited. He covered the courthouse and the city hall, the police beat, special news breaks, and did feature stories of his own devising rather than on assignment. Nearly all his work was by-lined, and his copy was clean enough and safe enough to escape rewrite. He had a desk assigned to him in the newsroom, but he did not use it very often, preferring to hammer out his copy on the old standard Underwood on the table by a living room window in the cottage. The paper went to bed at midnight, and it was the only paper in town, so the pressure was seldom noticeable.

He had learned long ago that if he spent too much time in the newspaper offices in the old pseudo-Moorish building on Bayou Street, J. J. Borklund, Ben Killian's managing editor, would rope him into any kind of dog work available, from obits to Little League. Borklund had a double-entry approach to journalism. You squeeze every dime out of advertising and circulation, and you put the minimum back into wire services, syndicated features and operating staff. And you take an editorial stand in favor of the flag, mother-hood, education, liberty and tourism, offending no one. And so the *Record-Journal,* on a county-wide circulation of 23,000 returned a pleasant and substantial profit each year.

Borklund had long since given up trying to make Jimmy Wing conform to his idea of proper diligence. He had given up after two disastrous weeks during which Jimmy, in order to prove his point, had reported to the newsroom every day at nine and quit at five, and had done exactly what Borklund had told him to do.

Jimmy Wing knew that the paper could not hope to acquire a man as perfectly suited to the job as he was. He had grown up in Palm City. He had an encyclopedic memory for past relationships and pertinent detail. He could transpose rough notes into solid and entertaining copy with a speed which dismayed the other reporters. When anything had to be fer-

reted out, he knew exactly whom to talk to. And he was
able to report about 20 per cent of what he learned.

But, as Jimmy Wing knew, and Ben Killian knew, and
presumably J. J. Borklund knew, it wasn't the way he had
planned it. For a time it had gone according to plan. He had
worked for the paper during the summers while he was at
Gainesville. After graduation he went onto the paper full
time, knowing he could use two or three years of that highly
practical experience before moving along to a bigger city, a
bigger paper. Gloria had agreed. And during those first two
years he had begun to place minor articles with secondary
magazines. That, too, was part of the master plan.

In fact, he had actually resigned and had worked for seven
weeks on the Atlanta *Journal* before Gloria had that first
time of strangeness and the doctor in Atlanta had said she
would be better off in the more familiar environment of
Palm City. Ben Killian had been glad to get him back.

During the bad years he had resigned himself to this
smaller and less demanding arena than the one he had
trained himself for. When the necessity to stay had been
ended, he had remained. The strain of the bad years had
somehow leached away his eagerness for a greater challenge.
Now he could adjust his effort to the extent that it filled his
days, amiably enough, with enough mild pressure to keep
him from thinking about anything which might make him
feel uneasy.

He went into the cottage, took the wad of folded copy
paper out of his hip pocket and tossed it onto the table beside the typewriter as he walked through the living room. He
took off his shirt and slacks, threw them on the bed, went
to the kitchen and took the last cold beer out of the refrigerator. He scrawled "beer" on his shopping list, carried
the cold can out onto the screened porch off the kitchen and
sat in a canvas sling chair. A blue heron stalked through
the shallows near his narrow crooked dock with attentive
caution. Forty feet beyond the end of the dock a mullet
made its three leaps.

He sipped the beer and looked out across the bay and
thought about Kat, drifting from reality to erotic fantasy
until finally he felt disgusted with himself. He went in and
phoned the paper and asked for the city desk extension.
Borklund had gone home. He would be back in at ten. Brian
Haas was on the desk.

"What'll you break down and give us, lover?" Brian asked.
"As always, old Jumping J. Jesus wants me to make it up
so he can tear it down and make it up his way."

"Let me see. About twelve inches on the Zoning Board of Appeals turning thumbs down on Ganson's trailer park."

"Boxed on page one?"

"Depends on what else you've got."

"What else I've got is practically nothing so far."

"And I won't be much help. I'll puff what I've got. So make it six inches on the Sheriff's car thief being wanted by Pennsylvania, six inches on the FHA squabble over Lakeview Village, four inches on opening the new parking lot behind Plummer Park and . . . one, two, three . . . five little filler-inners, five bits of lint from the public navel. Don't forget I left off all the County Commission stuff at two o'clock, Bri. Am I supposed to fill the whole sheet?"

"But your prose style has such an aching beauty, Wingo."

"I know. It sings." He looked at his watch. "You'll have this stuff by eight."

After he hung up, he turned the floor fan on, got his cigarettes and lighter, rolled paper into the machine, spread his notes out beside him on the scarred table and hammered the news stories out with four-finger efficiency, pausing very rarely to hunt for word or phrase, taking a familiar excusable pride in his competence.

When he was showering, his phone rang. It was Elmo Bliss.

"Jim boy, we got ourselves interrupted this morning before I finished all I had to say."

"I got most of the message, Elmo."

"But I never did get around to telling you where you fit in so good."

"Or where you fit in, Elmo."

There was a momentary silence on the line. Jimmy felt a quick apprehension, and was annoyed at himself for feeling alarm. He had a continuing compulsion to irritate Elmo Bliss, like a small boy's urge to stand too close to the lion cage. Though he could think of no ways in which Elmo could do him any serious harm, there was a flavor of wildness under control about the man which could cause alarm on a visceral rather than a rational basis.

Bliss chuckled. "You say things right out, Jim boy. Better you should wait until you know, and then say nothing. You come on out here to the place this evening, and we can finish talking. There'll be some folks around like always, but a better place to talk than the courthouse."

"I can't promise any particular time, Elmo."

"This will keep going until you get here, boy."

3

AFTER KATHERINE HUBBLE brought her two waterlogged children home from the Sinnat pool, she let them change into pajamas while she fixed the evening meal for the three of them. They ate at the round table on the enclosed part of the patio. Roy was eight and Alicia was seven. They had Van's coloring, and already they had a deep tan which she could never achieve.

In one sense it seemed the bitterest blow of all that Van should have lost the chance to watch them grow up. But sometimes she caught herself feeling a ridiculously unfair indignation toward Van, as if he had purposely run out and left her with all the problems of discipline, health, education and love.

And, as always when she was alone with them, she found herself fretting about whether she was handling it all properly.

Van's death had stunned the children. They had become irritable, whiny, quarrelsome and disobedient. And at just the time when she could feel that they were beginning to make a good adjustment, they had to turn the house over to the Brandts and move down to that small apartment on one of the back streets behind the main post office. Though they seemed to understand why it had to be done, in many ways it seemed a more severe emotional shock to them than the loss of their father. It destroyed the security of the known place. Roy, in particular, was a disciplinary problem during the first weeks of the new school year.

By spring they had begun to handle it better, and when they could at last move back to the Sandy Key house they knew so well, they ran and yelped and grinned the whole day long.

She tried to maintain as many of the ceremonies of being a family as possible, and she was grateful for the shortness of her work week, but it was still an abnormal situation to have them looked after by someone else during the weekdays.

She knew she could have found no situation more ideal than the one Claire Sinnat had volunteered. Claire had the twin boys, four years old, the big beach house and the pool and the grounds, a full-time cook-housekeeper, and a full-time girl—a Mexican girl named Esperanza—to look after her kids. Esperanza was chunky, cheerful and devoted to children. On her afternoon off, either Claire filled in or Natalie Sinnat took over. Nat was spending the summer with them. She was nineteen, Dial Sinnat's daughter by one of his previous marriages.

"My God, sweetie," Claire had said. "Shoo them up here every day, or I'll think you aren't being neighborly. The place is crawling with urchins all the time, and Di and I couldn't care less, really. Your two are sweethearts, and Floss will stuff a lunch into them on schedule, and Esperanza will keep them safe. In bad weather we've got that huge indestructible playroom."

After much argument, Claire had agreed to let her pay Floss and Esperanza an additional five dollars a week for the work and the responsibility. Roy and Alicia had begun to think of the Sinnat place as a second home. It was good not to have to worry about them. Van had had both of them swimming by the time they had learned to walk.

The kids were subdued at dinner, their brown faces drowsy, their voices slowed by the exhaustions of the long hot day. Their objections at being told to go to bed were halfhearted.

After they were asleep and the dishes done, Kat hesitated for some time, inventing and discarding plausible excuses, then phoned Sally Ann Lesser.

"I thought you might be at the Deegan's party," Kat said.

"Oh hell, no," Sally Ann said. "Sammy and Wilma go further afield for their weird guests. They find people nobody ever saw before." Her voice was slightly slurred. "Kat, honey, why don't you come on down here and help Carol and me destroy reputations? I'll send my idiot daughter up. She can do her summer-school homework just as well there as here. And don't let her shill you into a sitter fee this time."

Frosty Lesser arrived within five minutes with an armful of books. She was fifteen and looked older because of the maturity of her figure and her indifferent, impenetrable poise.

When Kat went up the walk toward the Lessers' front door, Sally Ann called to her, "Out here in the cage, dear. Come around."

She went across the lawn and around to the side door to the screened cage. The outside floods were on, and there was a faint reflected glow inside the high cage. Sally Ann reclined in a white chaise. She was a sturdy, muscular, brown woman with a heavy, affirmative jaw, curly gray hair worn very short. She wore swim suits in hot weather, slacks and work shirts in cool weather. On the rare occasions when she was forced to wear a dress, she seemed to lose her confidence and authority. She had a good deal of inherited money, and she was very careful with it. She had a rasping voice, complete domination over her husband, an offhand, derogatory attitude toward her three children. She drank quietly, slowly, and steadily all day long every day, without evident effect. She worked in her yard, swam every day, and was a ruthlessly efficient housekeeper and cook. She lied constantly and for no apparent reason, and became highly irritable when anyone tried to trap her in a contradiction.

Carol Killian sat in a redwood chair with her long legs hooked over one arm. She was a slender, dark, brooding beauty, just a few years past her prime, but still exquisite. She never had much to say. Her habitual expression was one of thoughtful intelligence, of perception and sensitivity. But when she did speak, her voice was high and thin and childish, and her every remark exposed the dull innocence and inanity of her mind.

Strangers often thought it was an act and tried to laugh with her, but they merely confused her and hurt her. They soon came to realize that she was a decorative object which had learned to dress itself tastefully, move gracefully, give itself good care and maintenance, and perform a narrow range of household duties. It could talk with a certain amount of animation about clothes, cosmetics and household furnishings. Ben Killian had acquired it long ago, and seemed content to live with it. Over an unstated number of pregnancies —Sally Ann insisted it had to be at least ten—she had carried one as far as six months, and it had lived in an incubator for six days before expiring.

"Fix yourself a noggin," Sally Ann said. "Carol just went in and brought out some new ice."

There was a weak, hooded light over the drink table. Kat fixed herself a weak gin and Collins mix and carried it over to where Sally Ann and Carol were, and sat on a redwood bench.

"We were saying that Sammy and Wilma Deegan have to keep finding new groups because they wear the old ones out," Sally Ann said. "Remember how they knocked everybody out when they moved into the Estates? My God, we thought they were the most wildly amusing people in the world. And in less than a year, dears, they ran out of material. They have these eight or nine routines they can do, and by the third time around you have found out they're very dreary little people. They have to have the laughs and the enthusiasm and the admiration, dears. They don't give parties. They give recitals."

"We were invited," Carol said. "I wanted to go. I think they're real funny. They keep me in stitches. But Ben had to be at the boat yard. I just hate to go to parties without Ben."

Kat said, as casually as she could manage it, "I wanted to talk to you about my house, Sally Ann. They say it's a better time to sell houses now than a year ago. I thought maybe Burt has said something about how houses are moving."

"But you can't sell out and leave the group!" Sally Ann said.

"I don't know. The effort of hanging onto it seems to be more than it's worth, really. I think that if I could sell it for a good price, I'd move over onto the bay side of the key. There's a little lot over there I could buy, and I could have one of those little Bender-Bilt houses put on it, and I wouldn't have anywhere near the taxes and maintenance. It wouldn't be like moving back into town. I'd be only about a mile from here. And I would have a little bit of bay frontage. I love Grassy Bay. I love to look out at that bay."

"Hah!" Sally Ann said.

"What's that supposed to mean?"

"Katy, dear, up until as recently as a month ago, I wouldn't have dropped you even a clue, but now I can tell you, *don't* plan on looking out at Grassy Bay very long. I'm dropping a hint for your own good, dear. I wouldn't want to see you make a terrible mistake."

Kat said, indignantly, "If you're trying to tell me somebody is going to fill Grassy Bay, you're wrong, Sally Ann. We didn't let it happen two years ago, and we won't let it happen now, or ever."

"Dear Kat, you sound awfully fierce, but there isn't a darn thing you can do about it. We're good friends, and I hope we can stay good friends, but you must know by now I don't go all misty about the birds and the trees and the dear little fish the way you do. We're going to have a nice big development over there, Kat, and Burt and I are going to have a nice cozy little piece of it."

"But it's such a . . . a wicked thing to do, Sally Ann."

"To warn you about buying a lot over there on the bay?"

"You know that isn't what I mean."

"Kat, you're a sweet girl, but you don't face up to reality. *Somebody* is going to fill that bay sooner or later and whoever does it is going to make buckets of money. So be glad your friends and neighbors are going to do it."

"I can't be glad anybody is going to try to do it. I'm going to have to spread the word, Sally Ann."

"But why bother, dear? It won't do you any good, you know. You and your conservation buddies will just waste a lot of energy and indignation. It's gone too far to stop it now. For God's sake, sweetie, do you think I'd be investing in it if there was any chance it could be stopped? Do me one little favor, though. In return for the favor I've done you. Don't let on where you heard it."

"Gee, you know, those kitchens in those little Bender houses are just darling," Carol Killian said. "I saw one and it made me want to be just married and starting out."

Kat Hubble stood up. "Thanks for the drink and the hot tip, Sally Ann."

"Now I'm getting nervous about telling you."

"I had to find out sooner or later, didn't I?"

"Yes, but I think we were all hoping it would be later than this. Dear, do you want me to ask Burt what he thinks he could do about selling your house?"

"Not for a while, I guess. I think I'm going to be too busy to think about it."

Kat walked slowly home along the dark street. She could hear distant music over the tinny little speaker at the Pavilion, half lost in a soft sound of the waves against the beach. A meager breeze made false rain sounds in the palms. A whippoorwill, far away, made his sound of weary astonishment. A nearby mockingbird made repetitive improvisation, with a silvery clarity and an undertone of anxiety. Bugs skirred and grated in the unsold lots of Sandy Key Estates.

Frosty gathered up her books when Kat walked in.

"They didn't make a sound," Frosty said. "I had a Coke. Gee, thanks a lot, but I couldn't take any money, Mrs. Hubble. I told my mother I wouldn't. Anyhow, it's hardly been more than a half hour. Well . . . thanks. Thanks a lot. Gee, any time you want me to sit for you . . ."

After the girl left, Kat went to the phone and called Colonel Thomas Lamson Jennings, A.U.S., Ret., the president of Save Our Bays, Inc. Colonel Jennings lived further north on the Key, on the bay side.

"Tom? Kat Hubble. I know it's an odd time to phone, but I have to tell you this. That Grassy Bay thing is going to open up again."

"Again? Are you kidding me?"

She quickly explained what she had learned and said,

"I got it from Sally Ann Lesser, but that's not for general distribution."

"Katherine, I could have used you as a staff G-2 in a couple of wars. Those idiots obviously thought they were going to catch us off balance. Can you come here at five o'clock tomorrow?"

"Let me think. Yes, I can make it."

"Good girl. I'll see if I can track down some more information on it tomorrow. I'll call a meeting of the Executive Committee. The big question now is to find out exactly when they're going to make their first move, and then we'll know how much time we have."

"Maybe . . . we can't stop it this time."

"Why not?"

"These are local men, Tom. They'll have things pretty much all their own way."

"Don't be such a defeatist, Katherine. Of *course* we'll whip them, just as we did before. Last time we whipped them in the very first round, the public hearing. We'll try to do the same thing this time, but if we don't, there are a lot more things we can do. Remember? We'll get it into the courts and we'll stall them until they give it up as a bad job. All we'll have to do is maintain a united front. I imagine there'll be some new pressures on our membership this time, local in origin, so it'll be up to us to keep the membership in line. I promise you one thing, Katherine, I'll never look out this window at Grassy Bay and see dredges out there."

After she had hung up it took almost a half hour for the hearty confidence of the colonel's voice to lose its persuasion. She recalled Van's sour comment on Tom Jennings. "That's the type who'd lead the Light Brigade up the wrong ravine, yelling 'Charge!' and grinning like an idiot."

But at the end Van had to admit Tom had organized it well.

It seemed a pity it had to be done all over again.

She finished her letter to her sister in Burlington, sealed it and put it where she would be certain to see it on her way out in the morning. She read two pages of a book and put it aside. She turned the television set on and searched the channels and turned it off. She walked back and forth through the silence of the house in a restlessness all too familiar.

When she went into her bedroom the arrangement of her cosmetics on the top of her dressing table did not look quite right to her. She examined it more closely and saw that several jars and bottles were not as she had left them.

It had been Frosty, of course. She examined a lipstick and found it worn down in a manner different from the way she had left it. Balled tissue stained with the same shade was in the bottom of her wastebasket. She was surprised at the extent of her own irritation, and tried to tell herself it was a perfectly normal thing for any fifteen-year-old girl to do.

But somehow having Frosty do it made it less palatable. She did not like Frosty, or Frosty's seventeen-year-old brother, Jigger, or the twelve-year-old sister, Debbie Louise. They were all superbly healthy, beautifully coordinated children, pale blonds with dark-blue eyes. Toward all adults they exhibited a watchful, impenetrable politeness which somehow had a false flavor, as though it were a mask for a contemptuous amusement. More than any other teenagers she knew, they seemed to confirm the assumption of the marketing experts that this was a new and separate race, a special people with only limited contact with the adult world.

It seemed too simple, somehow, to say they were spoiled. There had always been the pocket money in whatever quantity they seemed to need, and the use of the family charge accounts. Burt Lesser certainly imposed no disciplines on them. He was a big soft balding man with such mild indefinite features that he could be caricatured by drawing an egg and putting heavy black glasses frames on it. He dressed more formally than most of the businessmen in Palm City. He had a loud methodical baritone laugh which he used either too soon or too late, and generally too often. Burt had obtained his realtor's license soon after they had moved down from Wisconsin, fifteen years ago, the same year Sally Ann had received the final and most massive installment on her inheritance. Through a sweaty, earnest, fumbling diligence he had managed to do quite well at the trade. And Sally Ann had done well too, by buying in her own name those investment bargains which came up from time to time. Burt was an active work-horse member of a wide range of civic organizations.

There were those who said you just had to admire ol' Burt for the way he gets out and digs when, as far as the money is concerned, he could lay right back and take it easy.

But one night, on the Lesser's patio, while Van was still alive, Sally Ann, at one of the rare times when she was conspicuously in her cups, had given what was probably an accurate explanation. Somebody had been kidding Burt, asking him when he was going to retire. "Retire, for chrissake!" Sally Ann had roared. "As long as he can walk and talk, he's going to have an office to go to. I told him when I married him he wasn't going to clutter up the house all day long. That was the deal. It would drive me nuts having him around here trying to wait on me so he could feel useful." Burt had laughed, but it had been a hollow effort.

On reflection it seemed to Kat that Burt Lesser was an unlikely person to be heading up this new Palmland Development Company. He did not seem sufficiently directed, or properly ruthless. But he was well known and his reputation was good.

She was in bed by eleven-thirty. After she turned her light out, she stared wide-eyed into the darkness and kept trying new positions, hoping to find one which would relax her. When it was quarter after twelve by her bedside clock she gave up and took one of the green capsules Ray Coplon had prescribed for her. In a little while the familiar feeling of the drug began. The black world began to expand, moving out and back and away from her, leaving her smaller and smaller and smaller in an enormous bed—small and silky and dwindling away.

4

It was nine-thirty when Jimmy Wing arrived at the home
of County Commissioner Elmo Bliss, three miles east of
the city line, out on the Lemon Ridge Road. It was a huge
old frame house, and Elmo had put a lot of money into
modernization over the past few years. The house, and how
he had acquired it, had become part of the legend, and
had suffered distortions as had most other parts of the legend.

Jimmy Wing often caught himself in the act of exag-
gerating the man's past. Elmo had that inexplicable capacity
to seem just a little more thoroughly alive than anyone else.
Now, in his early forties, he looked like a leaner and younger
version of Jimmy Hoffa, but with a roan-brown brush cut,
and that tough sallow cracker skin the sun can't mark,
and eyes of a clear pale dangerous gray. He had Hoffa's
abrupt charm, his uncomical arrogance, and the same air of
absolute certainty, diluted not at all by the back-country
drawl, a lazier way of moving. In the past few years Elmo
had settled on the kind of clothing he would wear for all
except the most formal occasions. He wore slacks and sports
shirts in plain colors, in dull hues of gray, blue and green,
all in an understated western cut, along with pale hats
which were never quite ranch hats, but gave a subtle out-
door-man impression.

Jimmy Wing knew the bare outlines of the story, and it
always pleased him to be able to add little incidents which
had the flavor of truth. He came from a large clan noted
over the years for the frequency of their trouble with the
law, as well as a casual inbreeding which did the stock no
good. Poachers, commercial fishermen, guides, 'gator hunters,
brawlers. But Elmo was the one who became an All-State
wingback, and picked the best deal out of all the scholarship offers and went on to Georgia. When Jimmy had begun
senior high, Elmo had been gone three years, but the legends
still circulated in the high school.

Elmo lasted two years at Georgia before he was thrown
out. He came back with a big red convertible and money
in his pocket. The sheriff at that time had been Pete Nambo,
a solemn brutal man who believed that a Bliss was a Bliss,

37

no matter how many times one of them had had his name on the sports page.

When Elmo didn't have enough money left to pay his fine when Nambo arrested him the third time, the sentence was ninety days. Nambo put Bliss right onto one of the county road gangs, swinging a brush hook right through the heat of summer, living on beans, side meat and chicory coffee. And each evening, after the truck brought them back, if Nambo felt like it and had the energy, he'd have two deputies bring Elmo to him and he would work him over in an attempt to break him and make him beg. Nambo had learned he could break on the average of one out of every three Blisses he could give his personal attention to, and he had to find out which variety he had available this time. Not one of Elmo's avid fans from the old days came to his rescue.

When Elmo was released it was an even-money bet around town as to whether he'd take off for some friendlier place, or stay around and get into more trouble. But he sold his red car and apparently tucked the money away, and went to work as a rough carpenter. He kept his mouth shut, stayed out of bars, and ceased to be an object of any public interest. It wasn't long before he became construction foreman for old Will Maroney. Then he made some sort of complicated deal whereby he took a spec house off Will's hands. After he dressed it up and sold it quickly, the little firm became Maroney and Bliss. They tackled a bigger job than Will had ever attempted alone, and when they had made out well on it, suddenly Elmo broke with Maroney and went ahead on his own, calling himself The Bliss Construction Company ("Live in a Home of Bliss"), and Will Maroney went around town cursing Elmo for having walked off with the four top men out of his work crew, men who had been with him for many years.

The wise businessmen of Palm City said that Elmo was going to fold any minute, and all his creditors were going to take a beating. They said he was moving too fast, buying too many vehicles and too much equipment, taking on too many jobs, expanding his work crews too fast, doing too much damn-fool advertising.

But he didn't fold. As soon as it was obvious to him, as it would soon be obvious to the rest of the community, that he was over the hump and in the clear, he married one of the Boushant girls, Dellie, the next to the youngest. There were seven of them. Felicia, Margo, Ceil, Belle, Frannie, Dellie and Tish. They had all been born and raised in the big house out on Lemon Ridge Road. Their father had been a carnival concessionaire, their mother—until she got too heavy too young—a wire walker.

Not one of the seven girls could have been called a beauty, but they were uniformly attractive, all with vivacity, humor, their own brand of pride, and a good sense of style. They were affectionate, amorous, fun-loving, warm-blooded girls, and perhaps because there were so many of them, their reputation was a little more florid than their deeds warranted. Over the years of their girlhood, a thousand different cars must have turned in at that dusty driveway to pick one or the other of them up.

One by one, starting at the top, they eventually married, soundly but not advantageously, married sober, reliable electricians, delivery men, mechanics, and began at once to bear them healthy lively children.

In high school and during college vacations Elmo had dated several of the Boushant girls, and at the time of his marriage one of the sniggering jokes around town was that he had sampled every one of them and settled for the one with the most talent. Jimmy Wing suspected this was a partial truth. Elmo would have been too young for Felicia, and possibly too young for Margo. And too old for Tish. But a judicious weighing of all the factors of opportunity and inclination made it reasonable to assume Elmo Bliss had enjoyed three of his wife's elder sisters. He had gone with Ceil for a little while when he was in high school, and been seen often with Belle during the first summer of college, and had been dating Frannie at the time Sheriff Pete Nambo locked him up.

Also, Jimmy could remember the tone and expression of awe with which a local rancher had once described to him the young manhood of Elmo Bliss: "There was three or four of them, Elmo the leader, roarin' up and down this coast a hundred miles an hour any night of the week, all over Collier, Lee and Charlotte Counties, as well as Palm County, and inland to Hendry and Glades. I tried to run with them for a while there, but it like to wore me down. That Elmo, he'd do any damn thing come into his head. I'd say you could count on two fights a night anyway, and you could sure count on women because that's what Elmo was mostly hunting for. Lord God, the women! I'm telling you, Jimmy, he could find them where they wasn't. Schoolgirls, tourist ladies, waitresses, nurses, schoolteachers, all kind of shapes and sizes and ages, and we'd bundle them into the cars and go off, slamming down them little back roads, singin', drinkin', the girls squealin', and it seemed like we couldn't be anyplace in six counties where Elmo didn't know someplace nearby where we could take them. Anything warm, breathing and with a skirt on, Elmo seemed to get it without anywhere near the amount of ·fuss you'd expect."

So when Elmo married Dellie Boushant, and moved out to the big old house on the Lemon Ridge Road, the people decided he was settling for a smaller future than some had begun to predict for him. He would be just another of the men who had married Boushant girls. Many of the successful men in Palm County had, in times past, dated one or another of the Boushant girls, but successful men had not married them.

So Elmo had married Dellie and moved out into the old house, and she had begun the bearing of his children; there were six of them now, ranging from thirteen down to two. Nowadays people pointed to Elmo's marriage to Dellie as part of his luck and part of his success. Either the times had changed, or Elmo had changed them to suit himself.

Jimmy knew the story of how Elmo had acquired the big house and the sixty acres around it, and he suspected it was true. After Elmo had been married to Dellie a little over two years—she was twenty then and he was eight years older—Mama Boushant had dropped dead in her own kitchen, willing equal shares in the house and land to her seven daughters. Elmo was overextended at the time, so nobody knew quite how he managed it. At the conference there were thirteen of them at the huge dining room table, six daughters, six husbands and Tish, the unmarried one. They say Elmo let the arguments run on for an hour before he took the money out of his pocket, ninety bills, one hundred dollars each. As he started counting it into six separate piles, fifteen bills in each pile, the angry talk died away and for most of the counting there was a complete silence. Elmo said, "You sign the release, and then you pick up the money, in that order. If there's just one who won't sign, the deal is off for the rest of you."

Steve Lupak, Belle's husband, put up the biggest argument, saying the land was worth an absolute minimum of two hundred an acre, which would bring it up to twelve thousand even without the house. That started the rest of them off. Elmo leaned back with his eyes half closed, almost smiling, refusing to answer any of them. They appealed to Dellie, trying to make her admit it was unfair. But she sat close beside Elmo, placid and loving and heavy with her second child, the one who would be named Annabelle. By eleven Belle and Felicia were the only holdouts. By midnight Belle and Steve still fought it. By half past midnight they too gave up, and it was Elmo's house from then on.

Jimmy Wing had talked about that arrangement with Frannie Boushant a little over two years ago. Frannie Vernon, her name was at that time. It had come about in an unplanned way. He had known her in high school—she was two classes behind him—but had never dated her. He ran into her by accident in Miami. Borklund had sent him over to cover a Citrus Commission hearing. He had driven over, and when the hearing had been adjourned at four, he had phoned his story in and had been advised by Borklund that he might as well stay over and cover the session scheduled for the following day.

As he was walking toward his car he met Frannie on the sidewalk. It was a cool day. She wore a short cloth coat over a dark wool skirt and white angora sweater. There was such a family resemblance between the sisters, he did not know if she was Ceil, Belle or Frannie when she smiled warmly at him and greeted him by name. She detected his slight hesitation and said, "I'm Frannie, Jim."

They moved out of the pedestrian traffic, over toward the store fronts to talk. Like all the Boushant girls, she was dark, with high cheekbones, a long oval face, pretty eyes of deep brown, a heavy mouth which smiled readily, prominent teeth, an immature chin.

"What are you doing over here, Frannie?"

"Working. Living. God, it's a brute town, Jim. But I had to go somewhere. The Social Security was enough to get along on. It's pretty good when you've got little kids. But I was just sort of dragging through every day, and so a couple of months ago I parked the kids on Ceil, bless her, and came over here."

Suddenly he had remembered Dick Vernon had been killed six months previously. He had worked for General Telephone as a lineman. He'd gone out after tarpon with two friends on a Sunday morning in the small cabin cruiser one of them owned, and it had blown up in the Gulf a mile off Sanibel Island. The other two, with bad flesh burns, had made it to the beach. The boat had burned to the water line and sunk. Dick's body had been recovered the following day.

"That was a terrible thing, about Dick," he said.

Tears stood in her eyes and she laughed in a mirthless way. "Look at me. One kind word and I'm off. It's taking a long time to really believe it, Jim. So here I am, in Miami, which I guess is as good as any other place would be at the moment. I'm waiting table at that restaurant down the

block there, on the other side. Gee, it's good to see somebody from home."

"I'm covering a meeting. I have to stay over, and I was
about to find a place. Can I buy you a drink, Frannie?
Dinner, maybe?"

She looked thoughtful, glanced at her watch. "Sure. I
guess so. But I'd like a chance to get a bath and get fixed
up. You work in that place, you smell like grease all over.
How about you pick me up at six-thirty?"

She told him where it was and how to get there. He
went over and checked into a motel on the north end of
the beach. On the off chance, he rented better and larger
accommodations than he had planned to, feeling sly and
semiguilty as he did so. She was ready when he stopped
for her, and she did not ask him in. She looked very good
to him. She wore a sleeveless dress in a fuzzy pumpkin
wool, and a beige wool coat and a pillbox hat in a paisley
pattern. He took her to one of the big, quiet, shadowy
restaurants on the beach, a place for food and talk. They
spent a long time in the cocktail lounge. She was obviously
pleased to be taken out and happy to be with him. After
three drinks they talked about Dick and she wept. And
after that, he told her about Gloria, about this last nightmare visit, and how, after he had taken her back, they had
told him it was unlikely they would ever be able to give
her visiting privileges again. He told Frannie he was looking
for a buyer for their house, the home she would never
see again, and did not know he was weeping until his
voice clotted and he felt the tickle of tears on his face.
Frannie reached out to him and closed her hand around
his wrist with great strength.

"Please don't, Jim, honey."

He looked at her with a great earnestness. "But don't you
see, the terrible thing about it is the way it's all so phony.
I'm not crying about her, Frannie. I can't seem to cry about
it as a great loss. I'm . . . crying about me. I'm crying at the
great phony tragic figure I'm making of myself. And I
think I'm crying because I want to touch your heart."

"Let's eat now, Jimmy. We've had enough drinks. Let's
get a menu and order from here, please, and let them tell us
when it's ready, and not have any more drinks."

At dinner they had talked of trivial things which would
not trigger either of them. Over coffee, awkward as a school-
boy, he said, elaborately, "I . . . uh . . . found a pretty
nice place to stay. We could have a nightcap there and I
could show you my view of the pool."

When she didn't answer, he looked directly at her and

saw her looking at him with an expression he could not read. Her head was tilted slightly. She looked sad, rueful, slightly ironic, but with an undertone of tenderness.

"Yes, Jimmy. Yes, I suppose we have to go look at the pool. There's really nothing else we can do, is there?"

She was very quiet on the way out to the motel. They went in. He turned two subdued lights on. She threw her coat and purse on a chair, and they stood by the sliding doors and looked out at the pool. He put his hand on her waist and, after a little while, he turned her into his arms. After they had kissed with an increasing hunger, she backed away from him, sighed, smiled, took her purse and shut herself in the bathroom. He knew it would happen, and he knew it would not be very important or very good. He drew the draperies, turned out one of the lights, opened up one of the two double beds. The long fiasco of Gloria had made him jittery about all emotional relationships. He heard water running. He felt very tired. He wished he had not started it. He wished he had said no. He felt almost certain he would either be impotent, or it would all be over for him in a humiliatingly brief time. That was what had been happening to him lately.

She came out of the bathroom with her dress over her arm. She gave him a broad, friendly almost casual smile and said, "Hello, there!" and went to the closet and hung her dress and coat on hangers. She was constructed like her sisters. Their long oval faces and the long slender necks, the narrow sloping shoulders, gave them a look of slenderness. Yet their legs were long and heavy, their hips wide, their lower torso fleshy. Frannie had a slightly sway-backed stance which made her buttocks look the more round, thrusting and muscular, yet her upper torso seemed almost too frail and narrow for the size and weight of the wide-spaced conical breasts.

She came to the bed in such a matter-of-fact way, he was more convinced that it would not be anything worth remembering for either of them.

But her skin had a silkier texture than he would have guessed, and, more importantly, she quickly proved that she was frankly and enthusiastically concerned with the pleasure she could get from it, enjoying her own sensations without pretense or artifice or coyness. She gasped her small instructions, and she gave little throaty chuckles of pleasure, and she made a running commentary on just how good everything was. Paradoxically, her apparent complete unconcern for him made it possible for him to lose all his anxiety about himself, and soon find himself sharing the same pleasures he was giving her, tasting them in ways he had not known for a long time. So when it had ended, and they lay in a sighing contentment, sharing a cigarette, their hearts slowing, their bodies worn and leaden, he felt both gratitude and a quiet pride bordering on smugness. Each time she sighed, there would be a little catch of her breath at the end of it, like a hiccup.

"So nice," she breathed. "So fine and nice. I like the way we are, Jimmy darling. I like us a lot." Her hair tickled the side of his throat as she turned her face toward him. "What are you laughing at?"

"Well, if at anything, at myself. There wasn't any reason why anybody had to come over here to cover this hearing, you know. Borklund was trying to give me a change of scene. I was getting stale and jumpy and sour."

She kissed his throat. "Have you had a change of scene, dear?"

"Yes indeed."

"Are you still stale and jumpy and sour?"

"No ma'am."

"Then I must be good for you. You're good for me. You're the first one since I got married. I feel all over like warm marshmallow pudding. Darling, call the desk and ask them to wake us up at six." She rolled toward him and snuggled close to him. "Then we'll have a nap."

During the next two months he put a lot of mileage on his car. Every time he knew he would have enough time off, he would phone her and drive over. He stayed with her at her one-room efficiency. At first she didn't want him there. She said the room was too full of weeping, but it turned out to be all right for them. During those two months she mended him. She rebuilt the pride which the Gloria situation had eroded. She made him a whole man. They seemed to sense, simultaneously, when it was time to end it, and so they ended it affectionately and well, before it had a chance to turn into quarrels and accusations.

Later, at about the time of Van Hubble's death, Frannie met a man named Worley in Miami, married him and came back to Palm City with him. He got a job with the Palm County Highway Department. When Jimmy Wing would see her on the street he felt a faint retrospective stir of pleasure, and he felt glad it had happened just at the time it did, and in the manner it did. Once he bought her drugstore coffee. She was carrying her third child, the first child of the new marriage. She seemed very happy.

Whenever he thought of that two months and the fast narrow road across the Everglades, and her couch that unfolded

into a double bed, and the warm sleeping weight of her leg
across his hip, he would remember how they used to talk
after they had made love—lie and smoke and talk in lazy
intimacy of a hundred things.

He had asked her once about the way Elmo Bliss had
bought the Lemon Ridge house from the rest of them so
cheaply.

"Well, of course we resented it, Jimmy. But, later on, it
seemed all right. Nobody even thinks about it any more. Now
it seems as if . . . it's just the way it should be."

"How do you mean?"

"Elmo is sort of in charge of the family, so it seems right
he should be in the home place with Dellie. Three of the
brothers-in-law are older than he is, but he's the one everybody goes to. Sickness, jobs, trouble with the kids, anything.
And all of us are free to come and go just as if it was still
our house. It's sure crowded sometimes."

"So the family approves of Elmo."

"Gosh, not at first. Well, you know the reputation he had
and all the trouble he was in all the time. We didn't want
Dellie marrying him. She was only eighteen. But we couldn't
stop her. Dellie is a strange one. She's never had much to
say, but she's always had this idea that she was going to
have a lush life, like a queen or something. She just knew it
was going to be that way. We used to laugh at her. But the
way it worked out, she's certainly living a lot higher on the
hog than anybody else in the family, I'm telling you. We
never would have guessed she'd get that kind of a life by
marrying Elmo. He's real good to her. I mean if you don't
count keeping her pregnant most of the time. She's due for
number six any day now, but I'll say this, she doesn't seem
to mind. She's got all the help she can use with the house
and the kids, and she's never up before noon, and she certainly keeps her figure. I guess he's sweet to her, but . . .
you know Elmo. I don't know if she knows about other
women. Or if . . . she'd let herself know, or let herself wonder. Dellie is a realist."

"So is Elmo, I guess."

"I don't know what Elmo is. He has that way of talking to
you. When he talks to you, you feel as if you matter more
to him than anybody else on earth. He really listens to you.
Not very many people listen. He seems to really care about
you. I guess that's what makes him so good with women.
When a girl is with Elmo, she feels . . . I don't know, more
alive. You know it's an act, but you can't help yourself.
You don't ever really know if he likes you. Nobody knows.

We talk about him a lot, in the family. The way he helps us all, that seems to be kind of an act too."

"When he sold off fifty of the sixty acres of the home place, Frannie, I guess he did pretty well."

"I guess so," she said indifferently. "But he sort of sold it to himself, didn't he? One of those corporation things he keeps doing?" He remembered that she had turned toward him then and said, in a huskier tone, "Now, why are we wasting all this good time talking about my brother-in-law, darling?" She had reached her sturdy hand to him and said, with exaggerated petulance, "But it seems too early to change the subject, I guess. Isn't it too early? Gosh, you know, maybe it isn't. Now I'm sure it isn't. We're changing the subject, darling, aren't we?"

He grinned at that memory of Frannie as he slowed for Elmo's house. Eight or ten cars were parked in the field beside Elmo's house, nosed up to the big redwood fence. He parked and got out of his car. He remembered the eagerness with which he had headed each time toward Miami two years ago. Yet no part of it had been as compelling as what he now felt toward Kat. It offended his sense of proportion that this should be so. It was a meager feat finding a woman who would come to his Cable Key cottage. He had tried to cure himself of what he privately called his severe case of Kat-fever by using himself up upon some amiable and competent women during the past year, but it had not diminished the fever by a fraction of a degree. He resented being the victim of what seemed an adolescent compulsion. As an adult male he knew that in the deeps of the bed the differences between women are less important than the similarities. So why should this particular hundredweight of flesh seem touched with magic? What could she do that others had not done?

He walked through the open redwood gate and down the winding gravel path toward the pool, remembering the first time he had come to Elmo's house, three years and eight months ago, on election night, without invitation. He had come on a hunch. . . .

After Elmo had been married about five years, and Bliss Construction had become one of the largest home construction outfits in the area, Elmo had begun to devote considerable time to civic functions and duties. He joined service clubs and fund-raising ventures, and proved himself reliable and persuasive and dedicated whenever appointed to a committee. He had begun making sizable contributions to the Democratic County Committee, and had begun to electioneer on the behalf of Democrats running for county offices. Four years ago the top brass in the county organization had decided to give Elmo his first taste of running for office, so they put him up against Elihu Kibby in the primary. Elihu Kibby, Brade Wellan and Sam Engster were the ones who picked Elmo and talked him into it. Kibby was running for re-election to the Board of County Commissioners. It was to be his fifth four-year term, and everybody knew that it was an automatic re-election. Kibby would win the primary over anybody who was put up, and he would whip Stan Freeberry, the Republican opposition, handily.

On the evening of the primaries Jimmy Wing went out to Elmo's house at five o'clock. Elmo and a pack of friends and relatives were gathered in the big shed-type building beyond the swimming pool, the building Elmo called his workshop. It looked more like the main lounge in a rustic and expensive hunting lodge.

Elmo got him a drink and got him off into a corner and said, "Now, why in the world you killing time coming away out here for, Jimmy Wing? There isn't much of a news story out here tonight. You should be down to headquarters where the winners are all gathered round, slapping each other on the back."

"I've been thinking about you all day, Elmo, ever since I voted for you without really knowing why."

"You wasted a vote there, Jimmy."

"I wondered how many other people were doing the same thing. And then I thought about the big family you come from, and the big family you married into. I remembered how many people live in houses you've built, and how many people have worked for you over the past few years. I think it might all add up to a lot. It might just add up to enough."

Elmo had cocked his head, squinted his pale dancing eyes and grinned at Jimmy Wing. "Now, don't you start scaring me, boy. Anything like that would be a terrible embarrassment. Old Elihu asked me to run out of the goodness of his heart, so the voters could get a look at me in case I want to run for something later on, in a serious way. I haven't been hustling, have I? I've just been clowning around a little. I haven't said one unkind word about old Elihu."

"You made a few jokes, Elmo. Like the one about Commissioner Kibby wanting more county commission meetings because the doctor told him that at his age he needed more sleep."

"Just in fun, Jimmy."

"I came because I think you might make it, and if you do, this is where the story is. If you make it, how will you feel?"

"Let me see now. In your story, the way I'll feel will be

humble, proud, deeply touched, surprised, and real dedicated. You've done some nice stories about me the last couple months, Jimmy."

The returns were broadcast over local radio, WKPC. By six o'clock it was evident Elmo was the winner. After the initial furor began to die down, Elmo walked Jimmy out to his car.

"Humble, astonished and dedicated," Jimmy said.

"Right. I'll have to straighten old Elihu out. On the phone he was making out like I stabbed him when he wasn't looking. Like I told him, Jimmy, I've got to lean heavy for advice on those wiser heads in the party for the next four years." He took Jimmy Wing's hand in a hard clasp and said, "You come back, hear? You make it a habit dropping by. There'll be a lot of stories to write up in the next four years."

"Write them your way?"

Elmo laughed. "Jimmy, let's you and me write them our way, and see what happens. We're going to get along better than ever."

"Kibby could lick Stan Freeberry, but what if you can't?"

He rocked back and forth, heel to toe, and cracked his fist into his palm. "Old Stanley? If I was ever to get really worried, I'd tell you all about a little ol' Pigeon Town gal name of Darcy Miller, came and cooked and kept house for Stan about nine years ago, that time Miz Freeberry had to spend three months in California nursing her dying sister. I'd tell you about how this Darcy Miller has a slew of kids, and there's a bright yellow eight-year-old one she calls Stanley and keeps dressed up fine on some money comes in a plain envelope every month, money sent local."

Jimmy had stared at him. "That's if you get worried."

"If I get that worried. There's other things before I'd have to use that. Just put it this way, Jimmy Wing. Tonight I'm over the worst hump. I'm not about to be stopped short by things easier to do than whipping Elihu Kibby."

Jimmy Wing had other cause to remember that same night. After he had filed his stories, he went home to find that Gloria, after over a month of perfect behavior, had suddenly fallen back into her black private world. She had pulled down all the shades, turned on every light in the house, stripped, packed herself with pins, buttons, pencils and other small household objects, rubbed herself raw on the sharp edges of the furniture, and then had lapsed into a catatonic state more nearly complete than any he had seen. She sat on a footstool in a corner, her eyes open, snoring with every slow breath, bleeding, ropes of saliva dangling from her chin, gone so suddenly and completely away, unreachable, unknowing. That time it had been three months before she began to recognize him when he visited her, and six months before he could take her away from the hospital for short drives through the surrounding countryside.

By now he had been to the Lemon Ridge home of the county commissioner many times. He strolled through the humid night toward the lighted pool, hearing voices and laughter and music. There were always people around, friends, relatives, business associates, politicians. There was a protocol as rigid as any tribal ceremonial taboo behind the apparent casualness. Visitors were sorted into four categories. In the lowest group were the ones Elmo would talk to outdoors, usually by the pool, or, when the weather was foul, inside the "workshop" beyond the pool. The second category had access to the workshop in all weather. The third category were those whom Elmo would invite into his big study in the main house. The study had a separate outside entrance. Very close friends and relatives had the run of the house. Jimmy Wing was one of that group which could be invited into the study.

The gravel crackled underfoot. The night jasmine had opened, vulgar and sensuous as pink lace garters. When the path turned, just beyond a thickety patch of yucca and flame vine, he came in sight of the big screened pool. He stopped there in the darkness, thinking it looked so much like one of the color advertisements in magazines it was artificial and improbable.

The cage was so high the upper portion of it was in darkness. The screening had been recently extended to include the broad fan-shaped apron beyond the west end of the rectangular pool. The water was a brilliant, luminous green in the diffused radiance of the underwater floodlights. The pool lighting and the spotlights at the base of the plantings in the pool area made a reflected glow across the apron area where three men sat talking at an outdoor table. The double doors of the workshop were open, and the inside lights were on. He saw a couple inside the workshop, dancing to slow music, disappear and reappear. A big tanned girl in a white swim suit made a lazy backstroke the length of the pool, her arms lifting, turning slowly. A Negro in a white shirt and dark trousers came from the workshop carrying a tall drink on a small tray. He bent over and placed the drink at the edge of the pool and said something to the girl. As he walked away, she rolled over out of her backstroke position and swam at an angle toward the drink.

Jimmy Wing walked to the screen door and pushed it

open. As was almost always the case, there were fewer people around than the number of cars would lead you to believe. It always seemed to him there must be some place on the property he had never been told about, some activity he could not share—but he knew this was not true.

The girl on the far side of the pool turned and stared at him. He did not know her. She had a young, blunt, sensual face, and the hair water-pasted to her head looked like a smooth silver cap.

"Now, there he is!" Elmo said, his voice lazy and welcoming.

Jimmy walked to the table where the three of them sat. He pulled a chair over from the other table and said, "Evening, Elmo, Leroy, Buck."

Leroy Shannard, the lawyer, was in his late forties, a long, limber, indolent man, with the deep tan of golf course and offshore fishing. He had white hair cropped so short the tanned skull showed through the stubble. He had a harsh predatory face, so muted by his lethargic manner he looked like a sleepy eagle. Most of his practice was in real estate work and estate work. He was in partnership with Gil Stopely, a fat, bustling, humorless younger man who was a very keen tax attorney. Shannard was descended from one of the earliest settlers of Palm County. He lived with his mother in an old bayfront house three blocks from the center of the city. He had the reputation of being one of the most tireless and successful seducers of restless wives in all of south Florida, but he gave mild denial to any such accusation. It was said that his caution was in part responsible for his success.

Buck Flake was considerably more obvious. He was a relative newcomer to the area. He had been about twenty-five when he had come down from New Jersey ten years previously with some money he was supposed to have made in the scrap business. He had gone into some dangerous land speculation, saved his own skin with some tricky maneuvering, and finally traded himself into the huge tract which he had developed into Palm Highlands. He was loud, crude, huge and muscular, but now the muscles were softening rapidly as the belly expanded. His jaw was so wide and the space between his temples so narrow, he had an odd pinhead look. A good portion of his success had been gained at the expense of some of the unwary ones who had assumed Buck Flake was as stupid as he looked and acted.

With an awesome celerity, Major appeared at Jimmy's side and placed a drink on the table in front of him, saying, to himself, "Kitchen whiskey and one cube for Mr. Wing."

"Thank you, Major." Major and Ardelia, his wife, worked full time for the Bliss family. Their grown children helped out. The whole Major Thatcher family lived on a back acre Elmo had deeded them, in a frame house Elmo had bought when it was in the way of a new county highway, and had moved onto the land.

The girl was swimming again. Elmo gestured toward her and said, "Leroy here was just now telling Buck what a damn fool he is, but Buck won't listen to advice from a real expert."

"What's all this about advice?" Buck demanded, obviously annoyed. "Why should I have advice? I told you the score. She works for me in the office. She's been working for me a couple of weeks."

"Listen to the protestations of utter innocence," Shannard murmured. "That poor confused child bears the fabulous name—Charity Prindergast. Please understand, James, we have extracted this data from Buck a fragment at a time. She went down to Lauderdale from some midwestern university for the spring orgy, and apparently developed such a taste for gin she never quite managed to get back across the city line, until Buck went over to Lauderdale a few weeks ago and found her there, living in squalor and confusion on the pittance her dismayed parents were sending her. Out of the goodness of his great heart, he brought her back here and gave her honest work—at least honest to the degree that the Palm Highlands development can be considered honest."

"We build a damn good house for the money," Buck said.

"Our Mr. Flake claims that his employment of Miss Prinder gast has nothing at all to do with the fact his sweet wife Elizabeth and their two sturdy sons are spending the summer on her parents' farm in Pennsylvania. Yet, when questioned, Mr. Flake admits that though he writes his wife faithfully, he had made no mention of his charitable gesture."

Buck scowled and then grinned. "All right, you bastards, so I shouldn't have brought her over here."

"You probably couldn't help it, Buck," Leroy said. "You tend to consume as conspicuously as possible. The brightest colors, the biggest tail fins, the table closest to the floor show. Miss Charity is a spectacular morsel, and you have a great talent for vulgarity, Buck."

"Now hold it, you—"

"But you must face the fact you will pay a price for unseemly display. Even if you should send the nubile creature on her glazed way before Elizabeth returns, she will inevitably be told about her, due to your carelessness, and then, my dear fellow, that dear little wife of yours will flay you, salt you down, and hang your carcass in the sun. Your lies will not work, and finally you will be blubbering and whimpering for forgiveness. All you have to decide now is whether the lassie is worth it."

"Get him the hell off me, Elmo," Buck said.

"Consume conspicuously," Elmo said. "That's a nice way to put it, Leroy. I guess I do that too, in ways a little different from Buck here." He stood up. "Come along, Jimmy. You boys excuse us and yell for Major when you need him."

They went out through the door and up the path that branched toward the house. Elmo chuckled and said, "Leroy is teasing him, and Buck, he doesn't want to get too mad about it on account he knows I don't like him bringing that hard-drinking girl here to my house. Buck doesn't use much sense about a lot of things. That's the trouble with getting people together on anything, Jimmy. Everybody is a damn fool in his own way."

Elmo led the way around the side of the house and up the steps into the air-conditioned silence of his study. The big pale desk was shaped like a boomerang. Elmo turned on a single brass lamp on the desk. The floor was cork, the walls burlap, the chairs and couch of dark leather. Elmo had patterned it after the private office of a bank president in Jacksonville, even to the gun rack and built-in television and high-fidelity music system.

Elmo sat in the deep chair behind the desk and put his feet up and looked across the desk at Jimmy Wing. "I should have brought it up right here in the first place, instead of at the courthouse this morning. Then you wouldn't have spent all day wondering about the rest of it."

"I've done some guessing."

"Mostly what we need to go into is where we both are going to fit into this thing. Take me. I've made it plain I'm not running again. One term on the county commission is enough. I've told everybody I have to give more time to my building business. Do you have the idea I'm getting out of politics, Jim?"

"No. You took to it too well."

"Do you think it's been a good thing for Palm County, me being four years on the commission?"

"Elmo, that's a strange question, and I don't know where you're heading with it. I know damn well you're not fishing for compliments, so I'll give you an honest answer. On the whole, I think you've been of more benefit than Elihu Kibby would have been. Will that do?"

Bliss made a soft sound of amusement. The lamplight

was strong across his mouth and left his eyes in semishadow. His sports shirt was a soft shade of green-gray, with a tiny monogram on the breast pocket in black.

"Playtime is over, Jimmy," Elmo said. "We've had the four years of fun."

Jimmy Wing knew he had been invited into another room in that structure which was Elmo Bliss. Another door had been opened—another degree of intimacy. He could look back at all the other lighted rooms, at the connecting doors which stood wide open, and remember the time when each had been opened for him. Now here was another degree of closeness, yet with the inference there were still other rooms beyond. He felt a degree of excitement and alarm which he could not rationalize. Somehow closeness was in ratio to menace, as though, in the ultimate room, the door would slam shut and there would be darkness and a knife. He told himself that the suggestion of menace came merely from the awareness that it was contrived—that Bliss opened the doors for his own purposes when the time was right, that Bliss was using him.

"Four years of many things," Jimmy said, smiling, stalling.

"And four more years to come, and four after that, and God knows where we'll be by then, boy. Depends on the size bite I can take. I learned in a lot of hard ways that the way you set your teeth, and the timing of it, they're the only things that count. Bite too big and you strangle on it. Bite too small and you starve."

"Is that all there is to it, Elmo? The jungle approach?"

Elmo took a long time in unwrapping a slim cigar, lighting it. "I play a game, Jim. Nobody knows I'm playing it. What I do, I make out I'm the man I'm talking to. I add up all I know about him and I try to become him and look out of him at Elmo Bliss and see what he sees. You've got simple ideas about me, I think. You think I'm some kind of animal. Now when I look at you, maybe I see some kind of animal too, but sort of a sorry animal."

"Thanks a lot, Elmo."

"Because you got a weak connection between your teeth and your head. You worry so much about what you should want, you lose track of what you really want. You're a mixed-up animal, like a vegetarian dog. But that's the way most people are, Jimmy."

"Maybe my wants are small."

"Maybe it pleasures you to think they're small. Up in Georgia we had a school catalogue with the snap courses marked, so we wouldn't have to put too big a strain on our football brains. I took a marked one in philosophy.

Ethics it was called, a lecture course by a man named
Hoosin. Now don't bug your eyes at me like that, boy, it's
downright impolite. The lessons didn't take hold on me.
I listened good, but I thought it was a lot of crap. Those
lessons didn't jell until my time on the road gang, with
Pete Nambo beating on me of an evening, whistling between
his teeth and grunting when he wound up for a good one.
I came up with my own ethic right about then. I want
satisfaction, Jimmy. And I want to know when I'm having
it, and keep track of what it costs. I want the most people
possible saying 'Here comes Elmo' and 'There goes Elmo.'
I want people anxious to make sure I'm comfortable. I
want all the pretty things—like people writing down what
I say, and motorcycle escorts, sirens, steaks, secretaries, dollar cigars, mahogany boats, clothes tailored to fit, my name
in books, little girls fussing to pleasure me. To get it all,
and keep it coming, I have to take the right-size bite at
the right time."

He leaned into the light and banged his fist on the desk
with a force which startled Jimmy Wing. "I want the world
knowing I'm here, and I want it excited about Elmo Bliss,
and a little nervous wondering what comes next. Because
I *know* what comes next for everybody, boy, and that's a
black hole in the ground, and of all the people who have
lived and died in this world, maybe one tenth of one per
cent even got a name on top of the hole they're in."

He leaned back. After a long silence Jimmy said, "You're
uncomplicated in a complicated way, Elmo. How about good
and evil?"

"I'll keep doing enough good to make it no problem
living with the bad, and let somebody else keep score. This
is my time to be here, and I want the meat in my mouth
and room to taste the juice. There's getting to be so many
people crowding the earth, it makes it easier."

Jimmy was startled by the concept. "Easier?"

"Everybody fights hard to be ordinary and inconspicuous,
just one of the group. Fifty years ago there were so many
unusual fellas around, you had to be hell on wheels to get
any attention at all. Nowadays the people of the world
are so hungry for somebody different that a lot of half-
bright men stand out. Watch the news. Every month or so
some little piss ant will get up on his hind legs and say
something stupid and startling and find out he's a public
figure."

"Maybe it isn't that simple."

"We'll have a chance to find out, Jimmy. Right now I'm
not running again. I don't have to. I've got the county.

Old Elihu is being eat up by the cancer; and the heart has gone out of Sam Engster, so when two new commissioners go on this fall, they'll be the ones I put there, Brade Wellan and Willy Bry. In four years I've put a lock on this county nobody can shake off in a hurry, and I've made a lot of grateful friends in five other counties and in Tallahassee. I haven't been either so greedy or so pure I've made the boys nervous. I built up and run a successful business. I'm a family man. I've worked hard for the party. I come over real good on television. I've been on the right side of the issues that have come up. Four years from now, when I'm ready to make my move, I'll be forty-four. Now you tell me the size of the bite I'm thinking about."

Jimmy Wing considered it carefully. The nape of his neck felt cool. "Senator?"

"Not my style, boy, but you're moving in the right direction. I don't want to try to get elected to a club where you wait twelve years before you've got any weight or voice. Governor, Jimmy. Governor of the Sunshine State." He got up abruptly and went over to a cabinet, brought back a bottle and two glasses, poured drinks. "Twelve-dollar brandy, Jim. And right now we drink to setting up the machine that's going to do it. Right now that machine is just you and me. And years from now, boy, we'll both remember how we started it together."

Jimmy Wing sipped the brandy. "Forgive me, Elmo, but . . . it seems a little fantastic."

"With a whole four damn years to set it up?" He reached into a lower drawer of one of the desk pedestals, fumbled and came up with two fifty-dollar bills. He slapped them on the desk in front of Jimmy.

"And here's the first investment in the campaign, Jim. Go ahead. Pick it up. Don't look so worried. You'll keep right on at the paper until things get so hot and heavy you'll have to come over with me full time. But I sure want you to have regular expense money for the little things you'll be doing for me. It isn't salary, Jim. It's for expenses. I'll be accounting for it, so you don't have to worry about it. You'll get that every week, and when you quit the paper, I'll triple it. Pick it up, boy!"

"What will I be doing for you?"

"Gathering information. Writing speeches. Giving out news items. Sort of a public-relations job, I guess you'd call it, and eventually you'll be a personal aide and press representative. You'll be my Salinger. There won't be anything you won't know about, and you'll be in on the strategy.

You rate yourself too small, Jimmy. You've got a hell of a lot on the ball. It's time you got stirred up."

Jimmy picked the two bills up, put them in his wallet and noted a slight tremble in his hands. He hesitated as he started to return the wallet to his hip pocket. "Elmo, this isn't buying you any immunity in the work I do for the paper."

"If it did, Jimmy, I wouldn't have any use for you."

"I suppose the next question is, what do you want me to do first?"

Elmo poured two more shots of the fine brandy, took his glass and went over to the couch on the other side of the room. "I'll have to have backing, of course. But I don't want to go to Tallahassee as somebody's hired hand. And that means coming up with some money, a good piece of clean money I haven't got. I think three or four hundred thousand would do it just fine. And that means a capital gains. I've been hunting a good one for a year now. Once I'm out of office, I think those boys who've started this Palmland Development Company will let me buy in. Burt Lesser, Leory Shannard, Buck Flake, Bill Gormin, Doc Aigan. I've got reason to believe those five old boys would each let loose of a piece of their piece in return for my personal note."

Jimmy Wing had turned his chair around to face Bliss. Though he could feel the tension in the room, he kept his voice as casual as Elmo's. "For those shares to be worth anything, the county commission would have to approve changing the bulkhead line. When anybody runs for governor, the opposition takes a good close look. Somebody could make quite a thing out of it, a man voting himself into a piece of money."

"Now, I wouldn't want to do a thing like that, Jimmy. Look at the record and you'll find I was the one had most to do with getting that bulkhead line established in the first place. I believe in preservation of natural beauty. I believe in it so much that the record after the public hearing is going to show I voted against the Grassy Bay fill."

"But you vote next to last."

"Now, I would guess that DeRose Bassette and Horace Lander, being in favor of growth and progress and so on, would vote for it. Then Stan Dayson, being our only Republican right now, and against everything Horace and Stan are for, he'll vote against it and so will I. Then it'll be up to the chairman, Gus Makelder, to cast the deciding vote. So as long as it goes through in spite of my vote, I'd be a damn fool not to buy into it after my term is over, given the chance."

"So that's the agreement, is it, Elmo? You promise to deliver Makelder, Lander and Bassette in return for a good price to buy in at."

"I wouldn't want anybody to think there was a deal like that."

"Even me? I'm the guy who is supposed to know everything that's going on. Remember?"

"There is a sort of agreement, Jimmy. Just casual like. Nothing in writing. No options or anything like that. Gus, Horace and DeRose will be happy to vote for something that'll mean so much to the whole area. I'll buy syndicate shares, and when Leroy turns it into a corporation, I'll just sell off the shares I get, pay off my notes, pay the capital gains tax and put the money into something where I can get it out fast and easy when we come to needing it. See any holes in that?"

"Well . . . just one, Elmo. Voting to move the bulkhead line and voting to recommend the sale of the bay bottom by the IIF doesn't mean it will go through without a hitch."

"You keep proving to me what a good idea I had when I decided to make you the first member of the team, Jimmy. I watched you close two years ago when those outsiders tried to move in on us. Ben Killian tried to keep the paper neutral, but you got your licks in. You worked close with those Save Our Bays people, and you helped them a lot."

"Van Hubble talked me into it. He was a good friend."

"Jimmy, the way it stands right now, I'm pretty sure the bay fill group will win out over that Sandy Key crowd and all the damn fish lovers. But winning locally isn't enough. They'll want to take the fight right to Tallahassee and then into the courts. That'll take money, organization, enthusiasm. So what we've got to do right in the first round is take the heart right out of them. We've got to win it so big they'll have no stomach for carrying it any further. We've got to demoralize that bunch, Jimmy. So I want you to get just as close to them as you can. You know a hell of a lot about the people in this town. And there are some weird types on that executive committee. With enough private information, the kind they wouldn't put in public speeches, we can cut the head right off that organization by clobbering their executive committee."

"I'm supposed to spy on my friends?"

"First off, that's the ugliest way you could have put it. Second, nobody is about to know it, unless you tell them. Third, if you don't do it, Leroy will bring somebody in from outside who'll maybe do a nastier job on them than would happen if you handle it yourself. I hear you show up at the bank pretty regular to take that redhead Hubble woman out for her coffee break. If all of a sudden it should get gossiped around that she's took to screwing her dead husband's best friend, who's got a wife in the asylum—"

"God damn it, Elmo, I—"

"Easy, now. I didn't say you were. But somebody else could make it sound that way, and it could hurt hell out of that nice little woman. True or false, it would take her mind off Grassy Bay real quick. I figure if those people are your friends, you can do a good job of coming up with stuff that'll sink that executive committee without hurting the people too much. You're in the best position to do that job, aren't you?"

"I suppose so, but . . ."

"Jimmy, boy, when I was thinking about this little talk with you, I confess I started thinking about it all wrong. You see, I need you so bad and I respect you so much, I was thinking of ways to force you to join in with me. Hell, I thought of a lot of crazy things. I've got some wild kin who'd lay for you, grab you, run you way back up some slough and make you pray you could die. Then you'd jump fast every time I raised a finger, just to save yourself another trip up the slough, but once you do a man that way, it takes something out of him he never gets back, and he just isn't worth as much to you or himself from then on."

"I don't scare, Elmo."

"Now that's a damn fool thing to say! Are you all the man Pete Nambo was? After Wade Illigan beat him out for Sheriff, some of my cousins kept him back in the swamp for eleven days, and since then nobody's touched Pete all the six years he's been driving a transit mix truck for me, but his voice still gets squeaky when I say good morning to him. I don't bluff, Jimmy. I just decided I don't want to do that to you. It was a bad idea. Then I thought about your wife. It was out of pure friendship I got her put into that state special-care program up near Oklawaha. That was three years ago, Jimmy. And it would have cost you five hundred a month to buy her that much private care. I was going to bring it up to you, and ask you if you don't owe me something. But I wouldn't like myself if I took advantage of that poor girl's sickness that way. I even thought of hinting how easy I could work Killian around to firing you off the paper, but I guess you don't give that much of a damn about the job. Finally I came around to right where we are now. You got the facts, I'm leaving it up to you. You can put that money on the desk and walk out. But your walking out won't change any of the things that are going to happen. You're thirty-three damn years old, boy, and you've been telling yourself too long you like to live small and quiet. You sit back inside yourself and sneer at how crazy the world is, and you like to think you don't give a damn about anything. Okay, so here's your chance to prove you don't give a damn. Come aboard for the ride. Watch the animals. If you have to make excuses to yourself, you can tell yourself you're researching a book. You've got your world shrunk down too small, Jimmy."

Elmo stood up and came over to him and punched him lightly on the shoulder. The grin squeezed Elmo's eyes to bright gray slits and bulged the knots of muscle at the corners of his jaw. "Come on, boy!" he said in a half whisper. "Let's you and me stir things up. Ever since Havana that time, I knew you were going to fit somewhere. I need you, and what the hell have you got to lose?"

Jimmy Wing felt a sardonic amusement at how deftly Bliss was maneuvering him. Elmo had spread the possible rationalizations out in plain sight, inviting Jimmy to select the one which would make him the most cozy. Maybe, he thought, it isn't so reprehensible to be maneuvered when you can see just how it's being done, when you can see the foot on the pedal which controls the wheel.

"Suppose I want to say yes, but I'm afraid it might get too ripe for me later on?"

Elmo punched him again. "What the hell you think I'm operating here, boy? Bolita? Any time you want out, get out."

"Knowing, as you said, everything there is to know?"

"Ah, but you wouldn't use it! I use anything I can lift. But I've never crossed a friend. Or broke my word to a man living. You see, I don't ask for your word, Jimmy, because I don't have to."

Jimmy Wing sighed and stood up and put his hand out. Elmo's clasp was brief, dry and very strong. "We'll have some laughs."

"There better be some, Elmo. There haven't been too many lately."

They went out into the hot soft air of night, and for Jimmy Wing it was much like the transition from the unreality of a movie back to the ordinary casual world. He wanted to ask Elmo how he was to report what he learned, but he stifled the question as impossibly theatrical now that they were back in the summer night, crunching the gravel underfoot, strolling back toward the lights at the bottom of the lawn.

They went back down to the apron of the pool. Flake's girl had changed to a checked cotton dress. She sat on a cedar tub which had been turned upside down. Flake stood behind her, drying her silver hair with a big cherry-colored towel. The towel obscured her face. She sat with her legs braced, her hands in her lap, so bonelessly relaxed that Buck Flake's vigorous efforts rippled her body inside the snug dress.

As they approached, Elmo was slightly behind Jimmy. Jimmy saw Leroy Shannard give Elmo a quick, searching look, and he could not doubt but what Elmo returned a nod of affirmation. I shall have to be alert for these little things, he thought. I'll never know all of what's going on. I'll have to guess at a lot of it.

The dancers were gone, the music silent, the workshop lights out. "For chrissake, Buck!" Elmo said irritably.

Flake stopped immediately and backed away from the girl, leaving the towel draped half across her face.

"I'm not dry, Buckey!" she said in a sweet, complaining, little-girl voice. "Dry me more."

"It'll dry good in the car, Princess, with the top down. Come on. We're going."

She stuffed the towel into her beach bag, combed her hair back with her fingers and stood up, arching her back, taking a deep breath, smiling at all of them. "Thanks for the sweetie drinks and the sweetie swim, people."

Shannard said, "You were a joy to watch, child."

"Now cut it out, Leroy!" Buck said.

"What's he doing he should cut out, Buckey? Jeepers, you're getting so nobody can say a sweetie word to me any more!"

"Come on!" Buck ordered and marched her away.

They heard her thin sweet voice receding, and the angry gunning of Buck's big car as he backed it out, and at last the dwindling whine of it on the midnight highway.

"Where is he keeping her?" Elmo asked.

"He's got her stashed out there in one of his sweetie display houses," Leroy said. "He took the sweetie sign down. She seems to stroll over to the office once a day and type one letter, with two sweetie fingers."

"She's sure-God built," Elmo said.

"She'll weigh in at one-fifty," Leory said, "without a half ounce of fat on her. Buck should age visibly this summer."

"Won't you help him out?"

Shannard smiled into the distance. "Elmo, old friend, you

should know me well enough by now to realize that my libido operates in inverse ratio to the availability of the merchandise. That girl is without the old-fashioned restraint I'm accustomed to. She would accommodate me as merely a sociable gesture, like a healthy handshake, or remembering my name. I'm too old to think of sex as merely sensible hygiene. Mine has to be sharpened by the sense of sin and guilt. And it has to be difficult to arrange, so as to provide the stimulation of anticipation. If Buck's college girl could sunbathe, swim, drink gin and make love simultaneously, that's what she'd do every day, just because they all make her feel so peachy fine. No thanks, Elmo. Buck can struggle with this one all by himself. The hell with the new freedom. Give me a troubled, anxious, guilty woman every time. They think they're giving away something of value, at least. So they don't give it so often they tax me too much."

"Laziest lawyer in town," Elmo said. "But I like to listen to him talk. He belts me with fees that would take your appetite away."

"But I didn't charge him a thing the first time he came to me, James," Leory said. "He was in coveralls, wearing a carpenter hat, and he bulled his way in and dumped his records on top of my desk. He stared at me as though he was thinking about hitting me in the mouth. Then he said, 'The net worth is maybe four thousand. I owe eleven. I can take on a contract that'll make me twenty before taxes. I need ten thousand by tomorrow noon at the latest. Find it for me and you do my law work from now on. But find it as a loan, because I'm not selling any piece of my company.' On any average day, I'd have sent him right back out. But I was feeling euphoric. I had him sit in the outer office. I made a couple of phone calls to find out about him. Then I found him the money, right in my own bank account."

"At fifteen per cent for three months. Just a little old sixty per cent a year."

"Secured by a chattel mortgage on everything including the fillings in his teeth."

They grinned at each other. "Now I support you," Elmo said. "I should claim you as an exemption."

"Don't you?" Shannard asked. He hoisted his long body out of the chair. "You heading back to town too, James?"

They said goodnight to Elmo and went along the path together. When they reached the open gate in the redwood fence, the pool lights and garden spots flicked out. Only one car was left in addition to Shannard's Thunderbird and Jimmy's old blue station wagon, and it was an elderly Chevy with Collier County tags.

Shannard stopped in the darkness and said, "Being around Elmo is consistently interesting. He's never ceased to surprise me. He's impossible to predict, yet all the apparently meaningless things eventually fall into a pattern. Have you noticed that?"

"Maybe I haven't known him that well or that long."

"Let's stop at the Spanish Mack for a nightcap."

As he followed the multiple tail lights of Shannard's car toward town, Jimmy Wing had the feeling he was the victim of some vastly complicated practical joke, the point of which would be made evident to him later on. Charity Prindergast was a bit player. He carried prop money. Elmo had learned his lines.

But he knew that Elmo Bliss had probed for and found his special weakness, which was his understanding of his own role as an observer. Nothing could seriously touch him who watched. No blame could accrue to him who sat on the shady knoll and watched the armies at war. If you were offered a higher knoll, a better vantage point, why not accept? The invulnerable armor of the combat correspondent was the dry smile, the mental note, the clinical observation of self in relation to the furies observed. So all the breasts were wax, all the cries were recorded, all the blood was red enamel.

5

THE SPANISH MACK was a cinderblock tavern east of Palm City, right at the city line, just over the highway bridge crossing Foley's Creek. From there the creek wandered south and west, eventually emptying into Grassy Bay. It was a functional operation, without juke, pinball, bowling games or television. The habitual customer knew he would always find unobtrusive air conditioning, indirect lighting, comfortable chair or bar stool, enough soundproofing to keep conversations private, expert bartenders, local gossip, and package liquors at moderate prices.

Less than half the bar stools were occupied. They took two stools at the middle curve of the bar. Howie, the smaller bartender, greeted them by name and took their orders. As he placed Jimmy's drink in front of him he said, "Friend of yours was in, Jimmy. Left about a half hour back. The guy with the scar."

"Brian Haas?"

"That's his name. I always forget it."

"Drinking?"

"First he had tomato juice. Then two fast doubles. Bang, bang, and he slapped the money down. Don't look at me like that, Jimmy. They ask for it and I sell it, unless they're stoned coming in. The only reason I'm telling you, I remember it was a year ago, wasn't it, you were hunting for him all the time."

"Thanks, Howie," Jimmy said. He excused himself and phoned Nan. He looked at his watch as the phone rang. It was five of one. When Nan answered he asked her if Bri had come home.

"No, and I was beginning to worry, Jimmy. Do you want him to call you when he gets in?"

"No. By accident I just found out he had some drinks about a half hour ago, at the Spanish Mack. He must have come here from the paper."

He heard the long weary sound of her sighing exhalation. "Oh, damn it, damn it. God damn it, Jimmy. He's been edgy. He's had a lot of trouble sleeping. He didn't go to the last couple of meetings. He made excuses."

63

"I thought you ought to know, Nan. Is there anything I can do?"

"Thanks, no. I've got a number to call. They'll get people out looking for him. Did he buy a bottle there?"

He asked her to wait a moment. He came back to the phone and said, "No. No bottle yet."

"Well, here we go again," Nan said, with a kind of desolated gallantry. "Thanks for phoning me, Jimmy. I better make that call right now."

When Jimmy went back to his drink, Shannard said, "Trouble?"

"He's been off it fourteen months. The last time he went three years. His wife's alerting the AA's to track him down. Maybe if they grab him soon enough, they can steer him off it."

"I know Haas by sight, of course."

"He's been the route, Leroy. A sweet and brilliant guy. When he was in his twenties he was a top man in the business. Right after the war the drinking started. He drank his way through all the papers who'd take a chance on him, and drank his marriage away, and most of his health, drank himself right down into skid row. Then some kind of rehabilitation outfit got hold of him and picked up all the pieces they could find and put him back together, and scouted a job for him and sent him down here to Ben Killian. Ben tucked him under my wing. I never thought it would work at all. It was hard to communicate with him. He was like some kind of a refugee, like a man who managed to escape by some miracle when his homeland was blown to hell, so that nothing which can ever happen to him again will be very important. But when he started to do all right with routine assignments, he started to come back a little, and when he married Nan McMay about five years ago, he came out of it a lot more."

"Nanette Melton McMay," Shannard said. "I was in on that case."

"Were you? I didn't remember."

"Why it didn't destroy her, I'll never know. So that makes them a pair of refugees, in a sense. At least she should be strong enough to cope with anything."

"This is the third time she's had to face it. The last time he fell off, we got him hooked up with the AA's, and it seemed to work. Borklund wanted to let him go then. Ben Killian said he could have one more chance. If they don't get him in time, if he blows it, I don't know what will happen to him. He's forty-five. He's got no place to go, not from here."

"Howie?" Shannard said. "Once again here. Where were we, James? Oh, we were discussing the infinite variety of the commissioner. Did you get a tidy news story out of him tonight?"

Jimmy Wing felt an immediate wariness. "Nothing I can use right off, Leroy. More like background material."

"Over the last few years, Elmo has been the best source of any of the five commissioners, I'd imagine."

"Well, you could say a practical politician on any level makes use of the press. Some of them have a feeling for it. Elmo does. Sometimes it's a knack of saying nothing in such a way it comes out sounding like news."

"Would you think Elmo's knack is worth pursuing?"

"What do you mean?"

"Could he go further with it? Higher offices?"

"If he has the desire. But Elmo has the knack of making money too. Maybe that's more important to him."

"But you're talking about alternate roads to the same thing, Jimmy. Aren't you?"

"Power and importance? It would depend on what kind Elmo wants, and how much of it he wants."

"Let's assume his appetite is insatiable."

"Where are you heading, Leroy?"

The eagle face creased into a sleepy, knowing grin. "Hell, I'm just talking. He's an interesting man. I wanted to get your slant on him. He likes you, Jimmy. If you wanted, you could latch on and go along with him. That's what I've been doing."

"I'd have to wait for him to ask me, Leroy. I'd have to know where he was headed. You see, I can't think of anything I want very much that I haven't got."

Shannard put the money down and got off the stool. Jimmy thanked him and they walked out to their cars. "I guess I was too obvious about it, Jimmy," Shannard said.

"Too obvious about what?"

"He said you'd know how to handle it, but I had to check it out myself."

"I just don't know what the hell you're talking about."

Shannard got into the Thunderbird and grinned up at him. "You're perfectly right, you know. Elmo should clear it first. But welcome aboard anyway. Night, James."

By the time Jimmy drove out of the parking area beside the Spanish Mack, Shannard's car was out of sight. Three carloads of teenagers passed him, cutting from lane to lane, yelling at each other. The stop lights were off, blinking yellow down the length of Center Street through the middle of town toward City Bridge. The lift of the drinks was gone. He felt stale and sleepy.

A block before the bridge he changed his mind about going straight home. He turned right and cut back to Brian Haas's place. Brian and Nan lived in a garage apartment. The big house had been torn down and replaced by a row of connected one-story shops and small offices erected close to the sidewalk with parking area in the rear. The garage apartment was just beyond the asphalted area. It had a small walled garden at the side, shaded by an enormous banyan tree.

When Jimmy Wing parked by the garden wall and turned his lights off, Nan Haas came hurrying out.

"Just me," he said. "Anything new?"

"Not yet, Jimmy. They're looking for him. Come in and help me wait. Isn't this a hell of a thing?" Her voice was casual, but he could sense the strain behind it. He followed her into the tiny ground-floor living room. She wore white shorts and a dark blue sleeveless blouse. She was barefoot, and her hair was short, curly, brown-blond. Nan was a short, plump woman, ripely curved, light on her feet, firm in her skin, with a round, placid, pretty face and the beginning of a double chin.

"Coffee?" she asked.

"If you have some made."

"In this house, always."

He sat in a wicker chair. A big fan by a narrow window turned slowly back and forth, hesitating at the end of each arc, stirring the moist night air. He thought of what Shannard had said about Nan, marveling that what had happened to her hadn't destroyed her. She had been the exceedingly pretty daughter of a Palm City couple. Her father had been a city fireman. Nan McMay had started winning beauty contests when she was fifteen. She had been a frivolous, vain, uncomplicated child. At eighteen, after placing third in the Miss Florida competition, she had run away to New York with a photographer, planning to become a model. After two grubby years in New York she had the good fortune to meet a very decent boy who wanted to marry her. After she met the boy she broke up with a strange unsettled man with whom she had been having an affair. She and the boy came down to Palm City to be married. The man she had walked out on had been annoying her. He followed her to Florida. On the eve of the wedding he broke into her parents' home, shot and killed her parents, the boy she was going to marry, a younger sister, a younger brother and himself. Nan was not expected to live either. The bullet he had fired into her had done extensive abdominal damage before lodging against the spine.

Five murders and a suicide would have been given national news coverage in any case, but because the unbalanced man had termed himself a poet, and because Nan had been a winner of beauty contests, and because the suicide note they found on his body made it plain they had lived together, it was given exceptionally lurid and breathless coverage, spiced by her old publicity shots and by his "poetry."

After she recovered, guilt should have destroyed her. Heartbreak should have destroyed her. Public disapproval should have destroyed her. She should have killed herself, or gone mad, or disappeared. But she instead suffered the homely miracle of becoming an adult. She could never become a whole person. Torture had burned away all trivial things, but had also seared what was left. The radical surgery necessary to save her life had obviated any chance of children.

A year or so after she had stolidly, quietly put herself back together, she had started seeing Brian Haas, and they had married. It was, as Shannard had said, a mating of survivors, the way two travelers on a lonely journey might join together to share food, hardship and shelter. But any closeness which endures, no matter how guarded it may have been in the beginning, creates its own necessities, confirms its own new image, establishes its vulnerabilities.

Jimmy Wing knew he had become more of a friend of the marriage than a friend of either of them as individuals. He was a factor in the relationship, one measurable aspect of the balance they had achieved. From Bri, and with Jimmy's help, she had learned the art and pleasure of good talk. And from Nan, Bri had learned of the aspects of life which need not be complicated by introspection—a long walk, a swim, a picnic beach, making love. She soothed him and he made her feel alive, and so convenience became slowly transmuted into necessity.

She was receptionist-bookkeeper for a dentist in one of the offices in the building in front of their apartment. On their combined salaries they lived quietly and comfortably. Their sole extravagance was The Itch, a stubby, shallow-draft Bahamian ketch of great antiquity and, except for a temperamental auxiliary engine, great reliability.

She brought him the coffee and sat on a bamboo hassock near the tiny fireplace and said, "It's so damn airless tonight. Did you hear the thunder a while back? I could see the lightning out over the Gulf. It's crazy not to have any rain this time of year."

"What do you think started him off?"

"God knows, Jimmy. Anything or nothing. I've been going over the past week or so. I can't think of anything specific. How has he been down at the newspaper?"

"Perfectly okay."

"I just hope he didn't drive out of town. I'm glad you stopped, Jimmy. I wouldn't want anybody else here. I couldn't talk about it to anybody else." There was a look of wryness in her smile. "Whenever we need you, you seem to show up. I guess that's the best kind of friend there is."

"All I'm doing is drinking your coffee, Nan."

"That's all you have to do. If you came in here all terribly concerned and full of warmth and pity and so on, I think it would start me crying. Isn't that a hell of a thing? And I'd cry because I'm more mad than anything else. I'm mad at him and I shouldn't be. It's like he can't go very long having things be right. He has to spoil them."

"Not on purpose."

"No. But it's as if it was on purpose. For the last year things have been pretty good."

"I know."

"Better than either of us deserve, I guess."

"Could that be part of it, Nan? He spoils it because he thinks he doesn't deserve it? Self-punishment for guilt."

She shrugged. "Everybody feels guilty. It took me a long time to find that out. It doesn't matter how big or how little the thing is they feel guilty about, the guilt seems to add up about the same. And not everybody is a drunk. So where does that leave you?"

He smiled at her. "Interesting proposition, woman. No matter what I do, I won't feel any more or any less guilty?"

"You can't do things you aren't capable of doing."

"What if my capacity changes?"

"Nobody's ever does, really. Anyhow, that's Bri's theory. He says you can change your stripes in a lot of ways that don't really count very much, but when it comes to sin, everybody has a built-in limitation."

"So nobody can ever corrupt anybody?"

"Only if they're ready. Or, I guess, terribly young, so young they don't know what's happening."

He did not reply. Suddenly he did not care to follow that line of speculation any further. It was making him think about Gloria, and he did not know why. It was always easier not to think about Gloria. The wall-to-wall floor covering was of pale gray raffia squares. He put an imaginary knight on the square nearest his right foot and, using the knight's eccentric move, marched it to the square nearest her bare feet, then over to the kitchen doorway, across to the foot of the narrow staircase, and back to the original square where it had begun.

"Jimmy."

He looked at her and saw the tears standing in her eyes. "Yes?"

"I can't afford to lose much more, you know. I can't afford to lose this now."

"You won't."

"It scares me. I didn't want to ever have anything again I could give a damn about. I don't really know how I got so far into this. I didn't want to. Now, instead of thinking about him, I'm thinking about me, what I can stand, and what I can't stand."

"Now, Nan."

"I just wanted to . . . to sort of watch, and not be a part of anything." The tears began to spill.

Over the sound of the fan he heard a car outside. She got up quickly and hurried to the door. He followed her out.

"We got him," a man said.

"Thank God!" Nan said.

"It'll be easier getting him out this side, Joe."

Jimmy Wing hurried to help the two men with him. Brian Haas was a big man. He was semiconscious, incapable of standing. They got him out of the car, supporting him on either side. The light from the apartment illuminated his face. It had a mindless slackness. The long scar down his left cheek seemed more apparent in that light. He smelled of whiskey and vomit and made a mumbling, droning sound. They got him into the house and up the narrow stairway.

"Where was he?" Nan asked. "Where's our car?"

"He was down at the end of Sandy Key, down at Turk's Pass," one of the men said. "He drove into the sand and got stuck. He was lying in the sand beside the car. We'll get it back to you."

They offered to stay, but Nan told them she would manage. They arranged for someone to come and stay with him the next day while she was at work.

After the men had left, and Jimmy and Nan had gotten Brian to bed, he went into a deep sleep. She touched a red abrasion on his chin and said, "Somebody hit him or he fell. Can you cover for him tomorrow?"

"Sure. Can he make it back by Saturday, though?"

"He has Saturday off this week. He'll feel like death tomorrow. But he'll be able to make it all right by Sunday noon . . . if this is the end of it . . . if he's gone as far as he has to.

He'll claim it's all over. But I won't know. I don't think it will be over. It would be too quick."

"I'll stop by tomorrow, if you think it would be a good thing to do."

"Call me first, Jimmy. I'll be running over here every little while. I'll know how things are. I wonder how much he had."

She walked out to his car with him. "Thanks for letting me know. Thanks for stopping by. Maybe it will be all right. Maybe it's just one little slip, Jimmy, this time."

6

ON FRIDAY at a few minutes after five, Colonel Thomas Lamson Jennings opened the meeting of the Executive Committee of Save Our Bays, Inc. The meeting was held in the large living room of Colonel Jennings' bay-front home. The colonel was in his middle sixties, a lean, emphatic and totally bald man, whose height of forehead and steel-framed glasses gave him a scholarly look. But he was sun-blackened to the hue of an old copper coin, agile, tough and muscular. Kat had seen him in old swim trunks, stalking the mud flats with a throw net, tireless as any Calusa Indian who had stalked the same flats long ago. And she had seen him in the full heat of the midday sun, working with a peasant diligence in his garden beside his Chinese wife, Melissa.

The colonel looked up from his notes and coughed to quiet the random conversation and said, "I guess we can get started. This is all there'll be. Eight of us. I might say that this is perfect attendance for all those in the area. Four are in the north. I've asked Melissa to sit in and take notes for the minutes. Anyone object? All right, then. I've had a busy day tracking down the facts in this matter. I do not have all of them yet. I went into action on the basis of a tip telephoned to me. I can tell you this much. A land syndicate has been formed calling itself the Palmland Development Company. The five majority partners are Burton Lesser, Leroy Shannard, Doctor Felix Aigan, William Gormin and Buckland Flake. The syndicate may include many other local businessmen, but on a basis of merely token participation. They have an option on the Cable estate property fronting on Grassy Bay. They will soon petition the Board of County Commissioners for a change of the bulkhead line and approval of the purchase from the Internal Improvement Fund of eight hundred acres of bay bottom. In other words, ladies and gentlemen, we are right back where we were two years ago, except that this time we may expect a tougher fight. As these are local men and local business interests, we can anticipate a strong endorsement by the Chamber of Commerce, the Merchants' Association, service clubs, civic groups, et cetera, et cetera. From what I heard today, we can expect the petition to be presented quite soon. We are most

71

fortunate to have received a little advance warning. We can expect that the date for the public hearing on this matter will be set when the petition is presented, and that we will not be allowed very much time to prepare. We must organize the strongest possible opposition to this move, beginning immediately. I have roughed out a staff plan, but before I present it for your consideration, I would like to have some opinions from the floor."

Major Harrison Lipe stood up. He was a round little man with a fierce leonine face, a careful mane of snowy hair, a stance so erect he seemed in danger of tipping over backward. He was always in some stage of painful sunburn, blistered, puffy or peeling. His tone was stentorian and oracular. "Tom, though I am not familiar with the geology of this area, I do know that when the first . . . excuse me, *ever since* the first human feasted his eyes on the glorious beauty of Grassy Bay, untold generations have been entranced by its beauty. And once it is despoiled, it will be gone forever. In a few cynical months the dredges and the draglines can undo the glories of ten thousand years. Furthermore . . ."

"Harry!"

". . . experts have assured us that this is one of the most unique breeding grounds for shallow-water fish in the entire . . ."

"Harry!"

". . . west coast area of Florida. And—what is it, Tom?"

"Harry, I respect your sentiments. We all do. In fact, that's why we're here. You performed so well the last time, Harry, I hope you'll take the same job again. It will be up to you to coordinate all the hobby groups and conservation groups in the area. Boating, angling, water skiing, skin diving, garden clubs and the bird people. Locate their current officers, get the petitions written up and signed, and see that they come through with a maximum turnout at the public hearing. Form your own special committee as you did last time, Harry, picking anybody off the membership list you think you can use. Will you do that? We're all pleased and all grateful, Harry. Thank you. Mr. Sinnat? Were you about to say something?"

Dial Sinnat did not stand up. He had one brown, hairy, muscular leg hooked over the arm of the chair he was in. He was a hard, handsome enigmatic man in his early fifties. His coarse black hair was just beginning to gray at the temples. Kat remembered how surprised she and Van had been when Di had jumped into the fight two years ago. He had not explained his motives until after the fight had been won. On a late night beside his pool he had said, "It isn't atomic energy that'll do us in, buddies. It's sexual energy. Procreation. Billions of new bodies corrupting God's world. In their history books they'll read how once a man could walk all day long and not see another human or a house or a machine, and they won't be able to imagine how it was. There'll be oceans of squirming people, from sea to sea, fellows. So we kept them from gobbling one little bay, one little crumb, and it felt good, but it doesn't mean much. How long have we been sitting here? Two and a half hours? There's ten thousand more mouths in the world than there were when we walked out of the house. Rejoice, buddies. Mankind is on the march, heading toward that golden day when there's nothing to eat but each other."

Now Dial said, "Just thinking, Tom. This sounds rougher than last time. The clue is that option on the Cable property. Martin Cable has to be a convert, it would seem. He's the executor. How big a piece is it?"

"A little over six hundred feet of bay frontage, running from the bay to Mangrove Road," Colonel Jennings said. "And we can expect, this time, that Ben Killian won't be neutral."

"As it's a local operation," Dial said, "he'll have to go with his advertisers. I'm beginning to think we ought to try to lean hard on something we didn't give much attention to last time."

"Such as?" Jennings asked.

"Maybe we ought to develop some statistics to show that it won't help local business a damn bit."

"I don't think I follow you," Jennings said.

"They'll have statistics. Eight hundred new houses at umpty dollars apiece initial investment and umpty dollars a year upkeep and maintenance, and eight hundred new families in the area spending umpty dollars a year with the local business people. They gave us that jazz last time, those Lauderdale hotshots. I think we could develop statistics out of St. Pete, Clearwater and Sarasota to prove that all a big development does is bring in more butchers, bakers and candlestick makers, so that after all the dust settles, everybody has just about the same gross business they had before. In fact, they might be a little worse off, because residential areas never pay back in taxes the cost of the services they require, particularly in Florida with this homestead free ride on the first five thousand of assessed valuation. Industry is the only thing which takes up the slack in the tax billing."

"Could you get to work on that, Dial?"

"Better if it comes from some local businessman, Tom. I

unloaded the family firm up in Rochester twenty years ago,
took my capital gain and ran. I spend a couple of hours a
day in the biggest crap game in the world, buying a little
here and selling a little there, but I'm considered a playboy type, possibly because I am. Some yuk would question
me from the floor and ask me if I'd ever met a payroll. I
have, but it was too long ago. But I will see if I can find
a convincing pigeon for you. This thing may be spread so
wide it will be tough, but somebody is sure to be annoyed
at being left out, and not in a very good position to capitalize
on a big Grassy Bay development. I'll look around."

"Splendid!" Jennings said. "And I'd appreciate it if you'd
line up the Power Squadron people and the Yacht Club people as you did so well the last time." He made a check
mark on the pad fastened to his clip board, turned over another sheet and said, "And you, Morton, will you operate
just as you did the last time?"

Morton Dermond sighed in a somewhat dramatic way and
said, "I shall rally all the forces of culture. Yes indeed. But
it is tiresome, isn't it, to have to go into the same little act
all over again." There was a slight stir of disapproval in the
group. Dermond was a big waxy young man, apelike in construction—barrel torso, short thick legs, long meaty arms, a
head dwarfed by the neckless span of the solid shoulders.
His black hair grew low on his forehead, and his beard was
a blue shadow on the pale solid jaw. He had a light, flexible
voice. He wore lavender slacks and a coral sports shirt. A
ruff of springy black hair erupted out of the V neck of the
sports shirt. Dermond was a museum director, lecturer and
art historian. For the past several years he had been the
Executive Director of the Palm City Art Center.

"It may be tiresome, but it is important," Jennings said.

"Of course it is," Dermond said. "But I could agitate
my people a lot easier if we had some kind of vivid new
approach. I mean, some of them may actually yawn this
time. I realize that out here in the hinterland it is really
difficult to come up with truly creative ideas. Personally, I
can't imagine anything more *grim* than eight hundred new
dreadful contemporary houses. All those tricky white roofs,
blinding you. They'll look terribly modern for the first
twenty minutes, but in no time at all it will just be another
dreary middle-class slum, littered with tricycles, glass
jalousies, ceramic egrets and plastic lawn furniture. They'll
cram those tiresome houses in there, with no privacy whatsoever, and fill them with dreary fatuous little people, and
then we'll be just one step closer to utter mediocrity."

"That's defeatist talk," Harrison Lipe said sternly.

Dermond smiled at him. "I'm a defeatist, Major. I'll strain and strive, but as long as our society equates progress with quantity rather than quality, permit me my private dismals."

Jennings said, "If you feel you can do better with a fresh approach, Morton, please try to come up with one. Now, how about you, Mrs. Rowell?"

Doris Rowell cleared her throat. She was an ample billowy woman in her sixties. She wore a faded cotton dress and sneakers. She wore her straight white hair in a Dutch bob. Her voice was a pugnacious baritone. "It should be no great task updating my materials, Thomas. A team from the University of Miami has been doing another shallow-water ecology study, and I was of some small assistance to them, so I see no problems in getting access to their findings. Just as soon as we know the date of the public hearing, I'll make certain we have reputable marine biologists there to testify. And I'll coordinate this with state and Federal conservation authorities. We'll prove, as we did before, that filling Grassy Bay would have a disastrous effect on the local marine ecology, including, of course, game and food fish species. I can consider such a project no less than a criminal act."

"Thank you, Doris. By the way, Harry, add the commerical fishermen to your list, and use Doris's findings as the persuader."

"Yessir," said Major Lipe.

"Let's hear your appraisal of the situation, Wallace," Jennings said.

Wallace Lime stood up. He wore dark green walking shorts and a khaki shirt of vaguely military cut. Between the bottom of the legs of his shorts and the tops of his long dark wool socks, his bare knees were brown and sturdy, haloed with a curling crispness of sunbleached hair. He was in his early forties. He had a luxuriant mustache, reddish brown, carefully groomed. He wore glasses with heavy black frames. He used a pipe, lit or unlit, as a constant prop.

Whenever Kat saw Wallace Lime, Van's appraisal of the man came into her mind. Van had said, "Try to find the man behind the tricks, honey. Take away the glasses, the mustache, the mannerisms, the slight Limey accent, and take a good look. I know you can't, because behind all that camouflage is a man so desperately ordinary that he'd be practically invisible. Bugs and animals have protective coloration. Wally has spent his whole life going in the other direction."

Wallace Lime waited a long thoughtful time and said, "You must think of my function as that of creating a general climate of approval for what we are trying to do. Ektually, a climate of desirability. If I am to be denied all access to the means of public communication, press, radio, television, the tahsk becomes rather more difficult. I shall attempt to plant our little banderillas in significant places, of course. Largely, however, I shall be forced to operate on a personal-contact level. As soon as this matter is opened up, I shall see to it that our county commissioners begin to receive letters from the more thoughtful and articulate citizens of the community. I shall see what social and political pressures can be developed at this time, to counteract the commercial pressures which are obviously at work. And, as before, I shall put out mimeographed bulletins stating our position and see to it that they are properly circulated. Fortunately we ordered far too many bumper stickers and posters the last time. I have them in storage, and I shall get them out immediately. Tom, I will have the final draft of an emergency bulletin ready by tomorrow noon for distribution to our membership."

"We're going to get some drop-outs," Jennings said, "so we'll have to make every effort to increase the membership. And I plan to make an emergency assessment to build up our campaign fund. That brings us to the final staff mission. Jackie and I discussed it before the meeting. Jackie?"

Jackie Halley stood up quickly. She was a tall, gawky, spirited, attractive blonde. "Kat Hubble and I are going to handle the phone brigade this time. I'll have to blow the dust off the old card file and get organized. We'll be able to use most of the same team of gals we used last time. I guess you all know the system. By the time of the public hearing, every woman in this county we can reach by phone will have heard our little spiel."

"How does it go?" Dial Sinnat asked.

"We tell them that the bay bottoms are owned by the State of Florida, and the Trustees of the Internal Improvement Fund are supposed to administer them for the health and welfare of all the people. We tell them they own the bays. And their children and their children's children should own them too. But if we let the state sell that land to private enterprise, then it's gone forever, and they and their children and their grandchildren can't even go near it because it will be private property forever. We ask them not to let a few greedy men legally steal what belongs to them. It isn't a set speech, Di. We have gals who can sort of feel their way, depending on the reaction."

"Thank you, Jackie," Jennings said. "Kat, the last time we went to war, the newspaper was supposed to be neutral, but Jimmy Wing managed to slant things our way quite often, and I think it helped a lot. Do you think he'll help us this time?"

"I really don't know," Kat said. "He was Van's best friend, and he knew how worried Van was, and he tried to help us out. Brian Haas did what he could, too. All I can do is see if he'll be willing to help us this time. But if the paper comes out in favor of the fill, it might be impossible."

Dial Sinnat said, "Jimmy is a very bright operator, Kat. He doesn't have to be obvious about it. Lots of men have torpedoed projects by coming out very strong for them, listing all the wrong reasons. It's a standard device in politics. Tom, are we open for general comment? One thing I want to say to everybody: Last time we battled outsiders. Civil wars have a tendency to get nastier than the other kind. And men can do curious things when their pocketbooks are involved. I think we should all be ready for a game of dirty pool. I'm invulnerable. But there are others here who make their living out of the community, and the reprisals might get rough. How about you, Morton?"

Morton Dermond said, "I couldn't care less, Mr. Sinnat. I have a captive board of directors, a docile membership, and two years to go on my present contract. And, I might add, not the slightest interest in renewing it. How about your little bucket shop, Wally?"

Wallace Lime spoke irritably. "If I've given you the impression, old boy, that I'm dependent on the revenues from Wallace Lime Associates, I apologize. I would hate to lose all my little advertising accounts, but even in that unlikely event, I should survive . . . comfortably."

"I happen to work for the Cable Bank and Trust Company," Kat said, "and I can't afford to lose the job, really."

"That puts you in the target area," Dial said, "but I don't think Martin Cable would be that small-minded. Don't worry about it. I just wanted to say I think we can all expect some kind of pressure."

"I think you're right, Di," Jennings said. "We seem to be all set to go. I'll coordinate all the staff functions, and all of you will be hearing from me frequently. One thing I want to make clear before we adjourn. This is just our first line of defense. We'll fight like hell, of course, but if we lose this one, we'll regroup and fight just as hard on all the other ways we have of keeping the sale from going through and, if it does, enjoining the dredges from beginning. Anyone have anything to say? Meeting adjourned. Cocktails on the patio, everyone."

After talking with several of the others, Kat found herself with Melissa Jennings. They were standing near a clump of dwarf banana trees, looking out through the screening, across the quiet expanse of Grassy Bay. The shore-line shadows were beginning to lengthen out across the water. Against the distant mainland shore two cabin cruisers were heading north up the marked channel.

"Whether we looked out upon it or not," Melissa said softly, "I should not want such a lovely bay spoiled. The people who would live out there would think they had waterfront, but the true waterfront would be gone, with nothing left but little canals for their boats, and a few narrow channels."

Kat looked surreptitiously at Melissa Soong Mei Wan Jennings, at the classic, luminous, Oriental beauty of her face in profile. She was Colonel Jennings' second wife. His first wife had died several years before Tom had met Melissa in Chungking during the Second World War. She was almost twenty-five years younger than her husband, but the marriage seemed strong and close. Tom had grown children by his first wife. He and Melissa had three sturdy, popular boys, aged twelve, fourteen and seventeen. All the boys were away at summer camp. Melissa was tall for a Chinese woman, and it was only in these past few years, as she had reached forty, that her figure had lost its willowy, girlish configuration and had begun to thicken.

"If it happens, would you move away?" Kat asked.

Melissa turned toward her, frowning slightly. "I think not. Some years ago, yes. But now it is too late. This is where I brought my boys when they were small, and where the last one was born. We have planted so many things and cared for them so long we love them too much. Those trees of gold there, and the silk oaks. The house suits us too well, Kat." She smiled. "We'll have to learn not to look at the bay so much. I'll miss it. The light is always changing. Maybe all Chinese are peasants. This is my land, and it is more important than what it looks out upon."

"More talk of defeat," Dial Sinnat said, joining them. "What's the matter with all you people?" He stood close to Kat and put his arm around her casually, the hard warm weight of his hand against her waist. As always, his apparently unthinking touch created in her a strange indecision; a small despair. It made her feel like a fool, quite unable to cope with something so obviously innocent.

When Di Sinnat was near her, he touched her. It was that simple. He did not paw. There was no innuendo. He was fond of her. And he was evidently a man who automatically sought the tactile gestures of affection. But each time it seemed to freeze her. She had never liked being touched in casual ways by casual people. And people seemed aware of this trait, instinctively respecting that apartness in a crowded world. Yet Di seemed oblivious of the tension he created. She never knew exactly how to handle it. When he put his brown paw on her waist, her shoulder or the nape of her neck, she breathed in a constricted way, and mentally rehearsed the moves she could make to get away from him, yet could not move freely or casually. She did not want to be touched, yet she did not want to hurt him or, more importantly, create any special awareness between them by making such a point of moving away. So usually she endured it until there was some plausible excuse, and felt relief when it was over. She had tried to talk herself into paying no attention to it, but she could not accustom herself to it. And she was always aware of how very good Di and Claire had been to her since Van had been killed.

A few times she had even wondered if Di was deliberately sensitizing her to his touch, the way animals are trained by slowly acquainting them with the touch of their handler. But she had dismissed this as a paranoid idea which presupposed too much deviousness on the part of Di Sinnat. It was true that he knew women well, and that all of his wives had been beautiful, and that he was vividly male, but he did not seem to have the requisite subtlety to build toward seduction in such an unanswerable way. Somehow she had let pass her chance to stop him in the very beginning. She wished he would change the casual touch into a caress so that she could then stop him without loss of face.

Yet she was wise enough about herself to know that even though it might be the furthest thing from Di's mind, he was sensitizing her in a way that worried her. He was an attractive man. When he rested his hand upon her, it seemed at the time to have no sensual significance to her, yet twice in the last few months she had awakened abruptly from odd erotic dreams about him. In the last dream she had been alone on the beach down near the Pavilion, sunning herself, yet the beach had become so enormous that she was a tiny figure in a sandy waste, the Pavilion a tiny dot on one horizon, the Gulf a blue distant line opposite it. She saw an insect figure walking toward her from the Pavilion, taking a long time to approach across the sand. At last she recognized Di and was glad to see him because she had something important to say to him, but she could not remember what it was. He sat beside her on the blanket and began talking about Claire's plans for a studio over the big carport for his daughter, Natalie. Then, still talking, smiling, nodding, he put his hands on her breasts. In the dream it was the same as when he touched her casually, affectionately, at a party. She did not feel she could move or protest. She felt she had to say the right things about the studio for Nat as he described it to her, pretending she did not notice that he had pushed her back, loosened her swim suit, and was working it down off her hips, pulling it off entirely. Still talking, chuckling, he forced her thighs apart and his face was huge over hers, blotting out all the blue of the sky. She knew that if she could only remember what she was supposed to tell him, then she would be able to scream and make him stop and he would understand. She awoke, shuddering and sweaty, hearing the echo of her own night cry.

Now the warmth and shape of his hand came through the frail material of her blouse, and though it gave her no pleasure, it seemed to muffle the sounds of the conversation on the Jennings patio and make the colors of the early evening less bright, as though all other senses had become subordinate to her complete awareness of that unwelcome weight.

After the emptiness and the desolation of the first few months without Van, she had begun to wonder about herself and the need for sex, if need there was. Van was the only man who had ever known her. For the first year of marriage she had thought herself to be so cool as to be able to find only meager pleasures in the act, but in order not to be a disappointment to Van she had pretended the eagerness she thought would please him, and had doggedly and strenuously acted out the completions as she had read of them in various novels. But in time it became only half false, and at last it became entirely true, and like nothing she could have guessed—a gloriously sweet madness, inexhaustible.

The world seemed to believe that a woman so conditioned by a good marriage would be either unwilling or unable to accept a young-widow continence. She examined her own reactions with somber concern. Sometimes, in the empty night, her body would so yearn for Van's embrace it was as though ten thousand minute arrows pierced her flesh, poisoning her and sickening her. But it would always go away. She thought of all the men she knew, and imagined them, one by one, giving and receiving the pleasures she and Van had known, but instead of any fragment of curiosity, any crumb of desire, she felt a rising, curdling nausea.

On a previous February evening, Sammy Deegan had confirmed her suspicion. Other men had made oily little hintings, dropping little clues as to how well they could keep any secret, but Sammy, full of vodka confidence, had made the direct approach. His wife and his sister were out of town. He claimed he had seen her light. The kids were in bed. Thirty seconds after he was inside the house, he was fumbling at her, nuzzling her, murmuring to her, frightening her with his clumsy drunken strength. When she had wrestled loose and he had chased her into the kitchen, she had snatched a tack hammer from the counter top where she had left it after fixing a nail in her sandal, spun and chopped him squarely in the middle of the forehead with it. It made a deep gash and burst a vein. The alarming jet of blood sobered him and terrified her. He had lowered himself to the kitchen floor in a gingerly way, stared walleyed at her through the running mask of blood and said in a hushed voice, "Good Christ, Kat, where is there to put a tourniquet? Around my neck?" By some miracle she had managed to avoid hysterics. She took him to the bathroom. She found a place where she could press with her thumb and stop the regular pulsing. She made him hold his thumb on the place while she cleaned the gash, cut small strips of tape and crisscrossed them to pull it together. It stopped the bleeding. He was so full of guilt and shame he cried, but he tried to cry without moving his face very much, so it would not start up again. He walked off into the night with extraordinary care, as if he had a wineglass balanced on his head. After she had cleaned up the blood she went to the bathroom and vomited again and again. It was not the blood which had sickened her, or the fright. It was the memory of his wet wanting grin, and the rough fumbling of his hands, and the blunt, questing bulge of his sex against her when he had held her close. Sammy had answered the next-to-the-last question for her.

The last question was still there. Would another man ever have her? It would have to be with love. It would have to be like the way she had felt toward Van. But there might be no man in the world who could awaken that.

Wallace Lime had come over to talk to the three of them. Di took his hand away to light a cigarette. She smiled at them and murmured something about having to talk to Jackie, and went across the patio to where Jackie stood talking to Morton Dermond.

Morton said, "I was just telling Jackie she really does have the figure for one of those little sleeveless dresses, high at the throat, not fitted, no belt. I'd love to see you in one, Jackie. One of those fabrics that look like raw silk.

They're truly horrid on meaty women, dear, but you have a nice colty look."

"He doesn't know Ross," Jackie said. "I dress for Ross, Morty. He doesn't like the merchandise hidden under the counter. I've got to make the most of what I've got. Stretch pants and plenty of uplift."

Dermond looked pained. "But it's so obvious, isn't it?"

"Oh, yes indeed!" Jackie said, with a broad dirty grin.

Dermond looked at his watch and said, "I do have to run. I'll send you our current membership list so you can check it against your files, Jackie." He walked away from them, taking curiously short steps for a man of his size.

Jackie giggled. "I shouldn't tease the poor brute. He yearns for pretty dresses, but he hasn't got the build. He always wants to dress me, and it gives me the horrid feeling his taste is better than mine, so I strike back. He's really one of the nicer ones. He's not too obvious, and he has the good sense not to try to mix up the two worlds he lives in. When can we have our own little organization meeting, Katty?"

"No banking hours tomorrow. Do you want to come over?"

"You come to our house, honey. Two birds with one stone. I didn't get a chance to tell you before, but Ross wants to use you again. Now, don't look at me like that. It's a stinky little six bucks for an hour or any part thereof, and the sketch has been okayed, so he knows exactly what the pose will be. There's a swirly skirt of mine he wants you in, and it won't take more than fifteen minutes. How about right after lunch? Bring your kids."

"It always makes me feel like such an idiot."

"Don't be so self-conscious, honey. Ross loves your good bones, and he says you've got the best color values of any redhead he's ever used. And he says you're as easy to work with as a pro. And I'm so horrible at it. Poor guy. I freeze every time. I hunch my shoulders and the pictures come out looking as if I had one of those iron things holding my head steady like they used in the olden days. And I haven't got good arms, he says."

The group was breaking up. Kat said goodbye to Melissa and the colonel and went out to her brick-colored Volkswagen parked in the sandy shade next to the Jennings' semicircular driveway. As she drove a mile south on Mangrove Road toward Sandy Key Estates, she thought of the meeting and how it had disappointed her. Probably, from an organizational point of view, they were better organized than they had been the last time, but there was a quality of indignation and enthusiasm which was lacking. At the first meeting two years ago, everybody had tried to talk at the same time, presenting all kinds of ideas. Perhaps now they were better qualified to combat the Grassy Bay fill, but there did not seem to be as much spirit, as much righteous anger.

The side door key was under the mat, and she was glad Roy and Alicia were becoming so reliable about replacing it. She went into the empty house and felt a familiar twinge of guilt as she snapped the big air conditioner on. She took off her blouse and skirt in the bedroom and went back and stood in the cool wind of the noisy unit until she felt chilled by the evaporation of the mist of sweat on her body.

She phoned the Sinnat home. The cook-housekeeper, Mrs. Riggs, answered. She asked her to tell Esperanza to shoo the kids on home. Mrs. Riggs asked her to hold the phone. Claire came on the line and said, "I knew you'd be late on account of the meeting, Kat. So we asked the kids to stay for a hamburger cookout, and Gus is over here fogging us down. Here's the deal, dear. You come on up whenever you feel like it, and the upper classes will have steak later on. Then when my pair are sacked out, either Nat or Esperanza can take yours home and sit with them until you're damn well ready to call it a night."

"Claire, I just can't keep imposing on—"

"You've never imposed on anybody, Kat. Di wants you around tonight. As soon as he got home a few minutes ago he phoned Martin and Eloise, and they're coming over too, later on, but without the little Cable heirs, thank the good Lord. We were talking about it when you phoned. Di wants to nail Martin about why he's optioned that land to the developers. You know Di, so it ought to be something to hear. He thinks it would be a good thing if you were here."

"But I work for Martin!"

"You work in the bank and so does Martin. Don't be so darn timid, Kat, really. You were a friend and neighbor long before you worked for him. We'll expect you, dear."

"Well . . . all right, but I'm not going to get into any hassle. I'll just listen."

"Come along whenever you're ready."

BRIAN HAAS MUTTERED, stirred, opened his eyes at a few minutes before five. Jimmy Wing put his book aside. The small bedroom was hot.

Haas slowly fumbled the sheet down to his waist. His broad chest was shiny with sweat. His color was very bad. He looked at Jimmy.

"Still Friday?" he asked, his voice slow and toneless.

"Still Friday. Almost five o'clock."

"One long son of a bitch of a day. How long have you been here?"

"Fifteen minutes or so."

"Nan around?"

"She said she'll be here a little after five."

"Can you pour me some water?"

Wing poured a glass from the pitcher on the night stand. Haas hitched himself up in the bed and took the glass in both hands, shaking so badly he spilled perhaps a third of the water down his chin and chest. Wing took the glass, and Haas slid back down with a sigh.

"Been shooting me with something new," he said. "It's like the whole world was in slow motion. How about Borklund?"

"You've got a virus."

"A two-quart virus."

"Was it that much?"

"I don't know. Probably. I bought four pints. I always buy pints. It cuts the losses if you drop one, I guess. I think I finished two before the car got stuck. I can remember waking up on the sand and killing another and feeling around for a full one and not finding it."

"Couldn't that much kill you? Taking it so fast?"

"I guess so."

"Then what's the point?"

Haas stared at him and Jimmy Wing thought he saw a flicker of amusement in the dark deep-set eyes. "Only the drunks know there's no point in it, Jimmy. The civilians say it's immaturity, or a need for love, or a physiological deficiency, or an escape from reality, or some such crap. I'm a drunk. So I drink. It's that simple."

"We civilians have to find reasons for things."

"Happy hunting."

"Is it over for this time?"

"It might be."

"It's rough on Nan."

"It's no picnic for me, fella. My life is full of places I can't ever go again, and people I can't ever see again. If it gets too rough, she can join that group. I can't talk to you about it, Jimmy. You never joined the club. You haven't been there. We'll always be talking about two different things, so let's skip it."

"Okay."

"You're not sore?"

"No. I'll even change the subject. The Save Our Bays people are back in action. Emergency session right about now. There's a new move coming up to turn Grassy Bay into suburbia."

Brian Haas closed his eyes. It was a full minute before he opened them again and turned his head toward Jimmy Wing. "That's a good subject. Keep going."

He told Brian no more than Brian would reasonably expect him to know. As he finished he heard Nan coming up the stairs. She came in and said, "Howdy, Jimmy. My God, you got the uglies, Haas!"

"A thing of beauty is a joy forever," Brian said.

She sat on the foot of his bed, patted his leg and said, "How goes the remorses?"

"Same old ones. Familiar faces. Like abandoned children who finally tracked Daddy down."

"How are these shots working?"

"They're pretty good, Nan. Too good, maybe. I should be praying for death right now. I should be shaking the bed and gagging."

"I know. Do you miss it?"

"In a funny way. It's always been like paying my way. Maybe I've enjoyed the dramatics in some inverted way. It doesn't seem right to feel no worse than a flu case."

"He'll be here at six to give you the last one. Could you eat?"

"They're good, but they're not that good."

Jimmy stood up. "I'm off. You want to set up the board, I can give you one hour tomorrow, starting at high noon. Give me white, and I'll give you another crack at the queen's gambit."

"If I can see the board. Right now there's four of you. It's a side effect, I guess. How do you think we'll go on this Grassy Bay thing this time?"

"The paper? We'll come out for progress. Ben listens to
J.J., who is no idiot."

"Can we bore from within, like last time?"

"We'll have to wait and see, Bri."

He went down to his car and drove to the newspaper offices. To the old yellow-tan Florida-Moorish building on
Bayou Street, all courts and arches, dusty ivy and vivid,
unkempt flower beds. He parked quite close to the circulation shed where, in another life, when he was nine years old,
he had come in the first gray of morning to pick up the
papers for his route. He went in through the side door of
the main building, took some notes out of his box, and
went back to his desk in a relatively quiet, windowless corner.
One note asked him to call a number he recognized as the
number for Bliss Construction. He called. A girl switched
the call to Elmo.

"I'm going to be working late here, it looks like," Elmo
said. "So why don't you stop on by when you get a chance?"

"It won't be until about eight."

"I'll be right here."

He went to work on his accumulated notes. "At a special
luncheon meeting of the Chamber of Commerce, County
Planning Director Edison Kroot announced that fallout shelter builders will get full cooperation from county zoning and
building authorities. . . ."

"Five science courses in Palm County high schools will
become part of a Federally subsidized teacher-testing study
this coming fall, according to Dr. Wilde Sumnor, Superin-
tendent of Public Instruction. . . ."

"The El-Ray Snack House was burglarized Thursday
night . . ."

". . . went through the stop sign at the intersection of
North Street and Palm Way . . ."

". . . remains in critical condition in . . ."

". . . resigns post as . . ."

The copy girl took the yellow sheets to the news desk.
The evening tempo of work was increasing. Wire service·
material was being fitted into the makeup, along with the
ads and syndicated materials already positioned. Except for
late sports, the back pages were being locked up, one by one,
working forward to page one, which would be held open
until half past midnight. Borklund stopped by his desk, in-
quired about Brian Haas, and tried to load some phone
work on Wing, but he avoided it by saying there were still a
couple of things he had to go out and get. The teletypes chat-
tered, phones rang, linotypes clucked steadily, and the Saturday edition began to take on form and pattern. It was a kind

of work which, for many years, had given him satisfaction. But in this past year it had seemed to become smaller and less meaningful. The wire service reporting was leaden and clumsy. Each local story he wrote seemed to have been written before. Only the date had been changed. He could not know if his restlessness and sense of boredom was due to Gloria's final escape into her nonworld, or to the limits of all the demands made upon him, or to his increasingly obsessional relationship with Kat. But he knew that now it was all changed, and would all be different.

He welcomed the new and not yet known things that would happen, but at the same time he was alarmed, uneasy. You walk into a new room, close the door and pull a lever. Then you begin to wish you hadn't. But the lever has also locked the door.

When he had awakened, he had taken the two fifty-dollar bills from his wallet and turned them over and over in his hands. The money had looked theatrical, implausible. He had been offered all the usual things in the past, the junkets and free rides, the Christmas whisky and the unofficial due bills, the lighters and cigarette cases and desk sets. And, sometimes, cash. He had used a flexible judgment based less on morality than on convenience. He took what it had seemed plausible to take, measuring himself against what he believed others would take and did take, seeking that comfortable level where he could be labeled neither prude nor rascal, and avoiding those gifts which implied too direct an obligation for future favors. But he had returned the rare gifts of currency. Gift certificates had been the nearest thing to cash he had accepted.

But this money was not, of course, a gift or bribe. Elmo had made that clear. It was specific pay for specific employment. He had become a moonlighter. And, should the job itself become distasteful, or should the fact of having two jobs become burdensome, he would tell Elmo his acceptance had been a little too hasty. Elmo, of course, would take it gracefully. There would be no instructive visit to one of the back-country sloughs, not for a mildly recalcitrant member of the press.

But Ulysses S. Grant looked out from the money with a brooding, dubious expression. Hadn't he had some money trouble himself?

Now there was a summons from Elmo, and the money had given it a different flavor than had been apparent in the summonses of past years. His response to it had been altered also, in just as subtle a way. He wondered how many more there were who now played the same game, who had become

a part of the expanding universe of Elmo Bliss, willingly or
unwillingly—even knowingly or unknowingly. Frannie had
said that he made her feel alive. Maybe that was the most
effectively deadly subversion of all. All the children felt
gloriously alive, marching away from Hamlin.

The offices of Bliss Construction were in a small one-
story building in a commercial area on Bay Highway, south
of the city, just over the city line, about a mile and a half
north of the light where Mangrove Road turned toward
Grassy Key. Behind the office structure, and enclosed by
hurricane fence, were the storage buildings, a workshop and
the vehicle park. His transit-mix cement plant and his hot-
mix asphalt plant were in a heavy-industry zone north of
Palm City. Though Elmo had expanded with startling speed
throughout the fifties, he had the curious ability to give each
new venture the flavor of having been his from the very beginning. His expansion no longer seemed as brash and reckless as it had been. He had adjusted so readily to being one
of the city's most influential businessmen that it was easy to
believe he always had been. The tales of his early wildnesses
were told with that same fond nostalgia usually reserved for
incidents of a prior century. Jimmy Wing had wondered why
this could be true, and had finally realized that Elmo would
have been unable to achieve this quality of acceptance in a
more static community. Palm County growth had been dramatic. Total county population had been a little over twenty-
five thousand when Elmo had been swinging a brush hook
on a county road gang. Now it was over seventy-five thousand, and most of the newcomers had arrived after Bliss Construction was an established firm. To them, the Elmo Bliss of
the wild years had the quality of myth.

Elmo's office headquarters was set back just far enough
from the curbing of Bay Highway to provide room for a loop
of asphalt drive in front of the entrance. The long dusk had
ended when Jimmy Wing arrived. Tinted floodlights were
buried among the broad shining leaves of the shrubs in the
planting area that stretched the length of the front of the
building. The right half of the structure was unlighted. The
blinds were closed in the left half, but light escaped at the
edges of them. He parked behind Elmo's blue pickup truck.
It was, he knew, a considered part of the image, a truck
with the worn, battered, dusty look of the ranch lands, a
more telling symbol than any Cadillac or Mercedes could be.
Beyond the truck, in a more shadowy place, was a stubby,
elderly Renault, sun-seared and rusty.

He tried the door and found it locked. Over the hum of

traffic on Bay Highway he heard from inside the building a shrill yapping laugh of a woman. He pressed the bell beside the door. An inner door opened, and light streamed out into the reception desk area. A bright fluorescence flickered on, and a woman came toward the locked door, smiling, patting her hair, hitching her skirt. She was young, short, sturdy, her slender waist latched so tightly in a wide belt it accentuated hips and breasts far beyond their need for emphasis. Her face was broad, pale, pretty in a rather insipid way, roughened by acne scars. Her hair was dyed a dark red, and worn in a rather incongruous and inappropriate beehive style. She jounced toward the locked glass door on very high heels, coming down hard with each step. She looked cheap, trivial, empty and troublesome, but Wing had learned, during Elmo's term on the commission, that she was shrewd, competent and trusted.

She opened the door and said, "Hey, Jimmy."

"Evening, Miz Sandra."

She locked the door again and said, as they walked toward Elmo's office, "How about with my little sister in the Sunday paper, hey?"

"All set. They were going to make it a one-column cut, but now they'll use it three columns wide."

"It's only fair, her being the one in the family with looks, and marrying better than me or Ruthie. When I married Pat we didn't have the money to have a picture took, even."

Elmo was sorting papers on his desk. The desk and the room were like his study at his home. He looked up with an abused grin and said, "Rick Willis keeps telling me everything is running just fine, but whenever I spend two days away from this desk, I get all this here crud to sort out. Make yourself a drink, Jimmy."

The doors of the bar cabinet in the corner were open. He heard Elmo and Sandra Straplin talking about the work she was to do. He opened the small built-in refrigerator and found some beer on the bottom shelf, dark frosty bottles of imported Tuborg. He opened one and took it over to the long deep couch under the windows.

"You want I should do any of it tonight, like maybe the airmail to Costex, Elmo?" she asked, standing beside Elmo, frowning down at him.

"No. You have it all for me to sign tomorrow, so you just tell me when to come on in here."

She riffled the sheaf of papers in her hand. "About like two o'clock?"

He slapped her on the haunch and turned it into a little push, urging her toward the door. "Two o'clock will be just fine, Sandra. Goodnight, girl." He turned to Jimmy. "You follow along and lock that outside door behind her, boy, so we can talk easy. I got to get this desk cleaned the hell off."

Sandra put the papers in her desk drawer, took her purse from another drawer, turned out the reception room lights. They went to the door and she said, "What you do, you turn this hickey here to the right. Guess you'll be coming around more often?"

"Are you telling me or asking me, Sandra?"

The nearest light standard on Bay Highway shone a pale white light through the glass door, slanting across her wide white face. Her perfume was a very sweet and heavy flower scent. She smiled up at him. "Neither one, Jimmy. Just making talk."

"I wouldn't want you making that kind of talk too many places."

Her placid smile did not change. "Chrissake, honey, if I was to start now, I'd go down one hell of a long list before coming to you, so don't fret yourself. Thanks about my sister. We'll get along, you know. That's what he's good at, always knowing people will get along good together. Good night, Jimmy."

She left. He locked the door. He watched her little car turn out into the flow of traffic, heading toward town.

He went back and picked up the beer bottle and stood by Elmo's desk until Elmo looked up at him, and then he said, "Maybe what you should do, Commissioner, is take an ad in the paper. You know the usual form. We are pleased to announce that James Warren Wing has become associated with us."

"Are you sore, boy?"

"A little, I guess. Last night Leroy was so damn cute."

"You handled that real fine. Leroy likes the way you took it, and so do I."

"Thanks a lot. Does Sandra get to pat me on the head too?"

"Steady down, Jim, for God's sake. You know what Leroy proved? He proved something I already knew, but he had to check it himself so he'd feel easier in his mind about it. He had to make sure you weren't one of those people have to jump on every chance to make a brag. Most people are like that. It makes them feel bigger to hint around how important they are. I'm clearing you right now to talk right out to Leroy about any part of all this."

"Leroy and Sandra so far. Do you want to write out a list for me?"

"You got the ugly on you tonight, boy. One thing you

keep in mind, will you? What good would you be to me if everybody knew our deal?"

"Not very much I guess, but . . ."

"Sandra has been with me eight years. She'd just turned eighteen when she came to work here. Anything I do, she knows. Like Leroy does too. And like you do from now on. Man, I'm not a damn fool."

Jimmy went back to the couch. "I guess you've never given me that impression."

Elmo went to the cabinet bar and chuckled as he started to fix himself a drink. "Just don't worry about who knows what. Take a damn fool like Flake. He never gets to know more than I need him to know so I can get the use out of him I have to."

"But you have an arrangement with him on his share of this Palmland Development, don't you?"

"I got some ways of keeping him tame. Leroy and Sandra I don't have to worry about. They know they do good when I do good. So they like to come up with all the he'p they can give me. Hell, after Sandra married Pat Straplin, I made him a lend of the money to get into the contract electric business on his own, and I keep him busy. I got a couple of her kin onto the county payroll a while back." He pulled a chair toward the couch, sat down and put his drink on the coffee table. "What happens to a man, Jim, he gets a lot of other people fastened onto him in one way or another, so sometimes you have the feeling it's turned into a whole army, all pushing in one direction, everybody anxious to do all they can, because this is the way they make things better'n they've ever been. It's getting so it would be hard to find a public place around Palm County where a man could bad-mouth me and not get knocked flat and bloody."

"I suppose the biggest danger in that is beginning to believe it yourself."

Elmo looked at him narrowly, then laughed. "Hell, I believe *some* of it. Why shouldn't I? My name doesn't sound the same to me it used to. Elmo Bliss—it used to have a raggedy-pants sound. But I've pulled it higher than anybody thought I would already. It doesn't sound the same to me any more. You want I should be humble? It surprises me ninety-nine per cent of the human race can feed themself. Anything wrong with a man knowing he's in the one per cent on top?"

"As long as he stays on top, I guess."

"Women, liquor and gambling. That's what throws men, Jimmy. I do my gambling in a business way, where I know the odds. I got my drinking done early in life. And the women

I got are no more anxious for any scandal talk than I am, and anything new that comes along will be selected just as careful, boy."

"So you're safe, Elmo."

"It's something you should know, you betting your future on me. If I should go down, I'll fall heavy. And you might be right in the way."

"You better decide whether you're going to keep me in line by threatening me, Elmo, or by sweet-talking me. This way, you keep confusing both of us."

"It just goes to show how much I want to depend on you. It's making me too anxious. I guess once you get to work, we'll both feel better. I was awake in the night thinking about you, Jimmy. A good man should get paid what he's worth. I decided old Buck is going to sell a little bigger piece than he thinks he is, when the time comes. He'll sell you some, and take your note. You should clear ten thousand on it, which would be seven thousand, almost, keeping money, once you pay capital gain."

"Thank you very much."

"There'll be little things like that coming along ever' so often, boy. By the time you get out with a profit, I'll have a good place you should put it and watch it make you fat. I figure a man like you should feel more like a partner than somebody hired."

"I've been a hired man all my life."

"Then it's time you should stand on this side of the fence and see how it feels. I know what you're thinking right now. You're thinking I'm awful goddam anxious this land fill goes through. I am. But I'm not so anxious I'm losing track of anything."

"I wouldn't expect you to."

"They had their first meeting this evening, and the first one you should go after is that son of a bitch Sinnat. Now we're down to cases, boy."

"As I understand this, Elmo,' you want me to dig up some things about these people, things which can be used to get them off this Grassy Bay campaign."

"That's exactly right!"

"But what kind of things, damn it? How much proof? How are they going to be used?"

"Now you listen here, Jimmy Wing! What I want is that Dial Sinnat finding out it just isn't worth while for him to mix into this thing. He put up a good piece of the money the last time, and they'll be wanting to clip him for more. It's like a dog, he sticks his nose in a hole and a big yella bee stings it, he don't care what else is in that hole any more.

Just how it gets used depends on what it is you can come up with. And I don't think it has to be too much. You know why? It would take one hell of a lot to keep me or Leroy or Felix Aigan out of this deal, because we come out at the end of it with something you can hold in your hand, namely money. What's the word for the opposite of something you can hold onto?"

"Abstraction?"

"That's it. All the damn bird watchers and do-gooders and nature boys, they got an abstraction they've fell in love with. But the average man, you tell him that bay is a mess of mud flats likely to make his kids sick, he won't see anything pretty in it, and he won't want to save it. When the average man goes to look at nature, he wants something going on, like a porpoise coming ten feet up out of the water to eat a fish, or like pretty girls underwater, sucking air from a hose and eating bananas. There's nothing going on in that bay they can look at. But the goddam do-gooders got this abstraction they look at. They like the idea of nature being left the hell alone. Boy, it never is left alone. Never. Not when there's a dollar you can make out of it. Now, what I'm saying is that money in hand is a lot more persuasive than the abstraction of leaving it like it was when the Indians first found it. So it's easier to chase a man off an abstraction than it is to chase him away from meat and potatoes."

"Wait a minute, Elmo. A lot more men have died for abstract considerations, for ideas, than for money."

"Is Sinnat one of those, for God's sake?"

"N-no. He isn't one of those."

"So what can we use?"

"I don't know, Elmo."

"Then you find out. On his fourth wife, isn't he? Anything he's doing, or his wife is doing, or any of their kids are doing that he wouldn't want too many people knowing about, he could be cooled off real fast on this nature-lover business. You're the one can find out easiest and fastest of anybody in town, Jim. And he's the one I want discouraged first. Anything looks promising, you bring it right to me."

"And if there's nothing?"

"One thing I've learned. There's always something. Maybe you got to turn it a little sideways before you can use it, but it's always there if you look for it."

"How much time is there?"

"The petition gets presented to the commissioners next Tuesday morning. As far as setting the date for the hearing, I just plain don't know yet. The law sets two weeks' minimum time to wait after the petition is presented. I got to move a little easy on it, so the other commissioners won't get the idea I got a special ax to grind."

"Last time around, I helped the do-gooders all I could."

"That's good, boy. They'll want more help. Try to give it to them."

Jimmy Wing stared at the commissioner. "Maybe I'm not getting through. I agree with what they're trying to do."

Elmo finished his drink. "So do I, in more ways than you might imagine, Jim boy. If this whole coast could be just as it was when I was a boy, I'd be happy. Right in the middle of all those hundreds of little houses Earl Ganson built in that Lakeview Village of his, I used to get me my quail with an old single-bar'l Ithaca sixteen-gauge when I wasn't as high as it was long. Had a busted stock wrapped with wire, and every time you fired it you had to bang the butt on the ground to make the trigger spring back to where it belonged. Hell, you're old enough to know how it was around here."

"Remember that old dock on the north end of Cable Key, the long one on the bay side at the old Esterly place?"

"Sure do."

"I must have been about eight years old. It was a Sunday in May. There was a school of mullet in there like nobody has ever seen since. I'd say they were schooled up six miles long, a mile wide and ten feet deep."

"Say, I remember that! God damn! We gigged all day long until our arms like to fell off."

"Everybody did. Half the town was out there."

"And the fish house price fell off to two cents, finally, and then they wouldn't buy at all because they had no room. I remember we run a truck of them down to Naples, but it was a hot day and we had no ice, and the man down there didn't like the look in their eye by then. So we dumped 'em damn near in the center of town and took off fast."

"The whole town here stank for a week. That was the last big school, the last one on this coast, Elmo."

"It's a sad thing to think about, surely. And so are a lot of other things, Jimmy. All those miles of dead empty beaches. I was at a party at a big motel on Cable Key the other night. A political thing. Out at that Blue Horizon. I bet you Gidge Tucker put a million bucks into that, all told. And it's got places on either side of it damn near as big. I was standing out on the beach where they had a bar moved out there, and lanterns strung and all, and grass-skirt music going on, talking to a committeewoman from Tampa, and I looked at the way the shore line curves right about there, and knew where

I was at, and all of a sudden I had to laugh and I couldn't tell her what I was really laughing at. I had to make something up. You see, right about where we were standing, I'd spread me a blanket maybe twenty years ago, with a bottle and a fire and a little darkhead waitress from Estero, and we stayed right on there through most of the next day, the only time putting our clothes on to go all the way to town to get something to eat and some more wine. We had a game we were shipwrecked on a desert island, and we didn't see a soul all day, or expect to. Gidge paid three hundred a foot for that same shore line we blanketed on, and it's worth more now, but if it had been three dollars a foot back then, I couldn't have bought enough for a grave, except maybe lengthwise from the water. It'll all a sad thing the way it changes, all the wild things and wild places going, one by one, but you and me, we can't change it or keep it from happening. All we can do is get in there and get our piece of it. Hell, I know why you went along with those folks. Vance Hubble was a good friend, and I know for sure that the people who fought the fill the last time and will fight it this time make better people to be around, for a man like you, than the ones over on my side of the fence. But you did it to help your friends and be with them, not out of any great big complex about saving the world. You don't give enough of a damn about things like that to make it any great jolt for you to work against them instead of for them."

"I wouldn't want them to know what I'm doing."

"They won't know unless you tell them. I won't. Leroy won't. Sandra won't. And let me tell you something else. Once it's filled, the ones who were against it won't give a damn either. Maybe they'll feel regretful they lost, and maybe they'll scowl when they look out onto that fill and the houses going up on it, but after they've seen it fifty times they won't notice it any more, and they won't miss the bay unless they stop and remember how it used to be. The only thing left of that bay will be some old memories and some old photographs hanging around. And after it's filled there'll be thousands and thousands of folks coming down here who won't even realize it was open bay water, and will be bored if you try to tell them it was. Because they won't give a damn. Jimmy, what the common man wants is television, air conditioning, a backyard barbecue, healthy kids and a normal sex life. If it was the last bay left in the world, he might get agitated. But there's always more bays. And when he goes fishing, he doesn't compare how good or how bad he does to what he could have done ten years ago or fifty years ago. If he gets two runty little trash fish last week and three this week, he's happy to do better. If he sees one pelican and one blue heron all week, he's glad there's wild water birds around for him to look at. If they don't look at him, he'll yell and wave his arms to make sure they do. He likes nature to notice him. And that bay doesn't notice him worth a damn. It just sits there, and when it's gone he won't miss it. Neither will your do-gooder friends. But I would sure as hell miss the money I'm going to make out of it. I'd want to lay down and cry if it went bad on me. I got to have it, and it's not an abstraction, fella. It's the most actual thing there is in the world, and I mean to have it, because I got just the right use for it. And now listen close. Name me one son of a bitch in this world who can *prove* which is the best thing to have out on those grass flats, eight hundred houses, or eight million minnows. It'll be a nice high-class development, and the people who'll live there'll be happy they found such a pretty place to call home."

"I'll take the fish, Elmo."

"If I had any choice in the matter, I would too. But if I chose fish, boy, somebody else would choose to fill it, because it's close in, it's shallow enough to fill cheap, and the state is still in the business of peddling land belonging to the people."

"Which is a violation of trust."

"Maybe it's morally wrong, but it's as legal as marriage, boy. When there's next to nothing left worth saving, they'll put it all under the Conservation Department where it should have been put years ago. But so long as the door isn't locked yet, I'm walking through it before somebody else does. And I don't want any long-drawn-out law fights either. That's where you come in. And the first one I want nailed is Dial Sinnat. We set to go now?"

Jimmy Wing waited the space of three slow exhalations. "It should be interesting work."

"You'll get to like it, as soon as you break the ice."

"Elmo, I don't want to like it or dislike it. I just want to do it and get it over."

"Where will you start?"

"I don't know."

Elmo reached and thumped Jimmy Wing on the knee with his fist. "You'll figure it out. Boy, we'll find time to talk this way often. We'll get to know each other. The better I know you, the better I like you, Jimmy. You got a cool streak, but maybe that's a good thing. I got plenty of people can get too damn hot and excited. You lay back and keep account on how we're doing, huh?"

"Won't you know?"

Elmo laughed. "Hell, I'll know it when we go so slow on this thing I get nervous. Then I'd have to tell Leroy to get you some outside help on those folks. You'd still be in charge, sort of. But they'd be helping you dig. Leroy knows a damn good Tampa outfit with some smart ex-cops working for them."

"But you said it won't take much to scare those people off."

"It won't, Jimmy! It won't! But we've got to have that little bit."

Jimmy Wing wiped his mouth with the back of his hand. "If you want something to start with, I can give you something on Morton Derm . . ."

"Dial Sinnat first, Jimmy boy! Before he can fatten the kitty for them. Hell, I got to get on home before Dellie skins me. Get those lights over there, will you? I'll see that everything's locked."

Wing followed Elmo's pickup as far as Bayou, then turned off toward the newspaper building. Seconds after he arrived, a state highway patrol tip came in on a bad one ten miles south of town on Bay Highway, just north of the town limits of Everset. Borklund shooed him onto it, along with Stu Kennicott for pictures. They hurried down to Jimmy's car. Four blocks after they had turned onto Bay Highway an ambulance screeched by them. Jimmy tucked the old blue wagon in behind it, maintaining a minimum safe interval, and clicked on his illegal red flasher.

They had to yell at each other to be heard over the constant sustained scream of the siren and the hard roar of the old Plymouth engine.

"All you know is it's a bad one?" Stu yelled. He was an aggressive little man with thick glasses.

"That's all he said."

"Goddam death trap from Palm City to Everset. Same as Venice to Sarasota. I won't let Myrt drive it. You following too close?"

"I can see past him, Stu. If anything looks hairy ahead, I'll fade back."

"You do that. You know what I like?"

"What do you like?"

"I'm a beauty contest man. And animals. Long legs and cute kittens. I take a hell of a picture, man. These tore-up folks, they put my stomach off. Aren't you too goddam close!"

"Flash Kennicott, the fearless photographer. I have to move up so I can pass when he does, or I get nipped off."

"They'll still be there and they'll still be dead."

"Cheer up, Stu. If it's a bad enough schmear, maybe you'll get a wire-service pickup."

Stu kept both feet on imaginary brakes. Soon Wing saw the flashing lights ahead and he stayed close behind the ambulance as it slowed. Troopers with flashlights were moving the traffic through. He saw a state patrol car parked in a field, heading out, so he bounced through a shallow ditch and parked beside it. They got out and walked over to the mess. The sedan was on the near side of the road, upright, the front end accordioned. The old panel delivery was on the far side, on its side, damaged in the same way. Tow trucks were waiting to hook on, as soon as the state police gave the word. In the floodlights a heavy woman in orange slacks lay bonelessly spilling out of the open door on the passenger side of the sedan, face down, legs tucked under the dash.

Kennicott's power-pack bulb began to flash. Tires yelped far to the north and south as cars braked for the slow passage by the accident. They gawped as they went by, and pulled off when they were beyond the officers and came walking back through the confusion of lights and through the tall grass to stand and stare some more.

Jimmy Wing saw Cal Chadwicks, a patrolman he knew well, talking to another officer and a truck driver. He went over to them and said, "Evening, Cal."

Chadwicks turned, smiled, grimaced. "Hey, Jimmy."

"Head on, it looks like. We going to know how they did it?"

Cal gestured toward the truck driver. "This-here boy saw good. He lost forty dollars of burned-off rubber staying to hell out of it."

"Heading north," the driver said with that wooden tone indicative of shock. "The car there, the Nebraska car, passed me and come in between me and the truck ahead. Then he swang out to take a look, but the panel truck was too close, coming fast, so he cut back too far, tripped hisself on where the shoulder drops off and got flang back out right bang into that panel truck and got knocked right back again right across the front end of me to where it's sitting now. It was a hell of a noise. Seemed like it went on a hell of a long time."

When another officer came to speak to Chadwicks, Jimmy got the truck driver's name, and other pertinent information.

Kennicott came over to him and said, "I'll get back with this right now, Jimmy, they can get it in. You going to phone it in?"

"Yes."

"Then how about the lend of your car? Can you get a ride?"

Jimmy gave him the keys. "Leave it in the lot there. Put the keys under the mat on the driver side. Get anything?"

"What there is, I got. Who needs it?"

Kennicott left. Wing located Chadwicks again, over by the panel truck. It had Palm County plates. It was being rocked up onto its wheels. One ambulance was gone. "Who was in this one?" Wing asked.

"Claude Barnsong, from Everset."

"Which Barnsong is that, Cal?"

"The one runs a charter boat out of Everset Marina. His license here says he was . . . thirty-four. He was alone and he was in a hurry. Got a half ton of marine engine in that thing and it came frontwards when he hit." Wing borrowed the license and wrote down the RFD address. Chadwicks was able to lend him the identification on the other two deceased, a Mr. and Mrs. George Kylor, aged fifty-eight and fifty-six, with a street address in Grand Island, Nebraska, driving a 1960 Buick. They had lost control of it. There was ample evidence of the point of impact being in the southbound lane, all the fine scale and dust which is hammered loose from the underparts of cars in a head-on smash, the white powder of glass, burst of oil and spray of water, all captured on highway patrol cameras before traffic was permitted to roll over the place of impact. The police report would fix the blame on the Kylor car—and the insurance people would eventually settle. But who was responsible for a road too narrow for the traffic, or for shoulders scoured down by summer rains?

The other ambulance was gone. The panel truck had been hauled away. The burst and scattered luggage had been collected and shoved back into the Kylor vehicle. Patrolmen halted traffic while the wrecker turned out onto the highway with it. As Wing walked over toward the patrol cars to beg a ride back to the city, he kicked something in the grass and it rolled into the light. It was a carved coconut, with a bright clown face and a mailing tag. He squatted and used his lighter and saw the tag was blank. He straightened up and kicked it into the shallow ditch where some child might find it the next day.

A county deputy gave him a ride back into town. He turned his copy in, for the page-one space which had been cleared for it. After he had retrieved the hidden keys and gotten behind the wheel of the station wagon, he sat there in the dark parking lot for a little while without turning on the lights or the motor. There was always a carnival flavor about roadside death in the hot months. Flashing lights, the distant melodies of car radios, the abrupt nervous laughter at macabre jokes, the hot gaseous stink of engines mingling with the trampled fragrance of the grass, recognitions, greetings and farewells in the night, sirens coming and going, the holiday awareness of knowing strangers were dead, not you.

It had drained him, yet made him wonder that it could not touch him more deeply. The coconut mask was a sickly bathos. The fat orange slacks were clownish. He could believe that in these past few years of his life a crust had formed across some middle portion of his mind. He could perceive the relationships of his existence, yet he seemed to be required to explain them to himself in a search for reaction which was so studied that the whole procedure became meaningless. Sometimes he felt as if he had forgotton the first language he had learned to speak, and his acquired tongue had no meaningful words in it. It was not a cynicism. It seemed more of a process of a progressive deadening, depriving him of the internal dialogue he had previously enjoyed, that interplay of query and response which made awareness more acute. He had lost some textural, essential appreciation of reality, and felt himself to be in a dream of boredom, unresponsive to all cheap solutions, jeering at himself in a halfhearted way. And ready for Elmo's offer, ready for almost any change, just to see what it would do—thinking of himself as a small creature in a maze which it has learned too well, and now needs the stimuli of experimental complications.

A mosquito whined to a thirsty silence against his throat. He slapped it, started the car and drove slowly to Tamarinda Street. It was midnight. Number 27 was lighted. He parked several houses beyond it, and walked quietly back to it. He tried to remember the last time he had seen his sister, Laura, and could not recall. Eight months at least. She was his only blood relative left in the state, and she was seventeen years older than he. They had been close, a long time ago. But the relationship had not survived the loss of what she had wanted for herself and for him.

Laura lived with her invalid husband in a shabby little frame house. He went up onto the porch and looked through the living room window. She sat staring without expression at television turned so low he could barely hear the sound of it through the screen.

"Laura," he said.

She gave a violent start and put her hand to her throat and stared round-eyed at the window.

"It's Jimmy," he said in the same tone.

She pushed herself up out of the chair, turned the set off, and let him in. She wore a green housecoat belted around her thick body. Her hair was sandy gray. She had his long narrow head, beaked fleshy nose, pale blue eyes. But her mouth was tiny, pinched, set in a mesh of lines radiating from it.

"What's wrong?" she demanded in a low voice.

"Nothing. Nothing at all. I drove by to see if there was a light on. I just wondered how you are."

She shrugged and went back to her chair. He sat on a lumpy daybed. The small room smelled of fly spray, boiled food and sickness.

"How do you think I am?" she asked. "I'm queen of the May. Tomorrow I'm going to the south of France in my private yacht."

"How's Sid?"

She shrugged again, gesturing toward the back of the house by tilting her head. "Sometimes bad and sometimes worse. But he had a pretty good day today. He ate good. But he gets terrible depressed. It's eleven years now, and he was an active man. He's getting so heavy lately, it's almost more than I can do, getting him into the chair and back into bed.

"You ought to have some help."

"I don't like to bother all the servants with little things like that. On the pension I keep so big a staff I can't keep track."

"Can't Betty help out at all?"

She gave him a look of sad disgust. "Pregnant with her sixth? Three thousand miles away? A sixth grandchild I'll never get to see. Except the pictures she sends. She looks so little and tired in the pictures, Jimmy. How can she help out? You knew what he was when she run off with him. We all did, and there wasn't a damn thing we could do. He's a factory hand out there. A big car and big cigars, six kids and time payments and broke by Wednesday every week. I'll never see her again. They'll never get far enough ahead to come this far, and I can't leave Sid. What's the matter with you? How do you expect her to help out?"

"Don't get sore. I was just wondering."

After a long silence she said, "Do you remember how everything used to be, Jimmy?"

"Yes."

"I think a lot about how things went wrong for everybody, and I wonder why it had to be this way. I keep thinking of what Mom kept saying before she died. In those last weeks she got homesick for New York State, for the Cherry Valley, even though she hadn't ever been back since the day she and Dad left, when she was a young girl. And she kept saying that things had gone wrong because they'd come down here. You know, nothing seemed wrong then. Nothing at all, except her having to die that way, hurting. How old were you when she died?"

"Thirteen."

"That means Betty was six. Sid had a good job. Al was still alive. The family seemed to be doing pretty well. She made me and Al promise we'd help you get an education. We would have anyway. You know that. Already we knew you were the brightest of the three of us. We helped as much as we could."

"I know."

"It's like she knew things were going to go bad for all of us. Funny, isn't it? Sometimes I have a dream, and it's always the same. I'm having a picnic with Betty, in a beautiful place. And she has a little baby in her arms. There's sunshine and sort of music and we're laughing about something. Then we see Sid walking toward us, as if nothing had ever happened to him. Then I realize we're all at the Cherry Valley. I wake up smiling and crying. I've never seen the Cherry Valley."

"I drove through there once."

"Don't tell me about it, Jimmy. You want anything? Ice tea? Beer?"

"No thanks."

"How's Gloria?"

"About the same."

"When did you see her last?"

"Last month," he lied.

"You should go up there more often, Jimmy."

"What's the point in it? She doesn't know me. She hasn't known anybody for two years."

"But maybe she knows more than she seems to."

"Laura, don't for God's sake try to turn it into a soap opera. There's been a progressive deterioration of the brain cells, a physiological decay. Now they're willing to admit that possibly all those series of shock treatments may have made the process a little faster. It's something that destroys the actual brain cells. They talk about some kind of chemical imbalance or deficiency."

"Big words," she said. "Lots of big words."

"Do you have to have it in little words? She wears diapers. They feed her with tubes into her nose. Her eyes don't focus. They say it's interesting. They think they may be learning something from her."

"The big words help you, don't they? You don't have to

think of her as being Gloria. And you don't have to go see her."

He stared across at her in vast burlesque surprise. "Where'd all this concern come from? Aren't you my loving sister, the woman who celebrated my pending marriage by telling me I was throwing myself away by marrying a little Ybor City slut named Mendez? I was impairing my social standing, or something. And when we had that first trouble, you were plugging for a fast divorce, weren't you?"

"We didn't know she was sick then, Jimmy. And I got to like her. She's still your wife."

"She's nothing, Laura. She's breathing meat."

"You're cold as a stone."

"I went through all the kinds of feeling there are. I used up all there was. What the hell do you expect of me?"

"Nobody expects much of you, Jimmy. Nobody."

"That's nice."

"Maybe you got things just the way you want them. Kind of a little frog in a little pond. I saw you two months ago. Downtown, just going into the Bay Restaurant. You looked a little tight. You were laughing and you were with the Mc-Clure woman. I guess that's the kind of thing you like."

"Mitchie is an old friend."

"You don't pick your friends very careful."

"I've got a thousand friends, Sis."

She shrugged. "It's none of my damn business anyhow, I guess. You're grown. But I raised you, Jimmy. You remember that. Nothing is the way I dreamed it would be. I saw you, and I was on my way back here. I hadn't seen you in months, and then I saw you with that woman, and I was coming back here. The days go by so slow for me. They go slow for Sid too. I guess they're worse for Sid. I should be glad you came by tonight, instead of nagging you like this every minute."

She looked at him with a forced smile. On an impulse he took his wallet out and took Elmo's hundred dollars out of it. He had folded the two bills small and tucked them behind his credit cards. He unfolded them and took them over and put them in her hand.

She stared up at him blankly. "What's this?"

"Will it help?"

"My God, yes, it will help. But you act funny. Where'd you get it?"

"For a favor for a friend."

"What kind of a favor? Can it get you in trouble?"

"Do you want it or don't you?"

"I want it. Thanks a lot." She put it in the pocket of her robe. "Did you come here to give this to me?"

"Yes," he lied.

"One thing I'm going to do with it, I guess you should know, I'm going to talk to Betty on the phone. I talked to her at Christmas, just three minutes."

"It's yours. Don't ask for permission. Do anything you want with it. Maybe there'll be more. I don't know. I can't promise it."

"You don't owe me anything. You know that."

"I'll help if I can. Okay?"

"If you want to, I think it's very nice. You look awful tired, Jimmy."

"I'm sort of jittery. It was an automobile thing, down near Everset. A bad one."

"Oh, I heard it on the midnight news. Three people dead?"

"Yes."

"I heard it just before you got here: I guess that . . . just being alive is something to be thankful for."

"Sure. I'll be going, Laura."

She went to the door with him. She pecked him on the cheek, patted his shoulder and said, "Come back sooner next time, dear. You're the only brother I've got. You should take better care of yourself. Come back in the daytime. Sid would love company."

As Jimmy Wing drove toward his cottage on Cable Key, he felt better than he had all day. The nagging guilt about not having seen Laura in so many months was partially expiated. He could see her again soon. And, by giving her the money, he had somehow lightened his sense of obligation to Elmo. It made Elmo's assignment more of a game than a necessity. Tomorrow he would talk to Kat, and tomorrow he would find out something about Dial Sinnat which would please Elmo. If the money, or a reasonable percentage of it, could go to Laura and Sid, the whole venture seemed considerably more respectable. It was good to think about her talking to Betty in California. A nice long talk, courtesy of Elmo Bliss.

8

KAT HUBBLE, in a plastic and aluminum pool-side chaise at the Sinnats, tilted her head back and looked up at countless stars. They did not veer in the sickening way they had the last time she had looked. They were comfortingly steady in the heavens. She had had only two drinks before the steak and salad, but they had been made by Di Sinnat, and had hit her harder than she had expected. She had always been circumspect about drinking, less out of conservation than out of a reluctance to impair her awareness of everything around her. In this past year she had been doubly careful, having learned that it took very little alcohol to relax her control over herself. Grief was an act of balance on a high thin wire. Balance improved with practice. You hoped that one day you could walk it as casually as though it were a city sidewalk, but in the meantime you avoided anything which might imperil the careful balance.

The Sinnat twins were in bed and Natalie had gone home with Roy and Alicia to put them to bed and stay there until Kat came home. The night was hot and still. Claire Sinnat was in the pool, floating nearby in a hammock-and-pontoon arrangement, her heels hooked on the overflow gutter. She was twenty-seven, a pretty, merry, untidy little woman, brown as peat, muscled like an acrobat, her abrupt hair calicoed by the sun. She enjoyed people and laughter and horseplay. She played with the children like another child. At times she seemed more daughter than wife to Di. Her voice was thin and penetrating, her laugh a deep bawdy bray. She had no patience with malice, and was fun to be around, except when she drank too much. Liquor fouled her language and made her venomously quarrelsome.

Eloise Cable sat on the edge of the pool in her white swim suit, dangling her legs in the water. Superficially, Eloise seemed a lustier, more obvious version of Carol Killian. They both had tall bodies, dark hair, and an air of brooding reserve. But there was a rather pallid and sickly flavor to Carol's slenderness. Eloise had a fearful bursting health. Somehow she always looked freshly steamed, massaged and oiled. Her tan had a glowing depth. Her figure had a glossy ripeness which no style of dress could diminish or restrain. She had all the gleaming and somehow ludicrous over-emphasis of a calendar girl. She seemed both smugly aware of and obscurely disconcerted by these awesome riches, and carried herself slowly and with great care, as if she carried herself on a tray over rough ground, full to the brim. Her walk was constricted and circumspect, and there was no flirtatiousness about her. In another and more basic way she was unlike Carol Killian. Carol had the nervous, irremediable stupidity of an inbred dog. Eloise, from a far more humble background, had a tough peasant shrewdness.

If it ever astonished Eloise that she had married Martin Cable, the third, she did not show it. And it would have taken a very perceptive observer to detect that she had married better than her background warranted. Palm County had been astonished seven years before when Martin Cable, at the age of thirty-six, had suddenly married the nineteen-year-old daughter of a garage mechanic, a girl not long out of high school, then working as a file clerk in the installment loan department of the bank.

No one had expected Martin Cable to marry, probably because, at thirty-six, he had the bearing and mannerisms and fussy habit patterns of a bachelor of fifty. The first Martin Cable had been a St. Louis businessman who had come to Palm County to fish and hunt, had bought up large tracts of land, and had eventually settled permanently in the county after his retirement from business. The second Martin Cable had been a yachtsman, a drunk, a gambler, a lecher and an international boor, slain at fifty-one by a black Miura bull in a cobblestone street in Pamplona during a fiesta, spun on a dung-caked horn snugged into the lower bowel, dying in the middle of a scream nine days later. Despite cautious testamentary restrictions, he had worked a considerable diminishment of the involved estate the third Martin Cable inherited. The bank was the executor of the estate of the second Martin Cable, and Martin the third was executor of his mother's estate.

Martin had been a somber child, a dim and diligent young man, and had grown to become a humorless and exacting adult, a bit too jowly to be adequately described as Lincolnesque, vague and thoughtful in manner, aware of the social and civic responsibilities of his name, humble, distant, self-effacing, as is the habit of the inheritors of wealth.

Immediately after his marriage Martin took his bride on a three-month honeymoon, the only vacation of his adult life. Upon their return even the hastiest glance at his wife confirmed the gossip which had attended their departure. Yet even in the obviousness of pregnancy, the change in the girl was total and evident—Ellie Mikersy, the gum smacker, full of prance and halloo, snickerings and bobblings and hot blue glances, was gone forever, to be replaced by Eloise, wife of Martin, a woman who, with a ruthless and astonishing success, immediately patronized those who sought to patronize her. It was a seven-and-a-half-month baby, reportedly premature, but those few who saw it during its first few days were eager to report that the birth weight had been understated by a good five pounds.

A single mystery remained. How and where had the entrapment been consummated? How had such a total wariness been overcome? Yet most of the men of the community found it understandable. Eloise could induce a mild sweat at fifty yards. It was agreed that she had made the optimum use of her natural endowments within her hunting area, and when the baby, Martin IV, matured sufficiently to disclose the unmistakable Cable features, all agreed she had met the minimum ethical standards of the pursuit. Martin IV was now six years old, and his sister, Cooky, was three. They were beautiful children, completely out of control, sweet, active and savage as weasels.

Kat's chaise was angled toward the pool. Martin and Dial Sinnat sat at a table to her left. Eloise sat on the edge of the pool beyond her feet, with Claire afloat just beyond Eloise. The pool lights had been turned off to lower the bug count. Three flares burned atop tall metal stakes, the orange flames guttering and smoking when the night breeze stirred them, emitting a fragrance of aromatic repellent. The flames made patterns on the dark water of the pool, and on the naked glossy back of Eloise, tapered, smoothly muscled, with an ample breadth across the shoulders to carry the richness of the invisible breasts.

They had been talking, the four of them, carrying on two simultaneous conversations, and Kat had not been listening until Di said, "You keep side-stepping, Martin. By God, I'm going to nail you down."

The two conversations became one as Claire said, "I didn't marry a very subtle fellow, Martin."

"Let me try the question a new way," Di said. "Two years ago, Martin, you didn't get down in the mud and help us slug it out, but you were sympathetic when we were fighting that Lauderdale group. That big broad beautiful bay gives this town class. It's distinctive. For long-run business reasons, it's a good thing to have, particularly with the other west coast communities filling their own bays up as fast as they can so they all look alike. Now we find out you're going along with this new group, this Palmland Development outfit. I think we've known each other long enough for you to stop hedging and give me some reasons."

Martin said, vaguely, "I can't really give you a simple answer."

"So give me a complicated answer then. If I can't understand it I'll stop you."

"Well . . . my responsibilities as executor of my mother's estate come ahead of any personal feelings I might have, Dial. I'm accountable to the probate court. I'd have a certain amount of difficulty explaining why I turned down the best offer ever made for that land. Almost seven hundred feet of bay frontage at three hundred dollars a foot. It comes to more than two hundred thousand dollars. The estate retains the land to the south of that piece, and it will become much more valuable when the development is completed."

"Is the estate hurting for cash? Are there unpaid obligations?"

"Oh, no! If that was the case, that land would have been sold off long ago. Actually, I've been in the position of waiting for a good offer."

"So you could wait longer?"

"It isn't that simple. I'd have to justify waiting, on some kind of financial basis."

"But you have to exercise demonstrable bad judgement before the probate court gets agitated, don't you?"

Eloise spoke then. "But Martin has other responsibilities too, Di. Responsibilities to the community, as president of the bank."

"How did you get into this?" Di asked, astonished.

"Don't be rude, dear," Claire said.

"Eloise has been taking an interest in this," Martin said proudly. "She really has had some very sound thoughts about it. Tell Di what you told me, dear."

Eloise had turned toward the two men. "I told Martin a banker has to do more than just loan money and so forth. He ought to help get things started where a lot of people make money, like a farmer planting things. I mean it's sort of a responsibility to the community for Martin to do something to help such a big project get started, even though we all might rather have it stay the way it is. It would be different if he was in your position, Di. But a banker has to think of the economic health of the community."

"I didn't know you cared," Di said to her.

"Do you think it's wrong for me to take an interest in Martin's work?" she asked.

"No, Eloise," Di said. "It's very refreshing."

"In any case," Martin said, "the upland is optioned now."

"And you're certain you've done the right thing?" Di asked.

"I'm doing the reasonable thing, Dial."

"An option and a nice fat line of credit."

"That will be up to the Loan Committee."

"My God, don't give me that occupational sidestep, Martin!"

"What are you getting angry about? These are local men of good reputation, Dial. They have an option on access. They have their initial capital. Once they have the right to buy the submerged land from the IIF, they can present a very attractive operating picture. I've been assured the development will be in . . . good taste."

"Martin," Eloise said, "can we tell them about Turk's Island?"

"But we aren't ready to make any public . . ."

"Please keep it a secret," Eloise said eagerly. "It's being done through the Eleanor Marrinar Cable Foundation. The deeds and surveys and ownership of the land on Turk's Island were in a terrible mess, and the lawyers have been working on it for over three years, buying it through dummies, or however you say it. Pretty soon the foundation will have the last tract, and then the whole island is going to be presented to the State of Florida as a wildlife refuge, along with all the bay bottom between the island and the channel."

After a long silence Dial Sinnat said bitterly, "Very very neat, folks. It's too low and too far offshore to be developed. A sop to the bird watchers, at a very strategic time. We fight for Grassy Bay too, and we look greedy. I suppose you got it set up so that if the state tries anything cute, title reverts to the foundation?"

"Of course," Martin Cable said. "There are some squatters on the island. They'll have the right to stay during their lifetime. The foundation will retain a one hundred-acre piece of high land fronting on the bay for eventual use as a marine biology laboratory site."

"And this might just happen to be announced at the Public Hearing on the Grassy Bay development?"

"If it seems opportune."

"Martin, will you answer just one small silly question?"

"I'll try, Dial."

"You're chairman of the Board of Directors of that foundation. Eloise says you started quietly assembling the Turk's Island property three years ago. Was this the plan you had in mind in the beginning?"

"N-not exactly."

"When did you decide to do this with it?"

"I'd have to look at the minutes of the meetings. Perhaps six months ago."

"Martin, was that before or after you heard of the Palm-land Development Company plans?"

Martin Cable chuckled softly. "My word, Dial, I'm not that devious, really."

"Somebody is, dammit!"

"I hardly think so. Dial, I think you're trying to make a perfectly innocent coincidence appear to be a plot of some sort. As a matter of fact, Eloise and I had that inspiration one afternoon when we were out on the boat off Turk's Island last autumn."

"It was really your idea, darling," Eloise said.

"Maybe I'm turning paranoid," Di said. "I keep imagining some masterful hand behind this whole damnable deal. But when I think of the primary personnel involved, Burt Lesser, Bill Gormin, Shannard, Felix Aigan and that Flake animal, there just doesn't seem to be anybody that damn special. I hear there are others in it, but those are the big five. Leroy Shannard is probably the shrewdest of the lot, but he's never seemed to have the hunger to go with it. The way this whole thing is being shaped up so carefully, it has the mark of a bold and hungry man. It's as if we had a visiting eagle in our midst. Martin, is there any chance those five guys are fronting for some tough visiting talent? Is the Lauderdale group trying the devious approach, maybe?"

"On the option, I dealt with Burt Lesser, Leroy and Mr. Gormin, Dial. Not for one minute did I have the impression they were 'fronting' for anybody, as you put it. After all, isn't it a very straightforward development operation?"

"There's money in it. Lots of money. I'll feel better about the whole thing when they start to make mistakes, Martin. Then I'll know it's purely a local project."

"Aren't you in favor of the Turk's Island plan, Di?" Eloise asked in a chilly tone.

"I think it's just delicious, sweetie," Di said. "Let's all drink to the Eleanor Marrinar Cable Foundation, and to truth, beauty and all the little old lady bird watchers in tennis shoes, to marine biology, public hearings and all the good gray gentlemen of the Chamber of Commerce. Sorry you've resigned from our ball club, Martin, my boy. We're playing in a tough league this year. We'll miss you."

"If it wasn't for the bank . . ."

"I know. Eloise explained it to me, and very nicely indeed."

"I think we should be getting back, dear," Eloise said to

her husband. The Cables left about fifteen minutes later, disappearing into the darkness, and then reappearing thirty yards along Gulf Lane under the small glow of one of the few street lights in the Estates.

Di said, "Ladies, I am still paranoid."

"What's that supposed to mean?" Claire said. She had climbed out of the pool to say goodnight to the Cables. She sat on the foot of Kat's chaise. Dial sat on the redwood table, his powerful legs dangling, looking down at them.

"Our Eloise has taken a hell of an interest in the dreary world of commerce. Whenever poor Martin talked business, she'd yawn and whine. All of a sudden she's the helpful little woman. Martin thinks it's cute. I think it's very strange. How does it strike you, Kat?"

"It's a little out of character, maybe. But she could just have decided to take an interest."

"Or she could be working on Martin, as a favor for a friend. A shrew friend could tell her just what line to take with Martin."

"She doesn't act as bored as she used to," Claire said.

"Martin wouldn't be a very stimulating husband," Di said. "She'd be a damn fool to play around. She's got everything to lose. But she's a crafty one. I think she has a taste for intrigue."

"Have you checked her out, dear?" Claire asked, too sweetly.

"I haven't had the time, the energy or the impulse, sweetheart."

"I'll make sure you don't have."

"I'm sure you will, love. But forgive me for saying I do have a kind of an instinct for such opportunities. I'd mark her possible, but not probable. My interest is totally academic."

"See that you keep it that way, buster," Claire ordered.

"With your help, dear."

"I better be off too," Kat said. "You understand why I couldn't say much. I do work for . . ."

"We understand," Claire said. "Di wanted you nearby to listen."

"And now I want to know what you think," Di said.

"I guess I feel sort of depressed. The way it's organized, it's like a steamroller. I can't really blame Martin for what he's doing."

"But given a choice, Martin always prefers to do nothing. So he's been pushed. By Lady Eloise. That's what's odd."

"Well, thanks for the drinks and steak," Kat said.

"Walk her home, Di, and walk Nat back, please. That damn Gus makes me nervous this time of night."

They renewed their repellent spray and walked toward Kat's house through the dark night. Di carried a small flashlight.

They had not gone far before he sighed audibly and said, "I really think you ought to sit this one out, Kat."

"But I couldn't!" she said. "It's something I believe in, Di. Gosh, you know how hard Van and I worked that last time."

"I know, I know. But I have the feeling this one is going to be a little gamey. We fought outsiders last time. This time it's a civil war, and that's the kind which can get nasty. I'm going by instinct on this. I have the feeling I'd like to check Lady Eloise out and see if I could come up with something that would turn Martin against the whole scheme. Now, if I can think in those terms, the opposition can too. We're so damn vulnerable it scares me."

"Vulnerable? What do you mean, Di?"

"Take a look at our Executive Committee, honey. Pretend you're an electrician's wife, and the Grassy Bay deal will give your husband steady work for a long time. Who are the people trying to block it? First, most of them live down there on Sandy Key, so that makes them rich folks. Now look at the individuals who ramrod the S.O.B.'s. That name, by the way, is too sassy. This time it may hurt more than help. The Executive Committee is made up of two retired army officers, one man who retired too soon and got married too often, one dilettante advertising phony, one wife of a magazine artist, one widow of a young architect, one weird old lady amateur scientist, and one pansy gallery director. Who are those nuts to try to take the bread out of our children's mouths? They just don't want their view spoiled. They're just a bunch of rich, nutty, degenerate Communists."

"Di!"

"It can get that bad, kid, and we are a slightly strange group, you must admit. But I'd guess we're probably typical of the strange groups all over the country who are fighting with absolute sincerity to protect the countryside from the uglifiers, from the spoilers, the asphalters, the sign merchants, the tree haters. But, God, how vulnerable we are! I just hope they concentrate on trying to make us look silly, the way the Lauderdale group tried. But I have a feeling they'll use heavier weapons. Hell, it doesn't matter to me. There's no way they can touch me. But maybe you ought to make this one a spectator sport."

"I'm not hiding anything. There's no way they can hurt me either, Di."

They were in front of her house. He stopped her and took hold of her hands. "If they find a way to hurt, Kat, just don't get all choked up with valor. Get right out, will you?"

"But I don't see how . . ."

"Then be cautious, honey. Don't quack with strangers. Wear your life belt at all times, and be ready to abandon ship. The rest of us will understand, and Van would understand too."

"I'll be careful, Di, but I . . ."

"Let's get this sitter off duty. Miss Natalie Sinnat, the sweet dreamer."

"She's a wonderful girl, Di."

"Excuse me if I agree."

Natalie looked up quickly as they walked in. She put her book aside and stood up. "So soon?" she said, smiling.

"Martin Cable passed out early," Di said. "Fell right off his chair wearing a wide drunken smile. Eloise slung him over her shoulder and packed him off home."

"Again?" Natalie said, shocked and solemn, her eyes sparkling. "The kids were utter lambs, Kat, as usual. No phone calls. I dipped into the Coke supply."

Her father looked at the four empty bottles on the coffee table and said, "Don't you mean you wallowed in it, child?"

She blushed visibly and immediately and said most casually, "Oh, Jigger saw me walk the kids home and he came with us and hung around for a while."

"Indeed!" Di said. "Isn't he a little young for you? A gloriously beautiful chunk of muscle, I grant you, but that Lesser boy can't be over seventeen. I've made attempts to talk with him, but he seems to have the same shining emptiness as a brass spittoon, child."

She picked up the empty bottles to take them to the kitchen and looked angrily at her father. "I know he's young. And he has sort of a crush and I can't help that. But he's not empty! He's just very defensive with adults. He's a lonely, unhappy boy, and he's really terribly sensitive, Father."

"Excuse *me!*" Di said. "I wouldn't deny him the chance to unburden his troubled heart to an understanding older woman."

"You're terribly amusing, Father," she said tonelessly, and took the empty bottles to the kitchen. When she came back she said to Kat, "You don't mind Jigger having been here, do you?"

"Of course not, dear."

"He has to have somebody to talk to. If he didn't have, I'm afraid he'd . . . get into some kind of crazy mess."

"Like what?" Dial demanded.

"Let's go, Father."

After they were gone and Kat had looked at her children,

she remembered that this time she had forgotten to even go through the motions of trying to pay Natalie. Maybe, she decided, it was easier to forget the ritual, and not make the attempt.

Natalie was a very poised and adult nineteen. She was a dusky, very slender brunette, with a small piquant face, wide-spaced brown eyes, with a good sense of style and color, and a pert, trim way of handling herself. She was a child of divorce, and this was the first complete summer she had been permitted to spend with her father. In the fall she would return to the University of Michigan where she was taking an undergraduate degree in fine arts. Three mornings a week she was teaching a children's art class at the Palm County Art Center. She drove a little red Jaguar with a steely competence, sailed Claire's tender Thistle in hard winds, swam, sunned, sketched and helped with the house, the twins, the entertaining.

As Kat got ready for bed, she had a feeling of loneliness more acute than on the ordinary evenings of her life. For a long time she had wondered why it should always be worse after being out, and thought it was because of coming back to an empty house. Then she had gradually realized that it was worse because there was nobody to tell things to. She would come back full of things to tell, little observations of humor and drama, of things said and done, and there was no one to listen and care. On the ordinary nights nothing happened and so there was no fund of things to relate, and emptiness did not seem as critical. Whenever they had spent an evening apart, Van had enjoyed listening to her. She had liked making him laugh.

There should be a service for widows, she thought. Good listeners who could be acquired by appointment. One of them would be here for the ritual Sanka, eagerly listening, making little exclamations, laughing in the right places.

There has to be somebody to listen to you, because of you, not what you say. Without them, you walk around with the weight of all the untold things. When something happens you say to yourself, I must remember this, so I can tell it just the way it happened. When there is no one to listen, all these things clot in your mind.

When she was in bed she thought that she might talk to Jimmy Wing about the meeting. She turned her bed lamp on again, dialed all but the last digit of his number, and then hung up, clicked the light off and lay back in darkness. It was too late to phone him.

9

IN THE BRIGHT SUNLIGHT of the Saturday mid-morning Jimmy Wing saw himself sidelong in a downtown shop window, sandy and listless, slowed by the heat, squinting into the chrome dazzle of Center Street. It struck him that he should look so unremarkable, that the blackmail mission should have worked no change upon him.

"Blackmail" was the word he had awakened with, so apt and harsh it soothed him to use it, depriving him of pretense. Yet it had overtones of melodrama which gave it a twist of comedy. It needed wax on the tips of the mustache, and hidden cameras, tape recordings, pilfered letters, a lock box. Then they would set a trap for him, and the slug would smash him against the wall. He would fall, twitch and die, as the music came up and the good guy embraced the lovely girl.

But he had learned that most people who do questionable things are as unremarkable as the people who don't. Most people who are thrown into a cell for good reason are vastly astonished to find themselves there, because they look and feel like anyone else. It is all some kind of mistake.

Having faced the idea of digging up something Elmo could use against Dial Sinnat, he examined himself with care and concern, looking for some obvious alteration of the spirit. But he felt only a mild chagrin, a fussy anxiety about being successful at it—and not being caught at it, and a very subtle feeling of unreality, no more than a hangover or a slight fever would induce.

He had remembered old gossip, a fist fight, a damage suit which had been quietly dropped, and he had refreshed his memory in a microfilm booth at the paper. It seemed to make sense to go to a man's enemies first. Rule one for the amateur blackmailer.

He walked around the corner onto Veronica Street and into the old Central Commerce Building, and climbed one flight of stairs to the offices of the accounting firm of Malley and Rand. The door was unlocked. The secretarial desks were empty. Chet Rand was behind his desk, his office door open. He was a soft, florid, red-headed man. His scowl turned to a smile as he recognized Jimmy Wing.

"Officially we're closed, Jimmy," he said. "But not for big financial figures like you. What have they got you doing now? Selling advertising?"

Jimmy sat down and looked at him amiably. "If you're closed, why are you working? Too many accounts with two sets of books?"

"We recommend three these days. Four if it's a partnership. What I'm doing, pal, is trying to save the skin of a stupid son of a bitch who just happened to forget to declare a little windfall he got three years ago."

"What I want to talk about goes back a little further than that, Chet. I'm being the diligent reporter. Research. This is a confidential visit."

"I won't give you a crumb about any of our clients."

"I wouldn't ask. This is more personal. A story might break about an old buddy of yours. He might be getting into the same kind of trouble he got into once before."

"An old friend of mine?"

"Dial Sinnat."

Rand's mild worn urban face changed in a startling way. For a few moments he looked capable of a dangerous violence. In a soft voice a half octave lower than his normal tone he said, "Is this your idea of a funny joke, Wing?"

"I'm serious."

Chet Rand leaned back. "I get a lousy reaction to that name. But now I realize it isn't fair. I tried to kill him once, and I don't go anywhere where I might run into him. But I guess it wasn't his fault. I was in a lot better shape then than I am now. I'm nearly twenty years younger than he is. But he like to kill me before they broke it up."

"You dropped the suit, didn't you?"

"There was a lot of pressure on me from all directions. From Ruthie and Don Malley and from just about every member of the Board of Governors of the Yacht Club. So I dropped it." He gave Wing a strangely shy smile and looked away. "What I wasn't willing to admit then, even though I guess I knew it all the time, I had to admit later. Ruthie was a slut. After what happened with Sinnat, I watched her closer. I didn't lose my head the next time. I got the evidence on her and I used it to bulldoze her into a divorce. Somebody saw her in Phoenix over a year ago. I don't know where the hell she is now. I keep wondering about her."

"There was a dance that night, wasn't there?"

"Nothing special. Just one of the Friday night things they used to have. I don't know if they still have them. I resigned after it was all over. Sinnat had been at the hos-

pital most of the day. Claire had twins that evening. Di
came to the club from the hospital in a mood to buy
champagne. I guess he got there about nine-thirty. Ruthie
and I had a nice little load already, and the champagne
topped it off. I guess it was about midnight I realized I
hadn't seen Ruthie for a while. I'd been playing poker dice
at the bar. I went and looked in the car. She wasn't there. I
went out onto the docks looking for her. A wind had come
up. Any noise I was making couldn't be heard over the waves
slapping the pilings and the boats creaking. I went way out
on the end of the T and I wouldn't have seen them at all
if the moon hadn't come out from behind a cloud at the
right time. They'd pulled a bunk mattress out onto the cock-
pit deck of Johnny Shilling's old *Matthews*, and if they
hadn't been in such a big hurry and stopped to rig a side
curtain, they'd have been home free. It was a farce, I suppose. Like a dirty joke, where the husband always walks in.
But it isn't funny to the husband, Jimmy. It isn't funny at
all. They looked like farm animals, somehow. I went out of
my mind. I smashed a boat hook on him, they tell me, and
tried to skewer him with the splintered end. When he took
it away from me, I tried to strangle him, but by the time they
broke it up I had this new twist in my nose and I needed
two hundred bucks worth of dental work. He's a bull. We'd
been friends. I did some work for him. We'd been in their
house. They'd been in ours. Ruthie cried and lied and lied
and cried. I don't blame him now. I know she was a slut. I
don't blame him, but I still hate him."

"Did Claire ever find out about it?"

"How could she help not hearing about it, in this town?
But Claire is a tough girl, Jimmy. She's a realist. She
knows he's no angel. She has a good life. Why should she
mess it up because he did a little roaming when he was out
of circulation? Hell, I can talk about it now, but there was a
couple of years there when I couldn't. If I was alone and
began to think about it, I'd begin to cry. Isn't that the
damnedest thing? Not sad tears, but the way kids cry when
they get mad. What kind of trouble is he getting into now?"

"I can't talk about it, Chet. Wait and read about it in the
paper."

"What good does it do you to listen to all that old stuff?"

"Background information, Chet."

"I don't want it in the paper, by God!"

"It won't be, believe me. We don't run a scandal sheet."

"Is it woman trouble?"

"It could be in that area."

"I won't wish him any luck. But how can anybody bruise

the man? Name him as corespondent? There's nobody to
fire him, and she won't divorce him. I'm telling you, pal, I
spent at least a year trying to think of some way to mess
him up, but short of shooting him, I couldn't come up with
a thing. They don't give a damn for public opinion. He
spends five mornings a week in the brokerage outfit. He's
quick and shrewd and he does very well at it. He's healthy
as a pig. And I'm now willing to admit he probably wouldn't
mess with any woman who wasn't ready and willing. And
Claire certainly doesn't mess around."

"And I suppose that when you worked on something for
him, he wasn't trying anything cute?"

Chet Rand looked at Wing narrowly. "Boy, you're giving
me the idea you're fishing. The more I think about the story
you walked in here with, the fishier it sounds."

"What would I be fishing for? I'm just a newspaper type."

"His personal financial records are complete and accurate.
He's got fat holdings on tax exempts, a slew of blue chips,
and quite a lot of very very nice growth stuff. He
doesn't have to cut any tax corners. At least, that's the way
he was set four years ago. That closes that door. About the
only tender spots I can think of would be his kids."

Wing stared at him. "Four-year-old twins?"

"We keep the Art Center Books. There's a Natalie Sinnat
drawing twelve bucks a week teaching a class of kids. Nineteen and cute."

"I forgot about her. She's spending the summer down here."

"Maybe she isn't as tough-minded as Claire and Di."

"A man would have to be a thousand per cent bastard to
get at a man that way, Chet."

Rand shrugged. "It would depend on what he had to have,
and how far he'd have to go to get it. Bastardliness is relative, friend. Two months ago a partner in an old firm died.
The business is worth maybe three hundred thousand. The
surviving partner is buying out the widow for five thousand, because that's the figure given in the original partnership agreement drawn up in 1932, and never updated. The
partners and their wives have been close for thirty years.
Now the widow can't understand how good old Joe can do
this to her. But the law says he can, and he's doing it.
Don't talk to me about thousand per cent bastards."

"I wasn't fishing, Chet."

"Of course you weren't. This was a private talk, Jimmy.
Be at ease."

"Thanks for . . . talking about your own bruise, Chet."

"It doesn't bother me much any more, I just wonder where
she is, sometimes, and how she's making out. Listen. What-

ever you use on Sinnat, don't try a boat hook. It won't work."

On the short ride back to the newspaper in the bake-oven heat of his old station wagon, Jimmy Wing found his sense of unreality slightly enhanced. When a traffic light stopped him, he stared at his own hand resting on the steering wheel, a long hand, veined and freckled, fuzzed with pale fur, grasping the wheel with indifferent simian competence, as apart from him as though he looked over the shoulder of a stranger.

The hand is the animal reality, he thought, for blows and tools and caresses. Morality is an unreal conjecture, for younger men than I am. Morality is the conflict of rationalizations. I am trapped by myself, unable to do more or less than the old limitations permit.

He had a specific visualization of rationalizations, seeing a little apart from the commonplace furniture of his mind, a cave pink and membranous, where the things too easy to believe were like flat leech-creatures which inched up from the dark floor to affix themselves to the soft walls. If they were peeled away quickly they did no harm. But the longer they remained the more difficult they were to dislodge. Eventually they made themselves so much a part of the walls there was no way to find them, or even to know they were there. And so truth, forever out of focus in any case, was prey to these further distortions assembled over the years. They made a comfortable muffling, a padded toughened wall, as opposed to a Calvinist rawness.

The girl lives in the unreal context of wealth, youth and beauty. It would be a favor to her to show her the world has edges and thorns.

Besides, the time to make any decision is after you find out what, if anything, is usable.

And if you don't do it, somebody else will.

He phoned Kat from the place where he had lunch. She said she was just leaving for Jackie Halley's house. She said she wanted to talk to him, but she'd be at the Halleys' all afternoon. She said she had a lot to tell him and ask him. Could he stop by the Halleys' about six o'clock? He told her that if he couldn't make it, he'd phone her there and set up something else.

After he had turned in his Sunday edition copy, he drove to the Palm County Art Center building. It was on city-owned land at the foot of Center Street, fronting on the bay. The big tract also contained the Community Auditorium, the Teen House, the public library and the new headquarters for the city police. In the early thirties when the tract had been available for back taxes, the Cable family had purchased it and turned it over to the city for civic uses.

The Art Center was an incongruous piece of architecture for even that tropic coast, red brick Georgian with white pillars and fake shutters, more suitable to a shopping center in Williamsburg. He parked in the wide and empty asphalted area which served all the buildings in the tract. A sign on the front door of the Center announced that it was closed. The door was unlocked.

He walked through the arched entrance to the main gallery where Morton Dermond was supervising the efforts of a half dozen young people who were uncrating and hanging a show.

"Doris, darling," Dermond yelled, "the reds in that one will absolutely *slay* that wonderful Ricardi. You'll have to get it *much* further away. Try the west wall, dear."

He came smiling over to Jimmy Wing. "This show is so colorful, we're having a hideous time hanging it. How are you, Jimmy? I'm really terribly excited about this show. It's a shame we couldn't have gotten it during the season, but it's really much too good for us at any time of year. It's a traveling show. California artists. I was able to get it only because they had a little gap in their scheduling. It's on its way from the Delgado to the Four Arts. Please don't tell me *you* are going to review it! But you might do better than poor Dottie Grumbann at that. The dear thing comes to an absolute cultural stop over anything more complex than a Picasso."

"Is this a bad time to talk to you, Mortie? I'm just feeling out a possible feature story on these summer classes for kids."

"I can talk, if we stand here where I can see what's happening. Charles! I want to save that center wall for the Deibenkorn, please. Why don't you get it and hang it next, dear boy?"

"I had the idea of doing it as a sort of double interview, Mortie. One with a teacher, and one with one of the kids."

"But you'll have to clear the final draft with me, Jimmy. I have a *very* cowardly board of directors, you know. Let me see. I have just two teachers this summer. Peter Trent is sweet, but he's practically inarticulate. I think Nat Sinnat would be really ideal. And she'd look better in a photograph than Peter would, with that grimy beard."

"Then I have your permission to set it up with her?"

"Natalie! Come here a moment, dear!"

A girl at the far end of the gallery turned and came walking toward them, brushing her dark hair back with the back of her hand. She wore salmon-colored shorts and a white shirt with the sleeves rolled up. Her sun-dark legs were almost but not quite too thin. She walked well, with grace and assurance. As she came close Jimmy saw that she looked flushed and hot. Her hands and shirt and chin were smudged.

"Natalie, dear, this is an old friend of mine, Jimmy Wing, from the newspaper. We can spare you for a little while here, so why don't you take Jimmy into my office. He wants to interview you for a newspaper story about the children."

"How do you do?" Natalie said. "I've heard Mrs. Hubble speak of you, Mr. Wing."

"I don't want to take you away from your work, Natalie."

"She's earned a break, Jimmy. She's done as much as any two of the others."

The girl picked her purse up from a bench by the arch and, as they walked out into the lobby she said, "If you'll excuse me, I'd like to wash up. I don't know how the paintings get so filthy. If you'll wait for me in Mortie's office, I won't be long."

Morton Dermond's small office was a sweltering jungle of books, easels, paintings, sculpture, mobiles, magazines, posters, sandals and strange hats. He turned on the window air conditioner, cleared the junk from two contour chairs and positioned them near the only clear corner of Dermond's desk.

The girl came in, closing the door behind her, and went to stand in front of the cold wind of the air conditioner. "This is my first summer down here," she said. "It's really wicked, isn't it?"

"Once we start getting some rain every day it won't be so bad."

"That's what my father keeps telling me."

She came over and sat near him. He asked questions and made the few notes which would cue his memory. He made it clear to her that Dermond had suggested her as the person he should interview. She was quick, intelligent and more poised than he had expected. When he asked about the caliber of the children she was teaching, she said, "They are all recommended by the art teachers in the public schools. I probably shouldn't say this, but the ones who've had the least instruction are the most rewarding ones. What they get in the public schools seems to sort of tighten them up. They're afraid of their materials. Peter and I seem to spend most of our time getting them to open up, to be bold with their colors and forms."

"Are you planning to become an art teacher, Natalie?"

She frowned. "I don't know, really. I've had just one year of fine arts. I'll be a sophomore when I go back. I like this better than I thought I would. I want to be a painter. I know I have a knack, but maybe I haven't much talent, really. I guess you better put down 'undecided.' "

As he had talked to her he had become aware of a curious duality about her. Though her expression was placid, he thought he could detect the marks of tension in her young face. And her poise was a little too nearly perfect. She began to seem more guarded than poised. He guessed there could be a great amount of neurotic tension beneath the surface, the understandable product of sensitivity and a broken home. After he had told her he would make arrangements for photographs, and had gotten from her the name of a child who would be a good one to talk to, he put his notes away and said, "Aside from the climate, Natalie, are you having a good summer?"

"A very nice summer, thank you."

"Kat Hubble seems very fond of you."

"She's sweet."

"Her husband was one of my best friends."

"My father told me what happened to him. It seems so terrible and so pointless."

"Your people have been wonderful to Kat."

"They like her a lot. And her children are wonderful kids."

"Do you think you'll be coming down every summer while you're in school?"

"I don't really know. I needed . . . a complete change of scene this summer. I asked if I could come down."

"I guess it was up to Claire."

"What has this got to do with the interview, Mr. Wing?"

"Absolutely nothing," he said, smiling at her.

"Claire is one of the warmest, most generous people I've ever met."

"Well, I hope you'll come back every summer, Natalie. You improve the local summer scenery."

"Thank you," she said, startled and blushing slightly.

"Have our local young men gathered around with understandable enthusiasm?"

"I haven't been dating," she said, and stood up. "I better get back to work before they finish all of it."

After she was back at work he talked to Morton Dermond

again. The young people had almost finished hanging the show.

"Get what you need?" Dermond asked.

"Yes indeed. It should make a good story, Mortie."

"Nat is articulate and she's a darling and I love the way her mind works. She's superb with the wretched little children. I can't endure them myself."

"I got the idea there's more to her than meets the eye."

"Oh, you are *so* right! She arrived down here shattered, just getting over an absolutely sickening affair with some pig of a graduate student up there in Michigan, and her mother was no help to her at all. Recriminations and so on. That's why she came down. She told me about it in confidence. Broke down completely when I was criticizing her drawings, and it all came out. She seems to be coming out of it now, bless her. But she's terribly vulnerable. That pig destroyed her confidence. I think she yearns for someone to appreciate her. Too bad you're a little too old for her, Jimmy. Right now, to kill time, and maybe to help get herself back together, she seems to be running a little lovelorn anonymous club, being sweet and motherly to some dreary high-school boy, who seems to worship her. I saw him once in her car. I have no idea who he is. He's rather a beautiful boy, but he has a sort of bovine look. You know the type. Natalie is a very complex little person, and very troubled, but I can't tell you much about her because she spoke to me in confidence. You know how it is."

"I know. Like a sacred trust."

"Exactly, Jimmy. Did she tell you what child to talk to? Good. Do give us a nice big spread on this if you can, old man."

"Will try. Are you saving the bays again, Mortie?"

"What? Oh, that dreary meeting yesterday, of course. It was all sort of spiritless. You know? Actually, I'm beginning to wonder if it's worth it. People down here seem to despise natural beauty. It seems to make them terribly uneasy. They don't really feel secure until they can see asphalt in every direction, and they don't trust a tree unless they've grown it themselves. Oh, we'll fight the brave battle, mother, but I haven't as much zing for it this time, and I don't think the others do either. Except Tom Jennings. He's incredibly warlike, you know. And little Kat Hubble is very dedicated. Will you be helping us this time?"

"It won't be as easy, not with the owner in favor of the fill."

"All done?" he called to the young people. "Splendid! It's an absolutely glorious show, isn't it? And beautifully hung.

Thank you all so much! And I want you all at the reception
tomorrow, please. Four o'clock. You come too, Jimmy,
please."

"If I can make it, Mortie."

"Do try. When will the photographer come?"

"Next week some time, Mortie, during her class." He
started away and turned and said, "How were her drawings,
anyway?"

"Eh? Oh, they were competent. But very constricted. Tight
little exercises, as if her darling little knuckles were bone
white when she did them, and she bit her lip until it bled.
Absolutely virginal, actually." Mortie giggled. "But, gracious,
that certainly isn't accurate!"

Until Jimmy Wing had driven a few blocks, the steering
wheel of his car was so hot he had to keep shifting the
position of his hands. It was too late for a chess game
with Haas. He drove out to Cable Key, showered and changed
and had time for a beer before driving to the Halleys to see
Kat.

10

EXCEPT FOR THE FOUNDATION PILINGS and the post and beam frame, trued and bolted, Ross and Jackie Halley had built their house themselves. It was an oblong eighty feet long and thirty feet wide, set on slender pilings which raised it four or five feet above raked shell. It was on a small bayfront lot, and was nested so closely against a fringe of water oak and mangrove that the highest tides came up under the structure. It had a big roofed redwood deck on the water side, looking out toward Grassy Bay, and an unroofed deck on the other side, facing the parking area. The central part of the structure was one big living area, with a kitchen island in the middle completely encircled by a bar. The bedroom and bath were to the left, and Ross's studio was to the right.

From the parking area the whole side of the building was alternating rectangles of fixed glass, glass jalousies, and panels painted chalk blue, yellow-white and coral.

As soon as Kat had stopped the car, Roy and Alicia piled out, yelping and running toward Jackie's fond loud greeting. She was good with children, and Kat knew how desperately disappointed they were to be unable to have any.

"Go climb into the stuff Ross laid out on my bed, Kat, then yell for the mahster. I'm putting your brats to work. We're going oystering. The one that gets the biggest one gets to wear the straw sombrero."

Kat went into the bedroom and changed into the fussy yellow blouse and wide vivid skirt. When she called Ross, he came out of the studio with camera and sketch pad. "Hi, Lady Kat. Mmmm. Just about right."

"This shade of yellow makes me look like death."

"I don't want it for the color, m'am."

"Hair?"

"As is, I think. No, you better sleek it back a little. Give me more ears."

"I've got horrible ears."

"I've got a whole file drawer full of ears."

Smiling, she went and fixed her hair. Ross took her out into the side yard and had her sit in a garden chair under the shade of a punk tree. He squatted on the corner of

125

the deck above her and had her move the chair a few times until the angle was right and the play of light and shadow was what he wanted. He was a square quick man with a metallic voice, a tall black brush cut which looked dense and harsh as a nylon brush, a solid bar of black eyebrow, little black shoe-button eyes.

"Little more toward me. Chin up. You're looking up at a guy you didn't expect to see, but you're glad to see him. And you're going to get out of the chair. Lean just a little forward. Okay. Now start to reach out a little with the right hand. Okay. Chin higher. Okay. Not so much smile. Okay. Pull your feet back a little. Okay."

The camera ticked. Ross perspired in the sun. He changed angles slightly. He took two rolls of film, then made a few quick free sketches of details. After they went back into the house, he paid her in cash and she signed a receipt form. Jackie came back with the children, and a bucket of oysters. After Kat had changed back into her sun dress, she found that Ross had gone back out onto the oyster bar with the children.

"Can he take the time off to mind those two?" Kat asked.

"Heck, he's way ahead of the art directors for a change. Let's get going on our gals. I got the file out last night. Take turns? Here's your stack. I'll go first."

By five o'clock on that Saturday afternoon, Kat Hubble and Jackie Halley were depressed and concerned. They sat on stools at the kitchen bar, the phone between them, their file cards and notes in front of them. Roy and Alicia were out at the end of the Halley's narrow dock, catching bait fish on tiny hooks and putting them in the bait well of Ross's old skiff at the customary rate of two cents a fish.

Ross came out of his studio into the living room and said, "I developed the roll of black and white, Kat. It's fine. Hey, are you two about to break into tears or something?"

"Shuck the oysters, dear," Jackie said in a weary voice.

"Shuck the oysters, *please*, dear," he corrected. "Where's the oyster knife?"

"Please, then. Where it always is."

"Hey, Ross, we got eleven!" Roy yelled.

"Good work, men! What's with you sad ladies anyhow?"

"We're not scoring so well," Jackie said.

"Some of our best gals won't do it this time," Kat said.

"Word seems to have gotten around," Jackie explained.

"They don't even want to be members any more."

"Twelve!" Alicia yelled.

"Just one card left?" Jackie said. "Go ahead, dear. Who is it?"

"Donna Armstrong."

"Hmmm. Whose husband happens to be a car dealer," Jackie said. She laughed bitterly. "Make three guesses. Go ahead."

Kat dialed. "Donna? This is Kat Hubble. The S.O.B.'s are declaring a state of emergency, and we're calling you back onto active duty. What? Yes, it's Grassy Bay again. How did you know? Oh, I see. Well, you will help us . . . ? I'd like to know, of course."

Kat put her hand over the mouthpiece and looked hopelessly at Jackie and said, "She doesn't want it filled, but . . ." She listened for a few more moments and then said, "We'll miss you, Donna. You were so wonderful last time. But if Si really says you shouldn't, I guess there isn't much you can do. But please do ask him again, will you? And let us know if you can. Thank you, dear. I'm sorry too. 'By."

Kat hung up. "It seems a Mr. Flake buys his cars and trucks from Mr. Armstrong's agency. And it even seems that Si Armstrong has a teeny tiny piece of Palmland Development. And just last week Si let her in on the secret and laid down the law."

"Well, that's it. Let me check this thing. We called forty-two women. I'll mark Donna for a flat no. At least she's more honest than the ones who got so terribly vague about the whole thing. Thirteen acceptances. *There* is a nice lucky number. Fifteen refusals. Excuse me. Eleven refusals. Plus Donna is twelve. Nine couldn't be reached. Six gave us that let-you-know-later jazz. So out of the group who worked like dogs last time, its twenty-one to thirteen against. So we should pick up maybe three more out of that nine—sixteen when we'll need forty. And we've lost some of the very best ones, dammit!"

"I keep thinking about Hilda."

"I'd rather not think about her."

"Just how did she word it?"

"Oh, she just gave a merry little ho ho and said, 'But, Jackie, lamb, I've promised to organize a telephone campaign in favor of this project. This will be a delicious program, and it won't hurt Grassy Bay a bit, and my Danny says only the forces of reaction will be against it.' And so on and so on. Ugh! Her Danny was dragging his feet the last time. Remember? Eight hundred potential customers for dear Danny's appliance business. Do I sound like a snob? I'm not. Selling appliances is a good wholesome way to make a living in America. But damn if I like them filling the bay so they'll have a place to put them. Hilda was our best man, Kat."

"So we'll find other women just as good."

"You have considerable jaw on you when you shove it out that way, honey."

"And we'll make the sixteen work twice as hard as last time, and you and I will work four times as hard. And, as Tom says, if the commissioners vote the wrong way after the public hearing, we'll take the fight to Tallahassee."

"Stop glaring at me, for goodness' sake! I'm with you. Don't you think we've earned a drink?"

"I guess so. Weak for me, please."

"It'll have to be something with rum. Okay?"

"Fine."

As Jackie fixed the drinks, Kat walked out on the deck. The kids were quarreling over their fish count. Ross was finishing the oysters down on the dock. As she watched, he scraped the last one into the pan and waded out with the two buckets of shells and dumped them back onto the oyster bar.

"Jackie, would it cover that oyster bar?"

"Probably not that one, but it would cover the big ones out there, and it would block the tide flow to this one so that it would probably die. Here's your drink."

The first tall tree shadows were reaching out toward the dock, the intent children, the old skiff. The thunderheads were over the mainland, far inland, piled seven miles high, suddenly as monstrous in her mind as the tree shadows. "Seventeen!" Alicia called, her voice unbearably clear and sweet in the first silence of the coming evening. "That makes seventeen! Take him off my hook, Roy."

Kat felt a coldness along her back, like a leathery touch, reptilian. "Everything changes," she said. "Everything dies."

"Hey now," Jackie said gently.

"I'm sorry. Everything seems . . . like some kind of a dirty trick on people."

Jackie gave her a quick, rough, shy hug, a one-armed gesture which spilled some of Kat's cool drink on the back of her hand. "In the deathless words of my husband, dear, you can't win 'em all. He has a crapshooter's approach to eternity. He says he's small time at a big table. He drags back when he wins, and he covers so many numbers they can't ever hurt him too badly."

Kat turned and stared at her. "What does that make me?"

"The same as me, dear. We're hunch bettors. We win big and we lose big." She cocked her head. "Now who the hell is that dropping in?"

"Oh, I forgot. It's Jimmy Wing. I should have told you."

"Jimmy is welcome here any time, honey. You know that."

As they walked toward the front door, Kat said, "I wonder how Jimmy fits into that dice game idea."

"I think he just watches the game. I don't think he makes any bets," Jackie said.

"And Martin Cable owns the table?"

"We'll have to play that game with everybody we know."

Jimmy came smiling up onto the deck. Ross brought the oysters up to the house. Jackie fixed four oyster cocktails. They all sat on the rear deck with drinks and generous servings of the oysters, their chairs placed so they looked past the twisted trunks of the water oaks toward the quiet bay, the competitive children. Jackie and Kat reported the meeting, and told Jimmy of their bad luck with the women they had phoned. Ross took no part in it.

Jimmy said, "They're handling it well. It's the same doctrine we were up against last time. Growth, progress. Last time it was outsiders coming in, bearing gifts. This time it's our own people, and it's more persuasive. No absentee ownership. All the profits stay in town. Broader tax base. Nice new residents and so forth. I heard one of their battle cries today. Eight hundred families means sixteen million in new investment plus four million a year into the local economy. So they've been quietly lining up the local business people, getting them all set to be boosters."

"But that misses the point of the whole thing!" Kat said. "That bay bottom out there is public land. It belongs to *all* the people, all the people who don't have a prayer of ever owning a home there, or making any profit off it. It belongs to all the people now living in the state and all the future generations, and this takes it away from them forever, and turns it into eight hundred pieces of private land. It's like stealing it from the public."

"I know that," Jimmy said. "You know it and Jackie knows it and Ross knows it. The trustees are supposed to consider the health and welfare of the people of the State of Florida. But it's going to be used for the health and welfare of the bank accounts of the businessmen of Palm County, and done with so many reasonable arguments it'll be years before the public realizes what a polite screwing it took, here and all up and down this coast. Maybe what I'm saying is this, people. Nobody is going to listen to sweet reason. It's going to be a very emotional squabble. The fighting is going to get dirtier than you can imagine. So I'd say get out of it right now. Just as I told you the day before yesterday, Kat. It

isn't the same thing it was last time. It won't be a gallant battle and an honorable victory. So resign now."

"No," Kat said in a small firm voice.

"He's right," Ross said. "If you are lucky, they'll ignore
you. If you get too energetic, they'll clobber you. It makes me
damn uneasy."

"You're *always* uneasy, dear," Jackie said. "You've got the
idea the world is full of monsters."

"But it is," he said. He smiled at Jimmy Wing. "You see
what we've got here? A pair of innocents. Their strength is as
the strength of ten because their hearts are pure. Oh boy! I
mind my own store. Back when I was sure I was going to
be Van Gogh, I was full of social messages. I did a little
marching and a little poster work and a little singing and
carrying banners. I think I was coming out strong in favor
of human decency. Three Chicago cops took me into an alley.
They were real jocular. I told them fiercely I was an artist.
I was ready to die for mankind, but I wasn't ready for what
they did to me. They held my hands against a brick wall and
used a night stick on them. I couldn't hold a brush or a
pencil for eight months. Back in Dayton it cost my father
twelve hundred bucks worth of corrective operations. And I
can't even remember why I was marching that day. I mind
my own store. Messages are for Western Union. They always find a way to hurt you, some way you're not expecting."

"How do you stand on decency now, killer?" Jackie asked
in a deadly voice.

He looked at her for a long moment, then stood up. "By
now you shouldn't have to ask the question. Excuse me.
Couple of little things to do." He went to his studio and
closed the door.

"Me and my mouth," Jackie said. "I'm sorry."

"I'd always wondered about his hands," Kat said.

"This is awkward as hell," Jackie said. "I'm sorry. I'm no
good at the game of pretending nothing happened. So I'm
going to have to shoo you away and then go in there and
tell him he's a good man and I love him as he is, seeking
no alterations in the merchandise."

"I was going to have to leave in minutes anyhow, Jackie."

"And we've got to pay those commercial fishermen out
there," Jackie said.

The kids had caught twenty-six bait fish, eleven by Alicia
and fifteen by Roy. Jackie paid them the agreed rate to the
penny, wise enough to know that any careless generosity at
that time would have spoiled the game for them. As they
walked out to the cars, Jackie and the children lagging be-

hind, Kat said, "Can you come to my place, Jimmy? I didn't get a chance to tell you about last night."

He nodded. Just then Ross came out. "I didn't know you people were going to run off so soon."

"I tried to keep them around," Jackie said.

As Kat turned around to drive out she saw Ross move close to Jackie and, with a slight defiant awkwardness, put his arm around her slender waist and hold her close.

When she arrived home, Kat had a slight problem convincing Roy and Alicia it was too late to go up to the Sinnats for a swim. She took their minds off it by reminding them of tomorrow's picnic, and they went off to play in Roy's room. She made herself a rum drink and opened a beer for Jimmy. They sat in the coolness of the living room, the draperies closed against the glare of the western sun.

"That's the first time I ever saw any flaw in that united front," Kat said.

"I admire the guy for the way he came out to say goodbye. She hit him a dandy. It's easier to sulk."

"You think it's dramatic, and later you realize you were only being silly. It's pride, I guess. The wrong kind. Last night was strange, Jimmy. I didn't open my mouth. I just listened."

She told him the conversation Martin, Eloise, Dial and Claire had, and then spoke of how Dial had reacted to it afterward. "He seems to think there's somebody else behind it, Jimmy, somebody smarter than those five men we know about."

"Where would he get that idea?"

"I don't know. He's a strange man. He's big and hearty and sort of obvious, but there's something . . . almost feline about him too. Intuition or something. And you're never quite sure whether he's laughing at you. And he's also got the idea that somebody has been coaching Eloise, teaching her how to work on Martin, or Martin would never have gotten into this thing as deeply as he has."

"They need Martin," Jimmy admitted. "They need the access, and they'll need the line of credit to develop the land once they get it."

"If they get it. But they won't."

"That's going to be a matter of considerable opinion around this town for a while, Katherine."

"Why did you call me Katherine then?"

"I don't know."

"It's probably because you heard Van do it. Whenever he said anything to me like that, sort of dry and skeptical, when he thought I was getting a little too carried away, he'd call me Katherine."

"That's probably it. I'm sorry."

"I don't mind it, Jimmy. It just seemed odd."

She looked at him and looked away. The light was strange in the room. The draperies were blue, yet the light had a green tinge. His face was in shadow.

"I talked to Nat Sinnat today," he said, and she was relieved that he had interrupted the odd and awkward silence.

"Oh, did you? What about?"

"A story on the children's art classes she teaches. Mortie said she was the one to talk to, and he was right. She was articulate and she has good ideas. But she seemed a little ... odd."

"Odd?"

"That's not a good word, I guess. A little tense maybe. Not the tension of being interviewed. A more chronic kind."

"I guess there's reasons. Her mother was Di's second wife. And it wasn't a friendly divorce. I think Nat was about five at the time. Her mother is a real pinwheeling neurotic, according to Di. She didn't marry again. She's done a lot of traveling. She and Nat lived in France for a while. Her mother was bitterly opposed to Nat's coming down here this summer. There was a big stink about it. All in all, I think Nat is wonderfully well balanced, considering her background. But she isn't what you'd call exactly a normal girl of nineteen. She's independent, in more ways than financial. She's what I guess you'd call unconventional. She doesn't give a damn what anybody thinks, really. She goes her own way. But I guess she took some kind of emotional beating last year. Claire has hinted about it. That's why she came down here."

"She's a pretty kid."

"Unusual looking."

"Apparently she's dating some boy younger than she is, a high-school kid."

"Dating? Oh, no! That's Jigger. You know. Burt Lesser's boy. I guess he's got a crush on her. She says Jigger is a very unhappy boy. I would have guessed that. Anyhow, that would make two of them, misery loving company or something like that. Why do you ask?"

"I was just curious about her. Just making conversation, I guess."

"If you can stay, I think I can feed you."

"Thanks, Kat. But I've got some more work to do. The load is a little heavier the last couple of days. Brian Haas got taken drunk."

"Oh, no! Really? But wasn't it almost certain that Mr. Borklund would fire him the next time he . . ."

"We're trying to cover it, and maybe we have. If he got it out of his system it may come out all right."

"Nan must be terribly upset."

"She's handling it pretty well. I'm going to stop in later on and see how things are going. We have to get him back to work by noon tomorrow. It will be up to him to hide the shakes."

Again there was the heavy silence. She felt she should make some listless effort to break it. Perhaps it will rain? It's been a very warm day? She felt trapped within an almost unbearable slowness of the passing moments. Tomorrow—anniversary of death—would be the worst time, and then it would be over and the second year of it could start. A year from tomorrow would not be so bad a day.

He leaned forward, bringing his face into the unusual light. His forearms rested on his knees, his strong hands clasped. He looked at the floor, then raised his head slightly to look at her, his face almost without expression.

"Kat?" His voice was low and hoarse.

"What is it? What's the matter?"

He smiled and stood up, with that lithe and utterly relaxed elegance of movement. "Matter? Nothing's the matter. I have to go."

She walked to the door with him. "I thought you were going to tell me some terrible thing. Isn't that a crazy impression to have? Bad tidings. Now I'm chattering. Damn it, I hate chattering women."

He paused at the door and said, "Kat . . . if tomorrow turns out to be rough, call me, will you?"

"Aren't you going to be out of town?"

"I canceled."

"Not because of me, Jimmy."

"For several reasons. I should be handy to see how Brian makes it. Where are you going for your picnic?"

"Up to Sanibel so we can look for shells."

"The bugs will be fierce this time of year."

"We'll be plastered with goo."

She went to the window and watched him back out and waved to him as he drove away. She walked thoughtfully to the kitchen and began to prepare dinner. She was aware of a little area of strangeness in her mind, elusive and unidentifiable. It was like trying to remember a name momentarily forgotten. There had been a strangeness at the Halleys, when the four of them had been on the back deck. She and Van had spent many hours there with Ross and Jackie. Today, for the first time, there had been four of them again, but the fourth person had been Jimmy instead of Van. She realized, with a merciless honesty, that the situation had made her resent Jimmy for being Jimmy rather than Van. There had been at least one time when there had been six of them on that deck on a night of cool moonlight, drinking wine and talking wonderful nonsense. Jimmy would have just as much right to resent her because she was not Gloria. There was one awkwardness on that clear evening long ago. Gloria had been recently released, and it was her first social evening since her release. It had made the conversation more guarded and selective than it might otherwise have been.

Now, of course, she was as remote, as unreachable as Van. Her's was a subtler form of death, but no less final. Which was easier, she wondered, the slow regression to that point where there was, at last, no communication at all, or the sudden brutal stunning departure? And she wondered if Jimmy had made this same comparison, and envied her.

11

As JIMMY WING crossed the causeway to the mainland there was a strange lemon light across the land. The rays of the setting sun were almost horizontal. Every surface facing the west was touched with this luminous glow in contrast with the blue shadows of dusk which lay against everything else. From time to time a fitful rain wind turned the leaves and died away.

On the car radio the seven-thirty newscaster said, ". . . three tenths of an inch recorded for Palm County, far below the normal rainfall for this time of year. The current temperature at County Airport is ninety degrees, relative humidity ninety-five per cent, winds out of the southeast at three to five miles per hour. . . ."

He turned the radio off so as to focus himself with no distraction upon a special textural memory of Kat. When he had turned back at her doorway, she was a step closer to him than he had expected, standing tall and near in the aquarium light of the living room, so close for an instant that the detected fragrance of her hair mingled with the imagined feel of it, sweet and harsh against his lips, and he had come all too close to reaching for her. Another collector's item, he thought. Another image to file away.

He worked hard at his newsroom desk for an hour, and then walked down a dark block on Bayou Street to Vera's Kitchen. He was starting to eat his sandwich when Bobby Nest came in and sat on a counter stool beside him. Bobby at eighteen, concealed a fervent love for the newspaper business behind a pose of cynicism acquired from scores of movies and television shows. He had been the paper's official correspondent at Riverway High School during the past year, and this summer Borklund, for very small money, had him doing routine sports, the city and county recreation program events, summer bowling and golf leagues, shuffleboard, tennis, pram races. In the fall Bobby would go away to school and Borklund would find another serf, equally eager. Bobby was a small wiry boy with big glasses and a surprisingly authoritative baritone voice. He wrote pounds of copy which was never printed.

"This girl's old man is going to drive me nuts," Bobby said.

"Teach you to mess with girls."

"Who would mess with this one? She's fourteen and she looks like a twenty-year-old Marine sergeant. I think she shaves, even. But she can belt a golf ball two hundred and forty yards. It's her damn name, Jimmy. The Caroline is easy, but the last name is Smidt. S—m—i—d—t. I know how it's spelled, for God's sake. I print it in block letters. I put a note in the margin. But every time she wins something—not every time, but at least every other time—somebody decides it should be Smith or Schmidt or Smidth or some other goddam thing and then her old man calls up and chews out Jesus-Jesus and he chews me. There's gremlins in that shop, Jimmy, honest to God."

"Marry her and make her turn pro, Bobby. Nest is an easy name. And those gals make nice money."

"Nest is the name but I'm not about to build one. I wish she'd pick up a bad slice or something, so I wouldn't have to put her kook name in the paper." He sighed. "She doesn't seem to give a damn. It's her old man. He taught her the game. And he can sure talk nasty. Just coffee and Danish, Mike, thanks."

Jimmy Wing edited his next comment before he made it, then said, "Funny how unattractive most of those little girl athletes are. But some of them are worth staring at. Like that little water-skier, Burt Lesser's daughter."

"Frosty. Oh, sure. I think her real name is Frances Ann."

"There's the one for you, Bobby."

"Not for me. She runs with a pack of rich kids. She's only fifteen, I guess, but if you want her to look twice at you, you got to own a boat that will pull her all over the bay at forty miles an hour, and you've got to be seven feet tall and able to pick up the front end of a Buick."

"Sounds like a description of her brother."

"Jigger? I guess he could pick up the front end of a car. But he doesn't run with the pack. He's a year behind me at Riverway. He's sort of a fink."

"What does that mean?"

"He's a loner. And he's got a sarcastic way of speaking. He could make any team we've got, but he doesn't go out for anything any more. He gets good grades. But he doesn't mingle. You're walking and he's driving an empty car, he won't even slow down. He isn't the most popular kid around."

"How does he make out with the girls?"

"That's another thing. He doesn't try. He'd have no trouble, but he doesn't try. There's some talk."

"What kind?"

Bobby Nest looked uneasy. "I shouldn't say anything because I don't really know for sure. But you remember two years ago, the trouble at West Bay Junior High, the gay English teacher they had, and after one kid squealed, they found out there was a whole group of boys going over to the instructor's place, you remember, Jimmy."

"I remember. Was Jigger one of them?"

"He was there at the time. They tried to keep it quiet, the kids who got mixed up in that mess, their names. But that's what they say about Jigger, that he was one of the group, and he's a queer. This last spring two pretty husky guys tried to needle Jigger about it. They thought they could handle him, but they couldn't. He cracked them up pretty good."

"I guess the rumor must be wrong, Jimmy. This summer I've seen Jigger riding around with a pretty little dark-haired girl."

"In the red Jag? I've seen him too. But I don't know who she is. She looked pretty nice." Bobby snickered. "I saw him twice with her, and the second time I saw him, he didn't want me to. He slid way down in the seat, but he wasn't quick enough."

"Where was that?"

"You know that brand new motel, set way back, where Bay Highway comes out onto the Tamiami Trail below Everset? The Drowsy Lady Motor House, very fancy?"

"Yes."

"About a week and a half ago, when Jesse Gardner came down and gave the exhibition at Cabeza Knolls, he stayed there. He gave me a good interview, remember? Anyhow, he had to catch a real early flight so I agreed to go down there at dawn and pick him up and take him to the airport. I got there about twenty after five. He was in a unit in the building furthest back. You have to drive around behind it. Just as I went down the driveway to that building, the red Jag was coming out. It was just getting light. The girl was driving. Jigger didn't duck quick enough. I guess he hasn't got anything against girls."

Wing was tempted to ask more questions, but instead he finished his coffee and said, "We won't worry about him, then. We'll worry about you, Bobby, and how you're going to get friendly with Miss Frosty."

"No thanks. If I had the time and the money to have a steady girl, I wouldn't want one who could snap my spine in her bare hands. And I wouldn't want any sexpot pushover anyways."

"At fifteen?"

"Since thirteen, Jimmy. It's no secret. And she isn't the only one in West Bay Junior High. There's a whole crowd of them in that school, and, I don't know, they make me nervous. The way they look at you, you know they just don't give a damn. They don't even go steady. They just go around in a rat pack and do any damn thing. They know how to keep from getting in trouble, but it just doesn't seem right. I know I'm only eighteen, but those kids make me feel as middle-aged as you are."

"Thanks so much."

"Aw, you know how I mean it, Jimmy. Say! Why couldn't we do a story on it together? I could get the facts."

"Much as I hate to deprive you of the chance to do creative research, Bobby, we don't work for a crusading paper. Too many of our advertisers have probably fathered those little sluts. Borklund would drop in a dead faint if I suggested it."

"I guess he would. When I get out of college, I'm going to work for a paper with some guts. Why do you hang around this crummy town, Jimmy? You're good enough to get on a better paper."

"Thanks again."

"I mean it. Why do you stay here?"

"I left once, and it didn't work out."

"Oh."

"And I always get lost driving around a strange city. I haven't got much sense of direction."

"Don't talk down to me, Jimmy."

Wing stood up and put his hand on the boy's shoulder. "Okay. I won't. I'll tell you one of the great truths I've learned. Every place in the world is exactly like every other place."

Bobby, looking up at him, shook his head slowly. "I can't believe that. I wouldn't want to let myself try to believe that. If that's true . . . there wouldn't be much point in anything."

"It's just something you don't want to find out too soon," Jimmy Wing said, and walked out and back to the news room. He checked the files for the previous week and found that Gardner had given his exhibition of golf on a Wednesday afternoon at Cabeza Knolls.

It took him a half hour to drive to the Drowsy Lady. He arrived a little before ten-thirty. On the way out he had time to plan his approach.

Floodlights blazed against the lobby entrance to the Drowsy Lady. As Wing turned in he remembered, fondly, Van Hubble's explosive reaction to motel architecture. Van had been a mild man, until something offended his sense of taste and decency.

"They cantilever a great big goddam hunk of roof at a quote daring unquote angle and hang big vulgar sheets of glass off it and light it up like an appendectomy. You can't tell a bowling alley from a superburger drive-in from a motel from a goddam bank, Jimmy. They all turn people into bugs crawling across aseptic plastic. It's all tail-fin modern, boy. It's cheap, jazzy and sterile. It isn't architecture. There's nothing indigenous about it. It's all over the country, all the same, like a red itch, like junk toys dumped out of a sack. And it's so stinking patronizing."

A huge sign displayed a single heavy-lidded feminine eye, the trade mark of the establishment, repeated on highway signs thirty miles in every direction.

He parked and went into the tall lobby. The restaurant had closed at ten. A desk clerk placed a registration card in front of him with a hospitable flourish.

"Is the manager around?"

"What would you like to see him about? Maybe I can help you."

"I'm not selling anything, if that's what's worrying you. Is he around?"

"He's in the cocktail lounge, watching the fights. I could get him now, if it's that important. . . ."

"I'll go watch the fights too. What's his name?"

"Mr. Frank Durley. He's a heavy-set man, bald."

The cocktail lounge was very dark. Some lens spots shone directly down onto the bar, and there was a light behind the bottle racks. So much crowd noise came over the television set Wing got the impression there were a lot of people in the room. After he felt his way to the bar his vision adjusted and he saw there were but five people in addition to the bartender. A couple in a corner were leaning toward each other, ignoring the television set. Three men sat at the bar, watching it. The bald man sat alone. The other two were together.

Wing ordered a beer. He had taken a first sip when the fight was stopped in the seventh round. The bartender went to the set and turned it off, turned on some kind of background-music system, and increased the intensity of the light over the bar.

Durley got off the bar stool and said, "So you make another half buck off me, Harry."

"A pleasure," the bartender said.

As the manager started to leave, Jimmy Wing stopped him, introduced himself. When he said it was private, Durley led the way over to a table in the corner near the door.

"This is a delicate matter," Jimmy said. "I'm a reporter for the *Record-Journal*, but this isn't newspaper business. It's more a favor for a friend."

"That's how come the name struck a bell. James Wing. I've seen it in the paper. I've seen you before too. Out here?"

"I came out to your opening in April. I don't remember meeting you then. I met two of the owners."

"I'm one of the owners too, fella. And manager. What's this delicate matter you got on your mind?"

"A couple of kids. They've checked in here at least once, I think. Both the girl's parents and the boy's parents are friends of mind. I want to nail it down, prove it, so the parents can straighten those two out and get them off this kick."

Durley had a fleshy, unrevealing face, a casual voice. "You want to nail it down."

"I suppose the registration card would be the best way."

"You got any kind of writ or warrant to check my books?"

"Mr. Durley, that isn't a very cooperative attitude."

Durley leaned forward, wearing a rather strange smile. "You want to know about my attitude? I got this kind of an attitude. I got the attitude of a man with a heavy piece of money in this thing. I sold out a nice operation in Jersey. You know when we were due to open? December first last year. So we open in April with the season over. You know the occupancy I run? Forty per cent is a good night, a helluva good night. You know where the break-even is? Seventy-one per cent. So you come around doing a favor for a friend. I'm hurting, fella. I'm hurting real bad, and I'll rent units to anything that's warm, breathing and has money. Nobody around here ever heard of your kids. Anybody rents an overnight key here, they buy privacy too. You want something on anybody, fella, you don't get it the easy way, not from me. You go around the other way, like following them. If we got to do a hot-pants trade to keep alive, we'll do it until we get fat enough to pick and choose. You following me? In the meantime, they rent the key and they buy privacy. We need the local plates we're getting, and if I fink on any of that business, word gets around and we lose it. Right now I'm running a hot-pillow trade in a six hundred thousand dollar plant, which makes no sense at all and sometimes makes me feel ashamed, but I'm doing it to survive, and I'll keep doing it until I decide I don't have to. That's the kind of attitude I've got."

Jimmy Wing poured the rest of his beer into his glass. He smiled and shook his head and said, "Rough talk, Mr.

Durley. This local trade, you put them way in the back units so the cars are out of sight?"

"I got a lot of book work to do tonight, fella, so if you'll . . ."

"Wait a minute. You're in Palm County. I was born and raised here. I know a hell of a lot of people, Durley. I've done favors for so many of them, they'd do little favors for me without asking why. I know everybody in the courthouse."

"Where are you going with it?"

"You got hard with me, right sudden. I don't know as that's too smart. This isn't like Jersey. This is small town around here. Do all your signs conform to county ordinances? How much inspection are you getting on those county licenses you took out? How about sanitation? How about setbacks? All your kitchen help fingerprinted? Maybe it could even be a lot easier than that, Mr. Durley. Maybe a sheriff's deputy could take a swing through all your parking areas every hour on the hour all night long, with that big red flasher working so nobody would miss him. Now, I'm telling you just as honestly as I can that the biggest mistake you can make right now is to decide I'm bluffing."

Durley went over to the bar and came back with a drink. He sat quietly for almost a full minute. Finally he said, "I got so much on my mind, sometimes I forget how to be smart."

"It was a week ago last Wednesday. They were in a unit in the last building in the back. Dark-haired girl, small and pretty. Big husky blond boy. Red Jaguar."

"They would have checked in in the evening."

"Probably. And left very early."

"Let's go check it with Pritch. He was on."

They went into a small office beyond the switchboard. The desk clerk could not recall at first, and remembered when Wing said it was the night Gardner had stayed there.

"Oh, I think I've got it now. Let me check the cards."

Pritchard came back with a card in his hand. "The girl came alone and registered right after I came on. Here's the time stamp. Twelve after four. Haughty as hell. Wanted one way in the back. Went and looked at it and came back and paid cash. Eighteen fifty-four, with tax. She wanted to pay on her way in instead of out because she said she and her husband would be leaving early. Yes, I remember seeing the car out in front. Red Jag. She's got here on the card Michigan plates."

"That would be right," Jimmy said.

"She said they'd take occupancy later on. And she . . ." He stopped, snapped his fingers, and excused himself again.

Durley examined the card and handed it to Wing. The writing was firm, large, angular, yet unmistakably feminine. Mr. and Mrs. Nathaniel Tannis of Flint, Michigan. Wing was dryly amused to notice that Tannis was Sinnat spelled backward.

Pritchard came back and placed an identical card on the desk between them. "They're in the house tonight, Frank. I thought it was familiar. But Gil checked them in before I come on. Is there something wrong?"

"Nothing you have to know about, Pritch," Durley said. "All you have to remember is how Mr. Wing here is a man we're real good buddies with. We're such good buddies, you take these two cards in and run off a photo copy for our good friend Mr. Wing."

The clerk took the cards away. "I appreciate this," Jimmy said.

"That's why I'm doing it. So you'll appreciate it. So if I get in a jam I've got a local buddy to turn to. I wouldn't want anybody thinking of all the things you thought of, and wanting a shakedown."

"It isn't likely to come to that around here."

"That's nice to know. Funny, the girl doing the check-in."

"The boy looks too young."

"If you want to make my damn day perfect, now tell me the girl is fifteen."

"Nineteen."

"That's a small help."

"Are you going to make it?"

"We'll make it," Durley said. "If my wife has to make up every bed herself, and if I have to be desk clerk, bartender, chef and janitor, we'll make it. We can't afford not to. The trouble was, we missed the season that would carry us through the first summer."

"The rates seem high."

"The rear units have kitchen deals in them. We start at ten for a single. Once we hang out the low, low, summer rates signs, you'll know we've been whipped. We're not after the shoppers. It has to stay a class operation."

Pritchard brought him the copies of the registration cards. Durley walked him to the lobby door. Durley said, "I don't have to tell you what not to talk about and you don't have to tell me, right? We understand each other. Come out to dinner. Bring a friend. The food is good. It cost a hundred grand over estimate, and it was four months late opening, but the food is good."

Wing started to drive out, then turned and drove past the registration lobby and the big sapphire pool, back to the last unit. He estimated there were twenty rooms in the building. There were five cars parked in the darkness, faintly illuminated by a parking-area light on a tall pole. The little red car was nosed up to the low shrubbery in front of number sixty-six. The canvas top was up. The windows of sixty-six were dark. The little car looked more patient than furtive.

He turned around and drove out. Durley was standing in the parking area in front of the office watching him as he turned out onto the highway and headed back toward Palm City.

It was quarter after midnight when he knocked at the side door, the office door, of Elmo's home.

Elmo let him in. "Set, boy. When you phoned I was so far asleep Dellie liked to shook me to death waking me up." He yawned and leaned against the edge of his desk, looking at Jimmy sitting on the couch. "Saturday night I used to howl till break of day, but I'm slowed a lot. Wish you could have waited until morning."

"I don't want to see too much of you in the daylight, Elmo. Here or in public places. It might not be smart. And if I'd waited until tomorrow I might have changed my mind about the whole thing. And you had the idea this was urgent, the last time I talked to you."

"Everything is urgent, boy. The only un-urgent thing in the world is taking your pleasure, and that's a sometime urgent thing if you set it off too long. I hope to God you got something worth while on Sinnat."

"I don't know what it's worth, but I damn well know it's about the only thing you're going to get."

"Leroy said you'd get nothing at all. He poked around some."

"When you ask me to do something, I don't want a lot of other people I don't know about doing the same thing."

Elmo chuckled. He hitched himself up onto the desk, reached inside his silk robe and scratched his chest. "You got so many ideas about what you will do and what you won't do, you leave me confused. So far, Jimmy, right up to now, I can't see as you've done anything yet."

"Maybe I've done something about Dial Sinnat. I don't know how you can use it, or if you can use it. I don't want to be mixed up in that end of it. I want that clear before we go into it, Elmo."

"You keep this up, you're going to put me in an ugly

condition, boy. We're going to get along fine. I won't ask anything of you you can't do. We went into that. I want you for what you can do . . . better than other people."

"Sinnat is a tough-minded man. Pushing him the way I have in mind might not work out. By the way, he told Kat Hubble this deal is being handled smarter than any of the five men involved, and he wondered who could be the silent partner with the brains."

Elmo's eyebrows went up in wonder. "Well. How about that? So there's another real good reason to make him stop thinking about any part of it. What have you got?"

"I had good luck getting it," Jimmy said, and told him precisely what he had found out, and turned the copies of the registration cards over to him.

Elmo studied the copies, walked around his desk and sat down. "Too bad it had to be Burt's boy." He shook his head and smiled. "No beaches and back seats for that little gal. No bugs and bushes for her. She travels first class. Whether it's any use to us, then, depends on how much he thinks of his little girl."

"We can assume he's partial to her."

"You look beat and you talk mean, Jimmy. You tired?"

"A little. This isn't my normal line of work."

"It's a little special for all of us. But don't you start bleeding for her, hear? She's a little girl got herself a husky young buck to while away the long summer with. You sure Burt's boy is seventeen?"

"Positive."

"I'll have to check the law on it with Leroy, but I got the idea she's been tampering with the morals of a minor. And there's some kind of an ordinance about conspicuous cohabitation, but I don't know as it would fit this here situation."

"I hope this won't turn into some kind of a public mess."

Elmo looked benignly at him. "Now, if there is any way in the world of this turning into a public mess, this girl's father is going to be the first one in the world to want to prevent it. The way I see it, those men that run fast and loose through all the women they can reach, it's an entirely different thing when it comes to their own daughters. He might be right sensitive about this, Jimmy."

"He might be."

Elmo leaned back and looked at the ceiling. "There's another way to go at it too. There's no way in the world this little girl could prove it was Burt's boy with her these two times. She could be claiming it was Burt's boy just because if it came out it was somebody else, it would be a worse mess."

"I don't see what you . . ."

"She could be trying to hide the fact it was actual old Tom Jennings seducin' her. Two birds with one stone, you could say."

"Now wait a minute!"

"I was just thinking out loud."

"But I don't want anybody making it into more than . . ."

"Hold it!" Elmo said sharply, raising both hands. "Lord God, what the hell kind of game are we playing here? Get yourself back in focus, boy. What are we talking about? Robbing the poor? We got a snotty little rich girl playing around with Burt Lesser's innocent boy. And we got Dial Sinnat, with more money than Carter got pills, and a little cute-ass wife a quarter century younger than him. And they're *outsiders*, boy! They come down here from Rochester, New York, or some goddam place like that. You and I were born and raised here. If they died here, they wouldn't even be buried here. And if they decide they don't like it, they can go any damn place in the world and live fat. You look at that committee list. There isn't a *one* of them didn't come here from some other place. What the hell right have they got telling us what to do with the landscape we were raised in? Boy, you act as if I'm going to skin those folks, salt 'em down and fry 'em. All I'm going to do is give a little bitty nudge here and there, just enough to make every one of them take a sudden disinterest in Grassy Bay. I want to do it nice and gentle, with your help. If you haven't got the stomach for a little thing like this, a little job that's going to work out fine for everybody, with nobody getting hurt bad, then I can have Leroy bring some folks in who maybe set their feet down a lot heavier than you and me. Now, I'm not going to do any more thinking out loud. I'll maybe find a good way to use this, and maybe I won't, but you don't have to know about it if it makes you feel easier. This is the way the world works, boy. This is the way things get done. You should know that much by now."

"How *do* things get done, Elmo?"

"Why, I was just now . . . Is there more to that question?"

"I was wondering about Martin Cable the Third. And I was wondering about Eloise. How did you get things done with Eloise, Mister Commissioner?"

"She's a fine-looking woman."

"Lately she's taking a big interest in local economics. Martin says she's real bright about it."

"You know, you're being real bright too."

"Thanks."

"You ever see that shack Leroy has down in the Taylor Tract east of Everset?"

"No."

"He calls it a shack, but it's more a lodge, I guess. Fifty-some acres he's got down there, gate and cattle guard and a little old windy road going in, so you'd never know he had it fixed up so nice back in there. It's about the onliest place Leroy can get away from his maw. He's got power going in there. He's even got an unlisted phone. Real fine. I guess Eloise has been going down there off and on for six, eight months, little afternoon visits like. There were only three knew about it, them and me. Now it's four. He's been teaching her about business, you might say. Martin is a stubborn man, but when he won't listen to her, she just won't have anything to do with that poor man at all. And he's been coming around to her way of thinking. Or Leroy's way, you might say."

"Or your way."

"But she doesn't know that. She's just real anxious to help Leroy. Somehow she's got the idea that unless this development goes through, Leroy is ruined. She's got a tender heart."

"I'll be damned!"

"Leroy wouldn't like you acting all that surprised, Jimmy. Women take to that old boy."

"It's pretty stupid for her to get into something like that, isn't it?"

Elmo shrugged. "I don't guess Martin is the most exciting fella in the world for a woman like that to be married to. Granting you it's stupid for her to fool around at all, she's doing better with Leroy than if it was some fathead who'd get all carried away and get careless and get them caught. Or take it too serious. A man like Leroy, he understands women like Eloise. They want a little spice on account they get bored, but they don't want to take any chance on messing up their marriage. Leroy is careful, and he pleasures them nice and he talks the sweet way they like to hear. But if they try to take charge, if they get uppity with him, he takes a switch to them, and that's something new and different for them too, not getting any of that kind of treatment at home. Leroy, he says he doesn't see her as often as it could be arranged, because she's one godawful strenuous woman. He took up with her because we had it figured out that she could help us out with Martin. And she's done just fine."

Jimmy pictured Leroy Shannard, the thick white hair, the lean, hard, brown, sleepy face, the wise, remote, indolent eyes, the soft and cynical voice. He imagined Shannard with Eloise, and the match became more plausible—a cautious, civilized lechery appealing to her peasant shrewdness.

Jimmy sighed and said, "I've been around. I know a hell of a lot of things I couldn't put in the paper. But you are beginning to make me feel wet behind the ears, Elmo."

"Keep standing in the wind and you'll dry off fast. The next one on the list, Jimmy, is that Doris Rowell. Next to Sinnat, she worries me the most. She does too good a job lining up those fish experts and erosion people. You get onto her next. Get her out of the picture, and maybe we won't have so many people down here using big words and confusing the voters. But you get some sleep. You did fine on this, but you don't look so good."

As Jimmy Wing was heading north on Cable Key toward his cottage, he looked at his watch and saw that it was ten minutes of two. The neon of the Sea Oat Lounge was just ahead, on his left. He was exhausted, but he knew his nerves were so raw he would not sleep without some assistance, such as a couple of quick strong drinks. He braked sharply and turned in and parked. There were three other cars in front of the place.

He went in and sat at the bar, under the festooning of nets and glass floats. There was a noisy party of four in a corner, and one couple dancing, tight-wrapped and slowly, to the muted juke. There was a half drink and a woman's purse on the bar three stools away. Bernie, the fat bartender, was checking the bar tabs against the register.

He came over and said, "Long time, Jim. You off it?"

"Not so anybody could notice. Beam on the rocks, Bernie. Uh . . . make it a double. Slow for a Saturday."

"We did our share, earlier on. We made new friends. We carried out a few." He put the drink in front of Jimmy.

"Move over here cozy," a familiar girl-voice commanded. He turned and saw that the half-drink and purse belonged to Mitchie McClure. He grinned and moved to the stool beside her.

"How's the ink-stained wretching business?" she said. "Tuck the paper to bed, full of scoops and excitements?"

Her voice had the drawling quality which drinking always caused with her. She had a ripely sturdy body, a bland pretty childish face, so unmarked, so much in contrast with the knowing eyes, the sardonic voice, that it had a masklike quality. They had known each other for many years. Her hair was bleached almost white, paler than he had ever seen it, and piled in a contrived tousling which curved to frame her face and curled down almost to her eyebrows in a silky fringe.

"The hair is really something, girl."

"This week's hair. The only thing I haven't tried yet is shaving it off. Every time I get it done I feel like a new woman for twenty minutes."

"You alone? On a Saturday night?"

"Shocking, isn't it? There are clowns you can take and clowns you cannot take. I reserve the right to choose, Jaimie. I didn't send this one on his way early enough. I should know by now. Stick with a friend of a friend. It's when you get to a friend of a friend of a friend the system collapses. Look up good old Mitchie if you ever get down that way. God, what a boor! I'll tell you something, Jaimie. It makes a girl treasure her stinking little inadequate alimony, because maybe without it, life would turn into a wilderness of boors. Ha! Adrift in a sea of dullards. I'm a lucky girl. Right, Bernie?"

"Right, doll."

"One for the road, Bernie. And hit my friend again."

"Not right off like that," Jimmy said. "We go to the matches."

"That's my game. You can't win."

He tore matches out of the ashtray book. She went first, calling two. Their clenched fists were side by side. They glowered at each other. He had one match in his fist. "One," he said, displaying it. She opened an empty hand. "Horse on me," she said. "Your call."

He decided to use bad strategy. He used all three matches, and called four. She waited a long time, guessed three, opened her hand and showed one.

"You lucked out," she said indignantly. "Your lucky day, eh?"

"Sure. I'm up to here in luck, Mitchie."

She tilted her head and looked at him more closely. "I've seen you looking better, Mr. Wing. Much better. On the other hand, everybody used to look a lot better, every one of us. Right, Bernie?"

"Right, doll."

"I took canoeing and boating at Sweet Briar," she said. "It readied me for the world. Heavy weather. We run before the wind, Jaimie. No sea anchors."

The noisy foursome had paid and left. Bernie went and unplugged the juke. The dancing couple left.

"You have the look of a man trying to close the joint, Bernie."

"Right, doll."

They paid, said goodnight and went out. Bernie went to the door and they heard the click of the latch behind them. The spray of sea oats in yellow neon went off. A car whined by. The Gulf mumbled against the dark beach.

They stood between his station wagon and her ancient Minx.

"Old Saturday night," she said. "Sunday morning."

"One of each every week."

"You are down, aren't you, dear?" She moved closer to him, put her hands on his waist and looked up at him. "Got all dressed up and ended up with no place to go. We could share a little gesture of friendship. I'm not being brazen. Just cozy. And it wouldn't matter a hell of a lot either way."

He kissed the bridge of her nose and said, "Follow me," and got into his car. Her lights followed him up the Key and down his long driveway. She saved out some breakfast eggs and scrambled the rest. They talked aimlessly for a little while and went to bed. Just before they went to sleep, she rubbed the coal of her cigarette out in the bedside ashtray, settled back down against him and said, "Who is she, Jaimie?"

"Who is who?"

"Don't give me that. I told you my long sad story of unrequited love a long time ago, with tears and everything. Remember? Who is she?"

"She's somebody who isn't going to work out."

"On account of Gloria?"

"On account of a lot of things, Mitchie."

"She married?"

"You talk too much, honey."

She changed position, put her arm across him, nestled more closely and sighed. "I know. Anyhow, I feel more even with you. People like us, Jaimie, we have two things we can go with. One thing, you can wake up in the morning and know you're alive. That's something, I guess. The other is this. Having somebody close to hold onto sometimes."

"Mmm hmm."

"But neither is really so much, is it, when you think about it?"

"Go to sleep, Mitchie."

Toward dawn a great raw clangor of thunder awakened him. He heard the lisping roar of heavy rain moving toward the cottage, moving across water and tropic growth. He was trying to pull himself far enough awake to go see to the windows when he heard them being closed. He thought Gloria was closing them, and then he remembered Mitchie. The heaviest rain came. As it began to die away after ten minutes he heard a small thin whining sound. He was on the edge of sleep. He wondered if some animal was under the house. He tried to fall back into sleep and could not. Finally he sat up. The world was a drab dark gray. The rain was almost gone. Both the bedroom and the kitchen opened out onto the small screened porch on the back of the cottage. The door was open. He could barely see the pale figure of Mitchie standing out there on the porch by the screen, naked, making that stifled whimpering sound. He lay back. In a little while the sound ended. The rain was gone. He heard the sound of her bare feet on the wooden floor, heard the rattle of a towel rack in the bathroom. Soon the bed moved as she eased back into it. He rolled toward her, pretending to embrace her in sleep. Her skin was cool, freshened by the rain which had blown against her. He mumbled and held her and kissed her eye and tasted salt with the tip of his tongue. While they made love he wondered exactly what had been in her mind as she had stood out in the rain, crying. Perhaps she thought of nothing but her own tears.

She woke him at eleven. She had gone back to her place to change, and she had picked up some fresh orange juice on the way back. When he finished his shower, the eggs, toast and bacon were ready. He was glad she had awakened him, but he wished she had done it by phone. He did not relish having her around, not in the morning. She came cheery and too bawdy and too much at home. She came down too heavily on her heels when she walked. Her hips looked heavier than he had realized they were as she stood at the stove in her chocolate-colored shorts and her yellow blouse. And she made weak coffee. She could not possibly be the same person who had wept in the dawn rain.

She sat across from him with her coffee and said, "Cheer up, pal. I'm not here for keeps."

"It's nice to have you here."

"And it hurt your mouth to say it, poor boy. But no matter how churlish you feel right now, you do look better."

"I haven't slept this late in a long time, Mitch."

"We had a good rain. Did you hear the rain?"

"Vaguely."

"When I drove to my place the air was wonderful. All clean and fresh and sweet. Now it's like hot soup again. Are you in any kind of trouble?"

He looked up from the paper. "Huh?"

"Trouble! Are you in any?"

"I'm with you. My sister wouldn't approve."

"Laura is a dull, righteous frump, and she always has been. I remember you were about fourteen. I was eleven. You were teaching me how to throw a curve. I came over on Saturday morning. She chased me out of the yard with a rake. Called me boy-crazy. She was wrong. I was curve-ball-crazy. I wasn't boy-crazy until I was twelve."

"That's when you started teaching me how to throw curves."

"Not throw them, darling. Appreciate them. Oh God, remember how we were going to wing up to Georgia and get married? What was I then? Fifteen, I think. Look at us, honey. Could we have done any worse?"

"I forget why we didn't go to Georgia."

"Because Willy wouldn't loan us his car. Anyhow, Jaimie, you were my first. Remember the guilt? God, how wicked we felt! We pledged our sacred honor we'd never slip again. And we didn't, did we? Not for three whole days. Can you remember what we fought about?"

"No."

"You went away to school. End of romance. And here we are again. But without the romance. I wonder what kind of life we'd be having if we'd . . . if Willy had been a little more generous with his car. Have you slept with her, Jaimie?"

"What? Who?"

"With the gal who's messing you up."

"No. And it's none of your business, Mitchie."

She poured more coffee. "Maybe that's what you have to do. To break the spell."

"Get *off* it!"

She made her eyes wide and round. "Ho, ho, ho, yet. So with my dirty mouth I'm soiling some princess? This is Grace Kelly you're swooning over?"

"Mitchie, for God's sake!"

"Are you a grown man? What kind of a kid-stuff torch are you carrying? Listen to the voice of experience, dear. I have been around. Oh, way way around, and back several times and out around again. I've still got my disposition, half my looks, and twice my early talent. The bed part is pure mirage, until proven otherwise. Friendship is a bigger part of the rest of it than anyone will admit. One little smidgin is magical romance. Anybody who mistakes the smidgin for the whole deal is retarded."

He stared at her. "Mitchie, I am fine. I am nifty dandy."

"Then you got more on your mind than a girl."

"What I have on my mind is how late I'm going to be getting to the shop."

"I'd like to see you better adjusted to whatever the hell you're adjusting to."

"I don't cry in the rain, at least."

She narrowed her eyes. "You know, you're a bastard sometimes."

"You learned that a long time ago. You keep forgetting."

She stood up quickly, grabbed her purse and headed for the door without a word. She stopped suddenly. Her shoulders slumped and she turned slowly and came back to him with a small smile. She put her hand on his shoulder and kissed him on the mouth. "Enough old friends I haven't got, Jaimie. Last night seemed sweet. Even the tears were sweet. If I had any luck left, I'd give it to you. You know it. I wish one of us was happy. It would seem like a better average."

He smiled up at her. "You make horrible coffee."

"It's the only thing in the world I do badly, dear."

He sat and heard the rackety motor of the Minx start, and heard it fade as she drove out to the highway. He put the dishes in the sink and went downtown to work.

12

KAT TURNED THE LITTLE CAR into her driveway just after dark on Sunday. Alicia was asleep in the back seat, collapsed uncomfortably across the big wicker picnic basket. Roy slept beside her, curled against the door. For the last half hour Kat had become uncomfortably aware of having burned herself again. It had been a long dazzle of day on the beaches of Sanibel, the sand like snow and diamonds, the Gulf like a stream of hot blue milk. In spite of the wide brim of her coolie hat, the shoulder scarf, the big black glasses, the continual oiling, the time spent in patches of shade, the sun had found her. Her thighs stung, her shoulders smarted, and there were little needles of pain in her back. The all-day sun had merely deepened the brown-bronze of the tough hides of her children.

Never seem to learn, she thought. Now pray that it isn't the chills-and-fever kind. And that there won't be too many blisters, and they won't be too huge and wet.

But nothing could spoil her sense of relief and accomplishment at having gotten through the day. During the day she had tried to make herself lose track of the hours. She had hidden her watch in her beach bag. But she had kept stealing glances at it. . . .

About now he is finishing lunch in Venice, after talking to those men about the design for the new professional building.

Now he is in the car, heading south, heading home, thinking about the contract, planning the preliminary sketches, and at about that same time that drunken woman is storming out of the roadside bar in Punta Gorda, getting into that old pickup truck and heading north, with no license to drive, with the gas pedal flat against the floor, heading in a rage toward Venice where, as it has been reported to her, her common-law husband, missing for over a week, is now in a bowling alley with her sister.

Now both vehicles are entering that big curve north of Murdock.

Now they are a hundred feet apart.

Now the bald tire blows on the pickup truck.

153

Now Van is dead. Forty minutes from now, I will answer the phone. I will hear it ringing and come in from the yard, running and smiling because I am so sure it is him calling to give me good news.

"Miz Hubble, m'am? This is the State Highway Patrol. . . ."

She drove into the carport. In the sudden silence Roy made a murmuring sighing noise. She put her hand on his shoulder and shook him gently. "Come on, boy. We're home."

She got them roused and they each took their share of the things to be carried in. Mosquitoes whined around them in the hot crickety night. When they were inside, with the lights on, the children were astonished to find it was only eight-thirty.

Kat showered away the layers of sun lotion and the crust of sea salt. Then she used an antiseptic spray can, a medication which also contained some pain-deadening agent. She called Alicia in to spray it on her back.

It was so icy it made her yelp, and made Alicia laugh. "Get it on evenly, dear."

"Your back is pretty, Mommie."

"Thank you, honey."

"It's so smooth, but it's awful red."

Roy came into the hallway and yelled, "Colonel Jennings wants you on the phone."

"Please tell him I'll call him back in five minutes, dear."

"I don't care if they fill up the darn bay," Alicia said. "We don't have a boat any more anyhow."

Kat put her robe on and sat on the edge of the tub and took hold of Alicia's hands. "That isn't a very nice thing to say, dear."

"What's wrong with it?" the little girl demanded, looking sullen.

"Don't you like to look out across Grassy Bay?"

"I can't see it from here, can I?"

"You're being a little bit fresh. Now, don't try to pull away from me. I want you to understand something. You can't think of these things just in terms of yourself, 'Licia. You have to think of them in terms of pleasure for other people. Do you know about those huge redwood trees in California?"

"Sure. We had them in school. They're the oldest living things."

"Now just imagine that you're never going to see them in your whole life. I suppose if they were cut up into boards, they'd be worth a lot of money. Would you care if some men bought them and cut them all down?"

Alicia frowned and bit her lip. "And I wasn't going to see them anyway? Well . . . I guess I wouldn't like it. I mean it's nice knowing they're there."

"You own part of those trees, dear. If they were all divided into a hundred and eighty million parts, one part would be yours. Your part might be just a twig and a couple of leaves."

"That's silly!"

"And you own a part of Grassy Bay too. It's what is called an undivided interest. You don't know what part you own and I don't know what part I own, but if it was divided up, our parts wouldn't be worth very much. Maybe a little sand and a shell and a fiddler crab apiece. But with everybody's parts of it left together there, it's a beautiful thing, isn't it?"

"I guess so."

"Now, listen carefully, dear. This is hard to understand. If those redwoods were sold, or if the bay is sold, you won't get any part of the money, even though you own a part of both of them."

"That would be cheating, wouldn't it?"

"Clever men can use the laws to cheat all of us and make it sound as if they're doing us a big favor. That's what we're trying to keep from happening. Colonel Jennings and Mr. Sinnat and Jackie Halley and all of us. Do you understand?"

"I . . . I guess so."

"Now do you care if they fill up Grassy Bay and put houses there?"

Alicia frowned. "It wouldn't be right. No, I guess I wouldn't like it."

"Now, you run along, honey, and figure out what we're going to cook up for three tired beachcombers."

When she was alone, Kat looked at herself in the bathroom mirror. How can you know if you're doing it right? she thought. How do you know exactly what you're doing to them with the things you say? You could have done these things so much better, darling. You'd have the right words. They'd understand and remember. I don't think they really pay much attention to anything I say.

Tom Jennings' voice was not as forceful as usual over the phone. He sounded remote and windy and indecisive.

"I've been trying to get hold of you, Katherine. I don't

know if you can help or not. I hope so. This is very upsetting."

"What's the matter, Tom?"

"Di Sinnat phoned me about three o'clock. He was . . . almost formal. It was as if he was talking to a stranger. He said he had decided not to get involved in committee work this time. He said he was resigning. He said he was sorry to have to withdraw his offer of financial assistance to the committee. He wished us luck. I tried to find out why, but he was very terse and strange."

"I can't understand it!"

"Neither can I. I was counting on his help. I never thought he'd . . . Anyway, I called him back a half hour later to ask him if I could come over and talk to him. I got the house-keeper. She took my name. She came back to the phone and said Mr. and Mrs. Sinnat were gone for the rest of the day."

"But what could have happened, Tom?"

"I don't know. I really don't. I can't imagine him changing because he's gotten in with Burt Lesser and those people. And I can't imagine him being frightened off. I just don't know, Katherine. You're as close to them as anybody I can think of. I must tell you he did sound as if there's no chance of his changing his mind. But one always hopes. At least, maybe you can find out why this has happened. Without the two thousand dollars he promised for our campaign fund, we're going to have financial difficulty. It will . . . weaken our effort to have to spend time and energy raising money when we should be stirring up public opinion."

"Who else knows about this, Tom?"

"I decided that the fewer people who know about it, the easier it would be for him to change his mind back again. I don't know who he has told, of course. But aside from Melissa and me, you are the only one who knows about his phone call."

She looked at her watch. "I'll see what I can do. You understand, Tom, I can't get . . . rough about it. Di and Claire have been too good to me. I mean, if he doesn't want to talk to me, I can't get insistent."

"Of course I understand that. Of the eight on the com-mittee, he's the one I didn't want to lose."

"I have to feed the kids and stow them away, and then I'll see what I can do. I'll let you know."

"Phone me right away, please, no matter how late it is."

The kids were in bed by quarter to ten, their faces dark against the pillows. As she was wondering whether to phone, or whether to walk to the Sinnats and leave the children alone for a little while, someone rapped on the glass of the patio door. She turned the outside lights on and saw Nat Sinnat silhouetted there.

She opened the door and said, "Come in, Nat. Listen, dear, you've come along at just the right time. Could you stay here for a little while while I hurry up to your house and talk to Dial for a little while, if he's home?"

"What about?" Nat said, walking in. The tone of voice was so flat as to be almost rude. When the girl moved into the light, Katherine saw the compressed lips, the puffy eyes, the dark patches under the eyes.

"I want to talk to him about the committee."

Natalie walked slowly to a big chair, sat in it and looked toward Kat. She kicked her sandals off and pulled her legs up into the chair and said, "Then maybe you better listen to me. My father isn't going to talk to anybody, Kat. Not even Claire. And somehow I can't talk to Claire either." She lifted her chin slightly. "And I've God damn well got to talk to somebody or start beating my head on the trees. Do you mind?"

Kat sat down near the girl. "It's about the committee? I don't understand."

"Some person or persons got in touch with Dial this morning. They told him that his darling daughter was a tramp. They named the times and the place and they had it right, damn them. They told him they didn't want to interfere with any fun his little girl was having, but unless he severed every connection with Save Our Bays immediately, said little girl was going to be in the middle of such a stinking public mess, decent people would probably tar and feather her." Natalie Sinnat began to cry.

Kat went to her quickly. "Please, dear," she said.

"I keep c-crying because I get so d-damned mad. He's taking it so seriously." She started furiously at Katherine. "What the hell kind of a human being does he think I am? Certainly, people could make it sound ugly and horrible. I'm not a tramp! I don't feel messy! He should realize I don't care how anybody tries to make it sound. I don't feel as if I've done anything so terribly wrong."

"I can't believe you have."

"But now I don't know what to think. Maybe it was wrong. I have to tell you about it. And you have to promise to tell me if I was wrong. Will you?"

"Of course I will."

"Please go back over there, Kat. Could I have a drink? A strong one. Gin, if you have it."

"And tonic?"

"Please."

Katherine made drinks and brought them in. Natalie blew her nose and got her cigarettes out of her purse.

"You have to know how it started," the girl said. "When I first came down here, the second week in June, Jigger started sort of following me around. It was funny and it was annoying. I don't like the sort of boy I thought he was. Big and powerful and beautiful and arrogant. I thought he was trying to rack me up for a summer score, so he could brag to his seventeen-year-old friends how he made it with a college girl. It seemed as if every time I looked around, there he was. And I was waiting for a chance to chill him. After I was here about ten days they put on that big end-of-school beach party for all the kids in the Estates. I went because I didn't have anything else to do. He wanted to walk down the beach with me. I thought it was a good chance to clobber him. We walked a long way. I wondered when he was going to make the pass. He didn't. We'd started back. The bonfire was a long way off. I stumbled on some driftwood. He caught me and he didn't let go. His hand was here and he was trembling and it was as if he couldn't let go. That was my chance, and I let him have it. I've got a mean mouth, Kat. I chopped him right down to nothing, and I left him there. He didn't follow me. When I was about sixty feet away he made a terrible sound. A kind of anguish. I kept walking, but I kept remembering that sound. I'd said some truly horrible things to him. Finally I stopped and went back. I realized I hadn't been fair. I was taking out on him some of the pain and the heartbreak of the terrible year I'd had.

"He was sitting in the sand and he was crying. I circled around. I know he didn't know I'd come back. The crying wasn't faked. He was slamming his fist down into a little pile of shells the tide had left, hammering the shells with a terrible force so his hand was bloody. When I spoke to him he froze. It scared me. Have you ever seen a face with no expression on it at all? I knew there was something terribly wrong, and I didn't know what it was, but I knew I'd pushed him over some kind of edge. I knew I'd nearly destroyed him, and I had to see if I could undo the harm. I knew I had to make him talk to me. And I sensed for the first time that there was a real person, actually a scared person, hiding under all that poise and muscle.

"It took a long time to get him to talk. I didn't get all of it that night, or the next night, or the next week. But finally he was able to break through all the inhibitions and tell me what it was that was eating him.

"I won't go into detail, Kat. It's a lousy lonely home for those kids. There's no love in that house. Sally Ann is a domineering bitch. Burt is a dull, withdrawn man. The kids do as they please. Anyway, when Jigger was fourteen, he got drawn into a little group set up by a practicing homosexual teaching in the junior high. I gather that the man didn't actually mess with the kids until he'd made sure of them, and he took a long time making sure. Months passed before he got around to Jigger. The poor kid didn't know how to cope. He was fifteen when it happened. It shocked him, scared him and revolted him. He never went back to that house, and he never told anyone. But he couldn't stop thinking about it, remembering it. He carried all that guilt and shame locked up inside him. He went around with it like a dog with a rotting chicken tied around its neck. He began to believe he was queer. He began to get the idea people could tell it by looking at him. He worried about the way he walked and about his tone of voice. He thought the man had ruined the rest of his life. When it all came out—apparently there was a considerable scandal—Jigger knew his name would come into it, and he began to plan how to kill himself. When he'd made up his mind how to do it, he wrote a farewell note and put it on his pillow and swam out into the Gulf. He left in the early morning. He swam out until he was exhausted, until the shore line was just a little shadow he could see whenever he was on the crest of a swell. He tried to let himself drown, but he couldn't make himself go under and inhale water. He would go under, but he always came back up for air. Those Lesser kids were practically raised in the water. He doesn't know how long he was out there before he gave up and started swimming back. He was so completely spent he doesn't remember very much about coming back. He had to float often and rest. He came ashore a mile below the Pavilion. It was dusk. He said he fell down several times while walking home. His family was out. His bed wasn't made. The note was on his pillow, just as he had left it.

"Early this year he decided he would 'cure' himself by making love to a girl. He selected a little slut in his class who was reported to be ready to oblige anybody. He went to her house. She was alone. She kissed him hello, locked the front door, took him directly to her room, stepped out of her shorts, shucked off her blouse and bra and spread herself out on the bed and said, 'Hurry *up*, tiger!' Poor Jigger ran like a gazelle. He paused a block away to throw up, and kept running. The girl spread it all over school. By then if he hadn't already learned he couldn't kill himself, he would have tried again. It pushed him a little further from reality, that's all.

"Then I came along. I had two advantages, I guess. One, I hadn't had a chance to hear any of the talk about him. I wouldn't know, unless I suspected by just looking at him, which is ridiculous, of course. Two, I'm scrawny, not all big bazoom and fatty hips, which apparently the experimental girl had more than her fair share of, and he felt they had put him off. I guess you could say I had three advantages. He didn't want me to expect anything of him. Can you imagine what the poor thing wanted of me?"

"Just . . . maybe to be seen with you."

"Exactly! You're very wise, Kat. He wanted to have a girl to go on dates with, so the world would know he was dating a girl. He sensed I didn't want to get involved in any way, certainly not with a kid of seventeen. Actually, if he could have bought a robot girl, that would have been perfect, as long as everybody thought she was real. He wanted me to like him. He wanted to talk nicely to me so I would want to be with him. And I guess he wanted to practice being with a girl, walking with her and talking with her, so that he could be more at ease. He wanted a status he thought he didn't have, and I was to be the symbol. He really talked very nicely on our walk up the beach, but it was a little bit strained. I think he'd sort of memorized a conversational line he thought would keep me amused. I thought he was tense because he was working up to a pass. And then I stumbled and he grabbed at me in the dark when I half fell against him, and his big dear innocent paw clapped right over my left breast as if he'd planned it that way. And it was such a horrible moment, he froze. The very *last* thing he wanted to do was make a pass at me.

"It took a long time to get that out of him. He's terribly sensitive. And he's brighter than you'd think. I knew he was not homosexual. But how can you convince anybody who's gotten themselves tied up in such knots they can't listen to reason?" She lit another cigarette, shook the match out too violently. "I don't put much value on myself. Not after last year. When somebody takes everything from you, and decides it isn't enough. And you crawl and beg and humble yourself, and they laugh and walk out of your life, it doesn't leave you a hell of a lot to hold dear, does it?"

"Natalie!"

"I'm as much a woman as I'll ever be. You see, I felt *involved* in Jigger's problem. And maybe in some sick little way it made me feel better, because here was somebody messed up a little worse than I was. There's a kind of rare justice in it, Kat. I seduced that big scared kid. I took the risk I *could* seduce him, because if it hadn't worked, I don't know what would have happened to him. On that same beach, the first time, because it seemed to have to be something that happened by accident, almost. If he'd known I wanted it to happen, he'd have become impotent out of fright. Hours, it took. And all kinds of sneaky tricks. God, I was so tender and cautious. When it finally began to happen, I felt ten thousand years old, the mother of all, holding that great trembling scared lummox, that sweet whimpering ox. But he needed more assurance than that. So we've had a couple of motel dates. Are you shocked?"

"I guess so. Sort of."

"At the Drowsy Lady. I made the arrangements both times. It's like giving life to something. That bumbling shyness and all that fright is gone now. He can laugh at the way he was. He's a man now, and he struts and smirks and looks so incredibly smug. He makes love joyously now. That's the way it's supposed to be, isn't it?"

"Yes."

"Don't let me give you the idea it's something I just endure. He's learned how to make it good for me. Does it spoil the purity of the motive if I enjoy it?"

"Stop trying to hurt yourself, Natalie."

The girl made a face. "Now, of course, he is certain it is love undying. He's certain I'm not too old for him. He wants to come to school at Michigan. He's sure we'll get married. He has it all worked out. I don't want that, of course. I don't love him. He's a sweet, intelligent boy. If I stopped right now, he might just be trading one obsession for another. I had the idea I'd let him have . . . so much of me, the charm of the idea would kind of fade away after I go back to school. Do you know what I keep thinking when I'm with him? I keep thinking there is some girl he hasn't met yet, some girl I'll probably never meet, who can be grateful to me later on. Jigger will be a good husband. This isn't going to make him promiscuous. He's learning that, too, how promiscuity is such a silly shallow thing. Well, somebody found out about it. And they're using it."

"Does Jigger know?"

"The people who talked to my father didn't give him the name of the male involved. I refused to tell him. He's absolutely furious with me. No, Jigger doesn't know. I'm afraid of what it would do to him, and I'm afraid of what crazy thing he might try to do about it if he knew. If he knew somebody was trying to hurt me, he could be murderous. He . . . he hasn't got the stability he'll have later on, in a few more years. I don't feel soiled and messy. If you place no value on something, what harm does it do to give it to somebody who needs it badly? He writes poetry about me. Some of it is really quite good. I've watched him asleep. He doesn't look over twelve when he's asleep. I've felt proud to hold him, Kat. He was on some terrible edge when I found him. And now he isn't. Was I wrong? Is the whole thing dirty and cheap and wrong? Tell me, Kat. I trust you. I feel so defensive about it, too defensive, maybe."

"It isn't an easy question. There isn't any easy answer. If you could have gotten him to go to someone for help . . ."

"I tried, but he wouldn't hear of it."

"Natalie, I understand. I really do. It was the combination of two kinds of unhappiness, actually. But I think there's a part of it you don't understand, or you're trying to deny."

"Such as?"

"A masochistic streak in you. You're ashamed of last year. So you were willing to find some way to abuse yourself, if you could find a rationalization for it. You don't hold yourself cheap. If you did, you wouldn't be struggling so hard to justify the relationship with Jigger. You just wouldn't give a damn, would you?"

"M-maybe not. I don't know."

"But you can be awfully certain, dear, that few people could ever understand it. Very few women, and almost no men. They wouldn't comprehend the sacrificial flavor to it, and the kind of strange inverted motherhood. I've never liked that boy."

"He's never let anyone else know him. I didn't like him either."

"The world is going to turn it into filth, if it ever comes out."

"I pleaded with my father. I begged him. I told him to let them do their damnedest. I told him it wouldn't hurt me, and I didn't tell him that I wouldn't let it hurt Jigger. I despise the idea of anybody being able to get at him through me. But nobody can talk to him now. Claire is wandering around wondering what the hell happened. It's up to him to tell her if he wants to."

"Who found out about it?"

"I just can't imagine."

"There's an obvious answer, isn't there? Burt Lesser is anxious to have the bay fill go through. Di is tough opposition."

"Jigger? Oh, no. I have absolute confidence in him. They could cut him in pieces and he wouldn't tell. I told Dial I'd leave his house today. I'd pack and get out of there, and then he could tell them to pull anything they felt like. But he wouldn't hear of it. I'm telling you, Kat, for a man who's led the kind of emotional life he's led, he's a pretty primitive father. I'm supposed to be some kind of a golden princess or something. If he really believes that, I could tell him some things that would stagger him, charming little details of my great romance up in Michigan. I told Jigger a little bit. I didn't dare tell him any more. He would have headed north to kill the guy. No, somebody saw us. Here's the terrifying thing about it, Kat. We were there last night. That was the second time. They knew about that too. We took my little alarm clock with us, and set it for five, and creeped into our houses like mice this morning. Dial came and bellowed me out of bed as soon as he got the call."

"Who called him?"

"He didn't say, but I got the impression the other person didn't give a name."

"He said the rest of us were vulnerable and he wasn't."

"What?"

"Nothing important, dear. Jimmy Wing told me the other side might play dirtier this time. I didn't really believe him. I can't believe Burt Lesser would . . . approve of this sort of thing."

"I bet he doesn't know anything about it. It would be that oily Leroy Shannard, or that crude Buck Flake. Or maybe the rest of them, not Mr. Lesser, just hired somebody to raise hell with your committee any way they can."

"It's so stinking," Kat said.

"Isn't it, though? And it's such a darn . . . vulgar kind of melodrama. I didn't want it to be anybody's business but mine, what I did. I didn't want it affecting anybody else. My father is an idiot to let it change his mind about anything. What could they do, really?"

"I don't know, and I guess he doesn't want to test it."

"He isn't going to give himself a chance to change his mind, or anybody else. Poor Claire. This afternoon he told her they're taking a trip just as soon as he can get tickets. Her face fell. She loves it here in the summer. She loves the house and the pool and the beach. She asked where they were going, and he said he'd decide later. They'll take the twins and Experanza. She asked how long, and he said he'd decide that later too. They'll leave Floss there and keep the house open. I can stay there or not, he said. It's up to me."

"He's running away?"

"Kat, he's going away. That's what he's done with most of the problems in his life, walk away from them. I know I'll stay. I like teaching the kids. I can't run too. I have to find some gentle way to make Jigger independent of me, the way he should be. If I let him sink or swim now, all the rest of it would mean less . . . to both of us."

"Should I try to talk to Dial?"

"He'll be very sweet and very polite and extremely evasive, Kat. You won't get anywhere. I've seen him like this before."

"I'll have to tell Tom Jennings something. Natalie? Natalie, what is it?"

The girl was staring at her, her hand at her throat, her face stricken. "Oh, Kat, when will I ever get over being so darn young?"

"What's the matter?"

"I came storming in here, loading you up with all my infantile goopy problems, completely, utterly forgetting this has been such a miserable day for you."

"It doesn't matter."

"It *does* matter! I feel like an insect. You've been so sweet, listening to my silly mess."

"Stop it! Stop it or I'm going to get angry, Natalie. You had to have somebody to come to. And I'm concerned. I'm not pretending. What kind of a monster do you think I am? Do you think I'm so all wound up in my own problems there isn't any room to try to help anybody else?"

"But I should have remembered!"

"You just did. Now shut up about it, please. I think I asked you a question. I have to tell Tom Jennings something."

"Tell him the whole thing."

"Now you *are* being a silly little girl."

"I know. Righteous defiance. I'm sorry. My trouble is I'm old for my years, but not as old as I think I am, I guess. I'm about seventy per cent adult. The thirty per cent keeps making me feel foolish. I guess you'll have to hint."

"I wish you knew who could have seen you. Was your car parked where anybody could see it?"

"It was way around in the back both times. The first time we went there was a week and a half ago. When we were driving out, a boy Jigger knows was driving in, but we were both sure he didn't recognize Jigger. Both times I registered there was nobody there but the desk clerk. I've got Michigan plates, you know. And I certainly didn't meech around acting furtive about anything. I got over all that kind of maidenly shyness last year. The only thing I can think of, Kat, is what my father said about the bay fill being in the planning stage for a long time. So they could have been following me ever since I got down here, just for luck, for the chance of something to use. But I haven't felt as if I was being followed."

"It's so strange. All of a sudden it doesn't seem as if it's the same town. Do you think Dial will *really* go away?"

"Oh, yes. He's got his pack-the-bags expression. Very bustly and fussy and efficient. Poor Claire hates traveling." Natalie stood up. "Now I'm a little bit high, and very very tired, and very grateful to you."

"I haven't done anything."

"You could have made me feel like a degenerate."

Kat walked her to the front door and went out into the night with her. Natalie turned quickly and kissed Kat on the cheek, made a small snuffling noise, and strode off down the road.

Kat went in and phoned Tom Jennings. It was quarter of midnight.

"It's late to phone you, Tom."

"I wasn't going to be able to sleep until I heard from you. What did he say?"

"Tom, honestly, I don't think there's the slightest chance of his changing his mind. In fact, he's going to go away for a while. He's taking Claire and the twins."

"That's . . . very disappointing. But what *happened?* He was so determined to help us. . . ."

"Tom, somebody went to a great deal of trouble, somebody very sly and smart, and they dug up the names and dates and places, and phoned Di and said they would make a big juicy scandal of what they'd found out if he didn't resign from Save Our Bays."

"Claire? Is it something that Claire . . ."

"I can't say any more than I've said already, Tom. Maybe Di is reacting a little more violently than he should. I don't know. I'm sort of disappointed in him. You'd think it would make him mad enough to fight harder. But he's getting out. It would make very choice gossip. And it would probably do us harm if he stayed on the team and it did get circulated. But it wouldn't do us as much harm that way as this way. I'm going to try to talk to him tomorrow after he's had a chance to sleep on it, but I. don't think it will do any good." She waited a moment and then said, "Tom?"

She heard him sigh. "We'll all have to work just that much harder. I can put in a little bit more money than I promised, but I promised just about all I can afford to begin with."

"I can't help out, I guess you know."

"I know that, Katherine dear, of course. I was just thinking. Once we know the timing of the thing, when the date will be set for the public hearing, maybe we can arrange some kind of a rally and raise money that way. I have a feeling our regular membership is going to be . . . somewhat disappointing. I've been making a small telephone survey, sampling the membership list. It seems as bad as the report I got from Jackie. It looks as if we can expect a fifty per cent mortality in our old list. We'll have to go after a lot of new members. Well, it's a little late to be discussing organizational problems. And you have to work tomorrow. Thanks for what you've done, Katherine. I really appreciate it. It's alarming, isn't it, to realize they'd stoop so low."

"Yes, it is."

"We may have further losses. Depressing thought. Odd that our own neighbors should be so much more ruthless than those Lauderdale men were."

As Kat went to bed she thought the sunburn and the worry combined would make sleep impossible. But she felt herself falling away as soon as the light was out.

13

On that Sunday, Borklund put a heavy load on Brian Haas, and hovered so close Jimmy Wing could not help him with it. Whenever Jimmy tried to take a piece of it, J.J. would appear and put him onto something else. At two-thirty, when Jimmy went out to lunch, he phoned the news room and got hold of Brian.

"How are you doing, Bri?"

"Oh, it's you," he said, keeping his voice low. "The points are dirty and there's water in the gas. I keep cutting out, and the son of a bitch keeps running me uphill. I'd say he's got a strong suspicion."

"Will you make it?"

"I'm not even going to think about guessing. I'm taking the day in ten-minute chunks, and getting through one at a time. Thanks for what you've been trying to do."

"I'll be back in a little while to try some more."

"Bring me a big coffee, black."

"You should eat."

"I better not try. A quart container if you can manage it."

"Two pints if I can't. Okay."

As soon as Wing returned with the coffee, Borklund sent him to cover a call on a drowning. It had just come in. The photographer was there when he got there. The resuscitator people had just given up, and the young mother had been given a shot but it hadn't taken effect yet. The crowd could hear her shrieking in the small house. Wing got the facts from the neighbors. It seemed slightly grotesque to use a whole ambulance for such a small body.

On his way back into town from Lakeview Village he thought how this could be simplified by the use of a mimeographed form. "The (two-, three-, four-) year-old child was playing in the back yard of (his, her) home and apparently wandered away from (his, her) (mother, father, sister, brother, playmates) and fell unnoticed into a nearby (drainage ditch, pond, lake, stream, swimming pool) and was discovered approximately ———— minutes later, floating face down. Efforts to revive the child were not successful and (he, she) was pronounced dead at ———— o'clock by Dr. ————."

The purposeless death of a child is a horrible thing, he thought. If I unlock the little box labeled Empathy, I can even manage to squeeze a little water out of my eyes. But I have to work at it. We run about eight a year, and I have covered a lot of them, and somehow it has come to be the same child being drowned over and over, and I keep the little box closed. We could take one master picture, and always run it. When the small bodies are covered, they always look alike. It is always the same stricken mother, the same ambulance, the same pointless horror. Grief for a child is always mixed up with speculation about what it might have become. Yet, according to the odds, its life would most probably have been dull, discontented and unsung. Once it is dead, nothing can be proven. All glorious speculation is valid. Had I drowned at age two, Sister Laura might sometimes look at the ruin of her own life and think of the small brother, thirty years gone, and say, "If he had only lived, life might have been different for all of us." But I lived and nothing is different, and nothing is proven or disproven.

It was after five before he was able to give any attention to the problem of Mrs. Doris Rowell, she of the white Dutch bob, the academic baritone, the tennis shoes, the faded cotton dresses on the fat soft sexless body.

He reviewed what he knew about her. She had lived on Sandy Key, down near Turk's Pass for at least twenty years. She'd bought an ugly old stucco house down there when houses and land were very cheap. She lived alone, had owned a succession of very old cars, was an amateur naturalist, a savage conservationist. When the paper had some special research problem involving marine animals or plant life, bird life, indigenous trees and plants, Doris Rowell was the logical one to ask. If she did not have the information, she knew where and how to find it. Usually she had the information.

He drove down to see her. When he parked beside the house she came to the entrance to the shed in the side yard and stared at him as he walked toward her. She wore vast faded khaki trousers, a man's shirt, a baseball cap.

"From the paper," she said. "What is it this time? I'm busy. You'll have to talk while I'm finishing something, Mr. Wing."

He followed her into the shed. It was stiflingly hot. Lights hung over two large fish tanks in the back end of the shed. The water exchange system was bubbling. There were fingerling sheepshead in both tanks, about twenty in each. She was mixing some kind of fluid on a work bench near the tanks.

"What are you doing, Mrs. Rowell?"

"Are you making polite sounds with your mouth or do you want to know?"

"I'm naturally nosy. It helps when you're a reporter."

"I suppose so. These are *Archosargus probatocephalus*. I'm checking the relation of salinity to growth rate. That's the control tank on the right. I've got a control pen in the bay too. Proctor, of the University of Southern California, published a paper on the same experiment, using a somewhat similar fish, but a labroid fish, the *Primelometopon pulchrum*. I didn't like his conclusions. This is in the second month, but now I see perhaps he was correct."

"Will you publish your results?"

She turned and stared at him stonily. "Where? How? I'm a layman."

"Then why bother?"

"Are you trying to irritate me? I bother because it is knowledge. I bother because I am curious and I want to know. Why did you come here?"

"Just for a little general conversation about Grassy Bay."

"I have no time for general conversations."

"If I'm going to sneak any conservationist propaganda into the paper, which means running contrary to policy, I ought to have a little solid stuff to play with, don't you think?"

"Will facts have anything to do with what will happen?"

"A lot of people would like to think so."

She stared at him for a moment. "I can give you fifteen minutes. We will sit on the porch. I've been on my feet since six o'clock this morning."

He followed her to the porch of the house. She sat in a wicker chair and stared at him for a moment. "To start with a general statement, filling the bay would be a criminal act. It will take away forever something which cannot be replaced or restored. Depth, temperature, tide flow, composition of the bottom, all combine to make this bay unique. We have shallow-water species here which are not found anywhere else along this coast."

"I have to argue the other side of it, Mrs. Rowell, not because I believe it, but just to present the usual arguments on the other side. Isn't this uniqueness important only to a few marine biologists?"

"It is important to the sum total of human knowledge. We know painfully little about the world we live in. This is a living laboratory. Each new environmental fact is important to mankind, no matter how trivial it might seem to a banker or a newspaper reporter. You are where you are *because of* science, not in spite of it. A star and a snail are of equal importance."

"But when snails get in the way of man, they get eliminated. Hasn't it always been that way?"

"Always?" She stared at him incredulously. "For a million years, Mr. Wing, man shared this planet with other living things. The ecology was in balance. Now we are in a very short time of natural history when we have a plague of men."

"A plague?"

"I watch the cycles in the bay. For a few years everything will be favorable for certain species. It will become very numerous. It will dwindle the numbers of the other animals who share the same space, eat the same food. Then there will be too many of them. The climatic factors will change. The huge numbers will be reduced. The other species will come back. In this split second of time in which we are living, things have been too favorable for man. With science he has suppressed too many natural enemies. He is too numerous. He is poisoning the air and waters of the earth. He is breeding beyond reason. He is devouring the earth and the other creatures thereon. But it will come to an end, of course. Man has a longer cycle than do the small creatures. Geometric growth is insupportable. During this growth cycle it is the business of thinking people to protect and conserve the other forms of life, so when the cycle is reversed, the ecology will not be too badly distorted. A hundred generations from now, that bay might be supplying food for a mainland village just as it did thirty generations ago."

"That's a point of view so . . . so broad it takes my breath away."

"It's a scientific point of view, Mr. Wing."

"That would mean you anticipate a defeat of . . . civilization, of everything we stand for?"

"My dear Mr. Wing, the only victory is existence, and the only defeat is extermination. When a species cannot survive, it is defeated. We must keep mankind from making the planet unsuitable for existence without technology. In the criminal campaign against fire ants in this country, the poisoners have slain an estimated five thousand tons of small birds. *Tons*, Mr. Wing. Thirty to forty million in specific areas. Believe me, I am not snuffling over what happened to the dear, dear little songbirds. This is not a situation where sentimentality is applicable. This was nonselective elimination, taking the healthy and sick, the predators and sapsuckers, destroying not only that generation but all possible subsequent ones from that conglomerate of basic strains. It is a thoughtless ecological abomination, Mr. Wing.

It is like rubbing out one factor in a vastly complex equation. Due to the interrelationship of bird life, insect life and plant fertilization, the known characteristics of that area will change. To what? We do not know. We only know it will be different. I recognize a deity of interrelationships, of checks and balances and dependencies. Acts such as this are like spitting in the face of God. It is a dangerous temerity, Mr. Wing. It is, in its essence, stupidity, nonknowing, the most precarious condition of man. Filling this bay is a part of the same pattern of throwing away everything you do not understand."

"I can see that you have some very . . . strong opinions."

"I concern myself with facts, not opinions."

"You seem to be able to get some very noted scientists to come down here and speak out in favor of leaving the bay alone."

She shrugged. "They understand these things. I conduct a large correspondence. I help field crews when I can. They give me little research tasks. There is a little money sometimes. It helps."

"Where did you get your training, Mrs. Rowell?"

"I read. I study. I work. I think. I observe."

"You call yourself a layman. I assume that means you have no formal training in these fields of knowledge."

"That is the definition of the term, is it not?"

"That bothers me a little, how a layman can acquire such an objective viewpoint. Maybe some of your basic premises are wrong. How could you be able to tell?"

Her thick brown face turned pale, particularly around the mouth. "You are insolent, Mr. Wing. You should have more respect!"

"For what? Because you dabble in science?"

"Dabble! I had my doctorate before you . . ."

"You have a degree?"

Her agitation disappeared quickly. "Forgive me. It is just a manner of speaking. I have awarded myself various degrees, as a game, a joke."

"I see. I've often wondered about that slight accent you have, Mrs. Rowell."

"I have given you three minutes more than I promised. Please telephone me the next time to find out if I am busy."

"But you are always busy, aren't you?"

"Extremely."

She glanced back to the shed and disappeared into it without a backward glance or word of parting. He got into the car and headed thoughtfully back toward the city. There was something invincibly professioral about Mrs. Doris Rowell, something of the attitude of the professional lecturer, plus the austere philosophy of the trained scientist. He had heard no gossip about her, no rumors. She was thought of as merely a very strange and rather difficult woman. For the first time he had begun to wonder where she had come from.

When he had done a series of features on Palm County history, one of his more reliable sources for the Sandy Key area had been Aunt Middy Britt. She lived with one of her sons, a man of sixty, next door to the old Britt fishhouse on the mainland just below the Hoyt Marina. It was still the finest place in the area to buy smoked mullet.

Aunt Middy was dozing in her rocking chair on the shady old screened porch. He looked through the screen at her and coughed. Her eyes opened quickly and she began to rock. "Blessed Jesus, I tole you every last thing I know, and some that I didn't. But come in anyway, Jimmy, and set. Pretty sunset coming acrosst the bay now, isn't it?"

He sat with her and talked for a little while and finally said, "What about that Mrs. Doris Rowell, Aunt Middy?"

"Oh, her in the Faskett place way down the key? It set empty eight year 'fore she bought it. No history in her, boy. She's a come-lately. Nineteen and forty it was. These sorry teeth are getting loose on me again."

"Where did she come from?"

"Someplace north, where they all come from. Way it looks around here, it must be getting mighty empty up there. I wouldn't have no idea what special place it was she come from."

"Didn't people wonder about her when she first came down, a woman all alone?"

"Guess they did. Let me take myself back now. She wasn't too bad of a looking woman when she came down. There was talk she was a widow woman. Wasn't friendly. Nobody seen much of her the first year. Stayed in that house. Must have spent her time eating. Every time you'd see her, she was bigger. End of a year she was the size of a house. Then she was busying herself with plants and bugs and fishes, and the first hell she started to raise was on account of the size mesh in the nets around here, and she's been raising hell about all that kind of stuff ever since."

"But you've no idea why she came here, or what she used to do?"

"Jimmy, it's hard to keep up any interest in somebody strictly minds her own business most of the time. Smart woman, I guess. When the snooks got sick in the creeks that time, all rusty red around the gills and hundreds of big ones dying, she was the one traced it down. The Florida State folks took the credit, but Miz Rowell was the one actual found out. Forty-six, it was, back when snooks was a good money fish before the damn fools named it a game fish."

"Would anybody know any more about her than you do?"

"There's people know more about everything in the world than I do. I kept telling you that when you were writing up all the old settlers. Let me think, now. There was somebody around here knowed her before she came down. Or knew about her or something. Used to go visit with her, I think. Now who was that? Memory's as loose as my sorry teeth, boy. Hmmm. Wait now! Ernie Willihan, it was. He was fresh out of college, teaching in the high school. Ernie would be in his forties now. Aida Willihan's boy. She's dead now, God rest her sweet soul. She raised that boy singlehanded, and did her best by him. Sent him to school way up north someplace, Minnesota, I think it was. Of course he got a scholarship and he worked too, but Aida had to do a lot of scratching, then didn't live long enough to see him hardly started in life. Never saw a grandchild. And a wicked old woman like me gets to see a full dozen of her grandchildren's children so far and'll probably see more. You must know Ernie Willihan, Jimmy."

"I remember him all right. Where'd he go?"

"Oh, he's doing just fine. He got out of teaching, and he's up in St. Pete in some kind of scientific company he's a partner in. He was a science teacher in the high school. Now, if a person had to find out more about Miz Rowell, I guess that would be where he'd have to go. Why you so interested in her, boy?"

"Oh, Borklund wants to run a series of features on Palm County characters. He made up a list. I'm starting with the tough ones. She won't talk about herself. You're on the list too."

"Who else is on it?"

"You just wait and read the paper."

"Maybe she won't talk because she's hiding something."

"If I find that out, I'll have to take her off the list."

"Look how red that sun is going down, will you? Maybe we'll get to make a wish."

"You mean a flash of green? That's tourist talk, Aunt Middy."

"I seen it once, boy."

"You what?"

"Now, don't look at me like that. I'm telling you a true thing, boy. I'll even tell you the year. Eighteen and ninety-

eight, and I was a twenty-one-year-old girl, feeling older than
I do right this minute. My daddy brought us kids on down
to this piece of wild coast when I was ten. We were Foleys,
you know, and that's how the crick got named. We put up
the homestead on a knoll just a quarter mile south of where
we're setting. But I told you all that before, how I lost a
brother to the fever and a sister to a cottonmouth snake. So
I was twenty-one, married since fifteen to Josh Britt, and he's
dead now since nineteen and twenty-two, May ninth, hard to
believe it's so long. It was an August evening, and we were
in the fever time again, when folks died. I had only two
young then. I'd had three and lost the first to fever the
year before. There wasn't fifty of us in the whole settlement.
Josh's brother was down sick, and he was the one worked the
boat with Josh. I had to leave my two with my sister and
help Josh on the boat. We were food-fishing that day. My
two were both fevered, and I was sick in my heart with
worry, wondering if I was put on earth just to carry my
young and watch them burn with the fever and die. I was
two month along with my fourth, and I did a man's work that
day, helping pole that heavy old skiff and help Josh work the
net until my back was broke in half and my hands like raw
meat. We were poling back along the shore, coming home
with less fish than was needed, and we could see the sun
going down red like that, right out through Turk's Pass. I
was as low down in my spirits as a woman can get, and the
night bugs were beginning to gather like a cloud around us.
We rested from poling to brush away the bugs, and we
watched that last crumb of sun go, and the whole west sky lit
up with terrible great sheets of the brightest green you ever
could see. 'Make a wish!' Josh yelled at me from the stern
of the skiff. I wished, all right. There couldn't ever be
enough green for the wishes I had, boy. It didn't last over
ten or fifteen seconds. It was dark when we moored the skiff.
The fever had eased for my young ones. Life worked better
for me from then on, somehow. I raised six young out of
twelve, four still living, and that was better than most in
that time and place. I've seen children die and men killed
and women broke, but I never got so low again in all my
life as that one day on the net. So don't say it's tourist
talk, Jimmy. I prayed to God my whole life, and in fair-
ness I got to credit Him with doing good by me. But a flash
of green is something you see. We didn't see one tonight.
You act like you need one, Jimmy."

"What do you mean?"

"You don't set easy. You set like you got a knotted belly.
You're a man thinking of yourself too much and not liking it

much. I had one son like that. He lived a mean small life because he wouldn't do what I told him."

"What did you tell him, Aunt Middy?"

"I kept telling him until he was past forty to go find himself a healthy young girl and get as many young off her as she was able to bring into the world."

"I'm married."

"To what? A sorry piece of flesh that'll never know you again in this world, that they keep breathing just to prove they can do it when it would be God's mercy to let her go. Any lawyer would know what to do about crossing that kind of marriage off the legal books. But it pleasures you more to go around acting tragical."

He shook his head. "How can you sit on this porch and know everything about everybody?"

"People stop by and set and talk about things. You want a good young wife? You couldn't get her right off, but in six months she'd be ready. Judy Barnsong, down to Everset, widow of Claude that just got hisself killed without a dime of insurance money. She's twenty-three and got three young, bright as buttons. She's pretty and healthy and even-tempered, and built good for having babies. She's a good cook and she keeps a clean house. She's got three years of high school, and she'd make you a proud wife, if you got sense enough to go after her."

"Aunt Middy, you are an astonishing woman."

"There's been fine marriages arranged right here on this porch. You think about Judy Barnsong. You go sneak a look at her. She's a worker and she'll keep her looks. A ready-made family with more to come will keep you out of devilment."

"What do you mean?"

"A man snaps at an old lady that way over a little thing like I said has got a bad conscience. You doing something you shouldn't be doing, boy?"

"I drink and smoke and stay out late."

"Never knew a whole man who didn't. It's in the breed."

He stood up to go and said, "What do you think about them filling up the bay?"

"I'm eighty-four years old, and I've been watching the bay of an evening for seventy-four years. I'm not tired of looking at it. I just don't know how I'll be at looking at houses. I've got the feeling they won't hold my interest."

He went down off the porch, walking slowly to his car. A bay boat was at the old fishhouse dock, and two men were shoveling mullet into hampers to carry them up to the fishhouse scales. The fish seemed to catch the silvery dusk light and gleam more brightly than anything else in the scene. The old coquina-rock smokehouse was in operation, and there was a drift of burning oak in the evening air, flavored with the slight pungency of the barbecue sauce which had been rubbed into the white meat of the hanging fish. Somewhere nearby a girl laughed and a saw whined through a board.

Blessings on you, Mrs. Judy Barnsong, he thought. On your tidy house and fertile hips. I saw a little bit of what that marine engine did to your Claude when it slid forward into the front seat of the panel truck, and it was not anything I cared to look more closely at. But it left the face unimpaired, so you may safely have a viewing of the body. You'll never know how a dry and dreary man considered you almost seriously for half of one moment. Perhaps you would have said yes quite readily, because you sound like a person who would sense the kind of need I have. But the lust is for a more complex widow, and it is a little past the time when I could have escaped gently into you, into your tidy house, amid your busy button-bright children, to mist your memories of Claude and cushion my awareness of many dark things.

As he drove slowly toward town he remembered the sailor. Gloria had been missing for five days. They'd found her at that motel in Clewiston. They stopped the sailor as he was walking back there with a sack of hamburgs and a bottle of bourbon. The three of them had talked to the sailor out under the bright driveway lights. He was young, and at first he was defiant. He did not know how to handle being confronted by a deputy, a doctor and a husband. He thought it was some kind of a raid.

"Listen," he said, "all I did was I picked the broad up in Palm City. Okay? I was bumming to Montgomery, Alabama. I'm stationed in Key West and I got ten days. She has a car, this broad, and I changed my mind about going home. Okay?"

When he began to comprehend what they were telling him, the surliness and the defiance disappeared and he began to look younger, earnest and alarmed. "You mean she's nuts? You telling me she's a crazy? Honest to God, how would I know that? She doesn't talk much. She laughs a lot. We've been drinking some. Mostly, I never seen anything like it, all she wants to do is scr . . . Geez, I'm sorry, sir. You being her husband, I shouldn't say stuff like that. But how the hell would I know she was a nut?"

They told the boy what they wanted him to do. He agreed to get out of the way until they'd taken her away. He turned over the key. They said they would leave it unlocked, and he could come back for his gear after she was gone.

He went in with the doctor. She was asleep. A lamp was burning on the bedside table. Her face was puffy. She woke when he touched her shoulder. She looked at him without surprise and sat up and looked at the doctor. "Hello, Jimmy," she said. "Hello, Dr. Sloan."

"Better get dressed, honey. We're taking you home."

"Sure," she said, showing neither gladness nor regret, only a childlike obedience. She dressed quickly, used the sailor's comb on her hair, made up her mouth and came out to the car and they took her home.

That was back in the days when the doctors had thought it was psychological, when they were trying, with drugs and patience and depth analysis, to reach down into her darknesses and find the cause of this destructive behavior. Those were the days when they questioned him at great length, dredging up every detail of the sexual relationship between them, finding nothing of significance. Most of the time, under treatment, she was as mild and dutiful as a child, but when they would reach her with an awareness of what she had done, she would be torn by grief and guilt.

Then it was Sloan who had made the significant discovery about her, detecting the deterioration of intelligence and memory, then proceeding to other tests and pinpointing the parallel decay of manual dexterity. (She said her fingers felt thick.) They looked eagerly for the expected tumor and found none. Elmo helped get her into the special setup at Oklawaha.

"It would be God's mercy to let her go," Aunt Middy had said.

But she was gone. She was beyond torment. Dr. Freese at Oklawaha had explained the prognosis. "From her history we know there have been periods of progressive degeneration alternating with periods of stasis. She is in a period of stasis now, and if there are no other physical complications she might live a long time. The next period of degeneration, if we have one, could easily affect the motor centers of the brain, and death would follow, very much like the sort of death which occurs when the motor centers are gravely depressed through, say, the use of a heavy dosage of barbiturates."

"Why was the first symptom the sex thing, Doctor? I didn't know she was sick. I'm ashamed of what I did to her, the way I acted toward her when that started."

Freese had turned back to the first pages in the file. "But the sexual incontinence was not the first symptom, Mr.

Wing. It was the first to come forcibly to your attention. There was a parallel deterioration in her eating habits, her personal cleanliness, her attire, her speech. To attempt layman terms in this thing, you thought she was becoming crude and sluttish out of choice. Actually it was a deterioration of the ability to make choices. She was slowly retrogressing to an animal level of awareness. Animals, my dear fellow, have no table manners and no codes of morality. They sleep when they are sleepy, eat when they are hungry and copulate when there is an opportunity so to do. Many primitive peoples are on this level of existence too. Don't blame yourself for your inability to detect a condition which baffled several competent professionals for a relatively long period of time. Actually, Sloan caught the scent when he began to realize how closely her condition resembled that which we can expect after a successful prefrontal lobotomy, if that procedure can ever logically be called a success. In her case, of course, it has progressed far beyond that aspect."

When he arrived at the paper he was alarmed to see that Brian Haas was not in the newsroom. But they said he had gone down the hall for a moment. Borklund had left, saying he would be back about ten-thirty. Haas looked gray and his eyes were dull, but he had kept up with the duties assigned him. Jimmy Wing stepped into the situation and halved Brian's work load, giving the scarred man a chance to breathe between tasks.

"It's like housework," Brian said dolefully. "You try to keep it cleaned up, but all the muddy kids keep galloping through."

"And somebody keeps shaking the house."

"Every man does the work of three, and Ben Killian seeks tax shelters. What about this grapefruit release?"

Jimmy scanned it. "Pure flack, but cute. Let's run it."

"This is a magazine? A throwaway sheet?"

"Don't get the impression it's a newspaper. They don't have those any more. This is a write-cute outlet for wire services and syndicates, man. Fellow wants the news, he watches his TV and reads *Time*. If he wants think pieces, he buys *Playboy*."

"Grapefruit is *good* for you," Brian Haas said.

"Want to go eat?"

"I might not come back."

At a little after ten most of Monday's jigsaw was complete. The other departments were finished and gone. Pages one and two were the only ones still loose, with details on a TWA crash in Illinois still to come in, with fillers to piece it out if not enough came over the wire. And the page-one coverage of a meeting in Berlin could be readily truncated to insert a late box if anything came in worth it, wire or local. The press crew had come on, dour skeptical men who believed only in the rich full life of a tight union, despised the printed word and everybody who had anything to do with any other aspect of the business aside from feeding and operating the automatic presses.

Jimmy went to Vera's and brought back a sandwich and coffee for Haas. Haas said, "I just called Nan. First chance I had. To tell her I think I'll make it."

"It's a joke, isn't it?" Jimmy said.

Brian looked at him, his expression suddenly cautious. "What does that mean?"

"It's so jolly and boyish. Like in fraternities. Boy, was I ever hung! But I hit the biology exam for a C."

"It seems like that to you?"

"Sometimes, Bri. Sometimes."

"Then why try to help, you superior son of a bitch? So you can feel like an adult?"

"I almost never feel like an adult. I have my own little capsule dramas. Mine just aren't quite as obvious."

Haas picked up a pencil and put it down. He picked it up again and broke it, studied the pieces and dropped them into the wastebasket.

"You waited a long long time to give it to me, Jimmy."

"What am I giving you?"

"I don't know. I guess I don't want to know too much about it. With you, I had to make a guess about what was underneath. Everybody does, with you. There aren't many clues, you know. I made some bad guesses, maybe. You better get away from me for a while."

"More drama?"

"Not for me, Jimmy. I lost the drama way back. These days I adjust. To the job, to Nan, to you. That's all. Now I got to make a new adjustment to you, and it's easier if you stay away for a while. Just say I'm immune to drama, but not to loss."

"What have you lost?"

Haas smiled. "An imaginary something, boy. Something I invented. Necessity is the mother of invention? Thanks for getting me over the hump."

"See you around," Jimmy said and walked out. He had just gotten into his car when he saw Borklund drive into the parking lot. He did not turn his lights on, because Borklund solved all awkwardness of salutation by giving you something to do.

He sat in his car, feeling naughty. It was the only word which seemed to fit. A childhood word, involved with spanking and tears.

"Listen, Bri. I just had to take a hack at the nearest thing, and I'm sorry it was you. . . ."

"Bri, I don't feel that way about it at all. I mean I think you're handling it as well as you can, and I just . . ."

"Bri, I haven't got this much left that I can afford to lose . . ."

Friendships, like marriages, he thought, are dependent on avoiding the unforgivable. Sometimes the unforgivable is the way something is said, rather than the words. He told himself he would have gone back in, if Borklund hadn't arrived just then. He told himself that if he could have gone back in, he could have made things right again. So, in an obscure way, the blame could be divided between Borklund and Haas. Besides, Haas took it all wrong. It wasn't meant the way he took it. In fact, he seemed very damned eager to take it wrong. That's the way it goes. . You sprain a gut for a friend, and it just makes him anxious to resent you. Do a favor and make an enemy. What did Brian want? An apology, because he's too sensitive? What kind of a friendship is it, when you've got to watch every word you say? What's this crap about a loss? Is that all the credit he gives me?

Jimmy Wing started the car, jammed it into gear, and yelped the tires as he swerved toward the parking-lot exit.

14

THE CABLE BANK AND TRUST COMPANY had occupied the new building in 1957. Prior to that move, it had been on the corner of Center Street and Columbia Street, four blocks east of the causeway approach to City Bridge. An antique and idiotic law in Florida prohibits the establishment of branch banks. The new structure was on Center Street, a mile east of the old center of the city. It was an oblong of buff stone, aluminum and glass, set back twenty feet from the sidewalk, framed in grass and flowers. On one side of the building was the large parking area. On the other side were the drive-in windows.

Kat Hubble's desk was on the central floor area thirty feet inside the front entrance, facing it at a slight angle so that she could also see over into the bull-pen area where the minor executive desks were arranged in a spacious geometry.

Jimmy Wing had bird-dogged the job for her. He had learned that Mrs. Whindler, who had held it previously, had suddenly astonished herself and her husband by becoming pregnant after thirteen barren years of marriage. Jimmy had made Kat go directly to Martin Cable. Martin had been delighted to offer Kat the position. It had not occurred to him that his widowed neighbor would have to work.

The sign on her desk—lacy brass against white formica—said Information. But the job was considerably more complex than merely sitting there answering questions. She was expected to remember names and faces and greet the maximum possible number of customers by name. She was available for all manner of small miscellaneous errands inside the bank and in the neighborhood. She was assigned typing chores by departments which were temporarily overloaded.

It had been very difficult for her in the beginning. Her typing was rusty, her memory uncertain, and the clerical people assumed she was a spy for Martin Cable. But after three months she had learned the rhythms of her job and had gained the liking and the confidence of all the other employees. She worked from nine until three, five days a week. For the last hour and a half of each working day, the outside doors were locked, and the reception and information part of her day was over.

She had learned to like the special flavor and atmosphere of the main floor of the bank. There was a faint blue-green tint to the huge areas of glass, and as further protection against sun glare, there were outside false walls of pierced concrete. The patterned and tinted sunlight came into the coolness, into the spacious area where recorded music was just barely loud enough to cover the whir and chitter of the electric office equipment. Her desk area, with the aluminum railing around it, had become a pleasant and familiar place. She knew the jokes and the kidding and the personal troubles of the people with whom she worked.

On Monday morning, the tenth of July, she was troubled as she drove to work. The children had gone to the Sinnats. In her dismay at Dial's resignation from the committee, she had overlooked a more homely problem. If Dial and Claire went away, taking Esperanza and the twins, the pleasant summer arrangement would be no longer possible. Natalie could not be expected to hang around and watch the Hubble children. Floss could not be saddled with that responsibility. Any alternate arrangement would cost money, and she was operating on a very narrow margin as it was. During the school year, banking hours and school hours were so close to identical that the children were no problem.

At a few minutes after nine, Dennie McGowan, the elderly guard, moved over to her desk and said, "It's a blue Monday surely when even the redhead can't smile."

"Does it show that much, darn it?"

"What can the McGowan do for the lady?"

"Nothing, thanks, Dennie. It's just sort of a sitter problem. I have to work something out."

There was a surprising amount of activity for a Monday morning in the summertime, and she had no time to think about her problem until a little after ten when Claire phoned her.

"I hear that Nat told you the sorry news last night, dear."

"Yes, she said you were going . . ."

"He's in one of his states. Nobody can do anything with him when he's like this. He's in town now, churning around about passports and travel bureaus. He'll probably be in for a letter of credit or whatever he does when we go anyplace. We had one real howling match this morning, Kat, and I won one small concession. I love my children, but inasmuch as I'm being dragged away against my will, I absolutely refused to be a traveling den mother, with or without Esperanza. So my burdens will be staying here, and Nat will stay at the house, and your lambs will be as welcome here

as ever. I thought you'd want to know that. I knew you
must be worrying about it."

"I was worrying. It's so nice of you to let me know."

"Right now I'd be packing if the damn man would let me
know where to pack for."

"Claire, he's coming through the door right now."

"Honey, you nail him and tell him to call his poor confused wife and tell her where she's being taken."

Dial Sinnat gave Kat an absent-minded nod and walked by
her desk, heading back toward the vice-president compound.
Though she kept looking for him to come back, he came
up to her unobserved, startling her.

"Can you take a break?"

She glanced at the clock, regretfully discarding her hope of
taking her break with Jimmy Wing. One of the girls filled in
for her. She walked across Center Street with Di and had
coffee in a small booth at the rear of the new drugstore.

Dial Sinnat looked uncomfortable and slightly defiant.
"I guess I can assume Tom phoned you."

"Yes."

"And Nat saved a lot of explanations, didn't she? Sorry she
had to inflict it on you."

"I was glad she came to me with it, Di."

"I told you those people were going to play rough."

"Is this any answer, though, really? Going away?"

"It's my answer. I want it known, beyond any possibility of
misunderstanding, that I'm all the way out of the picture."

"And I suppose it makes it easier for you."

"That's a low blow, but I guess I left myself open. Yes, it
will make it easier. I thought of sending Nat back to her
mother and leaving it up to the opposition to try something
else. But I'm afraid they would, and I'm afraid it would
work. They'll leave Natalie alone when they find out I've left."

"Who phoned you?"

"Two of them talked to me, and I haven't the slightest
idea who either of them were. The first one was very suave
and indirect. The second one lost patience, I guess. He
took the phone. He sounded like a mean ignorant man. He
was very direct. He had a very dirty mouth." Dial leaned
forward and dropped his voice slightly. "I didn't tell my
daughter this. And I don't want you to tell her. I'm telling
you because . . . I don't want you to have too bad an opinion
of me, Kat. I want you to stand up for me, with the others,
but without telling them what I'm going to tell you. What do
you know about the Army of the Lord?"

She was startled. "Just what everybody knows, I guess.
It's sort of a crackpot sect down in the southern part of the

county, with a sort of a church near Wister. And a strange man who seems to run it."

"The so-called Reverend Darcy Harkness Coombs. Yes." His voice was strange. "It's quite a militant little group, Kat. They burn books. They preach on street corners. And they have . . . punished some evildoers."

"Like that woman last year?"

"And some other women you didn't hear about, and some drunks and some thieves. I can tell you almost the exact words the second man used. I've been hearing them ever since. 'If'n you don't unjoin that red Communist committee, Sinnat, we'll one dark night snatch that black-hair daughter of yourn out from that whore automobile an' run her off into the piny woods, strip her down, knot her up to a tree and flog the pretty hide off'n her back so as she'll realize how decent folks treats loose women and fornicators.' "

"But . . . that's horrible! They wouldn't!"

"They've done it to some other people, Katherine. That man sounded as if he'd enjoy it. You see, I can't take a chance on it being a bluff."

"She shouldn't stay here!"

"She won't consider leaving. I can't force her. If I told her what they told me, there'd be no chance of her leaving. You know the spirit she has. And she's too young to understand what a thing like that can do to any sensitive human being. And they could probably get away with it. There's been no identification made the other times. He said she would be in absolutely no danger if I quit Save Our Bays, so I'm quitting as obviously and completely as I can. I couldn't make her promise to stay away from whoever she's having the affair with, but I have the hunch that if she doesn't, she'll at least be a lot more cunning about it. How did she get into such an idiotic thing?"

"Di, I don't think it's . . . anything she's ashamed of."

"Obviously," he said with a bitter smile. "She's of the most vulnerable breed in the world—an idealist. Somebody sold her some good reasons. I respect her too much to accuse her of having cheap motives. But she can get into a cheap situation from the best of motives, even as you and I, Katherine. And she wouldn't be stable enough to take a public flogging. Who would? God knows what it would do to her."

"Have you told Claire all this?"

"Of course not."

"Are you being fair to her?"

"I am going to tell her the whole thing as soon as we are en route, Kat, when she can't try to do anything about it. She's got more fight than is good for her. She acts first and thinks later. We're getting on a ship late tomorrow afternoon at Port Everglades, en route to Lisbon. Tomorrow evening, when she can't turn the ship around, I'll tell her. By the time we get to Lisbon she should be settled down. Am I keeping you here too long? There's one other thing I want to say. I told you all this for two reasons. I guess you can guess the second one."

She stared at him blankly, then with a growing comprehension and horror. "Oh, no, Dial! They couldn't do that to . . ."

"Those people down there are blinded by their own righteousness, Katherine. But they are not going to go out and select a victim on the basis of rumor. Coombs is a fanatic, but I don't think he'd turn his army loose on anybody without proof which satisfied him. That's why they've been able to get away with these floggings. In the case of Natalie, they had the proof. I checked it with her. I'm saying that you and Jackie Halley should avoid . . . I don't know how to say this . . . the appearance of evil. You shouldn't, either of you, do anything which could be interpreted the wrong way. I say this with complete seriousness, Kat. Somebody with a lot to gain out of that bay fill is out to smash the committee completely. They want to take the heart out of everybody in any position to publicly oppose the bay fill. That's the pattern. That's what the rest of you are up against. Believe me, they've taken the heart out of me."

"I . . . I remember what that girl said. There were five of them, dressed in black, wearing black hoods. All they said was 'Repent, repent.' They were still trying to find out who the men were when she moved away. She was a nurse, wasn't she?"

"Having an affair with a married doctor. That was the rumor."

"I have to get back. I'm late now."

"Do you understand?"

"Of course I do, Di."

"Natalie has money of her own. She'd have just moved out of my house. She wouldn't leave, probably because of the man. I'm trying to keep myself from being the outraged father. I don't want to make moral judgments. I've lived in a lot of glass houses. If she'd had more security, maybe she wouldn't be in this mess now. I didn't give it to her. Maybe I could have. Maybe I was too lazy, emotionally. Katherine, keep an eye on her. She respects you."

"I'm fond of her."

She was late getting back to her desk. When she had a chance she asked McGowan if Jimmy Wing had looked in.

"Not today. I would have seen him. And he's not good enough for you anyway."

"It's not like that, Dennie. Really. It's not like that at all."

He winked at her. "Maybe not for you, sweetheart. But I say it is like that for him."

At quarter of twelve Burton Lesser and Leroy Shannard came in. Swarthy little Doctor Felix Aigan was with them. The three men were laughing at something as they came in. Doc and Leroy were in sports shirts. Burt wore a necktie and a linen jacket, and looked sweaty. This is three-fifths of the opposition, she thought. Ordinary men in a small southern city on a hot day. There is nothing menacing about them, nothing which could be involved in spying on a young girl or threatening her with flogging by hooded men. She felt the smile of welcome on her mouth.

"Gentlemen?" she said briskly.

"Katherine, dear, check Mr. Martin for us, will you?" Burt Lesser asked.

She picked up her inside phone and punched the button for Martin Cable's secretary. "Helen? Mr. Lesser, Mr. Shannard and Doctor Aigan are here."

"We're early, Mrs. Hubble," Doc Aigan said.

"Send them right on back," Helen said.

Katherine hung up and smiled and gave them the message. Leroy said, "Got yourself a burn, Miz Katherine."

"I'll never learn," she said ruefully.

Doc Aigan said, "I'll have my girl drop off a sample of stuff for you to try, honey. Supposed to make what little melanin you got in your skin do a better job for you. A good house puts it out so it ought to be okay. Matter of fact, I'd like a report on how it works for you."

"Thanks, Doctor. If it works on me, it'll work for anybody. I can get blistered looking at a colored photograph of a sunset."

Aigan hurried along on his short legs, his sandals slapping the terrazzo, catching up with Burt Lesser and Leroy. She turned and watched the three of them. Doc was an affable little man. Burt was a neighbor. Leroy Shannard had been Van's attorney, and he had been very understanding and helpful when he had handled Van's estate. Van had designed Doc's home. All three men had been at Van's funeral.

"Miss?" a voice was saying. "Miss?"

She turned and saw a man standing in front of her desk. "I'm so sorry," she said.

"All I want is to rent a box like to put something important in, Miss."

"You'll want to talk to Mrs. Harper," she said. "The lady with the white hair behind that counter over there to your right, sir."

As she watched Mrs. Harper greet the man and give him an application form, she thought, All I want is to rent a box like to hide in for a while. I don't want to think about the kind of a world where men like Aigan and Shannard and Lesser *could* know something about what is happening to Dial Sinnat, and approve of it.

When it was time to go to lunch and Jimmy had not yet appeared, she waited five minutes into her short time allowed and then went back across the street, hoping he would show up before she had to return to work.

15

"I REMEMBER YOU, Mr. Wing," Ernest Willihan said. "You interviewed me a long time ago when you were still in school, a reporter for a school paper. You reported the interview accurately and still managed to make me sound like an idiot. I predicted a newspaper career for you at that time. What brings you to St. Pete?"

Willihan was a brown and totally bald man in his forties. The tilt of his eyes and the baldness gave him a slight Oriental flavor. They talked in a small untidy office with a single large window overlooking a long concrete wharf owned by Stormer and Willihan—Marine Research and Development. Willihan's smile was inverted and his eyes were bright with amusement.

"Maybe I ought to do a feature on this setup, Mr. Willihan. What happens to public-school science teachers."

"You could get some of your material from your boss down there, Ben Killian. We've done some work for him. Tank tests on experimental hull designs. His little boat works there has done some fascinating things. It isn't commercial, of course. If you are interested in us, we wear two hats. We're an independent testing outfit for small boats, motors and boating devices. That's the bread and butter. Also, we are developing a few ideas of our own. That's feast or famine."

"What kind of ideas?"

"Right now we're fiddling with a sonar rig for small boats which can be set to give a warning buzz when the bottom shoals to within X feet of what you need to float the boat, thirty to forty feet off your bow. When the bugs are out of it, we hope to license it to somebody who can knock the unit price down below five hundred bucks."

"Sounds better than teaching."

"There's more money. There's no politics. But I miss the kids. I tell myself someday I'll go back into it. You hit me on a good day, Mr. Wing. Want a guided tour?"

"I'd like that, but I'll have to take a rain check on it. I came to ask you about something else. We're about to have a bay fill hassle down in Palm County."

"What do they want to fill now?"

188

"Grassy Bay again."

Willihan shook his head sadly. "Every place seems to have to make the same mistake, just as if it had never been made before. The fast buck. It's an illusion, Wing. Can't they come and see and understand what's happened to St. Petersburg Beach and Clearwater? Or what's happening to Bradenton and Sarasota? This whole coast used to be a shallow-water paradise. Spoiling it is so idiotic. A friend of mine made a very neat analogy about it. Once upon a time there was a mountain peak with a wonderful view, so that people came from all over to stand on top of the mountain and look out. The village at the foot of the mountain charged a dollar a head to all tourists. But so few of them could stand on top of the mountain at the same time, they leveled the top of the mountain to provide more room and increase the take. This seemed to work, so they kept enlarging the area on top of the mountain. Finally they had a place up there that would accommodate ten thousand people, but by then the mountain was only forty feet high, and suddenly everybody stopped coming to see the view. This convinced them people were tired of views, so in the name of Progress and a Tourist Economy, they turned the flattened mountain into a carnival area, and every night you could see the lights and hear the music for miles around. They still attracted customers, but it was the kind of people who like carnivals instead of the kind of people who like beauty."

"There's more people who like carnivals," Jimmy said.

"A fact the beauty-lovers find it hard to stomach."

"Anyhow, because of the pending battle, we want to be ready to run profiles of the key figures. I ran into some problems on one of them. She's always in the middle of our conservation battles. Some people told me you might be able to give me the background that she won't give. Doris Rowell."

Willihan frowned at the wall over Jimmy's head. He picked up a slide rule and began to toy with it. "As a newspaper man, Mr. Wing, I'd think you'd have come up against the fact that when people refuse to talk about themselves, there's generally a reason."

"As a newspaper man, Mr. Willihan, I resent historical blanks. I can't leave them alone. It's a compulsion."

"You better leave this one alone."

"I won't, of course. I'll keep digging. If you won't talk about her, it will just take a little more time and effort. And if it's anything discreditable, I might learn it from . . . a less sympathetic source than I think you are."

"If she's of value to the conservationists down there, Wing, and if you're opposed to the fill, you'd just hurt your own cause by printing something which happened a long time ago."

"It's going to be a rough fight down there. If somebody else comes up with whatever it is you won't tell me, I ought to be in a position to make it look better than they want it to look. She's on the committee opposing the fill. Everybody on that committee is going to be under fire."

Willihan swiveled his chair and looked out at the wharf. "It happened a long time ago and it seemed a lot more important then than it does now. I guess it would still seem important to a lot of people, though. She committed the ultimate academic sin, Wing, and was caught in the act and was thrown out of a world where she probably belonged. I might as well tell you about it. If you've traced it to me, you could discover the rest of it. It happened in 1939. I was a senior at Minnesota Polytech. She was on the faculty. She was married to Doctor Harris Rowell, but she used her maiden name for professional purposes. Dr. Doris Hegasohn. She's Swedish. She'd done her undergraduate work at Stockholm, and gotten her master's and doctor's at Polytech. She and Rowell were both instructors on fellowships when they married. She was a damned interesting-looking woman, very dynamic and impatient and intellectually merciless. Rowell was a very frail, rather unearthly man, a brilliant scholar. Doris was a competent translator. By 1939 Rowell had been an invalid for four or five years. She was teaching classes, doing research, writing papers and taking care of her husband. Maybe it was too much of a strain. Maybe she was too ambitious. She was making a name for herself and fighting for a full professorship, which would have eased some of the financial strain on them. Rowell needed special treatment beyond what they could afford. That year a man from Budapest was a guest lecturer. One of his associates was engaged in the same area of research as Doris was. The papers he had published were not available in English. Hungarian was one of the languages in which she was reasonably competent as a translator of scientific documents. Once the guest lecturer got on the trail of what had happened, a special committee was appointed to investigate. They found out she had taken a really enormous amount of the Hungarian's findings and published them as her own. They backtracked and found a long cribbed section in her doctoral thesis. By the time they were ready for a confrontation, Rowell was dying. There was a flurry in the newspapers.

They rescinded her two graduate degrees, fired her out of the profession. It is the final crime in learned circles, stealing a man's work and publishing it as your own. She made no attempt to defend herself. She immediately became a pariah. No one in university circles would care to have anything to do with the woman. Rowell died. There was insurance, and, I believe, a small income from her people. She 'retired' to Palm County. I saw her on the street and recognized her. It would have been strange if she had gone anywhere in the country and not have been recognized by one of us who were there at the time. It was one hell of a scandal, Wing. When I saw her she was becoming very fat, but I knew her."

"Could she have friends in academic circles, people who would know about what she did at Minnesota, and not have it make any difference?"

"No. It's a small, careful world. An insurance executive would not risk being friendly with a convicted arsonist. The relationship would be too open to misinterpretation. And there wasn't any two sides to the case. She was nailed. Also, I guess you'll have to admit she isn't the sort of person to inspire loyal friendship. She has all the personality of a snapping turtle. But she's got a fine mind. I used to go out there and talk to her. We got along. She was at ease with me because I knew what had happened to her, and nobody else in town did. She's made her own kind of adjustment, Wing. It would be very nice if she could be left alone."

"I can understand why she doesn't talk about the past."

"People still wonder about her. I was at a conference in Atlanta last year. When a biologist from Johns Hopkins heard where I went to school he asked me if I was there when they trapped the Hegasohn woman, and then he wondered out loud what had become of her. I didn't tell him. You could make a story of it, Wing. It would be, in a different sense, like those reviews of famous crimes of the century. But it wouldn't be a decent thing to do."

"Thank you for being so cooperative, Mr. Willihan."

"Remember one thing, please. She's a clever woman. She's clever enough to have been able to fake her way back into the profession with a new identity. But she didn't. She accepted banishment. She made a moral decision to live with it. I have to respect that."

"She's been doing odd jobs for marine biology groups working in the area."

Willihan frowned. "They'd be upset to find out who has been helping them. Even though it might be a perfectly

straightforward relationship, if it came out it would cast
a shadow on whatever they're publishing. I know how ridiculous that sounds, Wing, but every profession has its own
stupidities. Research programs are conducted with the assistance of grants from foundations and institutions. Boards
of directors are too easily alarmed. They'd be dubious about
backing any further work on a project where Doris Hegasohn
had been involved, even if the only employment they gave
her was brewing tea for the field workers. I suppose they
think of her and use her as a trustworthy layman."

"I guess that's the relationship."

"Can you stay and have lunch with me?"

"Thanks, no. I have to be getting back."

Willihan smiled as he stood up and held his hand out.
"I don't know why I have to feel so protective about that
fat old harridan. I think she liked me. You usually like
the people who like you. And that, I suppose, is just one
of the general forms of stupidity."

Jimmy Wing went from the waterfront offices of Stormer
and Willihan to the St. Petersburg *Times* offices. He checked
the annual index for 1939, and then viewed the microfilm
projections of the pertinent dates. He jotted down the dates
and page numbers involved, and left an order with the
library girl for photocopies, paying in advance for reproduc-
tion and mailing charges.

As he drove south in the heat of midday, he found
himself remembering a flight down the coast in a private
airplane three years back. He often remembered it as he
drove the Tamiami Trail. Jimmy had been on the port side
of the four-passenger aircraft, directly behind the pilot. The
sun had been setting as they left Tampa International. The
pilot flew at five thousand feet about a mile offshore, following the contour of the coast. The great dark mass of
the silent land stretched off toward the east, toward an
invisible horizon. The Gulf was a silvery gray and the
land was blue-gray. Stretching all the way down the coast,
almost without interruption, was the raw garish night work
of man, the crawl of headlights, bouquets of neon, sugar-
cube motels, blue dots of lighted pools. When the trip was
almost over, just before the plane turned inland to land
at Palm County Airport, Jimmy Wing had seen it all in a
fanciful way which he had never been able to get out of
his mind. The land was some great fallen animal. And all
the night lights marked the long angry sore in its hide, a
noisome, festering wound, maggoty and moving, draining
blood and serum into the silent Gulf. Now Doris Hegasohn

Rowell had given him a name for it. The plague of man. The sore was spreading. The dark earth endured this mortal affliction. Dead bright junk circled the moon, orbited the planet, hundreds of bits of it. Every living vertebrate, from a newborn rhino to a white-muzzled chipmunk, carried radioactive material in its bone marrow. Men were digging burrows in the ground, hiding away food and water, waiting for the skies to scream, for the earth itself to shudder, die and begin to rot.

In all this, he thought, in all this which diminishes me, no act of mine, or of anyone else, has consequence. Morality is a self-conscious posture. Dedication is delusion, based on a fraudulent interpretation of fact, a wishful projection of our present velocity. The only valid role is that of observer. Soon we will all eat stones.

He turned into the parking lot at the bank just as Kat was walking toward her little car. The lot was almost empty. He touched the horn ring. She turned and stared, then came swiftly toward him, such a smiling welcome on her face his heart seemed to move higher in his chest.

She looked in the car window at him. "Golly, Jimmy, I've been saving up so many things to talk to you about, I know I'm going to forget half of them."

"How was yesterday? You have a very red nose."

"And my forehead is getting crusty, and I have ten billion little pinhead blisters on my back and shoulders. Yesterday was okay. It got bad a couple of times. When it did, I'd run into the water and swim as hard as I could as far as I could. So along with the blisters, I'm lame. Where were you today?"

"Working on that feature I told you about."

"Are you busy now?"

"Later would be better."

"I promised Jackie I'd do two hours on the phone as soon as I get home. Can you come out about six and have a drink and stay to dinner?"

"Sure. What's going on?"

"Dozens of things, most of them bad. I want to tell you all of it, not just bits and pieces."

He arrived at her house at a little after six. She was in shorts and a halter, her sore back and shoulders greased. "Excuse how I look," she said. "Clothes hurt. And excuse how I sound. I'm hoarse from arguing and arguing over the phone. Jackie and Ross are coming to dinner too, but they won't be here until after seven. Now, sit down and I'll get your drink and I'm going to talk you blind."

She told him about Dial Sinnat quitting. She told him somebody had gotten at Dial through Natalie. It surprised him that Elmo had been able to move so quickly and effectively. It puzzled him that it had worked at all. Kat gave no details about Natalie. She merely said, "The girl did something that could be made to look pretty awful."

For a few moments his mind wandered. He did not hear what she was saying. He realized she was looking at him expectantly.

"I know it's a lot to ask of you, Jimmy."

"Sorry, dear. I wasn't tracking. What are you asking me to do?"

"Find out who is being so ugly about all this! Somebody spied on Nat, Jimmy. And two men talked to Di on the phone and scared him right off the committee, and he didn't recognize the voices of either of them. You know everybody, Jimmy. If you could find out who is being so terribly rough, maybe we could do something about it. Couldn't you sort of ask around, in a quiet way?"

"But people know I was on your side last time, and they know it will be the same again. If I start asking questions, why should anybody answer me?"

She sat on a foot stool, glowering into her drink. "Buck Flake, Leroy Shannard, Doc Aigan, Bill Gormin, Burt Lesser. Jimmy, maybe one of them is in real bad financial condition. You could find that out, couldn't you? If a man was worried, he might do terrible things. I saw that Buckland Flake with a *very* spectacular girl."

"I suppose I can ask around."

She stared at him. "Well, don't be overcome with enthusiasm."

"I don't know exactly where to start, Kat. But . . . I'll see if I can figure out something."

"When are they going to petition for a change in the bulkhead line?"

"At the County Commission meeting tomorrow morning at ten o'clock."

"So soon!"

"It'll be an open battle from then on."

"Excuse me. I thought it had already started." She tilted her head and listened. "Here's Jackie and Ross."

Jackie came striding in first, gawky, flamboyant and slightly drunk, wearing a denim dress, carrying half a drink in a huge old-fashioned glass. "Unless you had a lot better luck than I did on the phone, Katty love, let's not talk about it, because I find it extremely distressing. Hello, Wing. What have you done for us lately? Excuse me, dear. You probably have some adorable ideas. Meager but adorable."

"She's been working on this since about quarter of six," Ross said. "She's a swinging thing tonight."

"Give my little husband a weak drink, somebody," Jackie said. "Leave him in shape to take me home over his shoulder. Honest to God, Kat, this Dial Sinnat thing floored me. After you called Tom from the bank this afternoon to tell him definitely no dice, he spread the bad word. I never heard Tom sound so low. So I phoned Dial. He'd just gotten home. The son of a gun thanked me for my interest in his personal decisions. He brushed me off like an expert. Then poor Wally Lime phoned me and we wept together, and then I started belting these lovely things. Are we mice or people? Are we a committee or a burial detail? I've got the general idea, kids. Somebody pressured Di. So let's us pressure some of their boys. Walk me to a bay filler, fellas. I'll lunge at his jugular. Bring me a big one. Like Flake, or a little one like Aigan. Makes no difference to Killer Halley tonight."

"Can't she fill a room, though?" Ross said with awe and pride.

Kat's children came home from the Sinnats. Kat filled their plates and said they could stay up until nine-thirty if they played quietly in Roy's room, and didn't spill any food in there. Jimmy guessed that Kat was serving the small buffet sooner than she had planned. Jackie needed food and coffee.

"The trouble with us," Jackie said as they were all eating, "we're too damn nice. Even you, Wing. Perfect little gennlemen. What have we got left? A couple army types, you and me, Kat, a darling art gallery type, little Wally—our Madison Avenue South—and who else? Oh. Fat Doris. You know, it comforted me having Di on the squad. I thought he was the one with *cojones*, but he turns out to be a capon."

"Down, Jackie!" Kat said firmly.

"What? What's the matter?"

"You don't know all the facts or all the reasons or how Di feels. Maybe you'd do the same thing. How can you tell?"

Jackie looked at her with one eyebrow tilted abruptly. "Sweet Katherine," she said. "Sweet, gentle, forgiving, understanding Katherine."

"Now, honey," Ross said.

"The thing," Jackie said, "is to see him in proper per-

spective. Okay? He could fool around with our little
project as long as it didn't cost him anything except time
and money." She turned her bright stare toward Jimmy.
"The wise old owl that doesn't say a word turned out to
be a pretty stupid bird."

"Am I supposed to say something significant?" he asked.

"You could give it a try."

"I said it last week when I was talking to Kat about
this. I said people were going to play rough."

"And so are we!" Jackie said, banging her plate down.

"Fight, team, fight," Ross said.

Jackie stood up and looked solemnly at her husband.
"Funny man," she said, and walked out of the house.

"Should you . . . go with her?" Katherine asked, worried.

"She's okay," Ross said. "Good groceries, Kat. Oh, she'll
hike around with steam coming out of her ears. She gets
sore. She works it off. She'll be back."

They finished eating. Jimmy helped Kat take the dishes
out to the kitchen. Jackie came back, as noisy as before,
with Burt Lesser in tow. "See what I got!" Jackie said. "A
hunk of the opposition. He was home alone, helpless and
apologetic."

Burt Lesser acted as though it was some sort of party
game, as if he were the permissive, good-humored trophy
in a scavenger hunt. He wore a pale blue coverall suit
with short sleeves and a tricky brass buckle and his initials
in dark red on the breast pocket.

"Well, well, well," he said, and took out a handkerchief
and took off his heavy glasses, huffed on the lenses, and
stood wiping them, looking at them all with an uncertain
yet jolly look, his oval fleshy face naked without his glasses,
and his belly thrusting the brass buckle forward with a
look of comfortable arrogance.

Kat went to him quickly and said, "Burt, you know you're
welcome here any time. We didn't send Jackie out to bring
you back."

"Cowards," Jackie said. "Sit right there, Burt boy. This
is an inquisition. We're getting tough. We've got some questions to ask."

Burt sat on the couch. He put his glasses on and looked
hesitantly at Jimmy Wing. "I'm not in a position to make
any official statement."

"This is off the record," Jimmy said, "whatever you say,
Burt."

"Get him a drink, Kat," Jackie said. "Then you all sit
down. I'll be Perry Mason."

Jackie stalked slowly back and forth in front of Burt Lesser, scowling, darting fierce looks at him from time to time. She was the only one who didn't seem to sense the awkwardness of the situation.

"Now then," she said, "are you the president of the Palmlands Development Company?"

"Yes, I am."

"Is it the purpose and intent of this company to fill Grassy Bay and make a lot of money?"

"Uh . . . to make a lot of money for everyone. Yes indeed."

"You were not in favor of the Grassy Bay fill two years ago, Mr. Lesser. Is that true?"

"I wasn't in favor of it. I didn't . . . uh . . . actively oppose it, but I wasn't in favor of it either. But this is a different situation." He smiled at Kat and Ross and Jimmy, the smile of someone who is going along with a joke and wants to be appreciated.

"What's so different about it?"

"Several things, Mrs. Halley. Several important things. We're in a little business slump in Palm County, and we weren't two years ago. This could be a tremendous shot in the arm. Also, having local people in control of it assures a real tasteful development. We don't want to foul our own nest, you might say. Palmland Isles will be a credit to the area in every sense of the word."

"Is that what you're calling it? Ugh!"

"In every sense of the word. And we shall place all possible contracts and orders right here in Palm County. I have close contact with all the businessmen in the area, Mrs. Halley. I can assure you that the support for Palmland Isles is overwhelming. I think that you people are . . . uh . . . doing a disservice to the community by trying to oppose it."

Jackie paced for a few silent moments. She stopped, whirled, pointed her finger so energetically at Burt that it made him flinch. "You have the feeling that this project will go through?"

"Oh, yes! There'll be a clear majority in favor of it."

"And you think we are wasting our time and energy?"

"I guess you could put it that way."

She moved closer to him and lowered her voice. "Then answer this, Mr. Palmland Lesser! If you are so bloody sure of winning, why is your side pulling dirty despicable tricks on us, like blackmailing Dial Sinnat into pulling out?"

Jimmy saw that Burt Lesser was genuinely shocked and astonished.

"What? What are you talking about?"

"I don't know the details. But you probably do."

Burt Lesser flushed. "I don't like your tone of voice, Jackie. I don't know anything about Dial Sinnat and I don't know anything about blackmail. That's a damned dangerous word to throw around unless you know what you're talking about, and I'm not sure you do."

Jackie stared at him. "Now just one cotton-pickin' minute, Mr. President!"

Lesser stood up. "I'm a little tired of this game."

"Somebody on your team is playing dirty," Jackie said sternly. "If you don't know about it, you should. And if you don't believe me, ask Kat here, or Jimmy, or phone Tom Jennings. Who have you got on your team who'd pull such a stinking trick?"

Jimmy saw the momentary uncertainty on Burt Lesser's face. It disappeared quickly. "You know the five of us who have majority interests in this project, I'm sure. As far as the others who are on our team, as you prefer to call it, I can name Martin Cable, Ben Killian, Gerold Tucker, Willis Bry . . . in fact a long list of the influential men in this area. Every . . . uh . . . worth-while project attracts support from all . . . uh . . . segments of society. I can't be responsible, or be held responsible, if somebody in favor of the bay fill gets too anxious." He turned to Kat. "Thanks for the drink, Katherine."

"Well," Jackie said thinly, "you better check out your folks, because if they get too anxious, some of our people might get too anxious too."

"Is that some sort of a threat?" Burt asked her coldly.

"It's a promise, pal."

Kat said, "Burt, I'm sorry that this—"

"I know it isn't your fault, my dear. No harm done. See you tomorrow morning, Jimmy. Goodnight, Ross. Jackie, I think you make a mistake in combining alcohol with your . . . civic activities."

Kat went out with Burt. As soon as the door closed behind them, Jackie said, "The great white father! He's doing it all to help the poor. Honest to God, men, if there's anything I hate it's a hypocrite."

"You messed up pretty good, honey," Ross said.

"Messed up? What did I mess up? I believe him when he says he doesn't know anything about what they did to Di. So maybe he'll go find out who did it and raise hell. Big fat phonies like Burt Lesser get real upset about appearances. They don't mind stealing as long as it doesn't look like stealing. Right, Jimmy?"

"Burt has a good reputation in the real estate business."

"How would he do if he didn't have Sally Ann's money in back of him?"

Kat came back in and said, "He isn't really sore. He's just sort of hurt, I guess."

"What a dreadful shame!" Jackie said.

"Honey, I'm taking you home," Ross said.

"Oh, the *hell* you are! Not on your life, boy! I'm just beginning to swing."

Ross smiled and stood up and took her by the wrists. She tried to pull away. He kept smiling. She looked at him gravely. "Really? I'm due to go home?"

"That's what the man says," Ross said gently.

She gave a huge shrug and looked over her shoulder at Kat and Jimmy. "All of a sudden it turned into an early night. Goodnight, darlings. The food was nifty, Kat. You call me tomorrow and tell me how horrible I was. Okay?" She yawned and leaned against Ross. "Steer me away, lover."

After they had gone, Kat sat beside Jimmy on the couch and said, "It got out of hand, I guess."

"She's a very direct type gal."

"When she brought Burt in, you know the crazy thing I did? I started looking around the room for Van, knowing he'd take over and smooth things out. There was just a half a second of looking for him. I didn't want to have to cope."

"You coped fine."

"Did I? I didn't feel as if I was. Burt handled it pretty well, don't you think?"

"He kept his dignity."

"Which is more than you can say for Jackie, bless her." She yawned and hitched around on the couch to face him more directly. "Jimmy?"

"Yes, dear."

"What do you know about that Reverend Coombs down in Wister?"

He looked at her in mild surprise. "Why?"

"Oh, nothing special, really. One of the guards at the bank was talking to me about him. He goes down there every Sunday. He said I ought to go down there too."

Jimmy had the impression she was lying. "You don't need him, Kat. You don't need his brand of salvation."

"What's wrong with it?"

"He's found a button to push. A new mixture. A kind of militant revivalism. He took over an old school in the piny woods and turned it into a church. He keeps it filled with self-righteous, beat-down people who've always hated anybody better off than they are, and he gives them good reasons for the hate, and makes them feel like God's weapons. They're going to save all us wicked ones if they have to kill us to save us."

"Is that why they've whipped some people?"

"Yes. And maybe some day they'll whip the wrong one. I know of at least six cases which never even got into the papers. He works them up to a high pitch every Sunday and at least two evenings a week. They're the good right arm of the Lord. The Army of the Lord, they call themselves. Full of holy fervor to punish the wicked. Politically they're way to the right of the Birchers. They're flat out against perfume, make-up, television, birth control, divorce, big cities, modern painting, fiction, jazz, public swimming, dancing, liquor, movies, magazines, candy, cigarettes. They make public confessions. Anybody who disagrees with them is un-American, a red Communist dupe. I don't know how sincere Coombs is. If he's after power, he's getting it. They've cowed a lot of people down in the south county. He gives radio talks now, over WEVS in Everset, and I heard he's getting a pretty good-sized audience here in Palm City. He's a stocky guy about fifty, with huge shoulders and a great big head on him and a voice like a trombone. He claims to have spent the first forty years of his life in black sin, started reading the Good Book in jail, saw the light, started preaching on street corners and preached his way all the way across the country back to the swamps where he was born. Wherever he goes, there's a little herd of the faithful clumping right along with him, carrying weapons, because he claims the Reds are out to get him. There must be a hundred like him, scattered around the country. There's always a chance one of them will get to be big enough to be genuinely dangerous. I suppose his chance is as good as any of them have. No, Kat. That brand of salvation is not for you. Are you looking for some?"

She looked down at her hands. "I guess not. Not really. You remember, I took that trip home after Van died. I knew the whole world was a dirty fraud. I knew it was all a bad joke on people, without justice or reason or . . . decency." She raised her head and looked at him, frowning. "I'm more emotional than logical, Jimmy. The minister up home tried to help me. He'd sit with me and talk and talk and talk and try to make the whole thing *logical*. He was just fooling around with semantics. There was no logic in a world that could take Van away from me. But I . . . found my own way to whatever I believe, sort of in spite of him. I sat in a field on a gray stone. The leaves turn early there, you know. 'Licia came running to me with a bright red leaf. I turned it over and over. I wasn't looking for any deep thoughts or revelations or anything. I was just blue and empty, a woman looking at a leaf. I saw the pattern of the little veins in the leaf and I remembered hearing that no two leaves out of the trillions and trillions on earth are exactly alike. 'Licia had her hand on my knee, small and warm and grubby. I took her hand and turned it over and I looked at the patterns of it, the little pads and lines in the palm. It was unique too, like the leaf." Kat opened her own hand for him to see.

"It wasn't like solving a puzzle, Jimmy. And it wasn't any great blinding flash of comprehension. The leaf was as much a part of some . . . orderly process as my daughter's hand, both styled to live and die. I merely realized I wasn't as empty as I had been. I felt a kind of a comfort. Whatever the leaf was, whatever my daughter's hand is, even whatever the stone was I was sitting on, I was a piece of all of it, and all of it was a piece of me. And all that . . . that *flow* of reality, whatever it might be, it was certainly not something designed to benefit me. I felt ashamed, sort of. I felt I had shown a kind of witless, wicked arrogance to *blame* life for anything. A leaf could blame the tree for releasing it, and the stone could blame a glacier for carrying it away. You see, there's no logic in it. It's a kind of faith, I suppose. It's my awareness of God, or I guess I should say Godness, because I'm more aware of a process than an entity. That awareness doesn't make me miss Van any less. But it stops me from despising the other parts of life. It keeps me from poisoning myself. Jimmy. What do you believe in?"

"Me? Not very much. I don't know. There's as much chaos as there is order. There's as much randomness as there is pattern. I believe in accident, mostly. I'm accidentally alive, and by being alive, I'm in the process of death. I believe in luck and good footwork."

"With no purpose to any of it?"

"None that I can see at the moment."

"That's the emptiness I couldn't endure, Jimmy. I'm too much of a coward to stand so alone."

She looked at him in a quizzical way which deepened the small horizontal wrinkles above her rusty eyebrows. Her eyes were a shadowy gray in that light, her lips slightly apart. Her nearness was a magnetic field which pulled his mind into illogic, toward the threshold of words and acts which would mean nothing. He stood up quickly and with a great bursting effort, like a swimmer clambering up out of a pool.

"Did I say something wrong?" she asked.

"No. It's just . . . I have to stop by the paper. I'd like to stay and talk. Thanks for the drinks and dinner, Kat."

"You'll see if you can find out who made Di resign?"

"I'll try. I can't promise anything."

"I don't want to get you in trouble with the paper because you're trying to help us."

"I'm not worried."

16

THE PALM COUNTY COMMISSIONERS met in Room 100 in the County Courthouse. It looked like a small auditorium in a country high school, a room which could double as a gymnasium or small ballroom. There were rows of folding chairs, enough to seat a hundred people. The seating area was separated from the dais area by a golden oak railing with a gate at the end of the center aisle. On the dais, raised about a foot above the floor level, was the long table at which the five commissioners sat, facing the audience. In front of the table, but down on the main floor level, was a smaller table with two chairs facing the commissioners. Behind the oak armchairs on which the commissioners sat were the United States flag and the flag of the State of Florida flanking a large detailed wall map of Palm County. The press table was to the left of the commissioners, and the staff table off to the right, where the secretaries, assistants and county attorney sat.

In front of the place where each commissioner would sit there was a table microphone. There was a sixth one on the small table facing them. The system reproduced voices in a harsh and metallic fashion, and was frequently afflicted by feedback, a thin screeing, yowling sound that always infuriated the commissioners.

When Jimmy Wing took his seat at the press table on Tuesday morning, the five commissioners were just filing in, followed by the staff. Wing was astonished to see Borklund at the press table. He looked into the audience and saw Colonel Jennings and Major Lipe sitting together and alone in a front row, their expressions stern and watchful. On the other side of the aisle was a group of about fifteen persons, most of them women, all wearing an expression of rigid indignation. Behind them were several young men, none of them familiar to Wing. They stood near a bulky object draped in white, which was leaning against the wall. They sat down as Gus Makelder, the commission chairman, called the meeting to order. The young men looked brisk, competent and attentive.

The atmosphere of the meeting was informal. As the minutes and committee reports were disposed of, the commissioners made small conversational asides to each other, laughed at small private jokes. Elmo Bliss was in the chair at the end of the table nearest the press table. He turned and nodded at Borklund, winked at Jimmy. Commissioner Stan Dayson and Commissioner Horace Lander were arguing with some heat about the bids on the concession at the public beach on Cable Key when Burt Lesser, Leroy Shannard, Bill Gormin and Martin Cable came through the side door into the spectator section, eased the door shut and tiptoed to the nearest vacant seats. Both Jennings and Lipe swiveled their heads around and watched the entire process.

"Any new business?" Makelder finally asked.

"Mr. Chairman!" a woman yelled in a piercing voice, jumping to her feet. "Mr. Chairman, I got something to bring up." She came trotting down the aisle and through the gate and sat down at the small table. "I represent the Palmetto Circle Association. My name is Genevieve Harland."

"Just speak into the microphone in a normal tone of voice, Mrs. Harland."

"You put that wonderful storm sewer system in out at the circle, and it clogged up for that heavy rain we had last night, I mean night before last. All that water has tore out a big hunk of Palmetto Street. It come into four houses. And in the new houses out back of us, them septic tanks come a-floating right up out of the ground. Water is still standing around out there. I've been calling the County Health Officer, and the Road Supervisor and everybody I can think of and nobody has done one single thing, and we're all sick and tired of the mess and the stink and having to come all the way around by Thompson Street to come into town. We want something done and we want it done fast!"

The commissioners muttered to each other. Makelder soothed her. He told her the storm had caused damage in other areas too. Crews were at work. He said Commissioner Bassette would follow her case up personally and inspect the area and see that the necessary work was done.

She thanked them in the same tone of voice she would have used to curse them, and stood up and marched out, followed by her entire group.

"Mr. Chairman," Burt Lesser said. "My name is Burton Lesser. I am a realtor. I wish to petition the Board of County Commissioners, speaking as president of the Palmland Development Company."

"Come down front, Burt," Makelder said.

"Thank you, Gus. I have two of my associates with me, Mr. Gormin and Mr. Shannard. I'm sure you all know them. Mr. Shannard is secretary of the company, and Mr. Gormin is treasurer. I'll ask Mr. Shannard to read and present the actual petition. In the meantime, I'd like your permission to set up a couple of exhibits."

"You have it, Burt," Makelder said.

Shannard read the petition and presented it to the board. As he read it, the brisk young men set up the exhibits. One was a greatly enlarged aerial photograph of Grassy Bay and the surrounding area. They mounted it over the county map behind the commissioners. There was a glassine overlay over the photograph, with the area to be filled marked in red grease pencil.

The second exhibit was considerably more impressive. It was a detailed table-top miniature of how the entire development would look after it was completed and all the houses had been built. There was a landscaped entrance, a serpentine wall, a tiny sign that read *Palmland Isles*. Bright cars speckled the blue curves of asphalt roads and made a herringbone pattern in the parking area of a shopping center facing Mangrove Road. Indigo canals wound through the filled land, with cruisers at miniature docks. The young men had set it up in an open area near the staff table, on low sawhorses.

"If you would gather around, gentlemen, you can see it better," Burt Lesser said happily. "The news people too, if there's no objection. This model was built by Costex Associates of Atlanta. All the engineering on the project has been done by them too. They were very excited by the possibilities here, and think this project will receive national attention and acclaim. Mr. Steve Kerr here, of Costex, was in charge."

"Can Major Lipe and myself examine it?" Tom Jennings asked.

Makelder looked at the other commissioners and then at Burt. Burt nodded. "Come on right up, Colonel."

There was general conversation around the display table. Horace Lander said, "Now Leroy, you know dang well there isn't any zoning that far down Sandy Key to allow any shopping center."

"Artistic license," Shannard said, "plus a little plea for future dispensations."

"Mr. Kerr," Tom Jennings said sharply. "May I ask a question?"

"Yes sir."

"This model seems to show a surprising amount of bay area surrounding the fill project. It seems to reach-just a little more than half way to the mainland. According to the petition I heard read, Palmlands wants the bulkhead line changed to include a little more than eight hundred acres of bay bottom. Is this model scaled to that request?"

"All the roads and canals in the project itself are to scale, sir."

"Wasn't my question clear? Is the project scaled to the area?"

"It's to scale on the photo-map, sir, but not on the table model."

Everyone turned and looked at the map the young men from Costex had put up. On that the red mushroom outlining the land requested filled the heart of the bay, reaching almost over to the channel markers along the mainland.

"We have some other things we would like to pass out to the commission and to the news people," Burt Lesser said quickly. "I hope you will find them of interest. One is a study of what the project will mean to the area in actual dollars and cents, with a complete breakdown by types of retail and wholesale businesses. Bill, will you see that everyone gets copies, including the Colonel and the Major, of course. This second one shows the specifications as recommended by Costex. Roads, curbing, sea walls, elevations, sewage disposal system, street lighting, hydrants, drainage, underground conduits for power and phone. Please note, gentlemen, that in every single instance our specifications exceed county minimum standards for Class A Residential. What else do we have, Leroy? Oh, of course. This third study is an advertising and promotion plan, showing the dignified nature of the sales approach we will use. It shows the price range of the lots also. They will sell for a minimum of seven thousand up to a maximum of fifteen thousand five hundred."

"How many lots, Burt?" Stan Dayson asked.

"Eight hundred."

"If you average out at ten thousand, Burt, that would mean . . . eight million bucks."

"Our expenses are going to be very heavy, Stan. They have to be, to make this a project the whole west coast will be proud of. If it was going to be anything less than perfect, I wouldn't want anything to do with it. I might add that there has been a considerable investment in time, thought and money to bring the project up to this point of initial presentation. Beginning tomorrow this model of Palmland Isles will be on display in the Cable Bank and Trust Company, on the main floor. And right now I'd like to ask Mr. Martin Cable to say a few words to you about one aspect of this thing which may be bothering you."

Chairman Makelder looked up from his examination of the model just in time to look directly into the automatic flash gun wielded by Stu Kennicott. Makelder scowled and said, "Boys, let's all sit where we belong and listen to Mr. Cable."

Martin sat at the small desk, arranged his notes and cleared his throat. "One of the matters which should legitimately concern any government body which must pass on any phase of approval of such a project is the question of financing. I am not here to make a firm commitment to you gentlemen or to Palmland Development. I can merely say this. All of Palmland's plans and estimates have been examined by the loan committee of the Cable Bank and Trust Company. In the event—and let me stress this phrase—in the event all proper permissions are obtained by Palmland, and in the event there is no basic change in their plans of operation, the bank will be prepared to look favorably upon offering the financial assistance which will be needed to make this dream a reality. I . . . ah . . . speaking now as an individual, wish to add that my personal interest in this venture is attested to by my having made available to Palmland the necessary access land through approving an option, acting in my office as executor of my mother's estate. That land is the portion on the map behind you cross-hatched in green. Thank you."

"Thank you, Martin," Gus Makelder said. "Any comment?"

"I just happen to have a little something to say," Elmo drawled. "I just want to say I'm getting right confused here. Leroy certainly must know the public law on this thing. I'm not saying it's a good project or a bad project. But I do know we're sitting here, the five of us, getting buttered like breakfast hot cakes. Steve Merry, you being the county attorney, maybe you can straighten me out. We can't vote on a damn thing, can we? This Palmland is supposed to present a petition and then we set a date for a public hearing. Isn't the proper place for all this butter job the public hearing instead of now?"

Steve Merry adjusted his glasses and said, "Commissioner Bliss, I think these gentlemen were just explaining to the commission as a courtesy what they're planning. . . ."

"Steve, boy, I don't want you telling me what you think they're trying to do. I've got me a pretty good idea of what they're trying to do. I want to know the law."

"Properly, I suppose, this presentation should be made at the public hearing."

"Where the folks on the other side of this question have a chance to make their objections?"

"Yes sir."

"So what they're doing is trying to get us all on their side before the other side has a chance?"

"I . . . I guess it could be interpreted that way."

"Thank you, Steve. Gus, it looks to me as if we should just accept the petition and set a date for the hearing. I see no reason why the minutes should make any mention of all this other entertainment Burt and Bill and Leroy have given us."

"Do you so move?" Gus asked.

"I so move," Elmo said.

"Second," DeRose Bassette said.

"Moved and seconded we accept the Palmland Development Company petition and proceed to set a date for the public hearing."

"Mr. Chairman," Burt said, "before you set the date, I'd just like to say that our timing on this whole thing is running very very close and we would appreciate your setting it for as soon as possible."

"How soon can we do it according to law, Steve?" Gus asked.

Steve Merry bit his lip for a moment. "Two weeks has to elapse from the time of publication in the paper until the hearing itself. I could probably get the legal notification to the paper sometime tomorrow afternoon. That would put it in the paper Wednesday morning, the twelfth. The public hearing could be set for Wednesday, the twenty-sixth."

"That's real nice for Palmland, but how about the opposition? Gus, would it be out of order to ask Colonel Tom Jennings how this strikes him?"

"Colonel?" Gus said.

"Speaking as the President of Save Our Bays, Incorporated, I would respectfully request the Commission to give us a month to prepare our case against this bay-fill project. We did not even hear about it until last week."

"Move we set the date for the twenty-sixth of this month," Horace Lander said. Bassette seconded him. Bassette, Lander and Dayson voted for it, Bliss against. Lander suggested that the availability of the Palm City Municipal Auditorium be checked. A secretary left the room to phone and came back and said it was available. The time was set for 8 P.M. The commission meeting was adjourned, and the young men shrouded their display table and tenderly carried it away.

J. J. Borklund walked into the corridor with Jimmy. He said, "All I want from you today is more glowing copy than I can possibly use on this thing. Puff it all the way, James. Fatten it with interviews. Pie is raining out of the sky. Hosanna!"

"Then tomorrow you want a *really* glowing account?"

"That's the pattern, James. You anticipate me."

"And they'll come in for at least two hundred full pages the first year?"

"At the very least."

As Borklund walked away Elmo came up to Jimmy and said, "See me in fifteen minutes in Lupen's office." Jimmy nodded and Elmo hurried up the hall to catch up with Gus Makelder.

Jimmy stopped at a drinking fountain. When he straightened up he saw Tom Jennings and Major Lipe approaching him.

"They seem to be traveling first class," Jimmy said.

Jennings made a rueful grimace. "Rough. Very rough indeed. As a colleague of mine named Custer once said, where are all these Indians coming from?"

"I have a feeling there'll be more."

"And our recruiting is terribly discouraging," Major Lipe said. "I've just been reporting to the colonel. It looks as if I'm not even going to be given a chance to talk to some of the groups I'm supposed to contact. And I haven't found a single recreational club which will back us unanimously. You know, I can't even line up a decent committee to help me? I don't see how they could have done such a tremendous propaganda job without our hearing about it. Jackie tells me she's having the same problem. And Wally is going out of his mind trying to find reputable people to write the commissioners. It isn't *anything* like it was last time."

"You heard we lost Dial Sinnat?" Jennings said.

"Kat told me."

Jennings sighed and smiled. "We'll still make a good presentation at the public hearing. And losing this battle does not mean losing the war. That's our advantage, you see. They have to win every battle. All we have to do is win one. They won't be able to endure delay. Their money structure will collapse. And, best of all, Jimmy, we're right and they're wrong."

They walked toward the exit, erect and in step, chins up, arms swinging in unison.

When it was time, Jimmy got into the creaking elevator and rode up to the tower office of Calvin Lupen, the ancient man who held the job of courthouse custodian, and who had been on sick leave for almost a year. His office was a ten-by-ten cube with one narrow window. The scarred desk was thick with dust. One wall was papered with yellowing Playmates of the Month, many of them with anatomical oddities added with pen and pencil.

Elmo sat at Cal's desk, his feet on the low windowsill. He was staring at the wall of nudes.

"One thing I never noticed before, Jimmy. All different shapes and sizes of girls, but every smile is alike. Look at them."

Wing had closed the door. He blew dust off a chair and sat and looked at the girls. "I think you're right."

"How did I do down there? How did I sound?"

"Eminently fair, Mr. Commissioner."

"I didn't want to overdo it. That damn Gormin looked like he was going to crack up. Leroy is the only solid one in the group. And maybe Doc Aigan. Buck has got hisself so pussy-happy over that Prindergast piece, he's no damn good to anybody. I wish to hell his wife would come home and bust up that romance. Burt Lesser phoned me at home last night and talked like a crazy man."

"About Sinnat?"

"Hell, yes. The Halley woman chewed him out. Oh, you were there, weren't you?"

"What did you tell Burt?"

"What could I tell him? I said that if he thought I was the kind of man who'd use underhand methods on Dial Sinnat, then in the interest of harmony, maybe he'd better let me buy a hundred per cent of his interest after my term runs out on the commission. That slowed him way down. He's scared of that mean-mouth wife of his. She'd never let him forget I edged him out of his only chance to make any real money. He likes being president. I said if some nut was going around scaring people, it wasn't my fault or his. He finally apologized. But I haven't given up the idea of squeezing him out, that is, if he keeps getting in my hair. Worked out just fine with Di Sinnat, didn't it though?"

"What made it work so well, Elmo?"

Elmo looked at him too blandly. "Why, I guess he didn't want his little girl's name dragged in the mud."

"Maybe he didn't want his little girl dragged in the mud, personally. Maybe he didn't want her whipped by a bunch of south county nuts."

"What in the wide world are you talking about, Jimmy boy?"

"Di reacted pretty violently. I'm making a wild guess, Elmo. You got a heavy vote from those people."

"Man, I can't help who votes for me! Anyhow ol' Darse Coombs is kin of mine, about a fourth or fifth cousin. His middle name is Harkness, and my pa's great-aunt married a Harkness from Collier County. But I don't know as that means much to Darse. He figures me for a sinner. Told me so. Roared right into my face, sprayed me like a faucet."

"Elmo, I wouldn't want any part of this if you pulled something like that."

"Boy, I wouldn't want any part of it myself. You actually think that little Sinnat girl is going to get her tail whipped?"

"Not now, no."

"Then don't get all agitated. Damn it, Jimmy, I got a word for you. You're morose. You got the sour uglies most of the time. Look out there at that great big broad sunshiny world, crammed full of people having a time. It's a big world full of beaches and girls and sport cars. Full of bowling alleys and golf courses and cold beer. The things you get so broody about, why, they don't matter a *damn* to those folks. They want ball games, westerns, the next drink, the next steak, the next roll in the hay. They can get a little jumpy about being blowed up with atom bombs, but aside from that one thing, you can hardly attract their *attention*. We'll just be another part of the entertainment business, Jimmy, after we really get rolling. You give those people a few laughs and a little excitement, and they'll love you forever."

"If you say so, Elmo."

"Here's this week's bite, Jimmy. A pair of fifties."

Wing took the money. "Plus twenty-one dollars expenses."

"Plus what?"

"Twenty-one dollars I spent doing your work for you. If it's a hundred a week, the least I can expect is to have it free and clear."

Elmo shook his head, chuckled, took two tens and a one out of his wallet. "You know, you're making more sense as you go along, boy. I hope you run this up on that Doris Rowell."

Wing took the money, and told Bliss what he had learned. Elmo stared at him with a puzzled expression after he was through. "You mean there's people take a thing like that serious, Jimmy?"

"Yes indeed."

"Those eggheads that come down here when she yells for help, they'd stay away if they knew about this?"

"Very probably. Even if none of them had ever heard of the incident before. It works like this, Elmo. Industry will use people who have been tossed out of colleges. Industry is interested in ability and results. But other educational institutions don't want anything to do with anybody who has been caught in unethical practices. It's a sensitive area."

"My, my," Elmo said. "Think of that! I know how to handle a little case of where folks mess around in the ordinary ways, but what the hell do you do with a thing like this?"

"It doesn't have to be complicated, Elmo. She doesn't even have to know we've done anything about it. I can look up the list of the experts who testified last time and just mail them, with no comment and no return address, the copies of the news items, with 'Doris' and 'Rowell' underlined in red wherever those names appear."

"You mean that would do it? They wouldn't come down?"

"It would be very unlikely."

"And she wouldn't know what was wrong, would she?"

"She might guess, sooner or later, but she could never be sure who spread the word."

Elmo closed his eyes and pinched the bridge of his nose. "You go right ahead and do it that way, Jimmy. I think I like it. Tom Jennings will be leaning heavy on having those experts telling everybody how terrible it is to mess with breeding grounds and tide flow and so on. This way he may not find out until the very last minute they're not coming. I want him to walk in there with the heart tooken right out of him, with nothing left on his side but nuts and bird watchers opposing the march of progress and prosperity."

"Tom told me a little while ago that you have to win every battle to win the marbles, and all he has to do is win one."

"I know that just as well as he does. What I got to do is win the first battle so big there won't be anybody left to fight on his side. I've got lots and lots of people working, and now that it's out in the open, they can work harder. By the time of the hearing, boy, I want to have this county so worked up that if anybody should speak out against the fill in a public place, they get cracked right in the mouth by the first person who can get to him."

"Who's next on the priority list?"

"You gettin' eager, Jimmy?"

"Not noticeably."

"Come on around to the house tonight when you get finished up. There'll be some folks milling around out there. You an me and Leroy can have a little chat. Don't look so nervous boy. You're supposed to go where the news is."

"The morning paper ought to please you, Elmo."

"Ben Killian promised Leroy it would." Elmo slumped slightly in his chair. "You run along now and close the door, boy. I've got some quiet thinking to do. I've got to catch up on my mess list."

"On your what?"

"Whenever I get into anything, boy, whenever I take one

of those bites I was telling you about, I like to take time off
to just set and make myself up a list of every possible
thing that could go wrong, every bad break I can imagine.
And I decide just what I would do in each case. Then when
things blow up in my face, it doesn't take me by surprise. I
know just what direction to move because I've got it planned."

"Elmo, who phoned Sinnat?"

"Nobody he knew. Nobody you know. And they've got
no way of knowing either you or me had anything to do
with any part of it. One nice thing about this mess list is
the way you get in the habit of doing things in such a way
you cut way down the number of things which could go
wrong. The only time to get brave is when you've got aces
back to back."

"Is that what you have now?"

"It's more like queens backed, but the up card is the
highest one on the table so far. If I was raised, I'd bump it
again, because there is one hell of a lot in the pot. The
opener was forty thousand."

"From Mrs. Lesser?"

"Most of it." Elmo smiled and closed his eyes. Jimmy went
out and closed the door quietly. As the little elevator descended in the airless shaft, he decided he would work at
home that day, and bring his copy in by late afternoon.

17

THE TABLE-TOP MODEL of Palmland Isles was brought into the bank as soon as the doors were closed to the public. It was set up about fifteen feet behind Kat Hubble's desk. A railing was installed around it, just far enough to keep the public from touching the exhibit.

A placard on a nearby easel was inscribed, *Palmland Isles —A Planned Community—Styled for the Best of Tropical Living.*

Martin Cable and Burt Lesser looked it over after it was set up. After they left, the bank employees gathered around it.

Kat stood beside two girls from the installment loan section. "All the work in that thing!" one of them said.

"It's absolutely gorgeous!" the other one said. "Chee, would I ever love to live there! What a place for kids, huh? What I'd like is that cute gray house there on that kinda point where the road curves around."

"So tell Johnny you won't settle for less."

"Hah! Waterfront land? The only waterfront I'll see is the kitchen sink. The closest I'll get to that house is going by in a rowboat."

"That bay belongs to both of you," Kat said.

The two girls turned and stared blankly at her. "What do you mean, Mrs. Hubble?" the taller one said.

"You can use the bay now, Betty. Nobody can chase you off."

"What would I use it for? Nobody swims there. It might as well be houses for all I care. Because I can't afford it, it doesn't mean other people shouldn't have it that good."

"Hey, I like the little red house best," the other girl said. "On the wide canal there. A convertible in the front yard and a cruiser in the back yard. Wow!"

Kat went back to her desk. For the first time she had a hopeless feeling about their chances of defeating it. The model was the first tangible evidence that they were up against competence, imagination, money and a disheartening confidence.

She finished her routine typing a few minutes before three, and phoned Tom Jennings.

"They just set up a big model of that thing right here in the bank, Tom."

"I saw it at the meeting this morning. It was a little like being hit in the head. I've been a little dazed ever since."

"Somebody heard over the radio the hearing is two weeks from tomorrow. Is that right?"

"Yes."

"Golly, that's awful soon, isn't it?"

"It's being rammed through, Kat. The commissioners went along with it like lambs. All except Elmo Bliss. He gave me a chance to object, but they voted for that date. He was the only one who seemed to resent the very smooth job Lesser and company was doing on them."

"He's sort of an expert at the same thing."

"Yes. I suppose. Anyway, it was the only help I got in any form, so I was grateful. I've been alerting the others about how little time we have. No pleasant chore. Doris Rowell was very savage about it. By the way, Kat, that model is out of scale. There won't be that much of the bay left. I noticed that and called attention to it at the meeting. I hope the paper will make some mention of that. Both Mr. Borklund and Jimmy Wing were there. And a lot of pictures were taken. I'm going to go over the budget tonight with Harry and Wallace Lime and see what we can afford in the way of radio spots and newspaper ads. It won't be much, I'm afraid."

"I have to hang up, Tom. They want to close the switchboard."

"I'll phone you about the date of the next meeting, Kat. Don't let that table-top promotion scare you."

At home, after she changed, she walked to the Sinnats. The children, a half dozen of them, were on the beach with Esperanza, building sand forts and moats. Florence Riggs, the housekeeper, said, "Natalie drove them on over in the big car to catch that boat, Mrs. Hubble. She said she'd probably be back here about eight or nine o'clock if you want to see her."

"It's not important, Floss, thanks."

"Mrs. Sinnat sure hated to go. It was like he had to drag her. I guess it was it all being so sudden. When that man makes up his mind, he moves fast."

"I hope the children won't be too much trouble now that she's gone."

"They're no trouble at all! There's always somebody with them. You can be sure of that."

Well . . . you send them home about five-thirty, will you?"

"I certainly will."

When she walked back she saw some young people on the beach near the pavilion. She thought others were playing tennis, but when she neared the courts she saw that it was Sammy and Wilma Deegan playing doubles against Angela McCall, Sammy's sister and Carol Killian. Sally Ann Lesser sat in the shade of a beach umbrella, a thermos jug and a stack of paper cups on the bench beside her. She called Kat over.

"Sit and learn some new words," she said in a stage whisper. "This is for blood." She filled a paper cup and gave it to Kat. It was rum and fruit juice, icy cold, alarmingly strong.

Sammy and his sister were excellent players. Wilma tried to kill the ball whenever she could reach it. Carol had a model's superb grace whenever she was standing still, which was most of the time. When she had to go after the ball, she moved in a curious, floundering, knock-kneed trot and swung at it stiff-armed, turning her face away from the ball as she patted it.

Wilma Deegan was a spare, brown, savage little woman with a withered face and a cap of tight gray curls. She was some ten years older than Sammy. She and Sammy and Sammy's widowed sister, Angela, and Angela's strange, shy, frail ten-year-old son all lived well on the royalties from the books and plays Wilma's first husband had written.

"No tricks today," Sally Ann said softly. "No parlor routines. But Sammy and Angela will make it come out just right. Victory by a narrow margin for Wilma."

The players were sweaty. Tennis, Kat thought, like ballet, needs a little distance. Their tennis shoes slapped the asphalt. Their gasps of effort were audible. Carol Killian's long smooth golden thighs, exposed by her very short shorts, looked splendid when she stood still. When she lurched into her strange half-gallop, the thighs rippled into an unpleasant looseness, her breasts and buttocks bounced, and she made a squeaking sound as she bit her lip and swung the racket.

"Goddammit, stop poaching!" Wilma snarled at Sammy.

"Add here," Angela said, and crossed to the service court.

"What the hell did you do to Burt last night?" Sally Ann demanded. "He was very upset."

"Jackie Halley gave him a bad time."

"Burt said she was disgustingly drunk."

"He's wrong, Sally Ann. She was a little high. Mostly she was just angry about Dial Sinnat."

"Why should she think Burt had anything to do with that?"

"I guess because he has a lot to do with Palmland Development."

"So do a lot of people. Do you know how many *miles* of roads there'll be in the Isles?"

"I have no idea."

"It'll be a *very* substantial contract for somebody. Burt told me last night that he can't help it if people get so anxious to see it go through they . . . do unpleasant things to anybody opposing it. He wishes you'd get out of it, dear. He told me so."

"I couldn't let Tom down now, even if I wanted to."

"But he's such a dreary, solemn type. All those retired Army, they just can't stop *organizing* things. And fighting against the fill is really terribly unrealistic this time. *Everybody* is in favor of it. You know, dear, I sold some very happy little securities so I could put money into this, and I wouldn't have done that if there was the slightest chance of it falling through. I'm not a gambler. I'm much too stingy. Burt acts worried, but then he always does. Leroy and Martin are supremely confident. Burt was as fidgety as a bride this morning, getting ready to go down and talk to those dreary little commissioners. If you really want the truth of the matter, dear, Dial Sinnat probably spread some tale of persecution so he could ease out and save his face. He's a shrewd man, you know, and why should he make himself look silly by thrashing around for a lost cause?"

"But I happen to *know* that somebody . . ."

"Oh, I wouldn't deny that some idiot probably called him up and woofed at him. And that's precisely the sort of thing Di would ignore, *unless* he was looking for an out. You're too naive about these things, Kat, darling. It's a precious quality and I adore it, but it really isn't very realistic. Di will come back after it's all died down, and by then you'll forgive him, because by then it will be perfectly obvious that if he had stayed around, he couldn't have changed the outcome in the slightest degree."

"Sally Ann, sometimes you make me so darn mad I want to hit you!"

"People trying to live in a dream world always resent hard facts," Sally Ann Lesser said patronizingly.

"Set point!" Wilma Deegan yelled. She served to Carol. Carol patted the ball back to her. Wilma drove it into the far corner, past Angela. It hit a good eight inches past the base line.

"Beautiful!" Angela called. Carol Killian looked dubiously at her partner.

"We whupped 'em, pal!" Wilma said to Sammy. She gave

him a sweaty hug and they all came off the court, breathing hard, picking up towels, wiping their shining faces.

Angela, the permanent house guest, smiled at her sister-in-law and said, "Willy, you're putting a lot of top spin on that ball. It comes over real heavy." Angela was a graceful blonde with sturdy legs and ingratiating manners.

"But she wants to powder everything on our side of the net," Sammy said, and laughed.

Wilma stopped smiling. "I want to what?"

Sammy stopped laughing. "I meant you got an aggressive spirit, Willy."

"You're the one wants to cover the whole damn court."

"Just half of it, pet. Just half of it."

"So let me see you cover all of it for a while, darling. You and your sweet sister get on out there and show us some fast singles."

"Honey," Sammy said patiently, "it's almost too brutal a day for doubles. I'm dragging, and I'm sure Angie . . ."

"But I'd learn so *much* just watching you and your sister," Wilma said in a grave tone.

Angela finished her drink, stood up and picked up her racket. "Come on, Sam," she said and walked out onto the court.

Sammy Deegan hesitated, then followed her. Kat glanced at Sally Ann, and looked away quickly when she saw Sally Ann smirk and wink.

Carol Killian, with her customary lack of contact with the world around her, said, "Golly, I don't see how they can want to play again so soon. I'm so positively pooped I feel faint almost. They must be in wonderful condition."

"They're natural athletes, dear," Wilma said.

"I've never been good at games," Carol said sadly.

"You've never had to be," Sally Ann said.

Carol looked at her blankly. "Have Sammy and Angie had to be good at games?"

"It's been a big help to them," Sally Ann said.

"Get off my back," Wilma said gently to Sally Ann. She turned and smiled at Kat. "I don't see you for weeks on end. I hear there's a big broohah about Grassy Bay. Just don't propagandize me, dearie. I've had to shut Sally Ann up about it. It's too hot in the summer to get agitated about anything."

Kat stood up. "I wasn't going to mention it, Willy. I just dropped off for a drink on my way home."

Carol stood up quickly and collected her gear. "I'll walk with you, Kat. I'm so hot and tired I could die. All I want is a bath and a nice nap." She called goodbye to Sammy and

Angela. They waved rackets at her. Kat and Carol walked down the road.

"I didn't want to play tennis but everybody else wanted to. Mostly Wilma," Carol said. "What I am mostly is thirsty, and there isn't anything except that rum stuff Sally Ann makes. I had two cups of it, and honest, I've got such a buzz my mouth feels numb."

Carol stopped to fix her shoe. Kat looked back. Sammy and Angela were agile figures in white, bounding and racing dutifully in the afternoon sun. Wilma and Sally Ann sat on the bench in the shade of the umbrella, two brown women with gray curls, looking like sisters, one stocky and the other scrawny, two monied women who had ordered their world to their own liking, and seemed to spend most of their time wondering if they really liked what they had wrought.

Carol straightened up and began walking. "I should do more things like that to get tightened up. I'd like to be like Angela. She's hard as a rock. She's got dumpy legs, but she's in wonderful shape. Do you think if I swam more it would help?"

"Swimming is good exercise."

"You're real trim, Kat. But I guess you're naturally slender, aren't you? I mean you don't have to work at it. I weigh just the same as I did when I was nineteen, and my measurements are almost the same, but if I don't watch it every minute, my hips blow up like a balloon."

"I gain and then I take it off."

"Gee, Kat, I don't know about my spending so much time with them. There always seems to be some kind of a fight going on that I don't understand. But who else is there to be with this time of year? And Sammy is real odd, you know? I never know if he's making a pass at me, the way he kids around."

"I don't think he is, really. I think it's just his manner."

Carol frowned. "I guess you're right. I wouldn't want him really making a pass at me. I mean, it would be awkward. I've got nothing against passes. It makes you sort of confident, you know? Even if a girl doesn't want an affair, it's nice to know men think about it. I couldn't pull such a dirty trick on Ben anyhow. But I think a husband should know other men find a girl attractive, don't you?"

"I guess so. Will you come in and have something for that thirst?"

"No thanks. I think I'll go home. Uh . . . Sally Ann says Sammy is making passes at me. She says it's obvious."

"Sally Ann is a liar and a trouble-maker, Carol."

"Well. I guess so. Will you come over and have dinner with us some night?"

"I'd like to, after all the bay fill thing is over. It might be awkward right now, considering the stand the paper is taking."

"Oh, Ben doesn't have anything to do with that! That's all Mr. Borklund doing that."

"But Ben owns the paper. Mr. Borklund works for him."

"All Ben cares about is designing those darn boats and building them and selling them for a loss."

"Then the paper should stay neutral like the last time."

"Oh, Mr. Borklund explained how they can't do that again. He had a list of the advertising they'd lose. It was a lot of money. And there was something about zoning, something that might happen to the boatyard unless the paper came out in favor of it. Ben was mad for a week. He kept telling me he didn't want to be pushed around. Mr. Borklund was at the house almost every night, and he'd bring men with him and they'd argue. Finally Ben just said the heck with it. He won't even talk about it any more."

"What was that about zoning, Carol?"

"I don't understand that stuff. It was something about taxes and nonconforming. They could do something to him he wouldn't like."

"I guess the invitation had better wait until this is settled."

"Sure, Kat. If that would be better for you."

It was a little after five when Kat entered her house. As she started to close the door she watched Carol Killian walking away in her little white shorts, her gray-and-white-striped sleeveless blouse, carrying her racket and towel and little zipper bag, hair shiny-black in the sun, slow golden legs scissoring hips flexing. She was, Kat estimated, about thirty-four, a curiously teen-age thirty-four, childless, placid, a simplified, undemanding woman. Ben had provided her with a handsome home, a full-time maid, a new sports car every year, charge accounts, shopping trips. It had been Van's sardonic opinion that Ben Killian had acquired exactly what he wanted when he had married Carol twelve years ago. She was decorative, faithful, undemanding, unquestioning, healthy and as unabashedly sensual as any Micronesian maiden. She was always there when he wanted her, and she could be readily ignored when he did not.

Her days were without event. She slept late. When she got up she had the sober problems of what to do with her hair, how to fix her face, what selection of clothing to make from the yards of closet in her dressing room. There was music in the house, and daytime television to keep her amused.

Too many drinks made her sick to her stomach. She loved
oils and lotions and scents, naps and deep hot baths. She
had her own bathroom, with a large sunken tub and many
mirrors. She lived like a pretty cat on a cozy hearth. She had
her own bedroom, all quilted and cozied and dainty, with
a deep salmon rug, tinted mirrors and a draped canopy over
the bed.

Ben Killian was a remote man, complex, a listener who
made the more articulate ones uneasy through the uncom-
mitted quality of his listening. People were always asking
him, somewhat plaintively, if he agreed, and he could say
yes in a way that made it sound like no. His grandfather
had started the paper late in life. His father had driven the
competing paper out of business and had died early, when
Ben was still in college. Ben had spent every possible hour
of his childhoot afloat, and had planned to become a marine
architect and designer. But the brother, Arnold, the one
who relished the newspaper business, died in a war in an
unpronounceable village in Burma, and Ben was elected by
circumstance to publish the Palm City *Record-Journal*. He
went through all the necessary motions until he finally found
J. J. Borklund, and then he went through less of them. Gulfway Marine Designs took more and more of his time and
energy.

He was, as Van had once noted, a man constructed of
spare parts. He had the heroic torso of a beef-cake western
hero, the long leathery durable arms and curled thickened
hands of a dirt farmer, the domed head and large bland un-
focused bespectacled face of professorship, a pair of thin,
stringy, tough, bowed little legs. He was in constant demand
to crew for the ocean racers because he could do twice the
work of younger men with half the fuss and many times
the knowledge of the sea and the winds. He could cut, shape,
drill, fit and finish fine wood with the loving skill of a master
boatwright.

His attitude toward Gulfway Marine Designs was one of
utter dedication. His attitude toward Carol was avuncular,
gentle and slightly amused. His attitude toward the paper was
one of slight but evident embarrassment, as though it was an
affliction, a congenital deformity which strangers might notice and find distasteful.

Kat walked thoughtfully through her house, sat on the
edge of her bed for a little while, thinking of what Carol had
told her, and then phoned Jimmy Wing at the paper. When
they told her he was out, she tried his cottage. Just as she
was about to hang up, he answered.

"This is Kat. Are you in the middle of something? You could call me back."

"I was at the end of a shower. When I turned the water off, I heard the phone ringing."

"Oh dear! I hate to do that to anybody."

"No strain. I've been doing my public-relations job for Palmland Isles, and I'm going to take it in in a little while. Not much chance to stick any flies in the ointment, which I hope you and your buddies will understand when they see the by-line. I reported what Tom said about the model being out of scale, but that's no guarantee it will get by Borklund. Actually, it's a hell of a big local news story, Kat. The biggest we've had in some time. I can't legitimately underplay it."

"I understand that, Jimmy, and the others will too. What I called about, I was talking to Carol Killian, and she said something interesting, about why Ben is going to be in favor of the fill this time."

"I can think of a lot of plausible reasons."

"She said it was something about zoning, something to do with his boat works, about taxes and nonconforming. Would you know what she was talking about?"

"I think I do. He's got a very nice chunk of land there, just south of the Hoyt Marina, about three hundred feet of bay front adjacent to the channel. When the county was zoned four years ago, I think the commercial zoning extends down from the causeway onto Sandy Key to include the Hoyt Marina. But it doesn't include Gulfway Marine Designs. So that makes it nonconforming. Actually I think it's in Residential B."

"What does that mean?"

"It means he can't expand, and if it burned he couldn't rebuild it, and if he sold it, he'd have to sell it as nonconforming. But he's got all the buildings he wants there, and it isn't likely to burn down, and he certainly doesn't want to sell. Actually, it's fine for him the way it is. It was probably one of those favors local government does for newspaper publishers. He pays taxes on a Residential B basis. He loses money on that operation anyway, so the lower taxes are a help."

"How much help, Jimmy?"

"All I can do is guess. Three hundred feet. I'd say if they zoned him commercial it would cost him about eighteen hundred to two thousand a year more. His land goes all the way through to Bay Highway."

"That isn't enough to bother him, is it?"

"Not that alone. I wouldn't think so. Probably Carol

didn't get the whole picture. He's got a lot of little things scattered around, and he's probably getting the best possible break on all of them. If they went into rezoning and reassessment on all of them, they probably could bruise him pretty good. And he couldn't use the paper to fight back because all he would be doing would be disclosing the fact he *had* been getting some breaks."

"Carol said he was complaining about being pushed around."

"He probably was a little slow making up his mind, so they leaned on him. They're not taking any chances, Kat."

"But isn't it something you can use, Jimmy?"

"What do you mean?"

"Can't you sort of . . . track down what happened and let people know these Palmland people have blackmailed the paper?"

"Kat, are you comfortable? Can you listen to a lecture?"

"I'm stretched out across my bed," she said, "but don't you want to dry off?"

"I brought my towel along. Feet on my desk. Cigarettes handy. Now listen carefully, dear. You're an intelligent woman. I went into journalism out of a sort of idealism. I fell in love with a glamorous gal called the newspaper game, and after I'd lived with her a few years I found out she's a whore. She talks big sometimes, but she's bone-lazy, cynical, greedy and perfectly satisfied with herself. Do I sound like a college sophomore?"

"Maybe . . . a little."

"So let's look at the facts. I think these figures are close. There are seventeen hundred and sixty-one daily newspapers in this country. Sixty-one of them are in cities with more than one newspaper. The other seventeen hundred are monopoly papers. The *Record-Journal* is a monopoly paper. Now here is the crazy thing about a monopoly paper. It is the only form of monopoly not subject to regulation. Regulation would be interference with the freedom of the press. The A.N.P.A. would never let that happen. So, in seventeen hundred cities of America, including this one, the publisher decides exactly what he will give the public. We present the cheapest, dullest possible coverage of national and international news, and all the bargain syndicate items. In contrast, our local news coverage is maybe a little better than average. But the publishers—Ben Killian included—look on news as a tiresome but necessary evil, and they resent the public for expecting it. It's the only game in town, Kat, and it's main, basic, primary, unchangeable purpose is to sell adversiting and make money. Follow me?"

"Yes," she said hesitantly.

"Actually this is a better paper than the average, because Ben Killian doesn't have any particularly strong opinions. Our political stance is conservative Democrat on a local level, Republican on national issues, which precisely reflects the point of view of the advertisers. Suppose, as is true in many unhappy areas, Ben Killian was a confirmed John Bircher, a witch-hunter, an oppressor of every variety of liberal thought and viewpoint. Then, with no regulatory checkrein, no holds barred, he could make happen here what has been happening in, for example, Boulder, Colorado. He could have an outraged citizenship, indomitably ignorant, purging their community of everything which did not fit their standards of mediocrity. But Ben and Borklund have merely the simple touching desire to make the maximum amount of money with the minimum fuss. To do this, the paper must go along with the viewpoints of the advertisers. So, if Ben showed any sign of deviation, it is natural that the advertisers would arrange to move against him in the direct way of cutting their budgets for newspaper advertising as much as they dare. Because they can't cut it completely and survive themselves, they move against him in other ways, through the pressure they can generate through their indirect control of the agencies of local government. Clear?"

"It sounds so . . . cut and dried."

"It is. The only thing about that zoning thing which surprises me is that Ben hesitated so long they had to use it. And there's nothing there I can use, certainly. I work for Ben Killian. I am an agent of his policy. What if I want to expose this whole mess? What do I do? Go on the air? He owns thirty per cent of WKPC. And the men who own WEVT in the south county are certainly not interested in giving me a platform. I can't use Ben's paper to expose him. I couldn't get it past Borklund. Can I quit and go someplace else and expose the whole conspiracy? The next town I go to would have another monopoly publisher, and a readership vastly uninterested in what happens in Palm County. Do I start my own paper here? I don't have the million dollars required, and if I did have it and did get a paper going, neither paper would be profitable because the shopping area is too small. Do I still sound sophomoric?"

"No, Jimmy."

"So it's a little late for me to change professions, Kat. I have to go right on living with this lady I thought was so exciting. I'm an assistant advertising salesman. If I call myself a pimp, I sound too dramatically cynical, I guess. Put it this way. She isn't what I thought she was, but I'm used to

living with her now. I'm good at what I have to do. If somebody else did it, it wouldn't be done as well, and the lady
would be that much worse off. But don't ask for crusades,
Kat. No lance, no armor, no horse. We come out strongly
in favor of motherhood once a year, in May. We're in favor
of peace, education, public health, the right to work, church-
going, weak unions, lower taxes . . ."

"And filling Grassy Bay."

"You have the picture."

"If you'd *tried* to depress me, I don't think you could have
done a better job, darn it."

"You won't be really depressed until you see tomorrow's
paper."

"I can hardly wait. The thing that gets me, Jimmy, there's
just no way to . . . to present the other side of this to the
people."

"Not when the other team controls the communications."

"I hear the kids coming. Thanks for the lecture, Jimmy."

"I should have given it to you a long time ago. But I guess
I wanted your good opinion. I wanted you to think of
me as the fearless journalist, fighting for truth and beauty."

"I'll retain that delusion anyhow, Jimmy, because . . . well,
I know you would if you could."

After Wing had finished talking with Kat, he had a cautious euphoria which he could not identify. He knew he
should dress quickly and take his copy into town, but he did
not want to disturb this feeling of well-being until he could
be certain what caused it. He stretched out on his bed,
naked, resting the icy ring of the beer can against his belly. At
first he thought it was due entirely to Kat and to his awareness of her. She had said she was stretched out across her
bed. He had visualized her in a manner he knew was inac-
curate. He had made it night at her house, and put a weak
lamp beyond her, and dressed her in a diaphanous hip-length
nightgown, ribboned at her throat, her hair ruffled, her face
softened by desire as she spoke to him. . . .

Like in high school, he thought irritably. Sex visions. All
the hot swarming preludes to masturbation. You're supposed
to be grown up, lover boy. You are supposed to have arrived
at that male adult condition which has learned that strangers
are never very good in bed together, and that the similarities
shared by all women are of more moment than the differences
between them.

No, it was not the familiar compulsion which had given
him these moments of something which felt like a cousin to
happiness. He felt as if he had been released, freed of some

weight which had been pressing against him. He began to
wonder, with increasing conviction, if it was merely the result of having expressed his own attitude toward his work.
He realized he had never talked in precisely that way to anyone, about what he felt and believed. He had tried to tell
Gloria, but she had thought, each time, he was just in a bad
mood and needed cheering up. He had argued it with Brian
Haas, but Brian's disenchantment was so much more
thorough than his own that he generally found himself de-
fending a position he could not believe.

In stating his position to Katherine Hubble, he had felt as
though he were striking a pose with her, presenting a faulty
image of himself, but the pretense had been the reality he
had been suppressing. And he had experienced the familiar
phenomenon of self-illumination which comes through turning thoughts into words.

But as he tried to find the reasons for his sense of well-
being, it had faded to where it was too faint to identify. His
head was propped up on two pillows. He looked down along
his body, still lean, but softened by the sedentary years,
looked at the ruff of tan-blond hair on his chest, the slight
bulge of pallid belly with the dimpled umbilical knot, at the
nested peduncular sex, at the slight sheen of perspiration on
the long flaccid legs. My unloved engine, he thought, idling
along, working its gas-bag lungs, clenching its heart in resting rhythm, burning what it wants and making rubbish of
the rest—while way up here, behind the wet lenses to
see with, behind the fleshy bulge of the air intake, and behind that dual-purpose orifice which can make howling and
grunting sounds and also grind matter small enough to go
down the pipes, the gray jelly makes its pictures, its plans, its
excuses and confusions, arrogantly ignoring its dependence
on the engine which carries it about, ignoring all the dutiful,
clever combustions and hydraulics, the thermostats and
maintenance and repair procedures, the churning and pul-
sating and secreting which never stop until it all stops. Perhaps then, as the last bright picture fades, the final emotion
sustained by the bone-cased jelly is indignation that the
faithless engine has quit. Perhaps its last word is WAIT!

The phone rang. It was Harmon at the paper saying, "Borklund says to say he's wondering about the Palmland stuff."

"I'm just now tying it to the pigeon."

"Huh?"

"Tell J.J. it's Pulitzer material."

"Huh?"

"I've done it as a long dialogue between an empty bay and
a sexy bulldozer."

"Chrissake, Wing, what he wants to know is when are you bringing it in here?"

"Tell him to look up. I'm probably standing in front of him right now."

"Huh?"

Wing hung up, dressed quickly and headed for the mainland.

18

WHEN JIMMY WING parked in the field beside Elmo's Lemon Ridge home a little before eleven there were at least forty cars in the area. As he walked through the gate he could hear music that was almost drowned by the interwoven, incomprehensible texture of loud conversations, whoops, laughter. When he could see the pool area from the path, he saw that it was packed with people, most of them standing, most of them in large conversational groups. All the landscape, pool and apron lights were on. There were more people in the workshop, where the bar was set up. There was no uniformity of dress. A half dozen people were swimming. As he walked slowly down toward the screen doors, he saw women in shorts and halters talking to women in strapless cocktail dresses.

He stopped in the shadows to look at the composition of the group. He picked out the Palmland Development people, and many of the younger faces in the Palm County Democratic Party. He saw some of the wheels of the Palm County Chamber of Commerce, and a mixed bag of businessmen, those who might be the ones to benefit most quickly from a project to build eight hundred upper-income homes. One couple was leaving. The woman looked wan, tottering and drunk, and the man looked both concerned and angry. It was evident the party had been in process for a long time, and was showing exceptional vitality.

He looked for Elmo and did not see him. He saw Dellie Bliss on the far side of the pool. As he worked his way slowly through the throng, nodding to friends, acknowledging greetings, he saw Dellie leave the people she had been talking to. He hurried and caught up with her.

"Well, hi, Jimmy!" she said.

"Hello, Dellie. Pretty festive around here?"

"Isn't it a mess? It sort of just grew. That's the kind of parties you find around *this* house. I was just going to check and see if I ought to have more food brought down from the house, but I can tell you there isn't much left up there. If you're looking for Elmo, you come with me. I think he's in by the bar."

Inside the workshop the music was louder than the voices.

Inside a circle of spectators, Buck Flake was proving he could lie down on the floor and get up again without spilling any of the full drink balanced on his forehead.

Elmo saw Wing and left the circle and came over to him. They moved out of the doorway to talk. "How much is the paper doing?"

"Headline and half of page one, half of page two, one whole page of pictures and about eight little specials scattered around."

"Fine! It's been big on the radio all day too."

"What's the party? Premature celebration?"

"Keep the voice way down, Jimmy boy. Way down. Get a drink. You're way behind. This'll start to thin out some. You circulate and listen to the happy folk. We'll talk a little later on."

Jimmy carried a stiff drink out toward the pool. He admired a tanned and lovely back and, as the woman turned, he realized it was Eloise Cable, in a deceptively simple sunback dress. She was standing with Leroy Shannard, Martin Cable and young Connie Merry, the wife of the county attorney. Jimmy joined the small group. They all greeted him.

Martin said, "Tell me, Jimmy. You were there. Did I give the impression the bank was already behind this Palmland project?"

"That's not the way I reported it. There were a lot of ifs and whereases. Anyhow, Borklund got a copy of your statement and it's running on page three, I think, word for word."

"People seem unable to listen," Martin said gloomily. "It's a delicate situation. Palmlands has absolutely nothing worth loaning money on until they have title to the bay bottom."

"How about the sterling character of the participants?" Leroy asked lazily.

"Oh, each of you could borrow a certain amount on signature alone, of course," Martin said humorlessly, "but it wouldn't be nearly enough."

"You worry too much, dear," Eloise said.

"I couldn't go around obligating the bank like that," Martin said.

"We know that," Leroy said. "Everybody understands. And we appreciate your making that statement for us."

"Martin was glad to do it," Eloise said. She smiled at Leroy. Jimmy could see no meaningful emphasis in her smile or her expression. She looked hearty, handsome, confident and utterly relaxed.

"Maybe they could raise money by having Buck Flake put

that up for collateral," Connie Merry said, looking across the pool.

"Put what up?" Eloise asked. "Oh, is that the one? In the little orange dress?"

"That's the one," Connie said.

The orange dress was short, beltless and sleeveless, with a scoop neck. It made a striking color combination with her heavy silver hair. Each time she turned and moved, the dress clung for a moment to the warm lines of her strong young body.

"There is collateral the bank would like to accept, but cannot," Martin said with heavy-handed humor.

"I saw her and wondered who she was. I'd heard about Mr. Flake's . . . interest in her. I didn't put two and two together. Got his nerve bringing her to a thing like this, hasn't he?"

"He brought one of his salesmen along too," Leroy said. "That's supposed to make it all right. But it doesn't make it all right with Dellie and Elmo. Not at this kind of a deal. Buck realizes that, so he's been drinking to keep up his spirits. In spite of his knowing he's just making certain Betty will hear about it from some dear friend, he has to keep showing her off around town."

"She's something to show," Eloise said. "She must be over five ten."

"In that glass she's got is gin and ice," Leroy said.

"You seem to know her pretty well, Mr. Shannard," Connie Merry said, with a smile that wrinkled her freckled nose.

"As well as I ever shall, my dear," Leroy said. "When they're that young, they alarm me."

"Maybe it isn't any of my business," Martin Cable said, "but isn't it rather bad judgment on the part of one of the founders of Palmland Development to get mixed up with a young girl? Don't the rest of you disapprove of such . . . an obvious relationship?"

Leroy smiled. "Ol' Buck hasn't been much use to us lately. But what are we going to do about it?"

"I can tell you one thing you can do about it. You can tell your other associates that the bank, any bank, is always hesitant about loaning money to people of dubious moral stature."

Leroy looked at him sharply. "Do you mean that, Martin?"

"I was stating a fact, not an opinion."

Leroy shook his head in mild wonder and said, "You know, I think a romance just ended. Didn't it sound like that to you, Jimmy?"

Five men stood around Charity Prindergast. They all wore

the same glazed, bemused expression. He saw her pat one of them atop his bald head, hand him her empty glass. The man scuttled off.

"I heard a small crunching sound," Jimmy admitted.

"Suppose he won't give her up?" Eloise asked.

"A noble stance like that," Leroy said, "can happen in books, plays, and television, but not in the life of Buckland Flake. When anything stands between Buck and a dollar, he boots it out of the way."

"Are all men like that, Leroy?" Eloise asked, slightly coy.

"Most of them, my dear. There are exceptions. I try to have the best of both possible worlds."

"How nice for you!" she said acidly. "Isn't Leroy clever, Martin?"

"What? I wasn't listening, darling."

"Let me guess! You were thinking about the bank!"

"Well . . . as a matter of fact, I was."

By twelve-thirty most of the guests had left. Most of those who remained were drunk enough to have no intention of ever going home. There was one stubborn swimmer, and one girl who danced slowly, dreamily by herself, circling back and forth in front of the floodlights.

Jimmy Wing killed time, glancing at his watch. Elmo and Leroy were up in the office. Elmo had told him to come up at about quarter to one. Buck had passed out, face down on a long padded bench in the workshop. The bar was self-service. Major had gone home. When Jimmy went to make himself another drink he found Charity sitting cross-legged on the floor, going through the stack of records.

She smiled up at him and said, "These are sticky old disks, dear. Look. Wayne King, for the love of God!"

He leaned on a table near her and said, "You're trapped in the middle ages, Miss Prindergast. Rectangular types. We're not cool. We're not way out."

She laughed up at him. "Buckie does that too."

"Does what?"

"Tries the hip talk, but it doesn't sound. It's way over flat. Like I was to say 'twenty-three skidoo' and so forth."

"God, girl! I'm a more recent vintage than that!"

"What difference does it make? I mean when a thing is gone, does it matter how long it's gone? It's like memories, you know."

"No, I don't know."

"Well, you have a pocket to keep memories in. And there's a sweetie memory that happened when you were six, right? And you can take it out of the pocket and it's as shiny as what happened yesterday. And I have a memory of when I was six. In those memories, yours and mine, we're both six and it happened yesterday. I was twenty last week. You can be twenty with me by taking out a memory from when you were twenty. There isn't any age but young, dear. And the only time left is now. What is your name, anyhow?"

"Jimmy Wing. A momentarily confused Jimmy Wing."

"Oh. With the paper. I don't confuse myself. Why should I confuse you?"

"Stay where you are. I have to go now. I'll be back later."

"I'm not going anywhere. I always like being where I am best. I don't have to go looking for me because I'm never anywhere else but here."

"While we're apart, I'll think that over."

Elmo was sitting on his desk. Jimmy sat on the couch beside Leroy Shannard. "We could have banners made," Jimmy said. "The Palmland Panthers."

"You drunk?" Elmo asked, frowning.

"No. I was just talking to Miss Charity. I got into the habit of a stream of consciousness."

"Stream of unconsciousness," Leroy said.

"Leroy is as pleased as I am with the two little things you worked out for us, Jimmy."

"I'm pleased that he's pleased."

"We've decided that for a little while you're going to mark time," Elmo said. "We might not have to push anybody. They may drop off of their own selves."

"Particularly when they find out they're being un-American," Leroy said.

Jimmy turned and stared at him. "How's that?"

"I guess you just haven't thought it through," Leroy said. "What's the greatest strength of America? Free enterprise, of course. And what's more free-enterprise than reclaiming unsightly disease-breeding mud flats and turning those flats into a garden spot dotted with beautiful American homes? It adds strength to the economy. Why, my boy, if all over this great country little bands of Communist sympathizers and Communist dupes could put a spoke in the wheels of free enterprise by blocking progress and production, Red Russia could bring this mighty nation to its knees without using one single little bomb. Lenin said that in order to achieve victory over the capitalist nations, it is first necessary to bankrupt them. Leaving that bay untouched is one of the devices of a welfare state. It's socialistic in nature. It's part of the trend of the government owning everything. Naturally some of the people in Save Our Bays, Incorporated, have the best motives in the world. They love birds, or fish, or canoeing or some damn thing, but can you say they aren't being subverted by somebody working behind the scenes, somebody who will take every chance that comes along to divide and confuse us and cripple the free-enterprise system? And maybe that person has a Red Chinese wife."

Jimmy stared for a moment and licked his lips. "That's a hell of a dangerous thing to turn loose in this town."

"You mean people would believe it?" Elmo asked.

"A lot of them. Too many of them. It's just wild enough and absurd enough and idiotic enough."

"It's been turned loose in a lot of towns, for a lot of different reasons, Jimmy. And it's loose here already."

"Who started it?" Jimmy demanded.

"I did," Leroy said, "and I didn't mean to, and I'm ashamed of myself. A few days ago one of our more militant crackpots was in my office. Whenever he wants to sue some-body he comes to me and I talk him out of it. Jake Cooper. You know him. He heads up that big trailer park group."

"Fighters for Constitutional Action," Jimmy said. "Yes. I know him. He's a damned old bore."

"I was tired and bored, so I went into that little spiel just for kicks. Suddenly I realized he was taking it seriously. So I told him I was just making a complicated joke. He kept nodding and licking his lips and saying he understood. He's been hungry for some new liberty to suppress. Before he left he told me that he understood that I had to say it was a joke because I didn't want to get mixed up in that end of it. He said I didn't have to worry a bit. He said I could leave all those dirty radical nigger-lovers to him. He's already started making a noise, Jimmy. The other idiot-fringe groups will jump in. It was a stupid thing to do, but I console myself by saying it was such a natural that it would have happened anyway. So let's just lay back for a while and see what happens."

Elmo said, "You just write pretty words about Grassy Bay for us, and let me know if Jennings happens to come up with any good ideas. The money will keep coming."

"But weren't you talking about one little odd job for him, Elmo?"

"Hell, yes! I damn near forgot. You won't get much sleep tonight, Jimmy boy. You got to go pack that big blonde of Buckie's and stick her on an airplane. Here's a hundred dollars for a ticket."

"Where to?"

"She can pick her own direction, long as it's a nice long flight."

"Does Flake know about it?"

"He will in the morning, and when Leroy finishes talking to him, Buck will go down on bended knee and thank us for giving him a second chance. If she's long gone, he'll be easier to handle."

"Does the girl know she's going?"

"Leroy's going down there right now with you and have a little talk with her. Leroy's good at this kind of thing. I'll be down in a while, but I expect you'll be gone by then, so goodnight, Jimmy."

As they walked down toward the pool, Leroy said, "All you do is back me up if I have to bring you into it. Two work better than one on these things. She's just a kid."

Charity was fixing herself a drink when they found her. Flake was still in the same position, mouth open, arm dangling.

Leroy smiled at the girl and said, firmly, "You come out here for a while. We want to talk to you."

She came along willingly. Leroy took her to the far end of the pool and had her sit in a redwood chair. He pulled two other chairs close, facing her, and motioned to Jimmy to sit down with them.

"I want to ask you some questions, Miss Prindergast."

"I never give interviews except at the studio, sweetie."

"Where's your home?"

"Wherever I happen to be, sweetie."

Leroy Shannard made a sudden skillful motion. His hard palm cracked her face around to one side. Her drink fell and shattered. She was motionless for one stunned moment, then squealed with rage and lunged at him. Leroy shoved her back into the chair. When she tried again, he slapped her again.

"Settle down or I'll really have to hurt you. You're not among friends."

There were welts on her face and her eyes were streaming. "You . . . you dirty bastard!" she said.

"Exactly. Precisely. Now answer the questions without any cute talk. Where are you from?"

She hesitated. When he raised his hand she said, quickly, "Dayton, Ohio."

"That's better, dear. You met Flake in Fort Lauderdale. You went there for spring fun and games with the rest of the kids. Why didn't you go back home?"

"I was going to flunk out anyway."

"Buck Flake was stupid to bring you back here. Do you realize that?"

"I don't know what you mean. He offered me a job."

"You know what I mean. He's a married man."

"He's a lot of fun."

"The fun is over."

"You better ask him about that, sweetie."

"Buck has a lot of friends. He's tied up with a lot of people in various business ways. Those people want to take good care of Buck, whether he wants it or not. So nobody is asking him anything, Charity. In fact, nobody is asking you anything. We're telling you exactly what choice you have. Mr. Wing will take you home and wait while you pack and drive you to an airport, buy you a ticket and put you on a flight. If you want to be stubborn, I can have a sheriff's deputy and a jail matron here within fifteen minutes. They'll take you in and book you for theft."

"Of what?"

"Anything plausible. My wallet, maybe." He smiled. "Or it could be disorderly conduct, public intoxication, soliciting."

"Whatever you do, Buck would get me right out."

"Probably, if none of us could talk him out of it. But it's a funny thing about that matron at the county jail. Every time a pretty girl is booked, the matron looks her over and seems to find lice or the evidence of lice in her pretty hair. So, in the interest of hygiene, she orders the pretty tresses shaved off, before she puts the girl in one of her nice clean cells. Sometimes it takes four holding and one shaving to get the job done. But it gets done, Miss Prindergast."

She raised her hand slowly to her heavy silver hair. She stared at Jimmy Wing. "Could . . . could that happen?"

"It usually does."

"You're both trying to scare me."

"If you want to take the gamble, Charity," Leroy said, "go right ahead. It wouldn't be permanent damage anyway. Hair always grows back."

She snuffled, bit her lip and looked at the pool. "Can I even say goodbye to Buck?"

"You might say it too loud and wake him up, dear," Leroy said. "You have your purse. You better leave right from here."

"But I didn't want to leave. This is a fun place." She sighed. "They're all fun places. Hey! How about my pay?"

"What's due you?"

"Let me see. It would be about eighty dollars."

Leroy took out an alligator wallet, separated eighty dollars and handed her the money. "I'll get it from Mr. Flake." He stood up and said, "It wouldn't be wise to write or phone Mr. Flake, or to turn around and come back."

"I said he was fun. I didn't say he was a thing." She stood up. "Well, Jimmy Wing, let's go. I just didn't realize Buckie had such sweetie friends."

She was a tall girl to walk with. She had nothing to say. She sat in the car, subdued, as far from him as she could get. She did not speak all the way to Palm Highlands, except to direct him to the display house where she was living. It was several doors beyond the sales office. He stopped in the drive and said, "I'll wait here."

"Hell, come on in and help me say goodbye to it."

He followed her in. She turned on the lights in every room as she went through it. All the furniture was new. She had managed to strew clothing in every room, fill every ashtray, dirty every glass. She turned the built-in music system on at high volume, hauled two blue suitcases out of a closet, fixed herself a drink and told him to help himself.

"He belted me a couple of good ones," she said. "Look at the damn marks!"

"It surprised me."

"I know. Your mouth hung open. But it didn't surprise you as much as it did me. Go gather up clothes, dear. Start in the living room. Dump them in this suitcase."

In less than twenty minutes she was ready to leave. As she went around, taking a last look, she said, "It makes you feel like dirty, being hustled out of town. It makes me feel cheap. All clear, I guess. Help me get the lights. Key on the table, I guess. Should I leave him a note? Hell, no. What would I say? Four pieces of luggage and one sweater. Where are we going, dear? Which airport?"

"It depends on where you want to go, I guess."

"I'd like to look at what they have, and pick one out."

"Dayton?"

"Sweetie, if that's the only one they have, you can bring me back here for the new hairdo. I wore that place out." As she reached for the last light switch, she gave him an urchin grin, a bawdy wink.

"Shouldn't we do some phoning first, Charity?"

"That would be planning ahead, Jimmy. Makes for a dreary case of the dulls. Let's just roll the dice."

He carried the two big bags out and put them in the wagon. She brought the smaller ones. As he backed out of the driveway she said, "Maybe I kept you from phoning the little woman, eh?"

"No little woman. There is one, but she isn't taking calls."

"Separated?"

"That's a good enough word. Where do you want to fly to?"

"Let's see what they got first. Where's the nearest place with the biggest choice?"

"Tampa. But we can stop at Sarasota and see what they've got."

"Wing, sweetie, you're ugly in a kinda nice classy way. I usually don't like sandy men. They look as if they'd go fat and pink and start snorting."

"Thanks so much."

She carefully folded her white cardigan and placed it on his right thigh. She hitched around until she could lie on her side, using the cardigan as a pillow. The seat was as far back as it would go. The bottom curve of the steering wheel was within an inch of her forehead.

"Mind?" she said.

"Not at all."

"I'm a big girl. I need a lot of room. Wake me at the ticket counter." She breathed deeply a few times, and was asleep sooner than he would have believed possible. He was very conscious of the solid weight of her head against his thigh. When he slowed for a stop sign, there was a scent of her in the car, gin, and a soapy fresh smell of her hair and a faint fragrance of perfume.

It was a little after four when he stopped in front of the Sarasota-Bradenton Airport Terminal. She had stirred slightly in her sleep a few times. His leg was tired and numb from having held it in the same position so long. She sat up, rubbed her eyes with her fists, shook her glossy hair back, and then looked at him and said, "Oho! You again! Are you following me?"

"Want to wait while I check?"

"No. I'll go in too. You can check while I use the biffy." She got out and limped around in a little circle, stamping her foot. "Pins and needles," she said. She took the smallest suitcase out of the wagon and carried it in with her.

She came out in fifteen minutes, hair brushed, mouth fixed, looking incomparably fresh and rested. She came tocking toward him on her high heels, a big, gaudy, smiling young girl. She stood eye to eye with him, making him feel dwindled.

"Four hour and fifteen minute wait," he said.

"Where does it go?"

"It's Eastern, and it hops here and there and ends up in Idlewild in the later afternoon. There's room on it."

"On to Tampa, Wingy sweetie."

"After some coffee."

"Sure. But I could drive and you could sleep, you know. Show me a map. I'm damn fine about maps, man. I'm sober and I've got dandy reactions and I love to drive right into the dawn."

After slight hesitation, he skipped the coffee. He moved into the rear seat. She gave him her sweater for a pillow. He sat up until he saw that she handled a car with precision and competence. He stretched out. Moments later she was leaning in, shaking him. It was gray dawn. He sat up. They were in a parking area at Tampa International.

She handed him the parking tag. "Come on, sweetie. Wake up with the sun. I got lost once, but we still made pretty good time. You need a motor job. Let's leave the bags here until we know which lucky airline gets them. How do you lock this thing? How do you feel?"

"Wretched."

"You look worse than that. Come on. Get the blood moving. You didn't stir a muscle when I bought gas. You owe me five sixty, sweetie."

He stood beside the car and stretched, then locked it and followed her into the terminal. Every man within a hundred feet, sitting and standing, straightened up and stared at her. She went from counter to counter, airline to airline, standing at each long enough to read the dispatch board.

"Now the coffee," she said, and he followed her to the coffee shop. They sat at the counter. She ordered a large orange juice, cereal, hot cakes with sausage and a pot of coffee. He ordered juice and coffee.

"If you'd eat, you wouldn't get so tired, Wingy. This is like a new day. Fortify yourself. Now let me get straight. I name the place, you buy the ticket."

"Up to a hundred dollars."

She glared at him. "The hell with that! If I'm run off, I want the first-class treatment. You can get it back from all those dear old pals of Buckie's. How much have you got on you?"

He checked, his fingers slow and fumbling. With the money Elmo had given him yesterday morning, he had two hundred and fifty-six dollars.

"Of which five sixty is mine anyhow," she said. "No airlines credit card?"

"Not on my salary."

"Well, give me two-forty of it, and if it's more, I'll have to chip in."

"Damn decent of you. Where are you going?"

"Las Vegas. There's a couple of ways to get there. Any objection?"

"Nothing I can think of. Except the cost."

She had been eating with a considerable fervor. She finished and said, "Stand guard over my coffee. Give with the money. I'll get the ticket."

"Go see if you can get on a flight and then we'll go buy the ticket."

"Such trust," she said. She was back in ten minutes. She handed him a small package. "All for you, sweetie." He looked into the bag. It was a plastic kit containing comb, toothbrush, toothpaste, razor and shaving cream. "You don't owe me," she said. "It will improve your outlook." She patted his shoulder. "Run along and burnish."

When he came back to the counter she saluted him. "In a sense, you look human, Wingy."

"In a sense, I feel better. I was shaving and thinking about you. You're better organized than you look. Maybe Las Vegas makes some sense too."

"There was a spooky little bartender in Lauderdale. His brothers are all wedged into a thing out there, the Sahara, and they'd made a niche for him and he was on his way, wanting me to come along and share driving, saying I could make out, because there's so many ways out there. So he's there and he'd make some motions around and about but I could drop anyplace and land dancing, so it isn't a sweat. About my little airplane, dear, let's go buy it. But it isn't until three-oh-five, a jet thing, and the best I could do, except sprawling around Chicago for half my life."

"I'm supposed to be a working man."

"But you are working, aren't you? I didn't get the idea this was a pleasure trip."

They bought her ticket and checked the luggage through, except for the smallest suitcase. The sun was up and there was an early-morning fragrance, and a promise of heat and rain.

She stood in the terminal and looked at him with a great earnestness and said, "I really and truly, honest and truly, will get onto that thing and be gone, sweetie. I've got the ticket and the urge. So you can paddle back to Palmville and say you stoned me out of town. Okay?"

"All right, Charity. Sure."

She looked at the terminal clock. "But I am not going to stand around here like some kind of a nut for nine hours, rebuffing the chatty types. I saw nearby motels. You can drop me, and I'll leave a call and taxi back. One thing I can always do is sleep."

He drove her to a cluster of competing motels and she picked the one she liked. She strode in and registered and came out with a key, and he drove her back to a unit at the end of the court beyond a ludicrously small swimming pool. "She promised no maids clashing and bellowing around, and a taxi hooting for me at two-fifteen."

He carried the small suitcase in. The room was small, shadowy and chilly, with one bed and a giant television set and a faint institutional odor of antiseptic.

He put the suitcase on the luggage rack. She moved close to him and looked at him with a strange expression. "Well?" she asked.

"I was wondering . . ."

"Yes?"

"I guess it's none of my business. And you seem a lot more competent at twenty than I was. But that's a very hard town, Charity. I know you don't want anybody being protective. But there's a guy I know out there, works on the paper for Greenspun, I could give you a note to him you could hold onto and use if you have to, if things get rough for you somehow."

She shook her head slowly, her expression wry. "Here I stand, itching for the pass. Oh boy, did I ever have one for you! I was going to give it the swivel and a lot of back. I was going to give you one to make the pair I was given look like pattycake pattycake. So you don't pick up a single clue. Instead you keep on being a very nice sweetie guy."

"Do you want the note or don't you?"

"Now he's bugged. Yes, I want the note, don't I. Pretty please."

There was stationery in a drawer. He sat and addressed the note, and wrote, "This will introduce Miss Charity Prinderg . . ."

"Hold it!" she said. She was standing behind him, a hand on his shoulder. She reached over and crumpled the note and said, "This is a bigger departure than most, so I need a new name. For more reasons than you could guess. You give me one, sweetie."

"Is the Charity part okay?"

"It's even a character trait. Let's keep it."

He thought for a few moments. "How about Charity Holmes?"

"Mmm. As in Sherlock, eh? If it doesn't sound too much like a housing project for the aged. Charity Holmes. It swings a little. Charity begins at home. You know, I like it. I like it a lot." She kissed his ear. "I'm christened. On with the note. I'm ticketed as Prindergast. When I walk off the ramp I turn into Miss Holmes."

He wrote the note and gave it to her. She read it over, nodded, and put it in her purse. When he stood up, she put her arms around his waist and leaned back slightly and looked up at him. She had stepped out of her shoes, stepped down to a height where she seemed younger, smaller, more manageable.

"Poor old Wingy," she said. "The hard types using him for a handy man. Let's take ourselves a little lovin', just for luck."

"I just . . . thanks but I . . . I mean I really . . ."

She looked at him in a puzzled way. "You pledged, or something? Sick? Queer? Or you don't like great big girls? Sweetie, I may give it away, but I don't throw it around. There just aren't that many I need."

It was his intention to give her a friendly smile, a kiss, a perfectly polite and orderly and face-saving refusal of favors offered. But to his utter disbelief and consternation, the mild words clotted in his throat, he felt his face twisting into a sob, and the tears began to run out of his eyes. Through the distorting prism of tears he saw the sudden warm concern on her face. He tried desperately to laugh at himself, but it came out as a huge coughing sob. She led him over to the bed. He sat on the edge of the bed, slumped with his face in his hands. She knelt on the floor beside him, pressed against his leg, one hand on his knee, the other gentle at the nape of his neck. She made small tender sounds of comfort.

"I . . . I don't know . . . what the hell . . . is wrong with me," he managed to say.

"Sweetie, you're on the dirty ragged edge. Something chews your heart, Jimmy. It's a people-trouble. It can only happen to people, you know. Vegetables never get churned up."

"This . . . is so damn silly, for God's sake."

"It ain't manly, you mean?"

He struggled for control. "Today . . . yesterday, I mean, I felt good without knowing why. Now this. I'm cracking up."

"Darn you anyhow, James Wing. I don't want to know people can be racked up. Not elderly types like you. I had my little turn at it. It's a scene I don't want to make again. You coming out of it? Go wash your face, sweetie."

He delayed in the bathroom for long minutes, staring at his puffy red eyes in the mirror because he felt ashamed

to face her. When he came out, she was sitting on the
bed. She patted the spread beside her. "Come sit and listen,"
she ordered. She took his hand. "This is the story of a
girl bitched by biology, sir. When I was thirteen I looked
exactly like I look right now, almost. My face was a little
thinner and my hair was mousy brown, but all the rest
was as you see it. One minute I was in my happy little
world of scabby knees, hopscotch and bicycling, and the
next minute I came bursting up out of my girl-scout
uniform and discovered, to my alarm, I'd turned into a
big freak. And freaks, my dear man, either hide or turn
into clowns. So I went into my clowning era. The marks
of it are still with me. It didn't last too long. It lasted like
until I found out that what was freaky to other little girls
was just nifty for little boys. I was getting no appreciation
at home, for some dingy reasons I won't dwell on, so I
gloried in all the approval I was getting, and was too damn
careless, and got into a scandal bit which got nastied up
by the police coming into it, and I had to change schools.
Then began my sneaky era, where I still got cheers, but
kept it out of the papers. Then I fell in love. I was true
as blue. I trotted after him like a big dog, all happy and
panting. It lasted into college, my love era. I couldn't see
he was really a filthy little prig, I'd trusted him and told
all, so when he was ready, he bounced me out of his life
on the grounds I was a loose woman, all of which had
happened before I met him. Then I had the bad time,
Jimmy. The tears that come for no reason, and a kind of
reckless joy that comes for no reason. It's a pendulum
thing, like something came loose and starts swinging around
in your head. I wasn't mourning a lost love. By then I
despised the cruddy little stinker. I'd just gone raggedy.
But I came out of it, and soon thereafter I went to Lauderdale. Now are you all right?"

"How about your people?"

"Really and truly they couldn't care less, and never have."

"What do you think is going to happen to you?"

"I'm going to dally around, finding coffee and cakes,
until the President of the World finds me, sweetie. He's
going to fit the word 'man' as if it was invented for him.
When he laughs, they'll have landslides in the Andes. And
he'll be after a big, durable, true-as-blue girl, with so much
ready waiting love to give he'll be the only one who can
take the pressure. And every one of my kids will have the
living be-Jesus appreciated out of him. I'll kiss them and
applaud them all day long."

She raised his hand to her lips for a moment, then said,

"He won't be like us, Wingy, sweetie. All scabs and sores and busted feathers. We're the half-people, you know. It's the wise bastards who keep shoving us out into the traffic." She smiled at him, her blunt features oddly leonine in that light. "Nobody will push my President of the World around. He'll be solid and sound, scaled big enough so it'll take all day to walk around his heart. What, or maybe who, has bitched you up, dear?"

"I have no idea."

"So it's either something you are doing or something you're not doing. No fee for that analysis. And now if I should say make way for love, will you start flipping again?"

"Not this time, Miss Holmes."

She grinned and jumped up and pulled the orange dress off over her head. She held it by the shoulders and turned it to one side and then the other and said, "This little nothing in pumpkin is sadly rrrrrumped out, darn it. And I'm the gal who can do it. Sweetie, I think I'll take a shower first, with this little number hanging in there and see if it'll hang out some." She put the dress over her arm and went to her suitcase and dug around in it, taking things out. She smiled at him and said, "Feel free to stare your little pink eyes out, Wingy. A boy told me once I'm like Mickey Mantle—the more I take off, the bigger I look. Imagine a thirteen-year-old kid suddenly carting all this around? I went up through four bra sizes in three months. Why don't you pounce into the hay and have a little snooze? You'll have the time for it. I take long, long showers, dear." She got a hanger for her dress and went into the bathroom, humming in a small off-key voice.

He left the motel at a little after ten. She fell asleep while he was dressing. He bent over and kissed her on the temple before he left. She did not stir. A heavy tassel of the silver hair lay across her eyes.

As he drove by the airport a prop jet coming in startled him. It annoyed him to be startled. He did not wish to be roused out of a state which was neither trance nor lethargy, but an oddly quiet plateau, a place a little bit off to one side of reality.

After a dozen miles he recalled what it reminded him of. In his final year of high school he had been a third-string end, diligent enough and fast enough, but too brittle for the hazards of the game. They went into one of the last games of the season with three ends more useful than he out of action. He was sent into the game in the second quarter, and came hobbling out after the fourth play, with

a sprained ankle. During the half, the trainer injected novocaine into his ankle and instep in three places, and bound
it so tightly the flesh bulged over the tape. Within minutes
he could put all his weight on it without pain. It felt like
a hard rubber foot and ankle, springy enough, but not a
part of him. He started the third quarter. In the middle of
the final quarter he misjudged a tackle and broke the middle
finger of his left hand against a flying heel and came out
for good. All that evening he felt strange. The bloated ankle
had been cut free and retaped, but it did not hurt. They
told him it would hurt, later on. He had this same strange
quiet feeling then as now.

He had awakened in the middle of the night, bathed in
sweat. The pain of the splinted finger was nothing. The ankle
felt monstrous. It bulged with every heartbeat. It felt like
a balloon packed full of hot splintered glass. After he was
off crutches he had limped for nearly a year, and it still
ached when the weather changed.

So my sudden tears, he thought, were the sign of injury,
and Charity was the novocaine. It will hurt later, when
I try to laugh.

He had waited in the bed for her, wondering what she
would be like. After a long time she had come to him,
sweet and steamy from her long shower, friendly, talkative,
busy, utterly without artifice. She brought to the bed a flavor
of healthy, absent-minded innocence. It was strange and
casual, as though they had met at a party and were dancing
together for the first time, taking turns leading, interrupting
their conversation when the steps became tricky, apologizing
for any small miscues, attempting more ambitious twirls
and dips as they became more accustomed to each other,
then dancing some simple placid step when they wished to
talk. "So I found this stuff that doesn't make my hair brittle
and crack," she said. "A kookie name though. Silva-Brite."
"I like it," he said, "and I like the way you wear it." At
last her voice grew blurred and she said, in question, "Well,
here we go?"

It was ended. She kissed the tip of his nose. "Sweet," she
said. "Very sweet and nice. I'll sleep like stones now. Poor
Wingy. You have to stagger up and churn back south. Poor
dear man."

"You're quite a girl, Charity."

She yawned. "I don't like *that* tone of voice. You're
trying to patronize me. I'm just a girl sort of girl, bigger than
most, friendlier maybe, who likes you well enough for a little chummy kind of love. I thought I could loosen some of

those knots in your heart, that made you cry. So don't quite-a-girl me. It wasn't that big a scene."

He was beside her, facing her from such close range her eye looked enormous. She stuck her underlip out and blew a fringe of silver hair back off her forehead.

"You made it exactly right," he said.

"Good! I wanted you to have something good to go with the weeps."

"That's never happened to me before."

"Hell, sweetie, neither have I, so at least you aren't in a rut. Kiss goodbye. There. Now you can get up and scoot back and tell them the big pig has been shooed out of Buckie's precious little life." She winked that enormous eye. "Don't tell them I was beginning to think about leaving several days ago."

By the time he was twenty miles below Tampa, she had begun to seem unreal. He told himself he had merely reacted in the fashion of a normal male. He had taken a successful hack at a promiscuous, restless, rootless twenty-year-old girl. They passed out no medals for that. He told himself it was a pleasant, vulgar, meaningless little episode. But it kept being more than that. It was finding contact with someone in a place where all you usually touched were mirrors. She had a mangled wisdom of her own, suited to the lonely places. She made him wish he were fool enough to pack and drive to Vegas and try to be President of the World.

The novocaine was thinning, and pain was just a little way underneath it. The car roared down through the Gulf towns, toward the heat of the middle of the day. He sat and steered and was carried along, feeling disembodied, fragile, a husk-man, fashioned of cardboard and spit, dried in a hot wind.

The girl asked him if he had an appointment, and when he said he didn't, she checked with Leroy, and said Mr. Shannard could see him in about ten minutes if he cared to wait. He sat and turned the pages of an old magazine. The minutes ticked on toward two o'clock.

"Come in, James!" Leroy said with the sweet-sad welcome smile which crinkled the eagle eyes.

He went into the paneled office. Leroy closed the door and went around behind his desk.

"You got our problem lady off without mishap?"

"Off and winging."

"I didn't think she'd present much of a problem, somehow. Where did she elect?"

"Las Vegas. I had to put another hundred and forty into the kitty."

"She worked you over very nicely, didn't she?"

"Who reimburses me?"

"I guess that would be Elmo. And it won't make him terribly happy."

"She was going to be a problem otherwise. It seemed best to handle it quietly."

"I'm not saying you're wrong. I approve. But Elmo is our leader. And he will fret a little. By the way, our Mr. Flake is adjusting rapidly. He's sore as hell, but for the wrong reasons. He stayed at Elmo's place last night. This morning he learned he had been rude to her last night and she took off with some happy stranger for parts unknown, leaving him an unprintable verbal message. The switch in the story cost me eighty dollars, which somehow amuses the hell out of Elmo."

"How did the morning paper look?"

"Surpassed our fondest dreams. Stroll anywhere in our friendly little city, James, and you will hear an enthusiastic populace buzzing about our new golden era."

"And I've got more of the same to write," Jimmy said and stood up. Leroy walked toward the office door with him. Jimmy stopped and turned toward him and said, "You certainly handled that girl with a lot of authority, Leroy."

Leroy shrugged. "I picked what seemed likely to work the best with a girl of that sort."

Jimmy felt a mild and wistful sense of disbelief as he heard his own grunt of effort. As Charity had mentioned, you get a good swivel, and you get your back into it. He saw Leroy's eyes widen an instant before the pistol crack of palm against brown leathery cheek. His open hand blazed with pain. The slap spun Leroy halfway around, and he stumbled and braced himself, his hands against the paneled wall beside the door.

Jimmy stared at him stupidly, and suppressed the inane automatic apology which first came to mind. What do you say? My hand slipped?

Leroy seemed to stand for a very long time with his hands against the wall, his head bowed. He straightened up and turned around. Jimmy stood balanced and waiting, not at all certain he could whip the older man in a fair fight. He realized at that moment that it was not impulse, that he had brought the compulsion to violence all the way from Tampa.

Leroy was bleeding slightly from the left corner of his mouth. He looked at Jimmy with complete and hostile disgust. He took his handkerchief out and dabbed his mouth and sat down behind his desk.

"Feel better?" Leroy asked. "Sit down."

Jimmy sat down. He felt strangely bland, mild, uninvolved.

"Noble gestures cramp my ass," Shannard said gently. "Gallantry revolts me. It's always based on a faulty image. I didn't know you rode such a big white horse. What did you do? Bang her on the way to the airport and take a liking to her?"

"That's neither here nor there."

"You're so right. It doesn't illuminate the new problems."

"Such as?"

"You've just done an amazingly stupid thing, James. Would it sound too pretentious if I were to say that it is the sort of thing which could change your future personal history?"

Jimmy considered that for a moment. "You could be right."

"Thank you. It was a quixotic gesture, expressing moral disapproval at the risk of some form of martyrdom."

"Just defense of womanhood, maybe."

"If so, it came twelve hours late, didn't it? The main thing is this, James. I don't like people around me who are capable of such wild unexpected stupidities. I find them hard to predict. They can upset apple carts. Do you follow me?"

"Up to a point, the point being that I am not around you, the point being that Elmo brang me into this, as I recall."

"You know, I'm annoyed at myself for misjudging you so completely. I didn't want you brought into this. I told Elmo as much. But I think I had all the wrong reasons."

"Such as?"

"You're bright and you're capable, James. And you've done very damn little with those qualities. You seem satisfied to stay where you are and be what you are. You're not hungry. There isn't anything you want badly enough to go after it. The best way to control men is through their hunger, whether it's for money, fame, importance, power, liquor, women, gambling or what have you. You're a bored man, James. I told Elmo you'd go along with us, but without any particular conviction one way or the other, so it would be smarter to leave you out of it. He said he didn't agree. He said you like to be on the inside, to know a little more than the next guy, so your ego would make you useful. Also he said that you would be a sucker for the argument that you could keep your friends from being roughed up too badly by playing along with us. In a sense, James, it has worked out as he thought it would, right up until now. Now you disclose a new facet of the Wing character. And it bothers me. It makes me wonder what other dangerous impulses you might have."

"I'm just a bundle of neuroses, Leroy."

"You've been a help, but Elmo says you have a tendency to drag your feet."

"I haven't been standing at attention and saluting. Maybe I just didn't get the top jobs to do. Like Eloise Cable."

Leroy Shannard tilted his head, pursed his lips, stared intently at Wing. "Elmo tell you?"

"Yes."

"I'll be damned if I can figure out why. Everything he does usually turns out to have some reason behind it."

"Maybe he knew we weren't going to get along too good, Leroy."

"Believe me, boy, if I could turn Eloise over to you or anybody, I'd gladly do it. It stopped being much of a pleasure a long time ago. I can't wait for the money end of it to get all tidied up. There's been some dumb women I've enjoyed. And there's been some earnest ones who've pleasured me. And I've nothing against a woman with a real loving nature. Also, a woman who can't help being real active in bed is supposed to be a good thing to come across. But I'm telling you James, after the new has wore off her, a dumb, earnest, loving, passionate woman can give you the longest afternoons you ever spent in your life."

"Martin should be grateful, you mean."

"You've got a smart-pants way about you that just rubs me the wrong way, James. But now I'm quieting down a little. I'm going to tell Elmo about what happened here."

"I couldn't care less."

"The way I see it, we're both being used by Elmo. He isn't going to unload you because I don't like you and don't trust you. He's going to keep the people he can use, and get rid of the ones he's used up, so I can guess you and me, we're going to be in this right along."

"There's one thing about you which puzzles me, Leroy. Half the time you speak like a bad essay in the *Atlantic*. Then you switch to a southrun folksy lingo as thick as Elmo's. I have the feeling that when you get folksy, that's the time to watch you the closest."

"Watch me at all times, James. Watch me at all times."

"Do we have anything more to talk about, actually?"

"Since trying to slap my head off, you've handled yourself well. Very smooth and quiet."

"All I did was make the point I didn't think you had to belt that girl the way you did."

"You know the old story about the agricultural college that had a special course on mule training. The first day of class this old boy led a big skittish mule into the classroom, dropped the rein, snatched up an eight-pound sledge and give the mule one square between the eyes. The mule sagged, cross-legged and cross-eyed, tongue hanging, and nearly went down. The class gasped. The professor turned to them and he said, 'The first thing you do in training a mule is you get his attention.' "

Jimmy stood up and said, "So it worked both ways, didn't it?"

"What do you mean?"

"You got hers, and I got yours."

Leroy nodded very slowly. "Yes indeed, you can say that you captured my attention, James. Permanently."

PUBLIC NOTICE

NOTICE IS HEREBY GIVEN, *pursuant to Chapter 58–1855, Laws of Florida, and as amended by Chapters 59–1811 and 60–1866, Laws of Florida, that the Board of County Commissioners of Palm County, Florida, sitting as the* PALM COUNTY BULKHEAD LINE AUTHORITY, *will hold a* PUBLIC HEARING *at 8:00* P.M. *on the 26th day of July* A.D. *1961 in the Palm City Municipal Auditorium, Palm City, Florida, upon the application of: the Palmland Development Company for the:* PURCHASE OF SUBMERGED LANDS: ESTABLISHMENT, CHANGE AND LOCATING OF THE BULKHEAD LINE, *within the area of: Grassy Bay, lying in Section 8, Township 20 South, Range 15 East, Palm County, Florida, and more particularly described in map and addendum appended to this* PUBLIC NOTICE, *being a parcel containing 833.24 acres, more or less. A permit for* DREDGE AND FILL *will not be considered at such Public Hearing. All interested persons may appear and be heard at the time and place specified. Written comments filed with the Clerk of said Authority will be heard and considered.*

> AUGUST C. MAKELDER
> *Chairman of Palm County
> Bulkhead Line Authority*

C. L. ARLETTER, *Clerk of
Palm County Bulkhead Line Authority*

By: J. Z. Winslow, Deputy Clerk

PUBLISH: *July 12, 1961*

The morning papers for Wednesday, Thursday and Friday were packed with ever more glowing accounts of the glorious future which Palmland Development was making possible for each and every resident of Palm County, present and future. At midmorning on Friday, Kat Hubble went across the street with Jimmy Wing for her coffee break.

"I am so *damn* mad!" she said.

"I'd say you look pretty mad too."

"Wait till we sit down, Jimmy, and I'll tell you and I wish I had an hour instead of ten minutes."

After they had ordered, she leaned across the small table toward Jimmy and said, "You've got to *do* something about that horrible newspaper!"

"Like what?"

"Tom has phoned Mr. Borklund and Ben Killian and he can't get any satisfaction at all. He has carbons of sixteen very good letters to the editor, all opposed to the bay fill, and they haven't published a single one of them. Mr. Borklund says they're getting so much mail they can only print a representative selection. Hah! Like this morning's paper. Five in favor and one opposed, and the one that opposes the fill is from somebody I never heard of, who sounds totally insane. And another thing. Mr. Borklund won't handle a perfectly legitimate news item. They did publish our names and addresses to make it easier for everybody. Do you know, we're getting absolutely *foul* phone calls, all of us? Day and night. The phone company can't do anything about it. The sheriff won't do anything about it. Our telephone campaign has absolutely collapsed! The people we call up say *hideous* things. Most of our workers have quit. We can't keep a sticker on a car five minutes before somebody rips it off. We can't get anybody to put our posters up, and when we do, they get all ripped and scribbled. Darn it all, Jimmy, this is outright, horrible persecution, and everybody pretends it just isn't happening."

"Whoa now, Kat. Slow down a minute. Who phones you?"

"Women who yell. Sometimes men who whisper. That's worse, I guess. If you want to phone me, Jimmy, let it ring once and then hang up and dial again immediately. That's what I'm telling my friends. And that's the way we get in touch with each other. Otherwise I don't answer. And I don't dare let the children answer any more."

"What do these people say?"

"Filth, Jimmy. Absolute filth. They call me a dirty Communist slut and so forth. A lot of cars went by my house last night, blowing their horns. This morning there was garbage all over my lawn. Same thing at Jackie's house and Doris Rowell's, Tom's, everybody's. I'll be damned if anybody is going to intimidate me, but they certainly are making life unpleasant. Yesterday and this morning it's spread to the bank. This afternoon they're moving me to the Trust Department until this is all over. What's *happening* to people, Jimmy?"

"They've gotten worked up."

"Somebody has organized all the nutty people in the county."

"I'll see if I can get the county road patrol to check your house at night, Kat."

"I don't want that. I want some publicity about what's happening to us. Don't you see, they're *overdoing* it. And if all the decent people who are in favor of the fill could understand what's happening, it might turn them against it. Another thing, Jimmy. Golly, I wish I had more time. Tom Jennings talked to old Mr. Hotchkiss. He has fifteen hundred acres on Grassy Bay, on the mainland, just north of Turk's Pass."

"I know where it is."

"He's got two thousand feet of bay front, and rather than see Grassy Bay ruined, he'll sell the whole plot to Palmland for twelve hundred dollars an acre. That's way under going prices. They could dig canals into it and make a big development out of it without taking over any public lands."

"He's offered it to Palmland?"

"Yes. And they're not interested. They'd rather steal the land. But the important thing is to get it into the paper, and we can't even do that, so the people will know there was an alternative. Can you try to get it in, Jimmy? Can you get some of this other stuff in? Honestly, every day I read all that guff in the paper with your name on it and it makes me sick."

"You don't get to see the things I've tried to slip in."

"Of course not."

"I have to face certain facts of life, Kat. I can refuse to keep writing up the big stream of flack stuff Costex keeps throwing at us. So somebody else writes it. And maybe they fire me. Then I'm in a position where I can do no good at all."

"Which seems to be exactly where you are right now."

"Not because I want to be."

"I know. I'm sorry. Please *try* to do something. I promised Tom I'd beg you." She scowled at her watch. "Thirty seconds more." She spooned ice into her coffee. "Oh, by the way, who was the gorgeous chick you were seen with in Tampa the other morning? Heavens, Jimmy! You don't have to look *that* guilty!"

"Just one of those celebrities we newspaper types interview. Who reported me?"

"A girl coming back from vacation. She said it was a

show-business type in a wrinkled orange dress and platinum hair, about six foot seven. Who was she?"

"I was just doing a favor for a friend, putting her on a plane."

She gave him a puzzled look. "You act as if you think I'm being jealous. Good Lord, Jimmy! If it's none of my business, you've gotten your point across."

"But I was just . . ."

She jumped up. "I do have to run, dear. Try to help us, please."

Jimmy watched through the drugstore window as she hurried back to the bank, a redheaded woman, slender, agile and intense, a woman with the marks of life and marriage and loss in her face, a woman who, in comparison with the vivid Miss Prindergast, would look subdued, understated. But he knew he could never want anyone as badly as he wanted her.

He knew that in order to get a story into the paper he would have to make some special preparations. He visited Sheriff Wade Illigan. Using Kat's system, he phoned Jackie Halley, Tom Jennings and Major Lipe. Then he phoned Elmo Bliss at his office, told Elmo what he planned to do, and suggested that Elmo phone Burt Lesser, and then Ben Killian. Ben, he assumed, would speak to J. J. Borklund. After a fifteen-minute wait he phoned Burt Lesser, saying that he'd heard Burt had a statement to make. When Burt made it, Jimmy heard some of his own words repeated back to him. He wrote it up with great care:

"Mr. Burton Lesser, speaking as President of the Palmland Development Company and in behalf of the other partners in that enterprise, has expressed concern about the harassment being inflicted upon the officers and directors of Save Our Bays, Inc., a group actively opposing any change in the bulkhead line in the Grassy Bay area.

"Mr. Lesser stated to a Record-Journal reporter that support of the Palmland Isles Project is so overwhelming, the public hearing should result in a unanimously favorable vote. He said he and his associates are grateful for the support of every public-spirited citizen of Palm County, but deplore the activities of those who have been expressing their attitude by telephoning harassment of Save Our Bays members, and miscellaneous acts of vandalism committed on and around the private property of those members. He said that he has suggested to Sheriff Illigan that County Police protection be given the executive members of S.O.B., Inc., and the vandals be vigorously prosecuted if apprehended.

"Save Our Bays, Inc., is the only Palm County organization

thus far to have taken a public stand in opposition to the bay fill program."

He made a suggested head—PALMLAND CONDEMNS VANDALS—and took the copy sheet to Borklund's office. Borklund scanned it, initialed it, spindled it. He leaned back. His glasses caught the light and reflected the palm fronds outside his window.

"You puzzle me these days, Jim."

"How so?"

"You seemed so much more clever two years ago. This time I've blue-penciled forty clumsy attempts to sneer at Palmland, so clumsy you might as well have underlined them to save me the trouble. Brian has been much more subtle. He's even slid a couple of things past me that Ben chewed me out for."

"I'm probably turning into a dull fellow."

"Are you? This little item you just gave me is slick. Very, very slick. How did you get it?"

"On the phone, from Lesser."

"And you knew it would be all cleared by the time you got it to me. Funny how it got arranged so nicely. When I suggested we print something, I got turned down. I couldn't seem to get my point across. I said that if you miss a punch once in a while, it looks like a more honorable fight. You still win just as big, but it looks better. This will make the S.O.B.'s feel better, but it does them more harm than good. So I sit here wondering why you should do them more harm than good. Could you possibly have a piece of Palmland?"

"I think it will be tragic to fill Grassy Bay."

"But I have the strange feeling they're going to fill it."

"You mean you have a sort of a hunch?"

"Get the hell out of here, Wing."

Haas was in the newsroom. Wing went over and sat on the corner of his desk. "What is your opinion of a free and impartial press, Mr. Haas?"

Brian smiled at him. "It works on the valve theory, Mr. Wing."

"Would you explain that, please, for the benefit of our viewers?"

"Of course. When gas chambers are used to get rid of excess population, they have to employ a man to turn a valve. Right? Now, this man may not be in favor of gas chambers, and he may get very low pay for valve-tending, but he has to face up to a personal dilemma. It's such unskilled labor that if he refuses to turn it, somebody else will. This is known as facing reality, otherwise known as the facts of life. He can't merely pretend to turn the gas on, because when the chamber doors are opened again, they would discover his defection. Right? So all he can do is just turn it on a little slowly, and not quite all the way. This is known as learning to live with reality."

"God, Bri! Was that off the cuff?"

"Not exactly. It's sort of a short summary of the lecture I gave Nan yesterday. I lecture her every day now. Free association. The doc recommended it. It's supposed to be a form of therapy, to release the tensions which are supposed to build up and drive me to drink. I think it's asinine, but I'm going along with it."

"We never got to that chess session, you know."

Haas's smile was unchanged. "We'll have to do that some time, Jimmy. I'm too busy lecturing these days."

"When I popped off the other night, it was because I was . . ."

"I'm not sore at you, Jimmy."

"Well . . . I'm glad you're not."

"But I owe you a straight answer, I guess. I'm still a little precarious. After I get my feet braced, we'll get acquainted."

"Acquainted?"

"Yes. There's some things you'll have to tell me about some day. I've detected some contradictions. You could turn out to be a very interesting fellow."

Wing stared at him. He did not trust himself to say anything. The concealed anger made his knees feel weak as he walked away.

Late on Saturday afternoon, Kat phoned Wing at his cottage and said, "Are you terribly busy? Tom gave me a chore, and I sort of need moral support, Jimmy. If you could spare an hour or so?"

"I can take a break. What is it?"

"Something's wrong with Doris Rowell. Tom went out there this morning and she wouldn't talk to him. He wants me to try. I've always thought she's sort of creepy. You know? Would you pick me up? I'm at the Sinnat house."

"Half an hour?"

"Wonderful, Jimmy! Thanks a lot."

She was out by the pool when he drove up and parked. The pool was full of children of assorted ages from the Estates. As Kat came smiling toward him he looked beyond her and saw Natalie teetering on the end of the diving board, yelping, as Jigger Lesser bounced high at the middle of the board, trying to jolt her off.

As he opened the door for Kat he said, nodding toward the pool, "How is young love progressing?"

She gave him an odd look. "It's their business, Jimmy."

"I didn't say it wasn't."

As he drove off, she said, "You sort of sneered when you said it, Jimmy. I didn't like that."

"It isn't exactly Heloïse and Abelard, is it?"

"Are you cross today? To them it is, Jimmy. That's exactly the point, isn't it? I'm not going to classify it as a physical infatuation or love or whatever. And I'm not going to sneer at it or snicker at it. Love isn't dirty unless the people involved believe it is. And they don't. I don't want to quarrel, Jimmy."

"Neither do I. Not with you. Any trouble last night?"

"Rotten eggs against the front of the house. But I wasn't there to enjoy them. I paid Gus Malta to hose them off this morning. The kids and I are staying at the Sinnats. It was Natalie's idea. There's a lot of room. I'm glad that thing got into the paper this morning. Did you get it in?"

"Yes."

"But none of those letters have been printed yet."

"I don't think they will be, Kat. I'm sorry. They're too sane and reasonable. Just like the Hotchkiss land story. They'd spoil the image of the group of crackpot bird lovers. You said Doris Rowell wouldn't talk to Tom?"

"He wanted to know who's coming to stand up for us at the public hearing, and she wouldn't tell him a thing. He's very upset."

As they turned into Doris Rowell's driveway, Kat made an exclamation of dismay. "Just *look* at it!" she said. The yard was littered with trash and garbage. There were splats and stains and drippings on the front of the house. The mailbox was broken, and a car had ripped up thirty feet of the hedge.

"Do you think she's too scared?" Kat asked.

"Let's find her, if she's here."

She did not answer the front door. They walked around the house. There had been a heavy rain early Friday evening. Her skiff was tied to the dock, full of water, the lines taut. Wing called and there was no answer. They went up onto the porch.

Kat gasped Jimmy's arm suddenly, startling him. He saw the direction of her startled glance and turned and saw Doris Rowell. She was in the dingy kitchen, visible through a narrow doorway, sitting at a kitchen table, doing something with her hands, then lifting a hand to her mouth.

Jimmy rapped on the screen door and said, "Mrs. Rowell? May we come in and talk to you? I've got Katherine Hubble with me. Mrs. Rowell?"

He turned to Kat, shrugged, pushed the door open and

went in. Kat followed him back to the gloomy kitchen. Doris Rowell's face was shiny with sweat. She wore a torn shirt and khaki trousers, damp with sweat. There was a heaviness of body odor in the still air of the kitchen. She sat at a table covered with oilcloth in a faded flower pattern. In front of her was half a loaf of bread, the paper peeled away from it. There was a dish of butter, softened by the heat, a big jar half full of red jam, a knife on the butter plate, a tablespoon in the jam. The area in front of her was littered with crumbs and splatters of jam, as was the front of her white shirt. A ring of jam bloodied her mouth, and there were crumbs on her chin.

Jimmy felt Kat move closer to him as he faced Doris Rowell. Her motions were slow, but steady and unending. She would spread a slice of bread with butter, drop a puddle of jam onto it, fold it once and lift it to her mouth. She consumed each slice in three spaced bites, shoving the last one in with her thumb. The sounds of breathing and mastication were audible. She seemed to look at them, but her eyes were so dull, her glance so devoid of any impact of awareness, he could not be certain she knew they were there.

"Mrs. Rowell, Tom wants to know about the people you've lined up. Mrs. Rowell!"

He asked twice. She did not answer. Suddenly Kat went swiftly to the woman's side and grasped the heavy wrist, kept the sticky hand from lifting to the mouth. "Please, Doris!" she said.

"Numuny ummun."

"What did you say?"

Doris Rowell swallowed. "Nobody is coming," she said distinctly. "No one at all. You can tell the colonel that." Her voice was without regret, without emotion of any kind. The hand tried to lift but Kat restrained it.

"Didn't you ask them?"

"They expressed regrets. They are too busy. It will make no difference who asks them. The answer will be the same."

"But why?"

"Let go, please. I am very hungry."

"You have to tell me why, Doris!"

"They don't care to associate themselves with me in any way. Maybe they'll tell you why. I doubt it. It is easier to say they are too busy."

"Come on, Kat," Wing said. Kat released Doris Rowell's arm and stepped away. The hand lifted and then stopped. Doris Rowell was looking at Jimmy with placid speculation.

"You could have done it," she said, a flat statement rather than an accusation.

"I don't know what you mean."

She smiled to herself and nodded her head and poked the bread into her waiting mouth. Jimmy took Kat's arm and led her out onto the porch and down the steps. Just as he released her, he felt her shudder.

"That's horrible, Jimmy. We have to do something."

"I'll get Doctor Sloan out here. He'll know what's best."

"It's some kind of a breakdown."

"He'll know what to do about it."

As they walked through the side yard the wind shifted and a vile smell came from the direction of the long shed. He told Kat to go to the car. He went inside. He walked to the rear of the shed. The light was burning. The small pumps had stopped. All the striped fish floated, decaying, on top of the murky water in the two tanks.

He suddenly realized he had been standing there for a long time. His fists were clenched so tightly his shoulders and arms had begun to ache. His jaw was clamped so strongly there was a ringing in his ears.

He turned and walked swiftly back toward the rectangle of daylight. Kat was standing by the station wagon. "What were you doing?"

"She's let a lot of fish die in there. It'll have to be cleaned up. There's a billion flies in there."

"*Damn* them!" Kat whispered. "Damn all of them. Should I stay here with her until Dr. Sloan gets here?"

"I see no need of that."

"We can phone from my house. And phone Tom too."

Sloan said he would see Mrs. Rowell within the hour, and arrange hospitalization if he felt she needed it. Jimmy said he would phone Sloan again and check. As he hung up, Kat handed him a cold beer, and said, "I wonder what she meant by saying you could have done it. Done what?"

"I told her I didn't know what she meant."

"She's worked with those people for so long, I don't see why they should turn her down now."

"Tom has the list, doesn't he?"

"Of the ones she thought would come here? Yes."

"Then he better make the calls and see how he can do."

She took her drink over to a chair and sat and studied him. "Is there something you don't want to tell me, Jimmy?"

"Nothing very special. Just that you can't win, I guess."

"We know that. We know that all we can do at the public hearing is get our point of view on the record. People can't stay this hopped up, you know. We're working on the next step now, to force the trustees of the Internal Improvement Fund to hold another public hearing before they actually sell the bay bottom to Palmland. The things we can get into the record in both public hearings will serve as the basis for the lawsuits we're going to bring against Palmland and Palm County and the State of Florida. Two years from now, when Palmland finally gets out from under the last injunction and gets slapped with a whole batch of new ones, let's see how many people are going to be left around here throwing eggs and saying dirty words over the phone and giving women nervous breakdowns."

He looked down at her. "Kat, Kat, it's a brave point of view. But they'll just keep getting rougher."

"Good! Let 'em get real rough and real careless, and do something we can prove. Then they'll have some fat damage suits to defend too."

"That's Tom Jennings talking, not you."

"I've never been so angry, Jimmy. I'm too angry to be scared." She stood up. "Tom will be wondering." As she walked toward the phone it began to ring. She hesitated. When it had rung three times, she picked it up. She did not speak. She listened, making a wry face at Jimmy. "Thank you, dear," she said into the phone. "You're such a perfect lady." She hung up and said, "There isn't as much of that since I stopped answering. It spoils the fun when you don't answer." She picked the phone up, listened, dialed, waited a moment and hung up, and then dialed again. He heard her explain the Rowell situation to Tom, and could guess from her end of the conversation that Tom was agreeing to get in touch with the people Doris Rowell had thought would come to the hearing. Then he saw her face change as Tom kept talking. Her lips were compressed and her frown lines deepened. "I see," she said. "I know you predicted it last night, but I'd hoped you were wrong. Sure, Tom. I know. As I keep telling myself, you can't win 'em all. Yes, I'll let you know. Goodbye."

"What's the matter?" he asked.

She looked at him with a slightly startled expression, as though she had forgotten he was there. "We seem to be down to five little Indians."

"What happened?"

"Wallace Lime quit. He turned over his stickers and posters and so-called contact files and scuttled away. We thought he would. He's been getting awful jumpy the last two days. He tried to be fearless, I guess, but it was just like that mustache. It didn't quite suit him. And we aren't the same elegant civilized little group we were last time. We're not worth enduring slashed tires, garbage, dirty phone calls. His wife was getting hysterical. I think it was the paint bomb that broke his heart, Jimmy."

"Paint bomb?"

"They've got a little garden house. There's a record player in there. There's no way to lock it. Thursday night somebody sneaked in and plugged the record player in and put a record on as loud as it would go. Wally went charging out, and ran in the dark to turn it off. They'd put one of those spray cans of enamel in the middle of the record, so it was going around and around, with a big rubber band around it to keep the spray part going. If you look close, you can still see little flecks of bright green paint in Wally's mustache."

"Dear Lord," Jimmy said softly.

"It would be very very funny if it wasn't so very very sad. He wasn't doing much good. He was losing every other client he had. None of his ideas were working. Public relations! Hah! The poor little man. He'd have an easier job convincing the public that Jimmy Hoffa teaches ballet. Tom says he was so apologetic he was practically in tears. The group is getting very cozy, Jimmy. Tom can't get anybody to fill one vacancy on the committee, and now we have three. And he estimates we're losing an average of twenty regular members a day. By the time of the public hearing, at that rate we'll be past zero. We'll be minus twenty-seven or something. There are so many people we thought we could depend on, who've had pressure put on them in some unexpected way."

"I guess you have to expect . . ."

"Pressure through jobs, neighborhoods, clubs, even churches, Jimmy. It makes you feel so darn helpless. . . ." Her face twisted and she took one faltering step toward him. She stopped and straightened. "Whoa, girl," she said. She shook her head and turned away, her eyes shiny.

"Just eleven days to go," he said.

"I'll make it," she said. "I may never be the same, but I'll make it." The phone began to ring again. It rang fourteen times and stopped. "My public," she said.

He phoned her at the Sinnat house at eight that evening to tell her that Doctor Sloan had seen no reason to take Doris Rowell in for treatment. She seemed rational, even though her responses were sluggish. He had arranged for a woman to move in with her for a few days and clean the place up. He would stop again and see how she was coming along. He guessed that she would continue to follow the same pattern for a while, eating a great deal and sleeping a great deal. Some people responded to emotional shocks in that manner. She was, of course, overweight, but otherwise in reasonably good physical condition. She was dulling her mental responses by overworking her belly. In her own time she would begin to eat more moderately. Then she might be willing to talk about what was bothering her. But by then, of course, it would be of merely academic interest.

Kat seemed relieved. She told Jimmy that when Tom had phoned her at seven, he had been able to reach but four of the people on Doris' list. They had all been polite and evasive. They all pleaded other obligations, said it had really been very short notice, and had wished him the best of luck.

He told her that Wallace Lime had stopped at the newspaper office with a statement, and Borklund was going to publish it. It announced that Wallace Lime Associates had severed its connections with Save Our Bays, Inc., due to previous professional commitments.

"The louse!" Kat said.

"If it wasn't going in as a news item, he'd have put it in as an ad. Don't be surprised if Borklund has somebody fatten it to the point where he can run it under a three-column head."

"It would be very difficult to surprise me with anything lately. Almost impossible, Jimmy."

"Just for the hell of it, please don't go anywhere alone after dark, Kat. Don't open a door for anybody you don't know. Okay?"

"Where am I living, Jimmy? South Palm City, or East Berlin?"

"Take care."

"Sure. Sure, Jimmy. Thanks."

That night he bought a bottle on the way home. He sat in his sling chair on his dark back porch with the bottle and a bowl of ice until the world was tilted at a sickening angle. But he still saw the red jam and the dead fish. It was raining hard when he blundered off the porch into the yard in his underwear shorts and clung to the rough trunk of a cabbage palm and threw up. He stayed out in the rain until his head began to ache, and then he dried himself off and went to bed, remembering how Charity had stood out on his porch in the rain, crying. There was something wrong with the memory. As he slowly took it apart to see what was wrong with it, he remembered that it had been Mitchie McClure who had made squeaking sounds in the rain, not Miss Charity Holmes of Las Vegas, and not one of the sisters-in-

law of Commissioner Bliss, and not the white silent thing in
the bed up at Oklawaha, with the tubes in it.

The phone awakened him at seven. He had the feeling it
had been ringing for a long time. He could not comprehend who was speaking to him for several moments, and
then he realized it was Dr. Freese phoning from Oklawaha
to tell him that Mrs. Wing had passed away at 5:25 A.M.

"Are you there, Mr. Wing?"

"Yes. I'm here."

"We have an autopsy permission in the file. We'd like to
release the body to whomever you designate no sooner than
tomorrow afternoon, say by four o'clock."

"What's today?"

"Sunday the sixteenth, Mr. Wing."

"Tomorrow, eh. Well. Okay. There's stuff of hers there."

"It will be packed and ready, of course."

"I . . . I just can't think of anything to ask you or tell
you, Doctor."

"There isn't much to say, actually."

"I should say thanks for all you've done for her."

"There wasn't much anybody could do, Mr. Wing."

He sat by the phone in the early-morning living room for
several minutes. He rolled a sheet of paper into the typewriter and wrote: "Gloria Maria Mendez Wing—Born May
1, 1931—Married to James Warren Wing June 20, 1950. Died
July 15, 1961, at Oklawaha State Hospital after a long
illness. Mrs. Wing was born in Tampa and educated in the
public schools of that city. She is survived by her husband,
employed by the Palm City Record-Journal, and by her
sister, Mrs. Andrew McGavern of Toronto, Canada. She was
O God such a beauty at nineteen she could spin your
heart with a glance. . . ."

He went back and x'ed out the last sentence, left the
paper in the machine and took a long cool shower,
shaved, dressed, put coffee on and started making phone calls.
To his sister, to the newsroom, to Toronto.

Teresa, Gloria's elder sister, understood at once. Grief
thickened her voice. "Ah, the poor thing. The poor damn lost
thing."

"Are you going to want to come down? I haven't made
any arrangements yet."

"Down? How could I get down there? Are you out of your
mind?"

"I had to ask you. I had to know."

"I said goodbye to my sister two years ago. She looked
at me just once, and called me mama. I can't come way down
there."

"Teresa, there's people in Ybor City who should know, aren't there? I don't know who they are. Can you let them know?"

"I can do that, yes. But when I let them know, I should tell them about the burial. What do you plan?"

"Should it be in Ybor City?"

"For what? She can't be buried from the church. You know that. She gave up the church for you. She gave up a lot of things for you, Jeemy."

"Look. Let's not get into that kind of stuff."

"It doesn't bother you. No. Nothing bothers you. The way you treated her when she was sick."

"Nobody knew she was sick then, damn it!"

"Poor little thing. She didn't know what was happening."

"Cut it out, Teresa!"

"So bury her down there. Why not? What difference does it make? You have a place in a cemetery?"

"Yes. Look, Teresa. I'll phone you again about time and place and so on when I get things arranged."

"Yes, you do that, Jeemy. And you make me one promise. When you call me again, it's the last time forever. Okay? I want to forget you're alive on the same earth. Now she's gone, you're nothing to me. *Claro?*"

"*Si, seguro. Muchissima' gracia'.*"

The good connection faded suddenly. Her voice was frail and remote. "But I want the pin. You hear me? I want the pin with the pearls. It was never yours. You hear me?"

He hung up. It was eight-thirty. The coffee was tepid. He poured it back into the pot. He looked up the number for the Shackley Funeral Home and asked for Vern, Junior. The man said young Vern was at home, but he might not be up yet. Wing decided there was no special rush. He could phone later. He drank more coffee. He began to pace the length of the cottage, from the front door to the back. He tried to think of all the tender touching things he could remember of his marriage, feeling an obligation for tears, but he could not find anything to bring them on. He went out and got the Sunday paper and tried to look at it. He dropped it and began pacing again. He had the curious feeling his skin might split. He could feel exactly where it would split, down the insides of his arms, down the backs of his legs, and from the crown of his head all the way down the crease of his back, coming open with a gritty noise and peeling back, dry, ready to step out of. As he paced he kept thinking he could hear music and voices, but when he stopped, all he could hear was a slap and suck of water around the pilings of the old dock. He checked the radio to make sure it was turned

off. He found he was carrying his head a little bit to the
side, and realized he was tensed for some very loud and
unexpected noise. He had no idea what it would be. The
faint hallucinations of a hangover seemed mingled with the
jittery results of too much strong coffee.

Or, he thought, I'm losing my mind. He had an impulse
to turn that thought into a solitary joke. He made bulging,
grotesque faces and went into a wild prancing dance, stamping his feet hard, and on the final whirl, hit his forehead
against the front door jamb. He leaned against it, his eyes
closed, saying in a small random voice, "Yippee-i-ay, yippee-
i-ay." Then he could not remember or decide whether the
faces and the dance were something he had willed himself
to do, or something he could not help. A complete terror
stopped his breath and soaked his body. He went feebly to a
chair and sat down. He looked out the window and saw a
dark red dog trot diagonally across his small yard, an
exceptional length of wet pink tongue dangling. He felt an
almost tearful gratitude toward the dog. The dog was like a
hand on his shoulder, stirring him awake from a dream.

He called Vern at his home. Vern was having breakfast.
His voice deepened slightly and slowed to a careful professional cadence as soon as he realized what Jimmy was calling
him about.

A time was decided. Two o'clock Wednesday at the funeral
home. Form to be filled out. Freese would have certificate.
Sister Laura had suggested Reverend Kennan Blue, said she
was sure he would do it. Notice in paper. Arrange to select
casket. Calling hours? No, and best to have closed casket.
Pickup Monday between four and five, Oklawaha, right.
Bearers? No, it isn't required. Committal service at grave.
Limousines? Decide later.

He sent Teresa a wire containing the information she had
requested.

20

ALL THROUGH the short service at the graveside, Kat had been certain it would rain. More than half the sky had gone black and the thunder obscured the rather nasal voice of Reverend Blue. Jimmy looked so odd standing on the grass in the daylight in a dark suit. Beyond a row of pines she could see the pastel colors of the traffic on the Bay Highway.

There was that awkward pause when it was over, when nobody was entirely certain it actually was over. And then they began to move quietly to their cars. Engines began to start, doors chunked shut, the first cars began to move away. Jimmy moved back a little way. A few people spoke to him in low tones. To each he responded with a small stiff smile, a quick nod of his head.

At last there was no one left but Vern and some of his people. She hesitated, and then walked over to where Jimmy stood talking to Vern.

"Glad that rain held off," Vern said. "But it looks like that's it coming right now." They turned and saw the grayness slanting toward them, blotting out the distant trees and traffic and the buildings on Bay Highway.

"Come on," she said to Jimmy. He looked blankly at her. "Your car's at my house. Remember?" They ran to her Volkswagen and climbed in as the first fat drops began to fall. She sat behind the wheel and took her hat off. They rolled the windows up. The windshield steamed on the inside. The rain was a thousand small hammers on tin, roaring, surging and fading as gusts of wind rocked the car.

"I'll wait'll it lets up some," she shouted. An almost simultaneous flash-click-bang of lightning and thunder made her start violently, and the fright made the backs of her hands and the back of her neck tingle. She thought he had said something about the lightning.

"What did you say?"

He turned toward her. "I had no idea so many people would come. Not here. Come to Shackley's. I had no idea."

"You have a lot of friends. What's so surprising?"

"There weren't enough seats."

The intensity of the rain lessened. She wiped the steam off the windshield and started the car. By the time she made

265

the turn onto Mangrove Road, the rain had stopped. They rolled the windows down. She drove cautiously through temporary lakes, and steered around the larger palm fronds and branches littering the road.

When they reached her house, he came in and took his jacket off and loosened his tie. "What would you like, Jimmy? Coffee? A drink?"

"I want to thank you for everything. You must have other things to do."

"I have nothing to do except try to find out what you want."

"Oh. Well. If it doesn't sound weird and it isn't a lot of trouble, I'm hungry. I couldn't eat today. What I'd like, if you have it, is eggs. Scrambled."

"About four eggs? Bacon? Toast? Coffee, tea or milk?"

"Wonderful. Tea, I guess."

When she went back into the living room, he was at her desk, writing some sort of a list.

"What are you doing?"

"Oh. You can help, I guess. The people who were there. I've just been putting down last names. Killian, Borklund, Haas, Lesser, Jennings, Bliss, Halley, Shannard, Dayson, Sloan, Britt, Shilling, Cable, Tucker, Lime, Aigan, Lipe . . ."

"But, dear! There was a book to sign, near the entrance. Vern will turn it over to you."

He looked blankly at her, then snapped his fingers. "He told me about it, and I forgot. And I have a bunch of cards to send out to the people who came and sent flowers. I haven't got them yet. I ordered them. Now I know I didn't order enough of them."

"I'll take care of the cards for you. There's no rush about it, you know." She stood beside him and looked down at the list he had made. "Sort of a truce, wasn't it?"

"What? Oh, I see what you mean. Yes. The Palmland and the S.O.B.'s, all united in the common cause."

"I think you can come and sit down now, Jimmy."

She brought him the food. She sat with him and had tea and watched him eat with obvious hunger.

"Good eggs. Where are the kids?"

"At the Sinnats, as usual."

He finished and sighed. She refilled his cup. He smiled at her and the smile turned into an aching yawn.

"You didn't eat and you didn't sleep."

"Not very much," he admitted. "It's a strange thing. I knew it was going to happen. But I had my own reaction figured out wrong, all the way. I feel what I shouldn't be feeling, and I don't feel what I should be feeling. Do you know?"

"Of course."

"I've felt all day like a dummy, a black stork. I was afraid I'd either cry and couldn't stop, or laugh and not be able to stop, but I didn't do either. And either way, it wouldn't have been for her, somehow. It would have been for . . . for kind of the general idea of death. I can't even be sure I'm human."

"You are, Jimmy. Completely. Every kind of grief is ambivalent, because it's full of different kinds of emotion nobody can sustain. There isn't anything consistent about it."

"But is it grief, even?"

She put her hand on his wrist. "Jimmy, the most wonderful thing you did for me a year ago was let me talk and talk and talk. I said some very wild things, didn't I?"

"Yes, but . . ."

"And I'll listen to all the wild things you want to say, but not right now, because you're dead on your feet. The guest room is cool and ready and waiting, clean sheets all turned down for you, private bath with towels laid out. Now scoot."

As she was rinsing the dishes and stowing them in the dishwasher, she heard the sound of the shower. About fifteen minutes later she tiptoed down the corridor. His room door was ajar. She said his name softly. There was no answer. She looked in. He was on his side, breathing deeply and heavily. She tiptoed into the room and closed the draperies. She stood in the shadows and looked down at him for a little while, then tiptoed out.

She was doing some stealthy varieties of housework when Natalie came over. "He's having a nap," Kat said in a low tone.

"Oh. How about at the cemetery? Did the rain ruin it?"

"Let's go out on the patio and have a Coke or something. The rain held off just long enough."

Out on the screened part of the patio beyond the glass doors they could talk in normal tones. Natalie wore a swim suit patterned in dull shades of orange and yellow, straw slippers with thick cork soles. She seemed much less guarded, less constrained and tense than when she had first arrived in Florida. She seemed cherished and content, her small face less drawn, her movements more fluid, her spare body a little more mature. That unmistakable look of being loved gave Kat a little antagonistic feeling which she immediately identified for what it was and discarded, as being a most narrow and unworthy emotion.

"Won't the phone bother him?" Natalie asked.

"I had it put on temporary disconnect yesterday, before I knew he was coming here."

"Jigger is child-watching. He's really very reliable. He counts heads constantly. Kat, about Jigger and me . . ."

"Don't feel you have to tell me anything."

"Suppose I want to? Would you mind?"

"Of course not."

"I dumped the whole thing in your lap, so you have a right to know. And the way my father went off, it sort of left everything entirely up to us. We spend every possible minute together. I guess you couldn't help noticing that. Anyhow, what happened made it all kind of dirty and uncomfortable. We tried to tell each other it didn't, but it did. So we're being distinctly moral. I guess it's sort of a tantalizing game, after . . . knowing each other, but it's more than that, too. We slipped once, but we won't again. I'm finding out how much of a man he is, and I think I'm more than half in love with him." A blush darkened her small tanned face. "Isn't it absurd? He's seventeen years old! But I keep forgetting he is. He's found a summer job, starting next Monday. We think it will be better for both of us for him to have a job too. I know it's . . . really kind of egotistical for me to think you'd be interested when there's so much going on for you and people are giving you such a hard time and all, but I thought maybe you'd like to know that one . . . pretty good thing has come out of all this bay-filling war."

"Nat, honey, I'm glad to know and I'm touched that you've told me. I hope everything works out for both of you."

Natalie frowned. "We'll be apart when I go back to school. I can guess how these things usually work out. I feel sad when I think what will probably happen. But right now it's so good to be halfway in love. Some of it is very young love. You know. Silly things. Jokes and games. And some of it is very adult, I think. Because we sort of started backwards. What we have now is what we should have had first, I guess. But we had the other part first, the six times that we were together like that, with it getting more tremendous every time, as close as two people can get. So now that it's all a . . . younger kind of love, the things we already know about each other sort of shadow it, and make it more . . . I don't know if any word fits . . . marriageable? But we can't even think about that. I've got a terror complex about marriage. I've always promised myself I never would be. My father set such a dandy example."

"He and Claire are all right."

"Are they, Kat? They like the same things. A lot of people swarming around. And she gets the lush life she adores, and people to do the scut work for her. And he gets the girl-wife for his declining years, which is sort of a public advertisement of his manhood. Is it a marriage or a sort of a truce?"

"Most marriages are."

"Yours wasn't. I know that."

"No. It wasn't."

"What about Jimmy Wing's? What was she like, really?"

"Gloria was a very beautiful girl. Not a complex person. She had a lot of earthy vitality, and she was easy to be with before she got sick because she was essentially a merry person. I guess she was good for Jimmy because there's sort of a dark, involved, tortured side to him, and he'd need a marriage that would . . . would simplify the world instead of complicate it. Everyone who knew her knew she was a totally loyal and faithful wife. That's why it was so shocking and ugly and incomprehensible when she began to change. She seemed to coarsen. She seemed to stop giving a damn, about anything. Poor Jimmy thought it was something he had done. He thought he was inadequate or something. Then he tried to turn into the Biblical husband and wham the mischief out of her. So when they found out it was a physical thing, an illness she couldn't help, the guilt over how he had been handling it nearly destroyed him."

"The poor guy."

"She was put away for keeps over two years ago, and she's been in what I guess you could call a coma for over a year. It's supposed to be a very interesting case. Not very interesting for Jimmy."

"He's an interesting-looking man, you know. When he interviewed me at the Center, I was looking at him carefully. Every feature he has is actually ugly, all by itself. Those pale eyes that slant the wrong way and that big nose, the long head and sandy hair, and the crooked mouth and big uneven teeth. But he has all that darn presence, and that strange kind of . . ."

"Elegance?"

"That's the word. Lazy grace, I guess, plus complete confidence and that freshly scrubbed and polished look. Actually, I think he's wonderfully attractive."

"I can't think of him in just that way, Natalie. While Van was alive I didn't care for Jimmy particularly, even though he was one of Van's best friends. It wasn't jealousy. I just thought he was . . . a sort of contrived person. Artificial and sort of superior-acting. I didn't understand why Van was so fond of him. I found out this past year. He's a valued friend. An old shoe. When I'm with him I feel comfortable and safe and understood. When things were the worst I walked a hundred miles with him, said all the crazy things that came into my head, cried a gallon of tears onto his shirt fronts. He's seen me at my worst and still puts up with me. I love him dearly as a good friend."

"He could have other ideas, you know."

She stared at the girl. "Jimmy? Bless you, no. Not toward this raddled old redhead, honey. One man had the pleasant delusion I was a sexy exciting woman, and that was enough for one lifetime. Just because you're in the midst of romance, dear, don't turn those rosy glasses on the rest of us. Jimmy is racked up, and I am taking care, and if I ever made a pass at him, his little eyes would bulge with horror."

Natalie smiled and sighed. "I better get back to the younger set." She stood up. "By the way, Mortie was in rare wild shape this morning. Things are a mess down at the Center, you know."

"Tom told me Morton was having the same kind of problems as the rest of us."

"There's been a big membership petition asking him to either give up his S.O.B. activities or resign as director. My classes are down to about half what they were. Two of his people on the board have resigned in protest. People are canceling their pledges. All of a sudden his little empire has turned shaky, and Mortie is stomping on his hanky and dithering around all over the place. We're getting a lot of crank calls at the Center, and some absolutely filthy mail. It's such amazing reasoning, isn't it? The reason why Mr. Dermond opposes the bay fill is because he is a Communistic homosexual pervert, and opposing the fill is part of his long program of foisting degenerate abstract art on the duped citizens of Palm County."

"Do you think he'll knuckle under, Nat?"

"I don't think so. He's much too furious. But I don't think he'll have time to do you much good. He's too busy trying to mend the fences as fast as they're falling down around him. He had to have his home phone changed to an unlisted number."

"I know."

"Anyhow, one week from today it will be over. And then maybe my classes will fill up again. It seems so asinine to deprive those kids of something they love just because Mortie, for aesthetic reasons, thinks the loveliest bay in the county shouldn't be turned into a housing project."

They went out the terrace door into the side yard. Kat looked at her watch and saw it was almost five o'clock. "Send mine home soon, dear."

"Floss can feed them. Don't worry about them, Kat. I'll bring them on home later on, really."

"Well . . . they'd probably wake Jimmy up. If they won't be any bother."

"They never are."

She watched Natalie walk out the driveway and turn toward her house. As she turned to go back in, a soft voice near at hand startled her. "Miz Hubble?"

"Oh! Barnett, I didn't see you there."

He came forward, away from the screen of shrubbery, moving slowly, turning a stained old cloth cap in his thick dark hands. "I didn' get to this yard, yesterday," he said, staring beyond her.

"I know. I wondered where you were."

"Can't get onto it tomorra neither, Miz Hubble."

"Is something wrong?"

"Truth is, this time of year and all, I got me so loaded up on work, there's some I has to let drop off. That's the way it goes."

"Do you mean you can't work for me any more, Barnett?"

"Yassum," he said.

"I know it doesn't amount to very much money, and if you say you can't, I guess you can't. But I want you to see if you can find me somebody who can do it for me."

"I kin surely try, Miz Hubble. But I jus doan know who."

There was something very strange about him, the way he was standing, not even looking toward her, turning the cap around and around. Suddenly she understood.

"Who's making you quit?" she demanded angrily.

"It's just I got more then I . . ."

"Nonsense! Don't you *dare* lie to me!"

His glance drifted toward her, apprehensive, uncomfortable, and slid away again. He swallowed, licked his lips. "Maybe I could fit this yard back in a little later on."

"Who scared you?"

He looked directly at her. He straightened slightly and his voice had more dignity. "I'm not scared, m'am. I lived my whole life the way I got to live it. You have your head in the lion's mouth, you do like my daddy told me. You lie quiet. A man said words to me on my telephone. And there's other folks working for other white folks got the same words said. There's no colored cops in Pigeon Town, m'am. Not yet there isn't. Mister Van, he would have knowed how it is, without having to say anybody scared me. I'll do the most I can."

"I'm sorry, Barnett. It's just that . . . they don't seem to overlook anything. . . ." She realized that for the first time since it had all begun she was close to uncontrollable tears. She made herself smile. "I was angry for a moment."

He looked down into the cloth cap. "And it could be a lie about not being scared none. Decent colored people can always have their house fired by some boughten nigger." He looked around. "I got things pretty good here. If'n you could do a little and that Mister Gus would do some of the heavy things, I could be back soon as it looks all right. This isn't a lastin' kind of thing."

She had the television set on at ten o'clock, the sound turned low, so she did not hear Jimmy Wing getting up until he walked out with his jacket over his arm, startling her.

"Well! How did you sleep?" she said, turning the set off.

"So hard I had a hell of a time figuring out where I was when I woke up."

"I was afraid the kids would wake you. I made them be quiet going to bed, but when they whisper they sound like steam engines."

He sat on the couch and lit a cigarette. "Everything that happened today is a little blurred."

"That's the way it should be."

"What did I get? About six hours. And when I get back to the cottage, I'll want eight or ten more."

"You could have stayed right where you were."

"Makes a bad impression on the neighbors. And everything you do these days has to be above reproach, friend."

"Or I won't get any yard work done? Move to Palm County, the best of tropical living among friendly people. Brother!"

"What about yard work?"

She repeated the conversation with Barnett Mayberry, and said, "Two hours a week, for heaven's sake! I'm unclean. I'm not fit to work for."

"It'll be the same at the Jennings' and the Lipes's and the Halleys'. Part of the pattern. Make all you people as uncomfortable as possible, and keep you too busy to fight the bay fill. If Barnett ignored the suggestion, maybe nothing at all would happen. But why should he take the chance? You must be a trial to him, dear. You missed all your cues. You were supposed to understand just how things are, and go right along with his story about being too busy to work on your yard, and accept the fiction he'd try to find somebody else. Then a month from now he'd stop by and say things had eased up and he could come back to work if you hadn't gotten somebody else."

"I'm no damn good at your native folk dances, Jimmy, and I have no intention of learning them."

"Barnett will put up with you."

"Jimmy, you look a little better."

"Thanks to you. And thanks for helping me through all the red tape, too. Laura's got all she can do taking care of Sid. Kat?"

"That's a strange expression you're wearing, sir."

"I feel strange."

"Do you feel ill?"

"No. Nothing like that. You know what happens in color-plate work where the registration is a little bit off."

"What? Oh, the ghost people, like with three mouths, all different colors."

"That's me."

"But you've got to expect to feel a little . . ."

"Not just since I heard about Gloria. For longer than that. What if some time I want to talk to you?"

"You can always talk to me."

"Really talk to you, Kat. Peel off the lid. Show you where the snakes live."

"I'd listen. You know all my snakes by their first names."

"It wouldn't be that simple. All you'd have to do is listen to all of it, then give me no opinion, just let me go. I have all the opinions I can use."

"You know, you're pretty silly."

"Am I?"

"Of course you are. Everybody goes around killing people. Only the good ones know what they're doing. That's the penalty, I suppose."

"You're a fantastic woman."

"Just how do you mean that?"

"In the best of all possible ways. So goodnight before I open the wrong valve. To scramble the metaphors, dear Kat, I know the wheel is crooked, but I want to make my money last as long as I can."

She walked out to the car with him. For a time it looked as if the motor would not catch. But as the starter began to grind with an ominous slowness, it caught, ran raggedly and then smoothed out.

He looked up at her out of the car window and said, "The hell of it is, I can want a Mercedes, but not very much. Or a flight to Paris, but not as if I ached for it. I'm in the lousy middle, you know? The world is for people who either ache for the shiny things so bad their teeth hurt, or who don't want them at all at all. How about us slobs in the middle? Do I sound sorry for myself?"

"Not enough to bother either of us."

"Before I get really maudlin, farewell."

"Will you work tomorrow?"

"I'd rather than not."

"So I'll see you for the coffee break, Jimmy."

After he drove away she stood out in the driveway and looked at the sky for a little while. The stars were bright and close. She saw a shooting star, and with the wry habit of this past year, said politely, "No thank you." They were always giving you free wishes. Lately four-leaf clovers had become easy to find. But no thanks indeed. Not even for a flash of green, sir, if you should give me that notorious rarity. No flash of green, no monkey's paw, no star light star bright. We tucked another one into the ground today. This one was Jimmy's. And we'll take our turns when the time comes. With or without clover.

A car turned into the Estates, and as it went by, under a weak street light, she saw that it was Eloise in her little white car, alone.

Kat went back into her house, kissed her sleeping children and went to bed.

21

DURING THE FIRST PART of the week which remained before the date set for the public hearing, Jimmy Wing was intrigued and sometimes mildly alarmed by an apparently inter-related disruption of both his sense of time and the quality of his capacity to remember.

For a long time he had fitted sensibly into the steady progress of his days and nights, knowing without any effort of consciousness where the minutes belonged on the clock and the days belonged on the calendar. Now the internal time-keeping device had stopped. Three hours could disappear between heartbeats, and ten minutes could appear to last all afternoon. It had the remembered flavor of childhood, when Saturday was always a vast glad surprise, and Monday was a generation away. The segments of each day were protracted and compressed without reason. He would find himself startled by the idea of being late for an appointment only to discover it was still three hours away.

This disassociation seemed linked with a new vividness of memory, of fragments which came into his mind with such a force and color that he seemed to have to squint to look directly at these visions. The outside world was faded by comparison. These were all recent images, and they often had that ominous persuasive weight of dreams rather than reveries. He was absent-minded, forgetful. He sensed that people were being patient with him, and he smiled his gratitude. Sometimes, when his attention was on the person speaking to him, he seemed to hear the other's words a fraction of a second before the words were said. This was a hyper-sensitivity which made his brain feel as if it had been stripped raw, made all comprehension an immediate and painful thing. At other times he would see the mouth moving and he would hear nothing. He would search for the range of the person's voice, like moving a tuning dial, and suddenly he would hear him again.

The hot images in his mind were curiously static. A thing would come into his mind and last and finally fade, and when it was ended, then he would know whether it had been in bright focus for two seconds or an hour. The visions were random. One that came often was the image of Charity's eye, far brighter than it had been in the motel room, suspended slightly above him, big as a basketball, wet, fixed, anatomically exact, the lashes thick as lead pencils, iris big as a saucer, pupil big as a cup, utterly still. He could not force continuity onto such images, recreating what had come before or what came after. There were others which recurred. One was the bottom half of Elmo's face, the hard, chunky, knowing grin. And the motionless tumble of the orange slacks of a dead tourist woman. Aunt Middy Britt's leathery arthritic claw folded onto the arm of her rocker. Two flies, with the metallic sheenings of hummingbirds, feeding at a droplet of jam. Mitchie's mouth, wrenched sideways in a frozen sneer of sexual effort. The wrinkled brown nape of Shannard's neck beneath the feathery whiteness of his hair. The clean slant of Kat's shoulder, her fair skin oiled and angry red.

He would set out to drive to the courthouse and find himself at the entrance to his driveway. Once he sat on the side of his bed to change his shoes, and found himself in the bathroom, in pajamas, brushing his teeth at three in the afternoon. At times he was amused, but could not sustain amusement. At times he was alarmed. He knew he was doing his work reasonably well, but often when he would read his by-lined work, he could not remember having done it. And at all times he felt as if he was braced for some huge horrid unimaginable noise that might come at any time. He had always awakened in the morning remembering dreams. Now there were none, and he was glad there were none because he did not like to think of what they might be like.

Sometimes he thought of talking to Dr. Sloan, but he did not know what he could tell him, nor did he believe it could be of any significance to the man.

On Monday afternoon, two days before the public hearing, he had a phone call from Morton Dermond. Dermond asked him if he could come over to the Art Center right away.

Dermond was in his office. The Center was closed to the public. A good half of the clutter in the office was gone, and most of what remained had been dumped into a huge pile under the windows.

Dermond sat at his desk, the brute in colors gay, all brawn and hair, but without an essential ferocity, like a bulldog with rabbit eyes. He sat tired and remote, with a small self-deprecatory smile, handed Jimmy a fuzzy carbon of a typed statement and said, "Sit down and read it, Jimmy."

It was a brief, formal resignation as director of the Palm County Art Center, giving health as the reason.

"It has to be in tomorrow morning's paper, Jimmy," he said. "Please say that Mr. Oscar Grindle, chairman of the

Board of Directors, will handle the Center until a replace-
ment can be located. All activities will continue without interruption."

Jimmy made a note on his copy of the resignation. "Very
sudden, isn't it?"

"Suddener than anyone could have guessed. My car is all
loaded. My landlord has my key. Bobby is driving around
doing some last errands. He'll pick me up here in about
twenty minutes. Young Peter Trent is being kind enough
to crate the rest of my things and ship them north. Bobby and
I should be out of the state tonight."

"Do I get the news in depth, Mortie? The story behind the
story?"

"Just for your own amusement, I guess. You can't publish it, of course. You see, I knew something like this might
happen. When I saw how vicious and unreasonable people
were getting, I told Tom I should get out of it. I told the
dear man I'd do the group more harm than good. But he made
such an appeal to my loyalty, really. You see, Jimmy, we
develop a sort of sixth sense about these things. We should
never, never, never let ourselves get mixed up in public issues which get terribly emotional. I was lulled into a false
sense of security, I guess, because nothing happened two
years ago."

"What happened this time?"

"Tell me something, Jimmy. I want to be sure I haven't
been living in a fool's paradise. Have I ever been too terribly
obvious about my personal private life? Have people been
really *sure* about me?"

"Not completely, Mortie. And I guess most of the people
have had no idea at all."

"I know you have, because you ran into Bobby and me
that time in Key West. But I had the idea you didn't go
around smirking and gossiping, really."

"I didn't."

"I'm not an idiot, you know. And I'm certainly not a member of that *pushy* set, who go around demanding equal
rights and so on. I'm living in a world which disapproves of
my personal life, and I can't change that, so what would I
be trying to prove? I've kept my two worlds completely separate, Jimmy. I was down there three whole months before
I sent for Bobby Serba to come down. He's had that nice little
job in the gift shop at Cable Beach, and we've been terribly discreet. Actually, even though I know who most of
the locals are, and some of them might astonish even you,
Jimmy, we've neved mingled. And we've even maintained the
precaution of Bobby's having a little place of his own. I've

liked my work here, and I know I've done a very good job,
and I swear to you on my word of honor, Jimmy, that in all
the time I've been down here, I've never made the smallest
pass at anyone."

"I believe you, Mortie."

He gave Jimmy a look of despair, and suddenly there were
tears in his eyes. His voice broke as he said, "What they did
to me, Jimmy, they bugged my house. A dirty invasion of
privacy. And what good would it do me to go to the police?
It's a *shameful* thing, Jimmy."

"Who did it?"

"Two horrible men. Bobby came over on Saturday night.
Saturday was his birthday. I made my famous *paella* in the
big *casuela* I brought from Spain. You can't get all the right
ingredients here, but it was really very good. And we had
quite a lot of Spanish wine. Yesterday morning, just before
noon, we were lounging around the house, listening to
music, and those men rang the doorbell and came *muscling*
their way right in, grinning and laughing at us and talking
dirty. They had this battered little tape recorder, and they
set it up and made us listen to some of it. I don't care
what kind of a relationship you have, Jimmy, a recording of
completely personal things sounds vulgar and nasty and horrible. Bobby got quite hysterical and went positively *flying*
at them to turn it off, but they slammed him back against the
wall and he hurt his head. I was going to punish them, but
one of them took a gun out. Have you ever seen anybody aim-
ing a gun at you in your own living room? It is really impossibly theatrical. It's truly vulgar. That put Bobby in even
worse condition, and I had to quiet him down. Then they
told me I was resigning immediately and we were leaving
town. No place for us in a decent community and so on. Just
what you'd expect. If we didn't leave, the recording would
be played for some of the members of my board, and I'd be
publicly accused of being a deviate at the public hearing on
Wednesday, and their evidence would be turned over to the
police. You see, there's nothing I can do except what I'm
doing, Jimmy. All we can do is run. If we stay here and
brazen it out, not only will it be hurting a lot of people I'm
fond of, but we could really be sent to prison. The laws
down here are truly medieval."

"What were the men like?"

"Oh, rather beefy fellows in their thirties, ignorant types,
with meaty faces, dressed in cheap resort clothes. I've never
seen them before. Their first names were Ray and Andy. They
acted like cops. They had a southern accent, and a lot of
dirty language, and they acted like it was all very very funny.

They hadn't done anything very tricky. They'd just fastened a microphone onto my window sill with a long wire running all the way to the driveway next door, where they sat in their car and listened and ran the tape recorder whenever they felt like it. They were in a dark green De Soto with Tampa plates. The house next door is empty for the summer. One of them must have sneaked over and put the microphone where he wanted it as soon as it got dark."

"Where are you going?"

"I made some phone calls yesterday afternoon. We're going to borrow a friend's cottage on Fire Island and spend some time forgetting there is such a place as Palm County. Then I'll find something in New York. Jimmy, I know I'm imposing on you, but would you please tell Tom Jennings? I know I should phone him. I just can't."

"I'll tell him."

Mortie Dermond walked into the lobby with Wing. "Say goodbye to the others, the few who mean anything to me. Jackie, Kat, you know the ones. Explain it a little, so I won't look *too* bad."

"Sure, Mortie."

There were several huge raw-looking canvases hung in the lobby, predominantly black, red and white. The blacks were weighty and structural, like Kline. They were by a local young man named Sol Utica.

Morton Dermond stopped by the largest painting. "Poor little Sol. He's derivative, of course. But he's finding where he wants to go, and he'll have to have time. They'll find somebody for my job who won't give Sol gallery room. They'll pack this place with the hobby people, beach scenes, waving palms, picturesque fishing nets. I can feel wistful about that, Jimmy."

"People like to object to what they don't understand, Mortie."

"It's more than that. There's something we can't say to the public because it sounds so arrogant it makes people screamingly angry. Work like this is like mirrors. Cruel mirrors. They can't reflect a substance which doesn't exist. A person who is nothing will look at these and see nothing. They'll be baffled, angry, indignant. They'll think they're being had. They say a child could have done it, or a monkey. They'll think the whole world of modern art is some vast conspiracy. We tell them to make an effort to understand. That's nonsense, actually. They can't suddenly become actual people through an effort of will. This is a world they can't enter, so they claim it doesn't really exist. But it is more real than anything they can ever know. Dear God, if a man looks at a meadow and sees only a drainage problem, or something he thinks he can kill, why should he think he should be able to look at a painting? That's what angers them, Jimmy. They sense their limitations, and defend themselves by accusing the rest of us of fraud." He smiled. "My final lecture as director, my friend. I guess you are a reasonably sensitive man, but I shouldn't expect too much empathy from you."

"What do you mean?"

"You're adequately tolerant, I suppose. But the prejudice is still there, isn't it? 'Some of my best friends are a little queer. Some of them are real nice guys.' But I disgust you a little, don't I?"

"What's the point of talking like this, Mortie?"

"Turning the knife in the self-inflicted wound. Or maybe it's luxurious self-expression, my friend. Once you've burned a bridge, you can turn and yell anything you want. You see, *you* dreadfully viable types have a conviction of righteousness and decency which offends *me*. So the prejudice, like all prejudice in the world, works both ways."

"Is this doing any good?"

"It probably isn't even very good therapy, dear man. Out of pure reaction, I'll probably get progressively queeny as time goes by. Goodbye, Jimmy, and thanks for some small favors. No, I'd rather not shake hands, because at the moment it strikes me as a sort of gesture of tolerance."

Jimmy shrugged and walked out. Mortie's new red Falcon station wagon was parked near the entrance, down on its haunches with the weight of the luggage inside and on the roof rack. Bobby Serba was checking and tightening the lines which held the tarp. He was a willowy man, with an abundance of glossy dark hair and a minimum of chin. He gave Jimmy a slow glance as Jimmy walked by. He had long almond eyes, and in the glance was that same wary, remote, inhuman speculation he had seen in the eyes of penned cattle.

It was a little after six o'clock when he parked at Elmo's office. Elmo's pickup and Sandra Straplin's little car were there. The street door was locked. He pressed the bell but could not hear it ring because of the traffic sounds behind him. He alternately hammered on the door and pressed the bell button. After a long time he saw Sandra walking toward him, her heavy breasts bouncing, her eyes narrow, her mouth ugly with annoyance.

She unlocked the door and swung it open and said, "When you phoned, Jimmy, I told you he was too busy to see you. What's the matter with you anyhow?"

"I want to see him for a minute."

"Come on. You'll see him, all right. You got him in a dandy mood now."

Elmo was standing beside his desk. He dropped the papers he was looking at and stared at Jimmy as he came in. Muscles bulged and flexed along the hard angle of the jaw.

"Get out and shut the door, Sandra." As soon as the door closed he said, "You getting uppity, boy. You want to talk to me, you phone. She told you tomorrow. Not tonight. Tomorrow."

"Don't I have special privileges? As a member of the team?"

"You say that pretty snotty. Who all the hell you think you're getting to be?"

Jimmy went over and sat on the couch and looked at him. "I'm good old Jimmy Wing. That's all. I do odd jobs. Like at the Drowsy Lady Motor House. Like carting Buck's wench to Tampa. Like sidelining Doris Rowell. Like telling you every move old Tom Jennings plans before he makes it. When we get to Tallahassee, Elmo, will I have my own office? And a state car? I worry about things like that."

"Is this the way you were acting when you walked in and busted Leroy in the mouth?"

"I was a lot calmer, I think."

Elmo looked at him for a few moments. He finally sighed audibly, peeled a small cigar and took his time lighting it. "So what's got you all riled, boy? Dermond?"

"If you can guess that good, guess the rest of it."

"Sure will. When you come into this, the idea was how you were going to he'p me slow those Save Our Bay folks down. Knowing them the way you do, you could do it quiet and gentle. So all of a sudden you find you somebody else is in on it. And I guess you want to know why."

"I very much want to know why."

"Lots of reasons. You turned out to have a softer heart than I give you credit for. That doesn't mean I got no use for you now and in the future. It just means little things will come up best done by others. You bleeding about how Dermond got handled? Like my daddy used to say, a man with a plate glass ass shouldn't walk where it's slick."

"Leroy arranged the Dermond thing?"

"He found some fellas to take care of it. The thing was to run him out of town fast, him and his pretty boy, so as when the Reverend Darcy Harkness Coombs gives his little talk at the public hearing on Wednesday night, he can point to Dermond as being one of the bird lovers exposed and run out of the county by the forces of decency. You standing up for a goddam degenerate, boy?"

"Aren't you trying to win too big, Elmo?"

"In this game, Jimmy boy, there's no such thing. Then, you losing your wife, it kind of took your mind off all that's going on. And we figure you've been doing us a lot of real good by writing up how wonderful Palmland Isles is going to be. We figured you'd be a lot happier if you don't have to mess with the rougher parts of this thing. If you couldn't stomach it when Leroy give that big girl a little cuffing around, it's best we took some of the dirty work off your hands. Like how Dermond got convinced it was time to leave town."

"I don't care about Dermond, Elmo. I had to see you tonight to get something else straight. Jennings' organization is pretty well gutted now. There's four left on the committee, and about fifty members who haven't been scared off. I assume Leroy's little helpers are still on the job. I came here to tell you that nothing is going to happen to Kat Hubble. If anything is being set up, you better make sure it's called off. If anything happens to her, I'm going to make you the sorriest man in south Florida, Commissioner."

Elmo wore a tiger smile. "Big words. Maybe, as the years go by, Jimmy, and we get to know each other good, you'll stop wondering if I'm a damn fool. Leroy still wonders, sometimes. Ever since you busted his lip he's been especially nervous about you. But what he can't understand yet is how I got a lock on you that you couldn't bust out of if you tried. You're the most loyal man I've got. Now don't stare at me so bug-eyed, boy. Think it out. I'd say the one thing you value most is the good opinion and respect of that nice little redheaded woman who is the widow of your best friend. And every little thing you've done for me has give me a solider lock on you. But I don't want to push you past the point where you'd lose your own respect for yourself. I could make you do things you wouldn't want to think about. I could tell you that if you didn't do like I told you, I'd make sure that little lady found out just how you've been helping us and hurting them. Leroy has no call to be nervous about you, no more than I have. And that redhead isn't going to be hurt in any way. She's going to stay sweet and loving toward you, because that's how you want her to be, and you'll work to keep her that way. Before I ever talked to you I looked it all over careful. She's a spirited woman. She looks up to you. I knew you'd be awful careful not to let anybody know you have any deal with me, because she might find out. And I want you real careful, like you've been. You can't cross me, Jimmy, any more than Leroy could, or Buck, or Doc, or Bill, or Burt. Any one of you would be hurting yourself worse than me. So have no fear about anything happening to that little woman."

The office seemed slightly tilted, and Elmo Bliss looked half again life size. Jimmy moistened his dry lips and said, "It's so strange. The best reason you gave me for joining your team was that if I didn't, she might get hurt. That was the reason that meant the most to me. None of the reasons for it or against it seemed very important a few weeks ago. But that was . . . the one that counted."

"It was the heaviest one I had," Elmo admitted. "But why should you or anybody act like I'm a bad man? Chrissake, boy, we've been giving folks something to take their mind off the hot weather. What do they say? Bread and circuses. Dog packs need rabbits to chase. It angries up the blood and keeps folks young. I was going to get those two Army fellas pushed out of the picture too. We could have got to Jennings through his Chinaman wife, but then I got to thinking it would take the joy out of the public hearing if there was nobody to show up at all on the other side. They'll need somebody to boo at, and it might as well be Jennings and Lipe, standing all alone against the multitude. If Jennings has any idea of taking the fight further after the clobbering we'll give him, we can take his mind off it later on. And Lipe, without Jennings, isn't worth cutting up for chum. So who's been hurt too bad? Dermond, Mrs. Rowell, the Sinnat girl? They all *blameless,* boy? And look at the good that'll be done to more folks than you can count. There'll be fat pockets in this county."

"You . . . you can understand why I got upset."

"Because you didn't think it through. But I'll tell you one thing. I don't know how you can do it. But you'd best keep Miz Hubble away from that public hearing. She'll have no speeches to make. She's done all she can. You keep her away. It'll all die down fast afterwards. You'll see. But folks will be heated up Wednesday night. People could get roughed up, even if no real harm is meant."

For most of that Monday evening he had been without the bright static images in his mind. He sat at his desk in the newsroom and wrote about promotions and zoning appeals, meetings and resolutions, a Pigeon Town knifing, a drainage control project. He shrank himself into a little rubbery figure at a matchbox desk, running scrawled notes and short phone calls into rapidity-click, whappety-clack of pica black on yellow paper, bucked through rewrite, initialed at the desk, slugged, linotyped, copyread and locked up.

But later he was to remember that the image started before the phone call came. He did not know exactly what it was when it began. It was a shadowy something, and he could see the typed words well enough through it. Then it began to tower over him, a huge thing, ominous, silent. The words were gone and he was in a wild, still, lunar country. He stood in blackness at the foot of a bulge of mountain. There was some piercingly bright light beyond the mountain, shining on the long smooth concave curve of snow that led to the summit. To his right was a shadowy roundness where the light leaked around a wider portion of the great promontory. Suddenly perspective and proportion seemed to click into place, and he realized that it was a woman's breast, his eye so close to the base of it that for a moment he listened for the velvety thud of her heartbeat against his ear. The concave line of snow was the whiteness of her skin against the light beyond.

At midnight, after the phone call, as he was driving to the hospital, the image was still there. The lights of the oncoming traffic shone through it. After he had parked and was walking toward the emergency entrance, the vision left him. It did not fade as the others had. It merely moved slowly upward until it was beyond the furthest upward tilt of his vision.

Kat was waiting for him in the small alcove beyond the emergency room. She sprang up when she saw him and came to him, her eyes swollen. He held her in arms that felt wooden. She rolled her forehead back and forth against his shoulder, saying, "The dirty bastards. The horrible filthy dirty bastards."

"Where's Ross?"

"He's with her right now. He's waiting for the sedative to work."

"Has he reported it?"

"Yes. It was outside the city. Two deputies were here. They left a little while ago. What good can they do? She didn't know those people. She didn't get a look at any of them."

"Who's the doctor?"

"The one who was on duty in the emergency room. He's quite nice. He was very upset about it. Dr. Bressard."

"Does Ross expect me to go to her room?"

"No, dear. He was lucky enough to get a private room for her. He told me to wait for you down here, and for us both to wait for him. It shouldn't be long now."

"Can you tell me about it?"

"I think Ross ought to."

Ross came down five minutes later. He seemed to walk very carefully, like a man trying not to limp. His expression was thoughtful. "She's asleep now. It won't wear off for a while. I'll come back here so I'll be with her when she wakes up. Let's go get a drink someplace."

They walked to a small cocktail lounge two blocks away. It was a warm still night. They could hear the radios in the cars that drove by. They sat at a red plastic horseshoe booth in the back. Kat slid in first. After they had ordered, Kat said, "I haven't heard all of it, you know. How did they get the drawings?"

The low wall lamp had an opaque shade and a weak orange bulb. Ross Halley's face was in shadow. The light shone on his lumpy, malformed hands. He tore off small bits of the paper napkin, rolled each into a pellet and dropped it into the black plastic ashtray. "I didn't know the drawings were missing. I didn't know anything was missing. I haven't had time to check. Saturday afternoon we went to the beach. I took a camera along to get some casual beach stuff. Background for future work. I wanted to get her mind off this damn Palmland deal anyhow. We got back a little after four. Somebody had pied my studio. Dumped all my work, all my files and records and materials in the middle of the floor, poured everything onto it that would pour, and stirred it up with a broom. The tubes of color they squirted on the walls. The way they got in, they broke my outside studio door open. They wedged something in there and pried it open and splintered the door all to hell around the lock."

"Did you report it?" Kat asked.

He stared at her with a blank expression. "What was the point? Did it do any good reporting they cracked a window ten days ago heaving a rotten cabbage at the house? When Jackie saw what'd been done to my workroom, I've never seen her, or anybody, so mad. She scared me, she was so mad. When that was over she cried as if her heart was broken. Sunday she was still mad, but it was a deep slow burn. I fixed the door, put a new bolt on the inside. We worked all day long cleaning the place up, salvaging what we could. I haven't got any kind of insurance that covers that sort of thing. I checked and I don't. Actually, it's a hell of a loss. It made me feel sick. All the work I do for a long time is going to be just that much harder to get right. Now, understand, I'd been telling her to be careful, but when she went out tonight, I should have gone with her. She went out about eight o'clock, just to drive over to the mainland and pick up some cigarettes. We were nearly out. I guess they were waiting for her to come out, and followed her. I guess if we'd both gone out, it would have been the same thing. I don't think they were going to let me stop them.

"She went over to that shopping center at Bay and Mangrove. It was just about full dark by then. When she came back to the car, just as she opened the door, sombody eased up behind her and pulled some kind of big thick bag down over her head. She's a strong girl, but they didn't give her a chance. They grabbed her and hustled her into a nearby car and drove out of there. They'd wrapped some fast turns of line around her. It was so airless in that bag she panicked, and she thinks she fainted. But Bressard found a lump on the side of her head, so maybe she didn't. When she came out of it, she was being carried along a path in the woods. When they found she could walk, they stopped carrying her. They walked her with her arms twisted up into her back. The bag was gone and she wasn't tied. They had flashlights. She thinks there were at least four of them, and no more than six, all men, all in dark clothes, all wearing black hoods with big eyeholes and a big place for the mouth. They came to a small clearing. She could hear traffic a long way away. They spoke in whispers, and they used no names.

"They told her to take her clothes off, or they'd be ripped off. She tried to run and she tried to stall. Nothing worked. She did as they told her. They tied her to a big live oak tree, her face to the tree, so big she couldn't reach around it. She said she was blubbering and bellowing by then. There was a length of line fastening one wrist to the other. They wanted to show her something. They put the lights on it and held it where she could see it. Her head was turned to the side, her cheek against the tree. It was one of my drawings of her. I did a lot of them. I kept about twenty of the best ones. Some were charcoal, some pastels, some ink. Nude studies. Nothing lascivious, for God's sake. They were unmistakably her. I can get a good likeness. I did them years ago. I love her. I love how she's built and the way she looks. These were a private labor of love, something between me and my wife. Our business. Nobody else's. The head man whispered to her, 'Did you pose for this?' The question steadied her down. She said of course she did, and why not? Her husband is an artist, she said. Only a sick mind would see anything wrong in acting as a life model for your husband. He told her to answer yes or no, and he asked her again. She said yes. As soon as she said it, there was a sort of whistling, whirring sound behind her, and then such a terrible smashing pain across her naked back she bucked hard against the tree and screamed. The man tore the drawing in half, whispered, 'Repent!' and held up the next one and said, 'Did you pose for this?' Along about the forth drawing, she tried saying no, to see if that was what they wanted. When she said no they hit her twice, once for posing and once for lying. She said she would have done anything in the world to stop them. She begged. She said she repented. Toward the end she was going into a half-faint after each lash. She hung against the tree.

"Suddenly there were no more drawings. She heard them whispering to each other. They cut her wrists loose. She slid and fell. She heard them hurrying away, going away through the woods, and she lifted her head so she'd know what direction to go in. She rested for a long time, then, with her eyes more accustomed to the darkness, she was able to find her clothes. It took her a long time to put them on. She wandered off the path on her way back toward the highway. She forced her way through the brush and went through a deep ditch and up onto the shoulder. She was on the Bay Highway, about a mile this side of Everset. Two young boys picked her up, probably thinking their luck had provided them with a fine drunken blonde. She wasn't walking very well. As soon as she was in the car she fainted. Apparently the boys discovered the blood soaking through her shirt and slacks. Instead of dumping her anywhere, they drove her to the hospital and dumped her out there. She sat on the curb near the driveway to the emergency entrance. A nurse spotted her out there and came out and looked at her, then went back in and came out with another nurse and a stretcher. She told them to call me. When I arrived, Bressard was still working on her. He had a lot of cleaning to do, from where she'd rolled over into the dirt when they cut her loose. He thinks it was a heavy length of braided leather. Every swing sliced her open. The highest one is across the top of her shoulders, and the lowest one is across the back of her thighs a couple of inches above her knees. He says the worst places are where two marks cross. He did some stitching on those places. They had to treat her for shock and loss of blood. I saw her back. It's a dozen colors. If it wasn't for the shape of her, you wouldn't know what it was."

"Wicked," Kat whispered. "Cruel and wicked."

"She told me about it after we were up in the room. The pain isn't so bad. He froze it somehow. She told me in bits and pieces, not orderly like I've told you. There'll be scars for a long time. Maybe as long as she lives. She was always a girl who was proud of not having any scars and blemishes. And she never liked being hurt. If she'd scald a finger cooking, it would scare her and upset her."

"Don't talk about her that way," Kat said. "Don't use the past tense, Ross, please."

He gave her that strange thoughtful look. "Isn't it accurate? What makes you think the Jackie we know is still living?"

"Don't, Ross!"

"They took it all out of her, Kat. All the joy and the spunk and the spirit. It all leaked out of her back. You can't do that to a woman like that and expect to have much left. She's dull now, Kat. Her eyes are dull and her face is dull, and you can see how she'll look when she's old. She doesn't give a damn whether they fill your goddam bay or leave it alone. She's in a world she doesn't like any more, because now she knows there's no part of it you can trust. She trusted too much, and I didn't trust enough. I suppose I could go looking for those people. And if I'm as unlucky as I think I am, I might find them. Once I found them, I'd have to kill them. There's no other conceivable thing to do. And how much good would that do Jackie? So I'm not even going to look. When she's well enough, we'll move along. I don't think either of us will want to stay here." He looked at Jimmy in a slightly puzzled way. "Kat thought you could write this up. But you can't. And we wouldn't want you to. We don't want to advertise anything or fight anybody. We're going to take our losses and run, kids. And if you have any sense, Kat, you'll run too." He finished his drink and stood up. "I want to be right there in case she wakes up."

"Ross," Kat said. "Maybe it won't be as . . ."

He leaned one hand on the table to brace himself, reached with his right hand to cup her cheek in a clumsy way. "For everything you're thinking . . . for everything you're wishing . . . thanks."

He dropped a bill on the table and was gone, walking swiftly to the door and out into the night.

Kat looked down at her fists and said, "I wish it had been me. I wish it had been me. I'm tougher, Jimmy."

"Not that tough."

She tilted her head to give him a sidelong glance from narrowed eyes. "All that righteousness," she said. "That's the worst part of it. The way they must have enjoyed it. Repent! Shining those lights on her. Smacking their lips. A naked, painted, evil woman. Such a contrast she must have been, compared to their own women, their sorry, dumpy, drab little women. They couldn't have ever earned the love of a woman like Jackie. It was like rape, wasn't it, only better because they don't have to feel guilt. They can feel virtuous and stern. The mighty wrath of Jehovah." She rested her forehead on her clenched fists. Her hair was a sorrel gleam in the slant of the light. "What's happening to everything, Jimmy?" she said in an almost inaudible voice.

He caressed the shining hair. She leaned her head against the caress, pressing hard. Then suddenly she sat up, dug into her purse for a tissue, dabbed her eyes, blew her nose.

"Down to three little Indians," he said.

"These are bad times for Indians. Tom felt so damn guilty about Mortie. He kept saying over and over that he should have let Mortie quit when he wanted to. He's feeling responsible for the whole thing now. He's sick about getting all of us into it. I don't know what this will do to him, when he hears about Jackie. I don't think he'll give up. But he'll try to go the rest of the way alone. Of course, he's damn close to being alone right now. My car is at the hospital. I don't like to sound like a coward, but will you follow me home? And stay with me while I phone. . . . No, I can't phone him from the house, darn it. Anyway, it's so late. He needs what sleep he can get. I'll leave for work early tomorrow and stop there on the way and tell him."

"Are you back in your own house now?"

"Things quieted down. I thought it was all right."

"I think you better stay at the Sinnats."

"I guess so. Faithful Natalie is the emergency sitter. I guess we better move back there again tonight."

"I'll follow you home."

"Will . . . this be in the paper?"

"Wednesday morning. Yes. It'll get in through the emergency room records. Bressard will have to make a report. It will be picked up as a matter of routine, even though there's no complaint, no charges filed. Woman hospitalized, beaten by unknown assailants."

"I'm so tired, Jimmy. So gosh-darn tired."

"So let's get you home."

"I got a card from Claire from the Madeira Islands. She said it's a dreary boat, and get the filter unit changed in the pool please, and she hopes I'm having more fun than she is."

It was almost two-thirty when he drove out of the Estates. He hesitated at the gates, then turned right toward Turk's Pass instead of left toward town. There were no other cars parked at the pass. There was a high far fragment of moon and a moist steady breeze out of the west. He walked

around to the Gulf side. The breeze kept the mosquitoes
away. He sat on soft dry sand. The small waves spilled up
the gradual slant of the beach and slid back, leaving a
gleam which quickly soaked away into darkness. There was
a phosphorescence in the waves, a green flickering where
they broke. He found bits of broken shell in the sand
and snapped them toward the water.

Now then, he kept saying to himself. Now. He wanted a
beginning. He wanted to pick things up and build a plausible
structure. He wanted a starting place and a middle place
and an ending place.

"Now then!" he said, and was startled to realize he had
said it aloud. But nothing began. Things were in bright
fragments, and they were all static. They existed, and could
not be moved. He took off his clothes and waded out.
Fish sped away from him, leaving faint green lines of
phosphorescence. He stood where the incoming march of
the slow waves slapped his thighs. He felt the suck of water
around his feet, pulling the sand out from under them, settling him slowly, washing him in like a pier. He moved
out and swam for a little while, floated on the lift and fall
of the swell, looking at the stars, then swam in. He knelt
at the surf line and combed the sand with his fingers,
combed out a half handful of coquinas, then walked slowly
on the packed wet sand letting the wind dry him, eating
the coquinas, opening the small shells with his thumbnail
as if they were pistachios, licking out the tiny sweet bits
of living meat with the tip of his tongue.

When he was dry he put his clothing back on. He
stretched out in the dry sand and made a sand pillow
for his head. A night bird flew by, croaking with sad, habitual
alarm. Now then, he told himself. But nothing began. When
he awoke, the beach, the sea and the sky were all the
same shade of silver-gray. Far out over the Gulf lightning
made a small silent calligraphy between cloud blackness and
the gray horizon. A crab stood on tiptoe nearby, a small
ballet of wariness. Beyond the storm dunes and sea oats
was a crimson line over the mainland. He bent over and
brushed the sand out of his hair. A hundred yards away,
in shallow water, there was a turmoil of fish, startling him.
It was still too early for birds. The tide was running in
swiftly. He walked slowly along the shore line of the pass,
around toward the bay side where his car was parked.
When he was opposite the middle of the pass, an oiled
black arc of porpoise appeared, made a gasping huff and
sounded again.

He got behind the wheel of his car. Now then, he told

himself. But some essential connective pinions of his mind had rusted in place. He felt as if he was trying to glance at still photographs swiftly enough to achieve the illusion of motion. But the pictures were not in order. He had reasons, but he could not link them to acts. He could devise acts, but they were naked of reason and consequence. Memory had suffered a strange inversion, so that all that was to come seemed to have the quality of things remembered.

When he reached the cottage, he showered, knotted a towel around his waist and sat at the typewriter. During the morning the phone rang several times, but he did not answer it. By eleven o'clock he had it exactly the way he wanted it. He set his alarm and slept until two o'clock. When he woke up, he read it again. He had an original and one copy. He folded them separately, after dating and signing each one. He put the carbon in an envelope and addressed it to Kat. He mailed it in town and then went to the bank lot to wait for her to come out.

22

WHEN KAT WALKED around the corner of the bank building on Tuesday afternoon, she saw Jimmy Wing's station wagon parked beside her car. She saw him standing in the shade of the building, smoking a cigarette.

He came striding toward her. His color was not good.

"Where were you?" she asked. "Golly I called here and there."

"I want to come to your house. I want to talk to you."

"Of course, Jimmy! I want to stop at the hospital first though."

"At the hospital?"

"To see Jackie. What's the matter with you?"

"Nothing. I have to talk to you."

"Has something else gone wrong? You look sick, Jimmy."

"I'm fine. I'm perfectly fine. I'm in perfect shape."

"Do you want to stop at the hospital?"

"No."

"Perhaps later?"

"Can we go to your house right now?"

"But you seem so . . . All right, Jimmy. Right now."

He followed her. After a few blocks she realized he was following too closely. It was not like him. He was too good a driver. She concentrated on avoiding any traffic hazard which might cause her to stop too suddenly. When she had to stop for a light she turned and stared back at him. He sat motionless and expressionless, clasping the wheel high, his lips sucked pale, his mouth small. All the way home she invented things which could have made him act so strangely, but none of them fitted.

They went into the house through the patio door. The heavy noon rain had made the inside temperature more bearable than usual. She turned the air conditioner on. His strangeness made her nervous. And she heard herself talking too much, in the light quick way Van had called her society gabble.

"I was phoning you to tell you how Tom took it, which wasn't very well at all, not that I expected anything else. Would you like a beer or something? Do sit down. You want to talk to me and here I am doing all the talking.

When Tom heard about Jackie, he just seemed to sag all over. He turned into a little gray old man with shaking hands and tears in his eyes. He said he'd go there tomorrow night and speak out, but he would make it clear he was speaking for himself alone. He said he would not be responsible any longer for . . ."

"Is anybody coming here? Would your kids come here?"

"Have you heard anything I've been saying? Nobody is coming here. Jigger and Nat took the twins and my kids and Esperanza to an afternoon movie."

,He walked toward her with an expression so strange she instinctively backed away from him. He reached out and took hold of her upper arms and stared at her with an intensity which alarmed her.

"You're hurting me," she said in a faint voice.

"I wish I knew all it's costing. But I can't think that way any more."

"I don't understand, Jimmy."

He shook her slightly. It seemed a gesture of impatience. "When you can't figure out any of the possibilities, it's like walking around on a roof blindfolded. You don't even know what to be scared of."

She felt the tears well into her eyes. "I . . . I don't know what you mean, and you're hurting my arms."

He released her suddenly. He handed her some folded sheets. "Read this," he said harshly. "You'll get a signed copy in the mail."

He walked over and sat in a fireside chair, slumped, leaned his head back, closed his eyes. She unfolded the sheets and moved closer to the window.

"James Warren Wing, Record-Journal reporter, revealed last night a conspiracy between County Commissioner Elmo Bliss and the five majority owners of the Palmland Development Company. According to Wing, Mr. Burton Lesser, Mr. Leroy Shannard, Doctor Felix Aigan, Mr. Buckland Flake and Mr. William Gormin all entered into a verbal agreement with Commissioner Bliss some months ago whereby, after the commissioner's term of office was expired, they will each sell him, at a nominal figure, a substantial portion of their holdings. In return, Commissioner Bliss promised to aid Palmland in their acquisition of the submerged land in Grassy Bay.

"Wing stated that Commissioner Bliss, in his presence, estimated that his capital gain, after taxes, would be in excess of $300,000, a sum which Bliss has already earmarked as a campaign fund when he enters the next gubernatorial race.

"Wing further stated that he was taken into Commissioner Bliss's confidence on the sixth of this month when Bliss employed him, at a salary of $100 a week and expenses, to secretly assist Bliss in nullifying the conservationist efforts of Save Our Bays, Incorporated. Wing claims he was selected for this task because of his previous close associations with many of the members of the Executive Committee of Save Our Bays, Inc.

"Based on information turned over to him by Wing, Bliss brought pressure to bear on Mr. Dial Sinnat and Mrs. Doris Rowell which resulted in their resigning from the Executive Committee. Wing has kept Commissioner Bliss informed of all the promotional activities of Save Our Bays. Bliss, working quietly through various pressure groups and organizations in the county, has been responsible for a campaign of vilification and harassment unequaled in Palm County history. Wing stated that Bliss, through Leroy Shannard, his personal attorney, had employed Tampa operatives who, through the use of illegal tape recording, forced the resignation of Mr. Morton Dermond, another Executive Committee member, from his post as Director of the Palm County Art Center, and secured his immediate departure from the area.

"Wing also called attention to the fact that Reverend Darcy Harkness Coombs is related to Commissioner Bliss, and that Coombs may well have been implicated in the brutal and unwarranted flogging of Mrs. Ross Halley last Monday night when she was kidnapped in a public parking area and taken to a wooded area near Everset by several black-hooded men. The threat of a similar flogging was instrumental in Mr. Dial Sinnat's decision to resign from the Executive Committee and withdraw his financial support from Save Our Bays, Inc.

"Wing stressed the fact that, to the best of his knowledge, only Leroy Shannard, of the men in the Palmland group, has been aware of all the supplementary efforts of Elmo Bliss. He stated that it was Leroy Shannard, working through Mrs. Martin Cable, who has been most instrumental in securing a favorable financial climate for the Palmland Isles venture.

"When queried as to why Bliss should have gone to such lengths to smash all opposition to the bay-fill plan, Wing stated that Bliss wanted to be certain that Save Our Bays, Inc., would be in no position to offer any further opposition after the public hearing. Bliss also wishes public support to be so overwhelming that, in order to divert suspicion, he can be in a position to abstain or register a negative vote without endangering the bay-fill project.

"When asked why he had made this conspiracy a matter of public record at this time, Wing remarked that he had decided at the eleventh hour that the public has a right to know the details of this abuse of his office by Commissioner Elmo Bliss. He said that Bliss would undoubtedly attempt some retaliation for his having made this statement, but he could make no guess as to what form this would take."

Kat slowly refolded the sheets. She found she was making a special effort to fold them more neatly than Jimmy had, getting the edges in better alignment. She crossed the room to where he sat, feeling tall and severe and gravely speculative.

She knelt beside his chair. He put the folded papers in his shirt pocket. She knelt erect, her hands side by side on his forearm.

"It's true," she said. "It couldn't be anything else. It couldn't be some kind of crazy scheme . . . to help us."

He turned his head toward her, his eyes half closed. "It's true, of course."

"We all trusted you, Jimmy."

"I know."

"How does that make you feel?"

"I don't feel much of anything."

"But *why? Why* did you get into such a thing? Did you need the money?"

"No."

"Did they have something on you?"

"What's so astonishing? I'm a small-town cynic. I know a lot of people and I know the way things get done, and this time I was in on it. It would have come out the same way with or without me."

"Did they have something on you?"

"When you're bored, you want a closer look at the machinery."

"How did they make you do it?"

"They made it sound innocent."

"But you knew it wasn't."

She felt the muscles of his arm tighten, move, relax again. "It looks as if I'd gotten out of it now, doesn't it?"

She bit her lip for a moment. "But it's a little late, isn't it? A little late for Jackie and Morton and Doris. What do you want me to say? Bravo? Do you want absolution, forgiveness, a fat medal of honor? You've been mixed up in a terrible thing, Jimmy, and I think I owe it to you to try to understand."

"I'm not very good at explaining anything these days. There's no logic in my head. There's some pictures, and some darkness, and no way of knowing anything that comes next, or understanding what happened."

"They had some way of making you do it."

"They used you."

She stared at him. "Me!"

"That was just a part of it. I could play. Or they'd use rougher people. I thought I could keep it easy on everybody, especially you. I kept them off you. But they decided I wasn't suited to the real dirty work when they went after Mortie and Jackie."

"But I can take care of myself! Did I ask to be protected?"

"No."

"Why should I be that important to you?"

He put his free hand over both of hers. "You are. You have been. You will be, even though I've canceled myself out. And not a very romantic attachment, Kat. Not very civilized, even. Basic. Below the belt. Physical lust. Just a hell of a driving need to have you."

"But how could you have . . ."

"How the hell do I know! It isn't something anybody plans is it? It started seven or eight months ago, and kept building. I can't look at your mouth or watch you walk without feeling dizzy and sick with desire."

"I . . . I'm just a woman. I'm not that . . . special."

"I've told myself that and it hasn't done any good."

"I . . . don't think of you that way!"

"I know that."

"I've been . . . deeply grateful to you, Jimmy. You've been such a good friend to me. But now I find out you've been lying . . . I don't know what to think."

He sat up and took her suddenly by the elbows and guided her around so that she was in front of him, forcing her to hobble awkwardly on her knees, then pulled her close and wrapped her in his hard long arms and ground his mouth into hers. She fought for a few startled moments and then endured him. He gave a long shuddering sigh and rested his forehead on her shoulder. His hands moved gently on her body.

She felt very young, inept, confused. How do I get into such things? she asked herself. Why should I feel so uncertain, and why should I feel obligated? Why should I stop fighting him because I realized he was crying? Why should I owe him anything for being nice to me? How can he expect this of me? It's idiotic! And it's shameful. Does his wanting you give him rights? Make him stop.

"Jimmy," she said. "Don't, dear. Please don't."

He stood up and pulled her up and stopped her mouth again, and she knew her arms were around him. He was shaking with his need for her. What can you do now? she thought helplessly. You let it go so far.

He dipped and swung her up into his arms. "Please no," she whispered. "Oh please no."

She felt waxen in his arms. Beyond his still profile she saw the ceiling turn and move. She felt the cold whir of air against her as she was carried past the air conditioner.

"The guest room," she whispered, and hid her face and her shyness and her confusion against his chest.

While it was happening, she watched herself from afar, severely on guard against any thought of Van that might slip into her mind. He was more powerful than she would have imagined, and with deftness and skill that disheartened her. Her treacherous body threatened a participation she wished to deny it. She seemed to be apart from herself, off where she could watch the clever sequences lure the blind body into disloyal flexures and strainings, lead it into the dread ultimate gallop, the lungs gasping, the heart racing, the throat beginning its terminal whine, while the shocked mind, apart from all of it, seemed to be screaming, What am I doing? How did this begin? Why am I letting him?

It ended for him when she was a half step from the brink, from the long dark plunging fall. She lay in tension, in a bright agony of indignation and annoyance which was mingled with a deep and humble gratitude that it had stopped short of that most ultimate seduction, leaving her used but not using, a donor instead of an accomplice. She waited for it to recede, but found she was caught there, lodged precariously upon the edge. She gathered herself, then quickly and roughly tumbled him away, got up and padded out of the guest room and down the hallway to her bathroom.

By the time she had showered, the tension was almost gone. She brushed her hair, darkened her eyebrows, made her mouth up with care. She studied herself in the mirror. Her mouth looked slightly puffy. She put on an almost-new dress, high-heeled sandals, a touch of her best perfume. She looked at herself in her bedroom mirror, the short skirt swirling at her knees as she turned from side to side. She could think of no simple description of how she felt. She felt rueful about stumbling into one trap, yet smug about evading the second one, no matter how narrow the margin. In retrospect the second trap seemed the more deadly one because it would have made her hostage to the emotions her completion, at his hands, would have made inevitable. And she felt rather prim, as well as smug, filled with the severity of the one unjustly used, the one victimized by her own warm and generous heart.

She felt no shyness until she was a step from the guest room door. She lifted her chin and strode in quite briskly. He had pulled the draperies back, and he was standing at the window, slowly buttoning his shirt. He turned around as she walked in.

"Kat, I didn't mean . . ."

"Don't for the love of God start apologizing. I don't recall being raped, exactly." She went to the bed and with housewife dexterity, slapped and smoothed and poked the rumpled spread back to tautness.

"You're . . . pretty matter-of-fact about it."

She sat on the bed, crossed her legs, took one of his cigarettes from the night table and lit it. "How should I act? Grateful? All bashful and trembly? Heartbroken? I'm an adult female, Jimmy. You had your way with me, to coin a phrase. It wasn't my idea, and it wasn't an idea I was terribly enthusiastic about, but I couldn't see fighting a bloody battle over it." She made herself smile at him. "Let's just say I felt a lingering little feeling of obligation to you for past favors. And it isn't every day a girl gets to cure an obsession, does she? Now you've had me. Am I too matter-of-fact? When I think of it at all, and I certainly don't plan to dwell on it, I'll remember it as an invasion of privacy, Jimmy."

He moved closer to her. "You reacted."

She shrugged. "A little, I suppose. You seem to be a good lover. I haven't known enough men to be able to tell. And what was I supposed to do after we both found out I was willing? Lie there like a stick? I expect I was being decently hospitable, but no more than that. And it was like I warned you in the living room. I'm just another woman. And it didn't mean much to me, and hardly more than that to you, did it?"

"Kat, you're being so damned . . ."

"The least you can do now is to be honest with yourself. If we loved each other we might be able to make something special and magical out of the bed part of it. But this way, it was just a vulgar, sweaty little interlude on a sultry afternoon. And I'm not special to you any more, am I?"

He hesitated, then said, "No, dear. Not the way you were."

She was unprepared for her own quick sense of loss. She hid it with a smile and said, "So I've done you a favor, I suppose. Destroyed the illusion. Poor Jimmy. Pick somebody sexier for your next set of daydreams. It might work out better for you. Right now, all things considered, I think we're even. Nobody is obligated to anybody for anything. And there's a little sadness about it. Because there's no place to go from here. This is the end of us."

"I know."

"I did cherish you as my good friend."

"But that was over too, wasn't it, before I carried you in here?"

"I guess it was, Jimmy."

"So, either way, the ending is the same."

"Not quite the same. I feel sorrier for you than I would have. You have to live with yourself. You have to live with what's happened to all of us."

"I'll manage."

"I'm sure you will. Jimmy, how can you get that into the paper?"

"I've thought of a way. If it doesn't work, turn your copy of it over to Tom, will you? Don't try to do anything with it yourself."

"Tom will have better ideas, I'm sure."

"But if my idea works, you won't have to do anything with it."

"Best of luck."

They walked out into the living room. The shyness was upon her again when he looked at her. "You mustn't think it will change the Palmland thing to get this into the paper. It will cut Elmo back down to size, nothing more. Palmland has got too much momentum."

"I guessed that would be the case. But at least it's something." He stood in the middle of the room, looking around. "Did you leave something here?" she asked.

He ran a hand back through his stiff sandy hair and smiled in a rather apologetic way. "Maybe, but it's no time for cute symbolic answers, is it? I was just feeling . . . kind of nostalgic. You know. I used to come here and have good times. But that was a different person, I guess."

"Quite a different person."

When he was outside the door he turned, frowning, and said, "If you think of anything else I can do, any way I could . . . help fix things up . . ."

"There won't be anything else."

He looked at her, nodded thoughtfully and said, "No. I guess there won't."

She watched him from the window. He sat in his car for long silent moments, then started it and drove away.

The house seemed very empty. When she paced, her heels made noises that seemed too loud whenever she crossed the areas of bare floor. She turned the television set on and turned it off. Suddenly she remembered her other clothing and went swiftly to the guest room. The skirt was across the chair at the foot of the bed. The pale blouse was on the floor beside the chair. She picked them up. The skirt would do for another day. The collar of the blouse was faintly grimed. She found her bra on the floor between the bed and the wall. A gray ball of dust clung to the elastic when she picked it up. Her brief blue Dacron pants lay across the sandals she had worn to work.

She had picked the clothing up, and quite suddenly she felt so weak and faint that she turned and sat quickly on the side of the bed, near the foot of it, the clothing in her lap. She saw herself reflected in the narrow wall mirror, perfectly centered.

She gave herself a quick, vivid, social smile and said politely, "All dressed up and no place to go."

She gave herself a comic grimace. "Lo the faithful widow lady," she said.

And then, in her pretty dress and her perfume, she huddled over, hunched herself over the clothing in her lap, and began to cry, in a choking, gasping, hiccuping way, with the tears coming in a thin, scalding, sour way. As she wept she kept remembering that neither of them had said a word. They had made of it a desperate, silent struggle. And that seemed the most shameful thing of all.

23

AT TEN O'CLOCK Jimmy Wing found Brian Haas alone at
the counter at Vera's Kitchen. He went in and sat beside
him. Brian gave him a casual and rather guarded smile
and said, "Our Leader has been beating the bushes for you,
pal. That seems to be happening a lot lately. I seem to find
myself doing things you should be doing. Are you goofing
a little, maybe?"

"Definitely not! Everything I do is constructive. I have
been chugging around in the night, making up parables and
fables."

"You look a little bright around the eyes. You get the
needle into a vein?"

"Mr. Haas, if a man suddenly went stone deaf and then
suddenly got his hearing back again, he would go around
listening to the rustle of every leaf. Right?"

"Is that a parable or a riddle?"

"My gears have been locked for a while. I rocked them
loose."

"Okay, it's a riddle. So now you're racing your engine. Is
that the answer?"

"Mr. Haas, I will try out one small parable on you, one
that I made up concerning you. Once upon a time there
was a dog who had an undiagnosed case of distemper. Such
as the morbidity of the disease that the dog went around
blaming his low morale on his condition of doghood. He
had black thoughts about dogs and destiny. So, to prove to
himself that dogs are no damn good, he strolled over and
quietly bit the hell out of the dog next door. It gave him
considerable surly satisfaction, but when the disease wore
off, he was suddenly very very ashamed of himself."

Brian Haas put his cup down and swiveled his counter
stool and stared at Wing. His eyes were dark and mild under
the protective shelf of hairy brow. But there was a glint
of amusement in them Jimmy had not seen for a long time.
"In the first place, you illiterate bastard, when it has animals
in it, it's a fable, not a parable. In the second place, I know
a dog who gets a different kind of distemper. He reaches
around and bites hell out of himself. And is equally
ashamed. In the third place, Nan wonders when you're com-

301

ing around so I can whip your tail with a jazzy new variation of the Ruy Lopez."

"Tell her soon. I've got another one. This is a parable. No animals. This one is real deep."

"I'll pay attention."

"They shot this character into orbit, seven thousand times around the planet, and he took along seven thousand squeeze-bottles full of high-vitamin gunk, one a day. And almost as soon as he was up there, he started thinking about steak. He tried not to. Before the trip was half over, he was breathing, dreaming, seeing, smelling steak. And then he came down and had a steak. He gobbled it down. He gobbled it down so damn fast, my boy, that the only slight taste he got was exactly the same as what had been in all those bottles."

"So the second steak will be better, eh?"

"No chance. They shot him right back up there."

"Seven thousand more times around?"

"Aw, no, Bri! For keeps."

Brian Haas nodded. "You're right. That one is real deep."

"Ready for another deep one?"

"Let me get my feet braced. Shoot."

"This one will be a fable because it's got a monkey in it. One time there was a man who found himself a trick monkey. For a very small outlay in bananas, this man had himself a monkey who had a very quiet amiable personality. The thing was, this man could boost the monkey over transoms and through tiny windows, and when he was inside the monkey would unlock the house so the man could come in. The monkey thought he was pretty bright, and it was more fun than living in a tree. One day the trick monkey suddenly discovered that the kind banana man was . . . kicking the hell out of all the other monkeys . . . and . . ."

He put his fist on the counter edge and lowered his forehead until it rested against his fist. He heard the aftertones of his voice in the quiet lunchroom and knew he had gotten a little loud, somewhat shrill.

He felt Brian's hand on his shoulder. "Hey, boy," Bri said quietly.

Jimmy sat up. "I guess I didn't get that one worked out yet."

"It has possibilities. It has a plot line. It needs a kicker. You all right?"

"I'm brisk, Mr. Haas. Brisk and eager."

"And I've got to go make J.J. think I am also."

"That's what I had on my mind, Bri. I don't think you ought to go back there tonight. You ran into good old Jimmy.

He'll help J.J. put it to bed."

"So we'll both go confound him with our talent and intellect."

"I'd just as soon you wouldn't. Can you take it just like that? With no explanation, please? You go home to Nan. Tell her I love her."

"I want maybe just one crumb of explanation."

"If you go up there, there is something you might look as if you were mixed up in, and you wouldn't be mixed up in it at all, but people might not hang around and listen to any explanations. Okay?"

"I've been mixed up in a lot of things."

"This is mine."

Brian studied him for a moment. "Just so I'll know sometime."

"You'll know."

Wing walked back to the newsroom. Borklund looked at him with weary disapproval as he listened to Wing's story of Brian Haas's headache. "If you're as useful as you've been lately, James, it's a damned good thing there isn't much left to do. We aren't holding much open."

He worked with one eye on the clock. Finally he took an incoming call from a drunken woman and faked his end of the conversation, causing her considerable confusion. He went to Borklund and said, "I think I may have something hot, J.J. A man wants me to come down to my car in the parking lot. He wants you to listen to it too."

"Who is he?"

"A bartender I know. He's reliable. He says he overheard something that might give us a hell of a news break."

"It probably won't be worth a damn."

"He said to be down there in three minutes. Maybe it's something good. What'll it cost us but a short walk?"

Borklund hesitated. "Okay, okay."

They walked out to the parking lot. "I'm parked way over there in the corner," Wing said. As they neared the car, he let Borklund get a step ahead of him. He looked around and saw no one.

Borklund started to turn around, saying, "There isn't anybody . . ."

As he got halfway around, Jimmy Wing hit him squarely on the jaw with a short hard overhand punch. The blow opened Borklund's mouth and staggered him back against the car, his glasses dangling from one ear. As Wing moved quickly to catch the man, Borklund grunted and lifted his fists and struck Wing weakly in the chest. Wing measured him and hit him again. Borklund started to slide sideways along the car, and caught himself. The glasses fell and splintered on the asphalt. Borklund sighed and assumed a brave John L. Sullivan stance and pawed at Jimmy with his left. Jimmy's right hand was a throbbing lump of pain. In the shadows he could see a dark streak of blood on Borklund's chin. He had the frantic, nightmare feeling that Borklund would never go down. He hit him again, and the shock of pain that ran up his arm made him gasp. Borklund wavered. He leaned against the car. His knees bent and slid down to a sitting position, lowered his chin onto his chest, and toppled over onto his side.

Brian Hass appeared beside Wing and said, "*What* the holy *hell* are you doing?"

Jimmy took his knuckles out of his mouth and said in an exhausted voice, "I told you to stay the hell away, old buddy."

"You acted so damn strange I decided to come back."

"My God, that son of a bitch can take a punch."

"Are you out of your damn mind?"

"Shut up. You're getting highly nervous. Here. Take this over there by the light and read it. I've got something to do."

"Like what? Stomp him a little?"

Wing said with great patience, "I am going to tape his little wrists and tape his little ankles and tape a rag in his little mouth and put him in my car for a little while. So get the hell away from here before he comes out of it and thinks you're in this thing too."

Brian walked toward the light. Wing taped Borklund up and hoisted him in over the tail gate. Borklund seemed heavier than anyone would have guessed. Wing's right hand was beginning to puff.

He walked slowly over and stood by Brian as he finished reading the last few lines. "Holy Jesus in the mountains!" Haas said in a soft strained voice.

"How do you like J.J.'s nice little initials on it?"

Brian looked at them. "They should pass." He handed the sheets to Wing. "Where are you putting it?"

"Boxed on the right side of page one."

"*If* it gets by Harmon and Tillerman and Crawder."

"It will, with a nice two-column head: 'Reporter Accuses Bliss.' And the subhead: 'Bay-Fill Conspiracy Charged.' "

"But what kind of an angle have you got, Jimmy? Where's your protection? How much cover have you got?"

"None. Nothing. The sword of truth."

"A sword against heavy artillery, boy. But did you have to put an assault rap on top of everything else?"

"Name another way to handle it?"

"Hell, I could have decoyed him away long enough."

"Name another way to handle it where there's nobody in it but me."

Haas said slowly, "I see what you mean. But I know about it and I'm not doing anything about it, so that makes me part of it too."

"Go home."

"They'll believe two of us quicker than one. Let's go in there and spread some snow around, Mr. Wing. J.J. went home with a headache and or a sore throat. We'll snow them all, cut out some of the laudatory crud about Palmland and insert this little morsel."

"You'll get fired, Bri."

"I don't think so. They'll *have* to fire you. That'll make me more valuable. I'll be terrible shocked when I find out you actually struck poor Mr. Borklund, and then lied to me, your good friend. Okay?"

"So let's go."

After it was done, they waited around and picked a couple of the first copies off the press run. Brian had phoned Nan so she wouldn't worry. There was no one to worry about when Borklund came home.

"You better keep him," Haas said. "Like a rare butterfly."

Jimmy went to the car and checked and came back. "His eyes are open. He did a little thumping and grunting. I think he's annoyed."

"How's your hand?"

"I have pretty dimpled knuckles. I better not turn him loose until circulation is too far along to be stopped."

"Want to park him in front of my house for a little while?"

"I better not. I want to keep you clean."

They stood under the street light on Bayou, smiling at each other. Haas said, "You were a sneaky bastard, working for Elmo, you know."

"The job had small compensations. I got to take Buck's girl to Tampa and put her on a plane."

"I wondered what happened to her."

"She made Martin Cable nervous."

"When Eloise reads the morning paper, she's going to be the nervous one."

"Almost as nervous as Leroy."

"Mr. Wing, it has been a pleasure being associated with you. In a day when the newspaper business has become about as glamorous as chicken-plucking, you have created a new legend with a nice old-timey ring to it. May I suggest that you seek your next employment in Portland, Anchorage or Honolulu, and as quickly as possible?"

"After I stay and watch what happens."

"Don't stay too long. I'll say goodbye to Nan for you."

After Haas drove off, Jimmy walked slowly to his car. He had had little sleep, but he did not feel tired. He felt stimulated and mildly reckless, a three-drink condition achieved without drinking. But at unexpected intervals a little streak of fright would flash across the back of his mind, like a penny rocket. He kept thinking of a bloody old joke about a man reputed to be very quick with a razor. Ho, ho, ho, you missed me, boy. Did I, now? Just you try turning your head. Beyond old jokes, and the little gleams of fright, and the problem of what to do with Borklund, and the ache of his bruised hand, were the tangled sensory memories of Katherine, untouched, unsorted—all the jumbled, silky tumbling of her, white long clean lines and the gasping, all untouched, unsorted, and too soon over. For a time there had been one incredible answer to everything, a solution of such curious simplicity it had been overlooked. But, almost within moments, it had become a false answer to all the wrong questions, and she came tapping back in on her tall heels, her face cool, her mouth sucked to an unforgiving tightness, to tell him that little boys who write nasty words on the blackboard lose their chance to attend the school picnic.

He turned to look toward the rear of the station wagon and said, "Borklund, old buddy, what would you like to do? We're too late for the bars. They closed at two. We lost our chance to pick up a couple of girls. About the only thing to do is ride around. Okay with you? Fine. We'll just ride around." Borklund made a muffled growling sound and thumped with his heels on the tin deck of the wagon.

He drove aimlessly for nearly an hour, and finally parked at the small public beach at the north end of Cable Key. Two other cars were parked there, in search of love. There were hungry mosquitoes ranging the beach. He left the windows open a few inches, locked the doors on the inside, sprayed the interior of the car with the bug bomb he carried in the glove compartment, stretched out on the front seat and went to sleep. It was early daylight when he awakened. The other cars were gone.

He dropped the tail gate, hauled Borklund into a handy position and stripped the tape off. Borklund looked older and smaller, gray in the mild morning light. He sat on the tail gate, his legs dangling. His jaw was lumpy and discolored.

"Glasses," he said in a dusty voice.

Wing got them from the glove compartment. One lens was almost opaque with a network of fine cracks. Borklund put them on. He fingered his jaw tenderly. He spat onto the compacted shell of the parking area. He stepped down and walked in a small circle, slowly, lifting his knees high, flexing his arms. He stopped in front of Jimmy and said, "I don't want you sent to Raiford. I want you serving county time, so on the hot afternoons I can drive out and park and watch you swinging a brush hook on a county road gang."

"You're a hard man to put down."

"What the hell is it all about, Wing?"

Jimmy handed him the paper. Borklund leaned against the tail gate and read it. Then he slowly rolled the paper into a small hard cylinder. He stared out at the Gulf and whapped the paper against his thigh and said, "You poor damn fool. You poor sorry ignorant damn fool."

"Could I have gotten it in any other way?"

"No. That isn't what I mean. You going to leave me here, or do you plan to drive me back to my car?"

"I'll drive you in."

Borklund got into the car. As Jimmy backed out, he said, "Who was in this with you? Haas?"

"He was there, but he didn't know anything about you."

"I got to get my other glasses and change my clothes and go see Mr. Killian and then go sign a complaint."

At noon on Wednesday Jimmy parked on Center Street and walked a block and a half to the Bay Restaurant. He walked slowly in the hot sun. He had the feeling that if he looked down at the front of his clean shirt, he would be able to see his heart beating. There was a ludicrous flavor to the situation. It seemed that it had happened to him before, and then he remembered it was just a stock situation in ten thousand westerns. Ol' Jimmy Wing, the tumbleweed kid, has come into town a-knowing the Bliss gang has swore to shoot him on sight. Play a little *High Noon* music while the townspeople gasp and bug their eyes and scuttle out of the line of fire.

He gave a hitch at his gun belt, narrowed his eyes, and listened to the slow jingle of his spurs. But there were tourists who didn't scuttle, and glanced at him blankly, if at all. He went into the coolness of the lounge and stood at the bar where many members of the business community could be found at lunchtime, and had the small satisfaction of noting that he had put an abrupt end to about fifteen simultaneous conversations. When the conversations began again, they had a different character, a hushed sibilance. He ordered a drink and nodded and spoke to the ones within range.

"Hi, Les, Charlie. How you, Wade? How're things, Will?"

The responses were guarded. They left him ample elbow room at the bar. Leroy Shannard came in at quarter after twelve, heading toward the dining room. He saw Wing and stopped abruptly and came over to him.

"I've been boring hell out of our mutual friend all morning, James," Shannard said. "I keep saying to him I told you so."

"What's good word for him? Disgruntled?"

"That word has always bothered me. If you're not disgruntled, you have to be gruntled, don't you?"

"What's a better word for Elmo today?"

"I'd say hurt. Just plain hurt. He said if anybody was to see you, tell you he'd like a little chat with you. He should be at his office all afternoon. I guess he wants to talk to you like an uncle."

"You seem calm and contented, Leroy."

"I've had a busy morning, a right busy morning indeed, soothing some people down and chewing out other ones. I have to keep explaining how you snuck that into the paper without permission, and have been fired. Poor Eloise had hysterics over the phone after Martin left the house. Poor fellow has been adding two and two and coming up with twenty-two, but he can't back out on the financing now without confirming all the gossip that's going around. Darse Coombs was stamping around my office demanding we sue somebody. But, yes, I guess I'm calm and contented, James. The worst fuss is over already. It'll be downhill from here on. Tonight in a thousand happy homes, they'll use that paper to wrap the garbage. You'd better talk to Elmo. He's upset about what you said about retaliation. I guess he isn't entirely sure about what you meant, James. You've got no job with the paper and no job with him, and no chance of any kind of a job in Palm County. And of the people left who'll still speak to you, there isn't a one of them who'll ever trust you. So he seems to feel you've given yourself all the retaliation one man can use." He glanced at his watch, nodded at Jimmy and said, "Good luck, boy," and headed for the dining room.

After lunch he went to see Sheriff Wade Illigan at his courthouse office. Wade had the mild pink face of a fat man, and a stringy, durable body. After he was seated, Wade got up and shut the door and went back to his desk.

"I was expecting to be picked up by the city police," Jimmy said.

"Well, I heard about that, and the way I understand it, Jim, they decided against it. Borklund was for it, but Ben Killian was against it. They'll explain just how you worked it in tomorrow's paper, and publish it along with Elmo's statement calling it a pack of lies."

"Wade, we've known each other a long time."

"Don't expect much trade out of that, Jim. I'm an elected official."

"Elmo knows how badly I've hurt him. Maybe nobody else realizes yet except Elmo, and me. Wade, what happens to people who hurt Elmo?"

"He doesn't do anything without a purpose in it."

"How about Pete Nambo? Pete is nice and tame now."

"Maybe Elmo used to be rougher than he is now."

"Do you believe that?"

"Not especially. What are you getting at, anyhow?"

"I might not be worth taming."

"If there's any laws violated in Palm County, outside the incorporated areas, I intend to do my duty."

"Wade, damn it, I want to know what *could* happen!"

Illigan leaned back in his chair, and his face was still a fat man's face but, no longer mild. "There's a lot of people, some of them kin to Elmo, some not, thinking he's the second coming of Jesus. He's put a lot of meat in their mouth. They could just get the *idea* you'd done Elmo a hurt and he might like something done. But they wouldn't let it point back to Elmo. It would have to be one of two things, Jim. You'd have to have some kind of innocent accident. Or else one day you'd just be packed up and gone, which would seem likely."

"So, in either case, how close would you check it?"

"What are you trying to ask me? I'm an elected county official. I got half the budget I need. You know that. When, like they say, an aroused populace is on my tail, demanding justice, I have a hell of a lot of work to do. But with you, Jim, it's like this. Who is going to get aroused? Just who? I grease the wheels that squeak loudest. If it looks like you left, who's going to insist you get found? If you smoke in bed, who's going to order an autopsy? The county coroner?"

"So . . . I'm out in the cold."

"You knew that before you came in here."

"I guess I did."

Wade stood up, a sign that the talk was over. "I'm not saying anybody is going to even think of doing anything. I'm just saying you're awful short on friends. You've got nobody here. A sister you're not real close to. Who else? I were you, I'd leave. I surely would. You've wore this place out for yourself."

"I'll think about it, Sheriff."

Illigan said, "Good luck, Jim." He looked uneasy. "When I walk you out the door, I got to cuss you some and give you a little push. Don't take it too personal."

Jimmy Wing sat stiffly on the couch in Elmo's office. Elmo paced slowly back and forth in front of the couch, his hands locked behind him. He sighed audibly.

"Look at it this way, Elmo," Jimmy said. "This is the time you took too big a bite."

Sandra Straplin sat on Elmo's desk, swinging her beautiful legs, glowering at Jimmy. "The hell he did!" she said. "Everything was fine. Then you turned stinker. You *betrayed* him!"

Elmo turned toward her and said in a weary voice, "Now, you get on out of here, Sandra."

She crossed to the door with an exaggerated swing of her sturdy hips and banged the door shut behind her.

Elmo looked toward the door. "She got all worked up. Dellie got all worked up. My oldest four kids got all upset to hell. The other two are too little to understand. I tell you, when a man has so many folks depending on him and looking up to him, he carries a heavy load. Anything happens, he feels like he was letting ever' last one of them down. Sandra there was about the worst of all. You know you have a steady thing going with an office woman, and after a while she gets to take herself too damn serious."

"Should I take her to Tampa and put her on an airplane?"

"Don't you get smart-mouth with me, boy. I've got awful damn sick of you awful sudden. Here I am giving you the fairest offer in the world. You got a little upset and confused in your mind on account of your wife dying. You get up in the Municipal Auditorium tonight and confess you made it all up so as to help those bird lovers. You say you're putting yourself under a doctor's care. In return, I either get you back onto the paper, or I get you into the county somewheres at good pay."

"For the last time, Elmo. No!"

Elmo stood and looked down at him and smiled in a sad way. "Boy, you are not only stubborn, you are right stupid."

"So be it."

"You could wind up tied to a tree, boy."

"I could wind up a lot of ways."

"Are you too dumb to be scared?"

"That must be it, Elmo."

"The pity of it is you're causing me no real hardship, you know? Two out of that five are going to use it as an excuse to back out of their promise to sell me the share they agreed. I can smell that already. But when the time comes, they'll be brought around so fast it'll put a cramp in their necks."

"But what are you going to use the money for, Elmo?"

"I told you that once."

"But it isn't going to work now. You have to run against somebody, Elmo. And as soon as you start running, they'll start talking about Palmland, and they'll have names, dates, places and amounts. Your name will have a nice clinging little stink of corruption about it. You'll never get the state backing in the party you'd have to have. Elmo, I've cut down on the size of the bites you're going to take for the rest of your life."

Elmo studied him somberly. "What got you hating me so much?"

"I don't hate you at all. I think we both got trapped in a typical folk dance, Elmo. I think that every time—*almost* every time—a greedy little second-rater like you starts to get too big for his pants, some clown like me has to come along and cut him down. I don't think you or I could have kept this from happening, one way or another. Without me coming along just now, I think your chance of making governor was about one in five thousand anyhow. Now it's nothing in five thousand. I've drawn a line around you, Elmo. The border of Palm County. Get as big as you want to, but don't cross the line."

Elmo shook his head. "And the one I was most worried about was Leroy. Beats all, don't it? Anyhow, you're wrong. This will all die down. I just wait longer, that's all."

Jimmy stood up and moved a few steps toward the door and turned and looked curiously at Elmo. "Are you going to have me killed?"

"Killed! Lord God, fella, what kind of a man do you think I am? I'm a businessman who's got into politics a little. I got a wife and six kids and another on the way. Why, if I went around having everybody killed that let me down in some little way, I'd be busy night and day. Christ, I got to tell Dellie this. She'll laugh herself sick."

"I'll see you around, Elmo."

"Well, I'll say one thing to you. Don't hurry back. You've give me just enough misery so I can get along just fine if I don't see you again."

Jimmy Wing arrived at the Municipal Auditorium at twenty of nine. The large parking area was almost completely filled.

He parked at the farthest fringe of the lot.

"And *now* what?" Mitchie McClure said in a tone of bored impatience. "Christ, Jaimie, this evening is full of such dizzy excitement I don't think I can bear it." She was slumped in the seat beside him, the hem of her short white sheath hiked above her round solid brown knees.

He opened his door and said, "Sit tight. I'll be back in a little while."

She sat upright. "Oh, no! You can't *attend* that clambake. Please, dear. They'd shred you."

"I just want to listen for a couple of minutes. Outside. Wait right there."

She caught up to him when he was fifty feet from the car. "I'm coming along to see you don't get any dramatic ideas, lover."

The sound was audible a long way from the auditorium. A male voice would give a long impassioned metallic garble, and then there would be a hard concerted roar of enthusiastic approval. It would die away quickly and the voice would begin again. He stopped fifty yards from the building. It was a hot and windy night, and the air was not as moist as usual. There were many city police standing near the exits. Groups of children romped and rolled and yelped on the green lawns of the auditorium. Bands of teenagers were clotted in the shadows, making their obscure jokes, tilting communal bottles.

Mitchie took hold of Jimmy's hand and said, "Just *listen* to them! It makes creepy things run up and down my back. And it reminds me of something."

"Newsreels, Mitchie? From long ago. We couldn't understand what that voice was saying either, but they all yelled the same way."

"Jaimie, it scares me a little."

"It's a mob. Mobs always believe they are brave and strong and a thousand per cent right. There's an old definition of how to find out how smart a mob is. You take the I.Q. of the most stupid person in the group, then divide that number by the number of people in the group."

"Let's go, hon. Please let's go."

As they started back toward the car there was prolonged applause and cheering, then a frailer voice and then a great flood of jeering, hissing, booing, derisive yelps.

"They're expressing an opinion about bird lovers," Jimmy said.

"Take me to the nearest bowl of kitchen whiskey, driver."

At eleven they went back to Mitchie's beach apartment. It was tidy and spotless. She put a stack of records on and turned the volume low. She pulled the draperies open so that the only light in the small room came from the reflected glow of the floodlighting around the pool area, shining through the window wall. She fixed their drinks, then changed to a brief fleecy cabana coat and came back to sit close beside him on the broad low couch facing the wide window.

"This is the Class A treatment," she said. "This is for the very good friend of a very good friend. McClure Enterprises, a significant contribution to a vacation economy. No muttonhead conventioneers here, hon, because this is where I live."

"Nice," he said absently. He wondered how many drinks he'd had.

"It's worth more than I paid for it. It's co-op, you know. I had the sense to buy it with the settlement, and the stinking little alimony is the plus factor. I could sell it tomorrow."

"Very nice."

"The expensive ones stare out at the Gulf. Actually, I'd rather look at the pool."

"Sure."

"I like the way you keep yelping with sheer pleasure."

"I'm sorry, Mitch. I'm a drag. That drunk at the bar, I've known that guy for six years, at least. I did him a pretty good favor one time. So tonight he wanted to see if he could smash my face in. He was eager. He acted as if he was doing no more than would be expected of any good citizen. And he had some things to say to you, just for being with me."

"I didn't learn any new words, Jaimie. And he kept repeating himself. It was very dull."

"So who got asked to leave? Me."

She put her glass down and turned deftly to lie across his lap, looking up at him. All he could see of her face was a pallor of her hair, a bright highlight on her eye, another highlight on a moist lip.

"Rather be there than here, huh?"

"No, Mitchie."

"Darling, I still think you could be cheered up somewhat in a very ordinary old-fashioned way. So you should give it a small try, don't you think?"

After several minutes she moved away from him and sighed and picked up their empty glasses. "I guess we're down to one vice, hon."

"I'm sorry, Mitchie, I just . . ."

"Jeepers, Jaimie, don't get abject about it. At a time like this it isn't exactly a definitive test of manhood. If I thought it was necessary to your morale, boy, I would persevere, but we'd be up to our hips in raggedy nerves.

Honestly, I don't feel at all scorned or spurned or anything.
I was just making a small scorched offering anyhow."

She carried the glasses into the kitchen and turned the
light on. She hummed along with the gentle music as she
pried ice cubes loose.

"Mind if I use the phone?" he called.

"Your house, your phone, your woman," she said, and
came in and turned the music off, turned the small lamp on
beside the phone and went back to the kitchen.

Brian Haas answered and said, "I just came through the
door, Jimmy. I didn't note any fist fights in the audience, and
I didn't see anybody hanging from a tree when I left, so I
guess you didn't attend the festivities."

"How did it go?"

"Like hot buttered wax, friend. First off, our Elmo gave
a humble little address. He had been slandered. An irresponsible report had been published without the knowledge of
his great and good friends, Mr. Ben Killian and Mr. Borklund. A retraction would be published. But, in view of the
doubt it might have created in a few minds, he was ab-
staining from voting on the issue after the public hearing.
Long, loud applause."

"Naturally."

"Next came the Reverend Coombs. He too had been
slandered. And then he proceeded to slander all the Save
Our Bayers. Slur, sneer, smear innuendo. Gist of message as
follows: The soft weak do-gooders, the so-called liberals are
gutting the strength of this great capitalistic God-fearing nation, and it doesn't take any secret organization to put them
down, because the common man, in his wisdom, will rise
up as a multitude and smite them down. There is no place
in our grrreat community for irresponsible, pleasure-seeking,
Godless parasites and so on. Poor Tom got his turn next.
Believe me, not one single word was audible. Same with a
scared professorial type from Washington, from some national conservation group. Then Kat Hubble went up onto
the stage and faced the animals. Couldn't hear a word of
that, either. My God, she is a lady. She is brave and true.
That decency was like a banner in the sunlight. Then came
the perfect timing. Burt Lesser scolded them for being so
rude. He made his pitch. Then the golden voice of the
Chamber of Commerce made a financial pitch that had them
all breathing heavy. That was all. The commissioners called
a short recess to determine if they would vote on it at once.
They so determined. They voted yes. Gus Makelder gave a little sermon on the need for harmony, forget old differences,
hand in hand into the golden future and so on and so forth.

Not a peep out of the Costex people. The proponents had the sense to trim the presentation way down. With the S.O.B.'s whipped before they ever got started, there wasn't any need for the customary parade of talent. It was hot in that auditorium, Jimmy. Hot, sweaty, noisy and a little bit dangerous. They went swarming out with some steam left to release. When the hot dry winds blow, the natives get restless anyway. So we've had a little flurry of alarums and arrests tonight. Fist fights, car thefts, rapes and other little evidences of high spirits."

Mitchie handed Jimmy his drink. He said, "How are things at the zoo?"

"Your desk is empty. I've got your stuff in a carton in my car, and your check in my wallet. I'll stop by your place tomorrow before I go in, okay?"

"Fine, Bri. Thanks. How does that retraction read?"

"It makes you look like a thug, a liar and a person of unsound mind. Other than that, you'll love it. Borklund keeps staring at me the way the house cat watches the parakeet. He hates the news end. It complicates the money machine. I think he's wondering how he can cover the local scene without using human beings. You want to stop by and use our crying towels? You sound down."

"Thanks, no. And thanks for the report."

Jimmy hung up and turned the phone light out. The fresh drink was tall and strong. Mitchie had reversed the stack of records. She sat at one end of the couch, wedged some of the cushions behind her, and had Jimmy stretch out. He made small changes in his position until the nape of his neck was perfectly fitted to a curve of her bare strong thigh. Her fingers were gentle, smoothing his eyebrows, stroking his hair.

"How did Brian get that terrible scar? In a war?" she asked.

"In a saloon in Kansas, from a broken bottle. No fracas. He fell on it."

"Are they happy?"

"Huh? Nan and Bri? I guess so. Sure."

"Jimmy?"

"I'm right here."

"You know what the worst thing of all is? Really the worst thing of all? It's when you do some idiot damn thing, drunk or not, and later there's nobody you can go to and say you're sorry. It's when you can't disappoint anybody. Oh, the hell with having somebody to please. The worst is having nobody to be cross with you because you let them down. If they didn't have anything else, they'd have that."

"I guess so."

"Jaimie, it's like that old problem of the tree falling in the middle of the forest. If nobody heard it, did it make any noise? If you do a wicked, evil thing, is it really wicked and evil if nobody gives a damn? Or does it just happen in a vacuum?"

"Mitch, honey, I'm not exactly up to philosophical specu-lation."

"But this is heading someplace."

"Is it?"

"It might get roundabout, but if you don't fall asleep, you might find out how it comes out. My little girl was ten years old a week ago Tuesday."

"Uh . . . Carol?"

"Thank you for remembering her name." She leaned down and kissed him, then leaned back again. "When you're emotionally upset, you can do yourself a hell of a bad turn, you know? I really think my lawyer was playing footsie with his lawyer. I got careless, you know. When the dust blew away, there I was with my clothes and my car, a sixteen-thou-sand-dollar settlement, and two hundred a month until the moment I remarry. But he had complete custody of the kid. I told myself I didn't give a damn. He has the kid, and I am costing him less than seven dollars a day. For God's sake, our *phone* bill used to run more than that! But because I got careless—because I'd stopped giving a damn—they had me in a bind, and it was sort of take the offer, or nothing. I took it and came home. I can't see her, but they let me write to her. I write to her care of a lawyer. I guess they get together and fumigate the letter. Once a month is often enough, they've told me. I get formal, dutiful, polite lit-tle letters back from her. She sounds like a bright kid. When she gets to be eighteen, I guess she can decide whether to meet me face to face."

"That's a sad sort of . . ."

"Hold the sympathy, Jaimie," she said, touching his lips. "I'm making no appeal on that basis. I'm just buzzed enough to be terribly stark about all this. I make an appeal on a dif-ferent basis. It goes like this. I'm not happy. I accept that. I don't expect to be. But I'm not having much fun."

"I thought you were."

"Now let's get to the stark part, and take the cold apprais-ing look at Mitchie McClure. First for the deficits. I'm a party broad, Jaimie. I'm not on call, but I'm in scads of little black books. Buster, old buddy, if you get to Palm City on this trip, I want you to look up a pal of mine named Mitchie McClure. Here's her address. Tell her you're my friend. She's a lot of laughs and she'll show you the town, and whether or not she puts out depends on you, old buddy. She's no bum. Got the picture? Right. So there are the drinks and the dinners and the little gifties that piece out the budget. Sometimes a gift of money, tucked in a shoe or a drawer or a purse. The first few times that happened, it made me feel crawly. But we're talking deficits, aren't we? Okay. The girl is in the semipro league, and she drinks much too much, and she's letting herself get too heavy.

"Now for the assets, and leave us not indulge in any vulgar puns. She is selective, which I suppose is the dreary excuse and justification of all the semipros. She is reasonably pretty, and she is getting very bored with drinking these days, and even more bored with being horizontal, resort-type recreation for good old Buster and Charlie and Jack. She's clean, and reasonably intelligent, and she could hoe fifteen pounds of meat off those hips in a month or so, if she had reason to give a damn. And I think she has a capacity for loyalty which has never had a proper workout."

"Where are you heading with this?"

"Shut up. Jaimie, tell me true, does it mean anything to you that you were my first and I was your first? Can you feel any . . . tenderness toward those two love-dazed clumsy kids, the you and me of a long long time ago, full of dreams?"

"You know it means something."

"You know, I'm this here woman, this party broad, and I'm also the fifteen-year-old girl you used to take up into the storeroom over Getland's boathouse, both of us breathing so hard we sounded like marathon runners. We told each other it wasn't wrong, because we were going to spend our whole lives together."

"We squirreled the money up there behind a beam."

"Eighty-seven dollars it got to be. Runaway money, but Willy decided not to loan us the car. Jaimie, do you still love that girl a little bit?"

"Yes."

"I don't want you to love me. That would be a hell of a thing. Sooner or later you'd get awfully damned bitter about Buster and Charlie and Jack. But it wouldn't hurt to love that boathouse girl. She can't hurt either of us. You see, it was the sweetest part of my life. We invented how to make love. Nobody had ever done it before. We discovered it, and the rest of the human race couldn't know what they were missing. Oh, Jaimie, bless you, what happened to us?"

"Sundry things, here and there. But where is this taking us?"

"Don't be dull, hon. I'm proposing, of course. Stay right where you are! Don't get tense. We both know you're going to have to leave here, for the ordinary dreary reason you can't make a living here. No. Let me finish. If I list this place at eighteen, I can move it within two days. I'll go on the wagon. We'll trade in our two exhausted little cars on something big and new and sexy, winnow our belongings down to the minimum, and take off and keep going until we find a place to try new things in. A trial escape, Jaimie. Not a marriage. My two hundred will keep coming in. So you won't have to make a lot to keep us. Suppose we *do* get along. Then we can play it by ear. If we should decide we could live up to having kids, then we could see if we could start one, and then chop off my two hundred a month. You see, hon, what we'd have would be somebody to try to please, and somebody to say 'I'm sorry' to, and somebody to hold tight to when the nights are too black. And we start with that . . . that residue of tenderness from a long time ago. I think we know each other pretty well, and I think we're both gentleman enough not to prod the other guy where it might hurt. I would try very hard to be good for you, and keep things light and fun and unpossessive, and I know you'd be good for me. And I have just one last thing to say. This didn't just suddenly occur to me. It happened a couple of weeks ago, after I cried in the rain and came back to bed and you were gentle with me. I started thinking about it then. Since then, Gloria died and you've lost any reason to stay here. Jaimie, what do you think?"

He sat up and drank and settled back again. "I don't know what to think."

"Christ, it isn't exactly what you'd call the chance of a lifetime. You know, though, you wouldn't have to work for a while. You could get yourself sorted out."

"I have to do something."

"Yes, indeed you do. I'm neat. I make a lot of my clothes. I cook pretty well."

"But terrible coffee."

"I know. I know. So make your own."

He sat up. "It isn't every day I get propositioned."

"It isn't? *I* do. Oh, I'm sorry, hon. That's the kind of joke I won't make any more."

"Mitch, I want to think about it."

"I didn't expect you to tear home and start packing."

"But I do think I'll go on home."

"You could stay here. Please stay here, Jaimie."

"I have to go. I couldn't even tell you exactly why. Don't be sore."

"I'm not sore. It's perfectly all right. Really. Just drive

with care. I can't afford to lose you too many times, my Jaimie."

He stood just inside her doorway and kissed her. Barefoot, she seemed small. She tiptoed up snugly against him, her arm around his neck. Her solid weight moved him back against an angle of the wall by the door. His right hand, under her fleecy coat, traced the soft and heated planes of her back, down to the padded ledge of hip. At the end of the kiss he held her there, her lips at the base of his throat, her forehead pressing round and hard against his jaw. He looked beyond her and saw the palm fronds and the fat leaves of dwarf banana swaying violently in the inaudible wind.

"Goodnight," she whispered and turned away from him. He let himself out. He had to cross the pool area to get to his car. He looked toward her big window from the far side of the pool, looked into the dark room. She was standing at the window. Only the pale short coat and the lesser pallor of her hair were visible.

24

THROUGHOUT THE NEXT WEEK Jimmy Wing spent more time at his cottage than ever before. Mitchie stopped to see him a few times. At first she was confident and enthusiastic, but she became uncertain the more she became aware of his lethargy.

"So it was a dumb idea," she said at last. "So it was a dream, Jaimie."

"I didn't say that."

"You don't have to say it, dear. Your enthusiasm speaks for itself."

"I don't know what I'm going to do. I haven't thought it out."

She stood up and went to the door. He followed her more slowly. She turned, with a sad, wise smile. "It's one way to give me the message."

"It isn't like that, Mitch."

"Isn't it? Anyway, I'm off your back. You know where I am. Give me a ring sometime."

"Sure," he said too heartily. "I'll do that."

When the rackety sound of her little car was gone he searched himself for some feeling of relief, but, as during all the recent days, he felt nothing. He knew that it was implausible, and perhaps even dangerous, to have so little discernible reaction, but he could not summon up any sense of alarm.

The days were strange. Loella, the motel maid, had ceased coming over to clean the cottage, and it seemed too much effort to find out what had happened. The cottage grew increasingly cluttered. He had no routines, ate when he was hungry, slept often and heavily, sweating profusely in his sleep, dreaming of beasts and fleeing. He wondered how much money he had left in his account, but did not want to make the effort of reconciling his checkbook. He guessed it was about four hundred dollars.

He wrote to friends in far places, asking about the chance of a job. Usually the letters were too long, and he did not mail them. He tried to make a beginning on a half dozen ideas for magazine articles, but the prose seemed flat and artificial and he quickly lost interest.

The phone rang quite often that first week. He seldom answered it. Once, when he answered, a man offered him a free trip to Cape Coral and a free airplane ride over the new development, where hundreds of fine building lots were available, adjacent to the best fishing grounds on the west coast of Florida.

Another time a woman with a high, mad, whining voice chanted obscenities at him, terming him a Commie dupe.

He could not determine which of those two calls seemed more unreal.

He saved personal letters, unopened. One afternoon he decided to read them and looked all over the cottage for them and could not find them, and had to assume he had thrown them out accidentally.

He glanced at each day's newspaper. The things he had always covered had been divided up among several people. When they weren't by-lined, he could almost tell by the style who had written them. The paper constantly, stentoriously hailed the new era of prosperity which would enhance the area, courtesy of Palmland Development.

On his table was the carton Brian had dropped off, containing the junk from his desk drawers at the paper, a long accumulation. He did not open it.

Once, when he answered the phone, it was his sister Laura.

"I've been trying and trying to get you, Jimmy. I thought maybe you'd come here. I thought, being in so much trouble, you might come here."

"I was going to. I just haven't gotten around to it."

"I wrote you a note for you to phone me. Didn't you get it?"

"I'll stop by and see you pretty soon, Sis."

She lowered her voice. "Sid has been worse this week and I don't feel right leaving him here alone, but I was going to come out there. I've been worried about you, Jimmy."

"Everything is okay."

"You lost your job, and nine out of every ten people in the county think you ought to be ridden out of here on a rail, so things must be real good for you. Real real good. What are you going to do?"

"I'm not sure yet."

"Are you looking for a job?"

"I've got a couple of ideas."

"Jimmy, you sound so kind of blah. Are you facing up to things? You're the kind who always needs a push. You've got a wonderful education. You should get away from here. You know that, don't you?"

"I guess so."

"I don't want to sound cruel, but there's one thing I won't have you doing. I won't have you coming here and moving in on us, not unless you can pay your way. If you could, it would be a help, but I don't see how you're going to find any kind of a job around here. Jimmy, you come on into town and talk to me tonight."

"I'll be around to see you pretty soon."

"We have to talk."

"Sure, Sis. We'll talk it all out."

On Thursday, the third day of August, Brian and Nan came to the cottage at sunset. They had to sprint to the door through a hard rain that began to come down just as they had parked.

"You given up answering the phone?" Brian asked.

"Too many weird calls," Jimmy explained.

"They should be dying out by now," Brian said. "After all, they won."

"*Look* at this place!" Nan said, staring around. "If I can borrow a shovel and a wheelbarrow, Jimmy . . ."

"Don't bother with it," he said.

She gave him a questioning look. "I *am* going to bother with it. In fact, dear, it almost pleases me. You've always been such a Mister Neat, it made me insecure when you visited our cruddy little nest. I'm glad to see there's a little slob in you. You guys go sit on the porch and watch the rain while I housewife this shambles."

Brian and Jimmy sat on the rear porch. Brian said that at last he felt Borklund had stopped suspecting him of any complicity in what had now become famed as Wing's Forthright Editorial Policy. Brian began telling him of the changes on the paper, the new assignments, the foul-ups on the things Jimmy had always covered. He stopped abruptly and said, "I get the strange idea you're not tracking."

"Go ahead. It's very interesting."

"Sure. Sure. What are your plans?"

"I'm sort of formulating them, Bri."

"Nothing definite?"

"Not quite yet."

"Then I've got something for you. A coincidence. I tried to check it out with you but I couldn't get hold of you this morning, and I couldn't get away to track you down." He handed Jimmy a business card. "Scott is an old friend. And Jacksonville isn't too bad of a place to live. He's looking for a guy like you, Jimmy. It's a newsletter thing. *The Southeast Investor*. He'll pay a hundred plus expenses at first and work your tail off. He's got so many other things going for him, if he can find somebody who'll work out, he wants to give them the whole load, on a percentage of the net basis. It's a leg-work problem, plus good clear prose, with a captive analyst to give it the financial slant. It's made for you, boy."

"Interesting," Jimmy said.

"He flew back this afternoon. He'll be expecting you to be in touch."

"He just happened to drop in?"

"Just like that," Brian said with a wide, innocent stare.

"You're a good man, Haas."

"You'll go ahead with it?"

"It's something to think about."

"You can't stay here."

"These things die down," Jimmy said.

Haas looked at him in astonishment. "Lots of things do. Everything does, in one sense or another. But be a little realistic, for God's sake. You put a big crimp in Elmo's plans. He'll never be anything more than small time, but he'll always be as big as you can get in this county."

"I made him a noble speech. At the moment I almost believed it. He acted kind of sad and martyred, as if a pet hound had bit him."

"You bitched Elmo and you betrayed the business community and spat in the face of progress, and I don't think you could get a job washing cars in Palm County. Maybe you could get it, but I doubt you could keep it."

"I might be able to think of something."

"Why should you be anxious to stay here, anyhow? What is there here for you? Who is there?"

Jimmy smiled. "There could have been somebody, but I messed that up pretty good too."

"She asked me about you. She phoned you. She thought you'd left. She was surprised you're still around. A lot of people are."

"She still at the bank?"

"They moved her back out to the front desk, even. Sometimes I can't figure this damn town. She got up on her hind legs and talked to an unfriendly mob. She didn't let the situation rattle her. Same as Tom. So they're a couple of folk heroes. All of a sudden nobody is very mad any more. The heat is the common enemy. The purge of the degenerates has ended. But nobody is making room for you, boy. Don't count on that much amnesty."

The rain had stopped. Nan came out onto the porch. Soon it was time for them to leave. Brian had to go back to the newsroom. Jimmy thanked Nan for the cleaning job, forcing enthusiasm into his voice. Brian said they'd have to play some chess soon. Nan started to go out to the car with Brian, then sent him on ahead.

"You've done some taking care, Jimmy," she said. "You've done it when I was desperate."

"I was glad to."

She studied him. "Our turn now, Jim."

"I'm okay."

"Are you? I've been watching you. It reminds me of me, a long time ago. After I got out of the hospital. The body was mending fine."

"I tell you I'm all right."

"I kept telling people that too. But I didn't want to even wash myself or brush my hair. You sleep a lot, don't you?"

"I'm between jobs. That's natural, isn't it?"

"You can't read because you can't keep your mind on it. You stare at television, but the minute it's over you can't remember what it was about."

"Can anyone?"

"Don't make defensive jokes, Jimmy, please. You've had a serious shock, or a series of them. You're disturbed. I know the symptoms. I know them so well. You should see somebody, you know. Somebody who can help you."

"I don't know what makes you think I need any help."

"Sooner or later you're going to realize you do, and the sooner you realize it, the easier it will be to get over it. If you won't go see anyone, at least force yourself to . . . to stir around a little. Your world is getting smaller and narrower every day. You're putting up more walls every day. Try to break that pattern, Jim, please. For me. As a favor to me . . . and Bri. You're our friend. You know that. We love you. Try to do what we want you to do—for us if you can't do it for yourself."

"I keep telling you, I'm . . ."

"Please, Jimmy."

He shrugged, forced a smile. "Okay. I'll stir around, even if it does spoil my vacation."

On the following day it seemed much easier to stay at the cottage. He took a rusted spinning reel apart, cleaned it, oiled it, reassembled it, then felt so exhausted he took a long nap. After the nap he wrote a long letter of inquiry to Brian's friend in Jacksonville, telling himself there was no point in phoning or seeing the man before he knew what the working arrangement would be. In the late afternoon, with a sense of accomplishment, he took a huge bundle of laundry to the commercial end of the key and left it off. He drove over into the city intending to stop and see his sister, and then suddenly found himself slowing down for the turn into his own driveway. He went to bed early and slept late.

On Saturday afternoon he forced himself to drive to Kat Hubble's house. It took an alarming effort of will. His mind kept presenting a hundred plausible alternatives. He was able to make the final three hundred yards only by telling himself that she would not be home. But her car was there. He stopped in her driveway. As he hesitated, deciding to back out again, she came around the corner of the house, a garden trowel in her hand, a look of question on her face. She halted abruptly when she recognized him. He willed her to turn on her heel and go back out of sight. She flushed, then came slowly toward him, unsmiling, the flush fading to pallor.

He got out of the car. "Hello, Jimmy?" The greeting was a question.

"I've got no business coming here. Brian said you asked about me."

"I wondered about you. I phoned you. I guess I wanted to tell you . . . we appreciated what you tried to do, even if it didn't work."

"Regards from the committee."

"Not exactly."

She turned and moved into leafy shade. He followed her. Spots of sunlight made quick patterns on her hair.

"Are you all right?" he asked.

"I'm all right."

"He made a clumsy gesture. "About that other. I wanted to tell you something, Kat. It wasn't . . . all planned out, anything like that. It was wrong, but it wasn't from thinking about it and . . . waiting for a chance."

"I know that."

"Sometimes people do things that have no chance to turn out right."

"Yes."

"You can't calculate everything you do!"

"Dear God, don't plead with me, Jimmy. What do you want me to say to you? What is there I can say? It comes into my mind sometimes, and I push it out. It makes me feel annoyed, irritable. It's like when you go to a party and you are trying to be nice, and you pull some terrible social error, so bad you can't ever explain it to your hostess. We're adults, aren't we? We were tense and tired and upset, and we did a silly meaningless thing out of some sense of bravado, I guess. I'm not overwhelmed with guilt, you know. And there's no reason you should feel any either. I just feel . . . sort of ordinary and trivial."

He pulled a leaf from the pepper hedge and rolled it into a moist green ball. "Is there any starting place left?" he asked, not looking at her.

"For us?" She sounded startled. "But why?"

"Why not?"

"No, Jimmy," she said, her tone gentle. "There's no place to start because there's no place to go. What we used to be to each other, that doesn't exist any more, does it? And whatever new thing we tried to be, that didn't turn out to be much of anything either. And you shouldn't look at me like that, because I think you're trying to kid yourself a little, to make a justification. I don't hate you. Or myself. I just think any relationship would be . . . sort of dreary. It would be like wearing an albatross, don't you think?"

"Maybe."

"Don't you see that it doesn't fit? I'm too terribly P.T.A., dear, and you don't have enough self-esteem. We can't adjust ourselves into anything, you know. We can't neaten it up like a bad movie, because we can't change ourselves or each other, and we're both a little too wise to try."

"You're right, of course, but I didn't want to admit it." He smiled at her.

"Jimmy, you look pretty terrible. You look puffy. Are you all right?"

"I'm fine."

"What are you going to do?"

"I've got a good job lined up in Jacksonville."

"That's wonderful! When you get all settled, write me if you want to."

"I'd like to, Kat."

"When are you leaving?"

"Pretty soon, I guess."

"Isn't it definite?"

"Oh, it's definite. Yes. A good job."

She hesitated and put her hand out. "Good luck."

"Thanks. And to you too."

She winced slightly. "We need some. We haven't had much lately, have we? We haven't had much at all."

After he left her, he drove to the mainland and turned south on the Bay Highway. From the mainland road he looked out across the bay through Turk's Pass, and saw the dusky orange disk of the sun balanced precisely on the far clean edge of a purple sea. He drove slowly down through Everset and then through the twilight ranch land. He turned around in a ranch road, and it was night when he entered Everset again.

In the middle of the village he turned left toward the commercial dock area, and as he made the turn he had a strange feeling of inevitability. He felt as if a time of waiting was over. Barlow's Towne Tavern was doing a good Saturday night business. The old cars and the pickup trucks were lined up in front of it. Inside, the juke was loud, and the sweaty weight of people had overpowered the air conditioning. There was a smell of fish and labor, beer and perfume. The juke thumped against the shouts and the laughter. He pushed through the crowd, smiling, looking directly at no one. He found a single vacant stool at the far end of the bar. He ordered a shot and a beer. He smiled directly ahead at the bottle rack, and he could hear the change in the kinds of sounds the people were making. He could feel their eyes. He ordered a second shot to go with the rest of the beer.

A man he did not know pushed in beside him and stared at him. The man was short and heavy, with a wide weathered face, sun-bleached brows, little pale eyes. "What the hell you doing around here, Wing?"

"Having a drink."

"You know where you are?"

"Barlow's. I've been here before."

"Tell you where you are, you silly shit. You're right in the middle of Bliss country. There's anyway ten people here kin to Elmo. And the rest of us know he's the finest man ever walked the earth. He got my brother set loose from Raiford one time when Lonny had to get home and he'p care for his sick wife. Ol' Barcomb over there, Elmo he'ped him buy a boat when his old one got tore up in the hurricane."

"Nice fella, that Elmo."

"By now everybody in this here room knows who you are and they know you told a lot of stinking lies about the only man ever come into county government to he'p his own kind. Wing, you lost your damn mind?"

The last question was a shout. Barlow appeared suddenly on the other side of the bar and said, "Slack off, Walker. Nothing happens in here."

"Harry, you don't give a damn who you serve, do you?" Walker asked. He walked away, thick shoulders hunched.

Barlow leaned across the bar toward Jimmy Wing. "Could be you should git up and git, friend. There's some went off to bring some others."

"I like it here."

"You'll be all right here, inside, I gahrn-tee, but leaving is the thing. For leaving, a couple deputies might be a good thing."

"Would they come if they knew?"

Barlow thought it over, his forehead deeply wrinkled.

"Come to think on it, maybe not. But I sure wisht you'd go someplace else, or anyways try, before they get steamed up too damn much."

"Another shot and another beer, Harry."

Barlow hesitated, sighed. "Guess it would be cruel and unusual to refuse a man all the pain-softener he can hold."

The flavor of the place continued to change. More men arrived. The women left. The juke was stilled. The stool beside Wing was empty. From time to time there was a low muttering of voices. Bar business was good. They were waiting for him with all the heavy patience men can learn from the sea.

"Let's just take him on out," somebody said in a complaining tone. The others hushed him.

Jimmy Wing could feel no effect from his drinks. At times his throat would feel constricted and the back of his neck would feel icy. But it would go away, and he would feel capable of making bad jokes. He would manage something very flashy, agile, gallant. He would flee the lumbering pack, wearing the sparkling, infectious grin of the hero, disappearing like magic into the hot dark night, leaving an echo of his jeering laugh.

He picked up his change with great care. He left a tip for Harry. He turned slowly on the bar stool and looked at them. Several faces were familiar. He smiled at them all and nodded his head several times.

"Elmo Bliss is a monster," he said, articulating loudly and distinctly. There was no answer. "He is a smiler. He is a thief. He does cheap favors for meatballs like you, so you vote for him and pack his pockets with money. It's a good thing you love him so dearly, boys. I fixed his wagon. He's going to be your neighbor for the rest of his life."

He made a sudden dash for the door. He felt as if he was running in slow motion. They were coming after him, but it did not feel like pursuit. It felt as if he were leading them. Just beyond the door his arms were grabbed. There was a man on each side of him. The power of their grip made him gasp. It took the strength out of him. He felt as if he were a ridiculous rag doll.

Then they were trotting him along, around the side of the building and down a narrow dark area. He heard the sounds of their feet, and heard them panting as they jogged along with him. They were in grass, and then on boards, and then up against the back wall of something that stank of fish.

"Now make him last," somebody said softly, "or there'll be some people getting no turn at all."

The world slipped abruptly, and hammered his face. He

was lifted and jounced, he was danced and dandled as the thuds landed, the sky burst and rocked, as his mouth swung loose and his heart flapped free. He bounced to their gruntings and tried to laugh, but they gave him no time, and the world turned gray and slowly moved away from him, like a holiday ship leaving a small broken wharf.

25

By January, as the new tourist season began to approach its peak, the Grassy Bay fill was beginning to take shape. The drag lines waddled above the shallows, atop the dikes they built as they moved. The big dredges worked around the clock. By the outlets of the big pipes, where the dredges spewed their black foam of water and bay bottom, the gulls and the children herded, to snatch the living shells and the small fish.

The value of all property in the area zoned commercial went up in anticipation of the new community which would be built upon the marl.

On a cold day in late January, Jimmy Wing walked out of the hospital into the tug and bluster of a northwest wind. He carried a small canvas airlines bag. As he started walking slowly toward the corner where he could catch a bus, somebody called his name. He turned and saw Elmo Bliss in a pickup truck. Wing hesitated and then went to the truck. Elmo leaned across and shoved the door open for him.

"Get on in here, Jim."

He got in out of the wind and pulled the door shut. Elmo gave him a cigarette.

"You waiting for somebody?" Jimmy asked.

"Waiting for you. I heard you were getting out today. They didn't keep you long this time, boy."

"Not so much damage this time."

"Turn so I can see you better. Damn if you haven't got your face messed up for good. Jimmy, God damn you, what are you trying to do to me?"

"I'm not trying to do anything to you, Elmo."

"You trying to prove something?"

"I don't really know."

"What you're doing isn't making any sense to anybody. You should know by now you go down to Everset and bad-mouth me down there, you're going to get the ass knocked right off you ever' time. Twice you went down there and twice you got half killed and put in the hospital. Then you went to Jacksonville and I thought we were shut of you. But you have to come back and go down there again and get whipped again. Why didn't you stay in Jacksonville?"

"I got homesick, Elmo."

"You can't get no suitable kind of work here."

"Why are you worried about me, Elmo?"

"Don't you know I could have had you killed, you silly bastard?"

Jimmy Wing shrugged and sighed. "A lot of people knew that, Elmo, knowing how I cut you down to county size before you got a really good start. And so a lot of people were watching to see if I turned up missing. Then they'd have known I was on the bottom of the Gulf or down on the floor of some swamp. But if you let me walk around loose, the idea could get around that I'd done you no real harm. People would begin to say I'd made the whole thing up."

Elmo's voice went up a half octave. "But I was *fixing* to let you walk around loose, Jim boy! But you keep going down to Everset where they vote strong for me, and people are thinking it's me getting you beat half to death every once in a while."

"Then you're not really worried about me, Elmo. You just don't want me keeping the memory green."

"What the *hell* do you want, Jim? I got Darse Coombs run out of the area. People are forgetting fast. I want they should have a chance to forget the whole damn thing. What the *hell* do you want me to do?"

Jimmy Wing turned his battered face toward Elmo. He laughed abruptly and harshly. "This is pretty funny, Commissioner, or whatever the title is these days. You're a big man. A good business, a big family, big house, lots of weight and muscle. And I haven't got a car, a house or a job. Why should a big man like you have to ask me anything? People like me, you can buy us or scare us, can't you?"

"You wouldn't stay bought, boy."

"Think you can scare me?"

Elmo studied him for a moment. "I think I could have, last summer maybe. But now I got an idea it can't be done. A man has something he can't stand the thought of losing, that man you can scare. What I want to know is, are you going to go look for any more trouble?"

"I just don't know, Elmo. I just couldn't say right now. It may happen like this. I'll get another little job like the last one I had. Rough carpenter work, or kitchen help, so I can give my sister something toward my room and board. And some night I may go home and sit and start thinking about just how much of a coldhearted son of a bitch you are, and then I might get the urge to get on a bus and go down to Wister or Everset and give a few speeches around about you."

"But you don't really know?"

"Not at the moment Elmo."

"A thousand dollars cash money would take you a long way from here."

"I tried going away and I didn't like it."

"You want a foreman job? I can break you in on foundations, forms and finishing and block work."

"I tried working for you one time, remember."

Elmo banged his fist against the steering wheel. "Damn you, Jimmy Wing, you force my hand. I can't let this go on. You got folks laughing at me. There's other people trying to talk too much just because you get away with it. Now, you know I can't stand for that. I thought of two ways to stop it. One way, I spread the word nobody touches you, no matter what you say. But I thought that over, and I don't like it. You'd keep right on talking."

"Probably."

"So I got to do something that actual turns my stomach to think on it. But you're forcing me into it. I know you have nothing to do any more with the people you were close to. But they must mean *some* little thing to you. The very next time you get yourself put in the hospital making a fool out of me, you just take a look around and you'll see some familiar faces under them bandages. For a starter it will be Haas and his wife and the Hubble woman, and maybe Mitchie McClure. And if you don't learn from that, the list will be longer the next time."

Jimmy Wing looked directly into Elmo's eyes for a long moment. "Thanks," he said.

"What for?"

"I wasn't sure I was getting to you. How can you be sure I'm not out of my mind, Elmo? Your friends kicked me in the head that first time. How do you know I give a damn who you rough up?"

Elmo tilted his head and stared straight up in helpless exasperation. "What do you *want* from me? Just get off my back, will you?"

"Can't you figure out what I want?"

"I would be humbly grateful to know."

"I had to come back from Jacksonville to fight you, Elmo. I've been fighting you. I'm wearing the marks of it. But I'd rather fight you in a way I know more about. I had my gun taken away from me, so I have to use rocks and sticks."

Elmo's mouth hung open for a moment. "*You* want *me* to get you back onto the paper!"

"I think we'd both be happier."

"But I couldn't swing that, Jimmy boy. Not now."

"Not alone, but you can push the people who can. Shannard, Lander, Lesser, Cable, Killian . . . want more names?"

"But they'd figure me for a damn fool!"

"You aren't looking too good lately anyhow, Elmo. You heard any of those little verses people have learned by heart? I make them very simple, very easy to remember. 'A man in a house built by Bliss/Has one comfort he surely will miss./When the rain starts to come, he . . .' "

"I had an idea you were making those up."

"If I was back on the paper, I wouldn't have time."

"Hell, they don't bother me. They're good advertising."

"Got a lot of new contracts lately?"

"Honest to God, Wing, you got more brass than sense. How can you expect me to get you back into a spot where . . ."

Jimmy Wing opened the truck door and got out. He held the door open and turned and said, "I don't expect a thing, Elmo. You gutted me, like a trash fish. But I got over it. I healed up. You had no way of knowing I would. So I'll be on your back as long as we both shall live. And I'll be thinking of new ways to turn you into a clown. So play it your way or my way, whichever you think will work out best for you. You're half the size you were last summer. And one day it will be half that, and then halved again. And it's too late now to have me killed because the whole county will know it's because you couldn't stand having people laugh at you. People never forget that kind of weakness."

He slammed the truck door and began walking toward the corner.

On the evening of February tenth, at twenty minutes after nine, Jimmy Wing drove to Kat Hubble's house in a borrowed car, marched to the front door and knocked. The entrance light went on. She opened the door and stared out at him through the screen.

"Jimmy! Won't . . . won't you come in?"

"Just for a minute."

As he moved into the light he saw her expression change, saw her bite her lip. "Children no longer scream and run," he said, "so it must be improving."

"I heard about the times it happened. But I didn't know it was . . ."

"They like to mark you. It's an expression of outraged opinion."

"Will you sit down? Can I fix you a drink?"

"No drink, thanks."

"People say you . . . went down there expecting to be beaten."

"Let's say I didn't expect to win any fights down there."

"Wasn't that . . . a little childish, Jimmy?"

"Of course. A child has to find out if it is brave. It has to find out if it can cling to the things it wants to believe in. So I have a restyled nose, and some lasting lumps and a partial bridge and a slight impairment of vision in the left eye. But the childishness is intact."

"You've changed in other ways."

"Maybe. I can't tell yet."

"And you sit looking at me as if you're sort of defying me."

"That isn't the impression I want to give. It wasn't easy to come here. Maybe that's what shows. Anyhow, you know about the paper."

"That's all I heard all day, Jimmy. It's truly fantastic."

"I saw you a dozen times. But I went around corners and ducked across streets. Once you were at the Burger Den with the kids. In a booth at the left. I was supposed to bring a rack of glasses out of the kitchen and stow them under the counter, but I saw you through the porthole in the door and I didn't want to have you see me. Pride, I guess. I wanted to wait until I could see you on my terms. Like now. Like being back on the paper."

"How could it happen? Everybody was making guesses today. Some of them were wild."

"Sometime maybe I can tell you about it, about how it happened. If you want to know. If you have any interest in knowing. But I can't tell you now. Not because it's a secret. There's another reason. If I tried to tell you now, I might start to cry. That's pretty silly, I guess. I told myself I didn't give a damn. Then when it worked out, I realized today just how much I wanted it. I was on the edge without knowing it."

"Some day I'd like to know, Jimmy."

"All I want you to know, as of now. it isn't any kind of a deal."

"When I heard, I wondered about that. But I don't wonder any more. You . . . belong to yourself, don't you?"

"I think so. I hope that's the way it is. A funny thing. I understand Brian Haas better. I've got the same disease in a different form. So neither of us are going to be totally sure, ever. My escape routes were less obvious, that's all."

He stood up abruptly. "I just wanted you to know I got straightened out, Kat."

"I'm glad to know."

"But I don't want you to think it's like the last time I talked to you, asking you if there was any new place for us to start, asking because I'd bitched it so badly I wanted a chance to repair my own self-esteem."

"Neither of us did very well."

She had gone to the door with him. He looked at her with a speculative expression. "But it was two other people. Or is that just a rationalization?"

"I . . . I don't think so. Two other people, Jimmy." She walked out toward the car with him, hugging herself against the night chill, her shoulders slightly hunched.

"But even so, Kat, your good opinion is important."

"You have it, for goodness sake! I can't set myself up as a judge. I try to sometimes. But I shouldn't."

"Well . . . I'll see you around. How come you didn't rent the house?"

"I got a small raise and figured I could swing it this year."

"I guess the kids are glad of that."

"Oh yes."

"Say hello for me."

"I will."

He got into the car and rolled the window down. She looked in at him. "I've got a late lunch hour now, so I take the coffee break about eleven-fifteen."

"Same place?"

"Yes. Anytime you happen to be downtown . . ."

"Thanks, Kat."

"Good night, Jimmy."

On the way back toward town he pulled the borrowed car off the road and parked near the bay-fill project. He walked down to the bayfront and stood by the water and looked out at the dredges. Both of them were working, both brilliant against the black night in the glare of their floodlights. They made a vast wet gnashing grinding roar. He lit a cigarette. He could see tiny figures moving through the lights on the furthest one.

"Anything you want, mister?" The voice of the night watchman startled him.

"Just looking."

"This is private property."

"I know. And that's the trouble, isn't it?"

"Trouble with what? Don't you give me trouble, mister.

I'm asking you nice to get back in your car and go."

Jimmy Wing snapped his cigarette into the black and dwindling waters of Grassy Bay and walked slowly back to the car. Long after he had crossed to the mainland he fancied that he could still hear the sound of the dredges.